B[...]

by K.A. Mitchell

Bad Company

"…an entertaining, emotional, sometimes funny, oftentimes sensual story with two likable MCs…."
—Love Bytes

"Definitely, a must read! I was so enthralled with the characters Kellan and Nate! They were both charming, funny and oh so stubborn."
—Diverse Reader

"This is a great read that I'm adding to my favorites. Thank you, K.A. for bringing these men to light."
—Rainbow Book Reviews

Bad Boyfriend

"I really really loved this book. It was sexy, fun, quirky, heartwarming and everything amazing."
—Gay Book Reviews

"Fake boyfriends, a little age play, and a whole lot of chemistry between Quinn and Eli come together to make this an unputdownable read."
—The Novel Approach

By K.A. MITCHELL

BAD IN BALTIMORE
Bad Company
Bad Boyfriend
Bad Attitude
Bad Influence
Bad Behavior
Bad Habit

READY OR KNOT
Put a Ring on It
Risk Everything on It
Take a Chance on It

Published by DREAMSPINNER PRESS
www.dreamspinnerpress.com

BAD

INFLUENCE

K.A.
MITCHELL

Published by
DREAMSPINNER PRESS

5032 Capital Circle SW, Suite 2, PMB# 279,
Tallahassee, FL 32305-7886 USA
www.dreamspinnerpress.com

Bad Influence
© 2018, 2019 K.A. Mitchell.

Cover Art
© 2018, 2019 Kanaxa.
Cover content is for illustrative purposes only and any person depicted
on the cover is a model.

Mass Market Paperback ISBN: 978-1-64108-075-0
Trade Paperback ISBN: 978-1-64080-422-7
Digital ISBN: 978-1-64080-421-0
Library of Congress Control Number: 2018931591
Mass Market Paperback published November 2019
v. 1.0
First Edition previously published in Trade Paperback by Samhain
Publishing, Inc., April 2014.

Printed in the United States of America
∞
This paper meets the requirements of
ANSI/NISO Z39.48-1992 (Permanence of Paper).

For my readers.
Thank you for making it possible to keep coming
back to the characters I love.

Chapter One

SILVER HEADED out into the night, the noise and bass beat of the club still ringing in his ears. Or maybe the pounding was rage from finding one of his few escapes contaminated by the nuclear blast from his past. Why the fuck did Saint Zebadiah Harris have to show up in Baltimore?

He wasn't headed in any direction but gone, but his legs found a familiar route. That brick wall separating a parking lot from a park should have held an imprint of Silver's spine from how often he'd leaned against it in his rent-boy days. Though those days were never far away enough for Silver's liking.

"What are you doing back here?" Tanner yelled as Silver came around the corner of the wall. "Thought you moved on."

"Missed the life."

"The fuck you did." Tanner gave him a big hug.

"Missed you, anyway." Silver thumped Tanner's heavily inked shoulder. Silver was glad to see him. A lengthy career wasn't part of street life, and shit happened. Better to not give a fuck about anyone, but it was hard to not like Tanner.

A kid who couldn't be more than fourteen flipped a butterfly knife open. "Next one's mine."

"Fuck off, Eddie." Tanner grabbed the kid's wrist, twisted it, yanked the knife free, and threw it over the brick wall lining the lot. "He's not here for trade."

With a sneer and glare at Silver, Eddie vaulted over the wall. Silver resolved to keep the bricks at his back.

"You aren't, yeah?" Tanner muttered in Silver's ear.

"Nope. Just came to say hi." Since a night of forgetting everything by dancing at the Arena had gotten totally fucked when he caught a glimpse of Zebadiah Harris there.

Dancing with Silver's friend Eli. Zeb had the whole goddamned world to be self-righteous in. But no, he had to show up in Baltimore.

"You too good to be a whore?" Eddie was back, playing with his blade. As long as he didn't make a move toward Silver, they were cool.

"Silver moved up in the world. Got himself a studio gig."

"Fancy word for porn." Silver laughed. "So where is everybody?" Aside from Tanner, there was no one there he knew.

"Troy left town. Matty OD'd. Dakota is now working the other side, if you know what I mean." Tanner made a little feminine swing of hips and shoulders.

"Gotcha. James?" Silver asked.

James had looked smaller and younger than Eddie but swore up and down he was fifteen. Didn't have Eddie's ready-to-fuck-you-up attitude either. Tanner had tried to look after him, the way he'd looked out for Silver when he first hit the street.

Tanner shrugged and glanced away. "Disappeared. So, how's the high life?"

"Money's good. Shoulda come with."

"Oh, hon. My life ain't much, but it's all I got. No way am I risking it barebacking."

Silver worked at keeping his face still.

"'Sides"—Tanner shoved Silver with a hip—"mug like mine would break the camera."

Tanner was tall and muscular, torso ripped enough to be an anatomy poster. But a long jagged scar on his face twisted his eyelid and pulled at his mouth. His souvenir from an uncle who caught him sucking off a cousin.

Lights streaked across the wall, a car turning in. "Here comes one. Do your thing, Silver."

Eddie's knife flashed.

"Put it away, hon," Tanner said. "He's going to give you a hint about the john. He does this thing with the cars. He's really good."

Silver made a quick study. "Red Pontiac, 2006, nonvanity plate. He's white, around thirty, lives in the far suburbs, maybe faking it married or could be too scared to show his face in a bar. First-timer—or that'll be his story. Total bottom."

"Guess you're screwed, hon. Or not." Tanner winked at Eddie, then nudged him. "Take your shot."

Eddie approached the car. "Whatcha lookin' for?"

Silver tuned out anything except trouble and asked Tanner, "Where'd they find Matty?"

"Right up the block. The old theater."

The tweakers had been hanging out there as long as Silver had been in Baltimore. "Jordan?" The name Silver had left behind came out of nowhere. His head turned automatically.

Then his mind went gray-white with static. One word burst into it, a flashing alert.

Zeb.

Then, *Here.*

Fuck.

Silver's hand slapped the wall, feet leaving the ground almost before he made the conscious decision to run.

A rough tug on his wrist dragged him back. "Jordan," Zeb said again.

First the club, now here. Was Zeb looking for him? Silver tried to shake him off. "Got the wrong guy."

Tanner laughed. "What's the matter, Silver? You run out on a trick?"

Zeb grabbed Silver's other arm, eyes searching his face like there was some kind of proof written on it.

Yes, it's me. Yes, I'm a fucking whore. Yes, it's all your fucking fault. Silver clenched his jaw and fought Zeb silently, getting in two kicks to his shins and preparing a knee for higher up until Zeb body-slammed him against the wall.

"Get off me, you crazy fuck."

Silver had handled bigger guys than this, then run like his ass was on fire. How could he not get away from Zeb?

"Silver, five-o." Through pounding blood, Tanner's urgent whisper penetrated Silver's brain right as his eyes picked up the flash of lights across Zeb's face.

Silver panicked. Writhed and twisted like he was back at Path to Glory and they were going to stick him in that room again. The Reflection Room. But like back then, it didn't make any difference.

The cops had ahold of him and Zeb.

Hands shoved him facedown over the hood. One hand pinned his neck while a foot kicked at his ankles. "Spread 'em."

"Like he's never heard that one." The other cop actually sounded like a pig as he snickered.

Silver didn't move or speak. He knew how authority worked. Whether it was the cops or the counselors at Camp Path to Glory.

The cop's hand took a long time on Silver's balls and dick. "Gotta make sure we put your pretty face in the right jail."

The cuffs were tighter than Silver had imagined. The cop cranked them another notch as he said, "You are under arrest for prostitution."

"He's—I know him." Zeb's face appeared behind the cop's shoulder. "He's not a prostitute. We weren't—"

The cop held Silver under one arm as if displaying his skintight jeans and blue tank top with *Fresh Cream* written in white cursive letters.

Zeb shook his head. "Listen. I was just driving, and he looked like someone I used to know. I stopped because I wanted to talk to him. That was all."

"Uh-huh. Excuse me, *sir*." The cop pulled Silver toward the passenger door. "Feel free to come down to the station and give your statement to the judge on Monday. Now go home."

Zeb had been glad enough to do that the last time they saw each other. Shut his door, refuse to answer his phone. Pretend Silver had never existed.

"Wait." Zeb reached forward, but he didn't touch the cop or Silver. His hand hovered in the air. "How can you arrest him and not me for…?"

Was he insane? Did he want to get arrested for—come to think of it, Silver didn't know what the word for it was, besides being a john.

With a disgusted sigh, the police officer spun Zeb around. "Hands on top of your head. I'm placing you under arrest for obstruction and patronization."

So *that* was the word.

Thank fuck being shoved in the back of a cop car with their hands cuffed behind them finally shut Zeb up. Silver was having enough trouble swallowing back a total mental freak-out. It wouldn't be like the Reflection Room at Path to Glory. Each time his chest got tight enough to block his breathing, he reminded himself it wouldn't be the same tiny cell. There would be normal lights, not complete black or that blinding spotlight. He was pretty sure he wasn't going to find Bible verses painted on the walls. But mostly, there would be other people. Even if one of them had to be Zebadiah Harris.

Separate processing. Prints, mug shots. Every step took Silver in deeper while every nerve and muscle screamed at him to run. No matter how still he tried to be, how much he tried not to get any extra attention, he couldn't completely hide the desperation in the twitch of his fingers, the tap of his toes.

He held his breath as the cop examined the laminated card with Greg Carter's name on it. The fake license had better be worth what Silver had paid for it in blood, sweat, and come. He'd debated giving the name he'd been born with, but the cops were going to find the Greg Carter ID on him, and then he'd be screwed for sure.

The cop tapped away on the computer. "Is this your current address?"

"Uh, not right now. I meant to get it changed."

After Silver rattled off the Tyson Street address, he felt the cop's eyes back on him. As long as the cop wasn't staring too hard at the ID, Silver didn't care how creepy the look was.

"Supposed to be done within thirty days. Could suspend your license."

"I just moved."

The cop made a grunt and handed Silver a thick envelope. "Wallet, phone, belt, shoelaces, and anything else in your pockets in here."

Silver eyed his phone as he slid it in. "Can I call someone?" Not that there was a long list, but Eli's sugar daddy might help post bail if it wasn't too high. Silver had always heard that if he got picked up by the cops, he'd just get a release ticket. Not actually get hauled to jail.

"Later." The cop had scanned the contents of Silver's wallet. "Thirty-two dollars." The cop's eye roll suggested he didn't think much of Silver's street value. Back when he'd done it for money, he'd made a hell of a lot more than that. Tonight he'd only been hanging out.

Through mug shots and fingerprinting, he caught glimpses of Zeb. Silver was glad they were being processed separately. The last thing he needed was Zeb calling Silver "Jordan" often enough to make the cops look closer at the fake ID. When he'd needed Zeb to stand up, he'd been too much of a pussy. Now he wanted to act like some kind of knight swooping in to defend Silver's honor.

As Silver watched, the cop turned Zeb sharply away from the fingerprinting station. They were fucking with him because he'd been an ass down by the park and made them arrest him, so they were giving him the full treatment. Probably do a cavity search on him. It should have made Silver laugh, but he only wished Zeb hadn't gotten involved. Wished he'd stayed wherever the fuck he'd been, acting all pure and honest like he didn't love a fat cock in his mouth, didn't want it fast and hot and dirty as much as any guy Silver'd had since.

He looked away and tried to turn off. Shut out the whole humiliating, boring mess of it. He wasn't embarrassed to be called a whore. Hard to argue when he'd done plenty of fucking for cash—usually on camera. But he couldn't believe he'd actually been caught—especially when he wasn't doing anything. Another thing to put on Saint Zebadiah Harris. Fuck. The whole reason Silver had been hanging out over on Eutaw by the park instead of dancing with friends at the Arena was because Zeb had been there with Eli and Quinn in the first place.

They ended up getting fitted out with the double set of cuffs and chains at the same time, and Silver could barely touch his forehead if he hunched over.

Right as he was about to follow a guard uniform downstairs, one of the cops called him back.

"Grab that one. Bring him back. Gregory Carter."

Silver had been hanging on to one thought. He'd stand in front of the judge and get a court date. At which point he'd make a few calls and earn enough money to pay whatever fine he got nailed with. Hell, he could probably even cover the fine if he could get extra shifts at With Relish.

But when they hooked his chains through a loop on the edge of the desk, his hands went ice-cold and started slicking up. He wanted to clench them into fists to hide the tremble shuddering down his arms but didn't want to get in more shit with the guy behind the desk. The one who wasn't a uniformed cop anymore, but with a half-loosened tie and detective as the first part of his name.

"So, kid. You want to tell me why I got a hit here that your prints don't match Gregory Carter's, formerly of Bookert Drive?"

Silver would have been happy to say anything that would get him out of that chair. Even if it meant going down to wherever they'd taken Zeb. He tried unsticking his dry lips, but since he didn't have the right answer, nothing came out.

"Kind of a good thing for you, considering this Gregory Carter's been dead six years. Except that instead of you maybe skipping out of here after you see the judge, you're now looking at felony fraud and identity theft."

If he could only sit on his hands. He tried not to grip the edge of the desk, tried not to let the man see how shook he was.

"Let's try this again. With a real name."

Silver wasn't sure he was going to have any better luck prying open his mouth this time. He heard his friend Marco's frequent complaint—*Where is your happy place,* cuate?

Silver didn't have a happy place. He had a cold, dead place. And if he could survive those six weeks at Path to Glory and force himself to open that sealed envelope to read the like-I-didn't-know-I-was-fucked result, he could live through this. The trembling stopped.

Silver gave the cop the name he'd sworn he'd never use again. "Jordan Samuel Barnett."

Chapter Two

SILVER SCOPED out the situation as they led him to holding. Zeb had clearly been watching for him, but Zeb wasn't what worried Silver the most right then. One tweaked-out guy jonesing for candy, someone fucked-up enough to be puking steadily. The other three looked like they were no strangers to a holding cell. One took up as much space as possible on one bench—but everything about the way he sat said he wanted to be left alone. The one leaning on the opposite wall looked dangerously bored, the kind of guy who might stir shit up just to amuse himself. The third guy was tough to get a read on, but Silver worried that if Bored Guy started something, Mr. Mystery might want in on it.

Two points of immediate danger. Plus having to fight the panic that wanted to choke off his breath when he heard the lock on the door. It echoed, heavy

and thick, like the one on the Reflection Room. And
he didn't think getting out of here would be as basic
as finding someone who'd trade a blow job to leave a
door open.

Breathe, act bored, and don't look at anyone, he
reminded himself. *Don't give them anything to use.*

He planted his back on an empty spot on the wall
near the quiet guy on the bench and slid down to a half
crouch, keeping an eye on things while pretending not to.

His keep-away glare drove off the tweaker but
didn't work on Zeb. He only stared back and hunched
down as much as the shackles would let him. "What
happened?"

"I know your memory isn't that bad." Silver
peered over Zeb's shoulder, half to make it clear the
conversation wasn't welcome, half to keep an eye on
the potential for trouble. "You grabbed me, the cops
showed up, and here we are."

"I mean, why didn't they bring you down with me?"

Right now was when Zeb decided to take an interest in what happened to him? Wrapping himself in
anger hadn't been much of a shield at Path to Glory,
but after four years on the street, Silver had built it up
to an effortlessly thick second skin. "Fuck. Off."

"Jordan, after almost four years, don't you
think—"

Silver bolted up straight. Zeb no longer had an
extra inch on him, so they were eye to eye. "Don't
you think you've fucked me over enough for one
lifetime?" Even with his voice low, that got a snicker
from the bored leaner.

"You offering someone else a chance at it, pretty
meat?"

Acting like a jealous boyfriend, Zeb moved between them. Like that was going to help. The big guy on the bench didn't open his eyes, but Silver was sure they had everyone's attention. Even the guy hunched over the can stopped ralphing.

Silver shifted around Zeb and mimed a blow job at Bored Guy. With an exaggerated purse of lips, Silver blew him a kiss, then laughed. "In your wettest dreams, man."

"No touching." The guard banged against the bars.

"Jordie." Zeb lowered his voice to an urgent whisper. "Not the time for attitude."

"Not the time to be seen as a pussy either. And don't call me that."

"What should I call ya?" No-Longer-Bored Guy made his way over to stand right behind Zeb.

For an instant Silver considered that there had to be a dozen ways to cause serious harm to another human body even in shackles, assuming you were willing to take some pain to do it. He preferred a quick assault and then running away, but right now Silver could use the distraction.

The guard banged his stick against the bars again. "Collins."

The guy went back to his previous post, and Puking Guy let loose with something that echoed around the walls.

Zeb moved up to the front of the cell near the guard. He probably thought good manners and a sincere smile meant he'd get special treatment. Silver eavesdropped.

"When can we see the judge and use a phone?" Zeb asked.

"Phone in about an hour, when they finish cleaning in there. Judge'll be here when he gets here, which might not be until Monday morning."

Silver glanced at the clock over the guard's little table in the hall. One thirty on Sunday morning meant seeing the judge was over thirty hours away. Now it wasn't only about getting bail. Silver had to take his pill in the morning. A few hours was one thing—though the lady at the clinic had been really emphatic about sticking to a schedule. They couldn't deny him medication when it was life-or-death.

Before the panic could get a good squeeze on his lungs again, Silver felt Zeb's gaze, intent, hot. What kind of intent? Silver met the stare, then lowered his lids partly, let his mouth soften. Zeb swallowed thickly. *Really, Zeb, here?* At least Silver knew that still worked. He rolled his eyes, and Zeb flushed and glanced away.

A jangle of keys and the slap of feet on the stairs brought Silver's attention back to the hall outside the cell.

"All right." The new guard unlocked the door. "Blondie and Jesus." He pointed at Silver and Zeb. "Phone calls. Follow me."

Silver pinched his lips against a sarcastic laugh. With shoulder-length wavy brown hair and the stubble filling in around his mouth and chin, Zeb had always gotten some mileage with his Jesus look. The only question was which had come first, the look or Zeb's martyr complex.

The phones were in a space between two larger cells, a much bigger space than the first cell they'd been in, reeking of wet, moldy mop and industrial disinfectant. Silver wanted Zeb on the phone first, distracted enough so he couldn't hear Silver's side of it. Who would Zeb call? Did he have a boyfriend now? Silver watched Zeb fish a scrap of paper out of his jeans and start dialing. Since that was all the privacy Silver was going to get, he took a deep breath and punched in Eli's number.

His friend might have traded in the night life for a sugar daddy in the suburbs, and it was almost 2:00 a.m., but Silver knew Eli would pick up his phone. He had a clinical addiction to drama—and Silver was about to supply one hell of a dose.

Chapter Three

AS SOON as they were off the phones, the guards put Silver and Zeb into one of the bigger holding cells. There were more benches in this one. Silver could only manage a halfhearted warning glare when Zeb followed him to the bench farthest from the toilet. Zeb might have been the cause of every miserable thing that had happened tonight, but at least he didn't reek like some of the guys in the other cell.

Silver had always managed to do what he had to to survive. Tolerating Zeb's ridiculous idea that he was somehow saving them both with his presence was cake compared to breathing the air around that meth addict or the puking drunk.

"Are you ever going to say anything, Jordan?"

Silver tried to put one foot up onto the bench to rest his head on a bent knee, but the chains wouldn't let him. He braced his feet against the cement floor and stared at the crack between them. "Like what?"

"Like what happened. I don't mean tonight. How—I mean—what were you doing with those—?"

"Hustlers? Streetwalkers? Prostitutes?" Silver looked over to see Zeb flinch at the words. "Maybe I was doing the Lord's work. Spreading the gospel to Christ's favorite professionals."

Zeb glanced away.

"What do you think I was doing?" Silver prodded. "Exactly what do you think happens to gay kids who have no place else to go?"

Zeb's cheeks turned patchy red. "Your parents didn't turn you out."

"No. They sent me away. Someplace much worse."

"I'd heard it was a camp."

"Camps are supposed to have tents and marshmallows and swimming. Not cinder block cells with bars on the windows and forced labor." Not to mention the Reflection Room. But Silver wouldn't. Because now wasn't the time to let that memory in.

Zeb reared back, like Silver's spat-out description was something he could escape from. Good.

Silver hadn't planned to answer Zeb, wanted Zeb to know what it was like to be shut out in the cold, alone, with no explanations. But that wasn't enough. Anger burned up Silver's spine. He wanted to slam all that pain and fear into Zeb.

Silver turned toward Zeb as much as the shackles would let him. "You want to know what you were telling me to go back to when you sent me off that night? Did you think conversion camp would fix me too?"

Trapped in the dark, no sense of time, no sound but his own shaky breathing, waiting for them to switch on that light. Craving that moment when he knew they were watching him. For his moment to read his Bible verse and tell them he had learned his lesson.

"Conversion?" Zeb's brow furrowed.

"Yes, to convert me straight. What the fuck do you think they sent me to? Bible camp to put on an all-new production of *Joseph*?"

"I'd heard"—Zeb placed a lot of emphasis on that word, like it excused him somehow—"that it was a place for teenagers who had made bad choices, to keep them safe."

"Jesus fucking Christ." Silver watched Zeb's wince with satisfaction. "A bad choice? Is that all it was? You and me, fucking for over a year? Just a bad choice?"

"You lied to me from the day we met." Zeb had some of his cool back now, the self-righteous idiocy Silver had always been able to chase away, first with a joke, then with his hands and mouth. "I wouldn't call that good."

Silver would use a different tactic to throw Zeb off his game now. "You know how fast everything happened when Tina opened her big fucking mouth about you being my boyfriend? Normally my parents might have kept me under house arrest for a bit, but a spot opened at Path to Glory. Guess how? Kid killed himself. In the dorm room they put me in. Killed himself because of how much fucking fun he was having at the camp to keep him safe from making bad choices."

Silver drank in the emotions so plain on Zeb's face. Shock and then sweet, sweet anger.

"Yeah, from the first day I was there, I slept in a dead kid's bed. The other kids weren't supposed to talk to me because I was on entry-level, but they let me know just the same. Told me how he'd taped plastic over his head and hands. I swore I could still smell puke and shit in that room every night."

Lines tightened around Zeb's mouth. Silver didn't remember them being there before, but he liked being the cause of the emotion that made them surface.

He rammed another point home. "Some of the kids were addicts, but most of us were there because our breeders didn't like what we were doing. Having sex. With the wrong people or wrong gender. Couple kids bought into it, really thought Path to Glory would fix them. Make them straight."

Zeb's throat worked like he was swallowing around something thick. Silver wished he could imagine it being a cock, but he was too pissed and too sick with reliving this shit to go there.

"Did they have counselors or—?"

"Fuck, didn't you read that letter I smuggled out?"

Zeb shook his head. "If you sent something to me, I didn't get it."

"*If*, right. Because everything Jordan says is a lie. Does thinking that make it easier? Especially knowing what you told me to go back to?"

Score one for Silver. A shot right to the nuts, because Zeb dropped his gaze and glanced away. Silver had never managed to make Zeb flinch before, always those changeable hazel eyes stayed focused and earnest on Silver's face, like everything he said mattered.

The flash of triumph didn't do anything to clear the ache in muscles held tight enough to snap. He pushed harder.

"Would you have bothered to read it if you had?"

That backfired. Zeb looked back at him, all emotion smoothed away, covered with a calm Silver knew was fake. He knew everything about Zeb, had studied every expression, shared his body and his breath until they were living in each other's skin, they felt so close. If they were ranking lies, Zeb's was bigger. Because you don't love someone like that and then walk away because of some stupid rule.

"Jordan," Zeb began with the same patient affection that used to make everything inside Silver get warm and soft until he had to get them kissing. Had to make it hard and rough because if he let himself give in completely to safety and warmth, he'd never drag himself out Zeb's door and back to the cold house where Silver still had to live for another thirteen months.

Right now disgust for the name he'd left behind took care of any old feelings the tone might have stirred. He could have corrected Zeb, but it seemed pointless when Silver was the one dragging their past over hot coals. As long as Zeb's ass came out equally barbequed, Silver could stand a bit more of it.

"You can't think I wanted to—I'd have lost my teaching license." Zeb went on in that same tone. "Jordan, I could have gone to jail."

Silver cut his eyes toward the cell bars and then looked back with a smirk. Zeb started to chuckle, a smile so broad it turned his eyes to slits. Silver felt the laugh start in his own chest and fought with everything he had to let nothing show but a disdainful smirk. It was too easy to remember the sense of the absurd they'd always shared.

The guards saved him when they came back with the big black guy who'd been sitting on the bench and the skinny white meth head. After asking them if they had any candy or gum again, the meth head started pacing some more, dancing a little to whatever he heard in his head. The black guy sat on the bench opposite them, head back against the wall, eyes closed.

"I called." They hadn't been speaking loudly, but Zeb's tone dropped to right above a whisper. "On your eighteenth birthday—assuming you didn't lie about the date as well as the year."

"It's still August fourth." Gary Carter's was May first. Eli had thrown Silver a birthday party for the date on the fake license, and Silver had learned Zeb was in Baltimore. God, was it only two weeks ago?

"It wasn't your number anymore," Zeb said, doing the thing where his eyes were wide and intent, like he was so full of honest goodness, in a minute Silver would be apologizing to Zeb.

"Ya think?" Silver sneered. "They took my phone and computer first thing. As soon as the little bitch opened her mouth."

"I was in Haiti," Zeb threw out like it had some meaning.

"And?"

"When I called. I was in Haiti. I couldn't do anything about finding a new number for you."

"Right. Because a happy birthday would have made it all better."

The look Zeb shot him wasn't one Silver had ever cataloged. Maybe Zeb had found it in Haiti. If he didn't know Zeb better, Silver would have sworn it was cynicism.

"Exactly what was I supposed to fix, Jordan? The fact that you lied about your age from the beginning, or what you decided to do after that night?"

Silver stared back at the crack on the floor and dug the edge of his rubber-soled sneaker into it. "Absolutely nothing." He willed himself to slide away inside the black space.

When he was younger, Silver escaped most of what sucked by imagining he was starring in the movie of his own life. No matter how much he'd tried, high school refused to completely blur into a longed-for montage, Linkin Park slamming on the soundtrack, drowning out all the fucking assholes with their endless refrain of *Die, faggot*. And no matter how many times he'd willed the montage into existence in his head, Silver never managed to emerge triumphant and successful, bursting from the school with the last power chords, flipping off the deaf-to-bigots teachers and epically moronic hicks as he got the hell out of New Freedom, Pennsylvania, forever.

The only movies Silver ever starred in were straight—*ha*—to DVD or available for subscription online, not much of a soundtrack beyond the slap of flesh, grunts and gasps, interrupted by the occasional gag-inducing *Take all that meat, little boy*. At least it had beat hustling on the street.

The awkward and sometimes painful process of faking passion for the camera should have cured him of the fascination of pretending he was in a movie, but he still played the game, zooming out of his body to watch from as far away as he could get, convincing himself it was happening to someone else, poor fucker. Right now the script called for a flashback. Something with a rippled effect, maybe special lighting or a filter like on Instagram to make it look really cool. But he wouldn't flash it back to the night when he'd begged outside Zeb's apartment.

Nope, hit rewind all the way back to the day when Silver had seen Zeb looking a little lost while pouring himself a coffee in the basement of New Hope Church. For most of the congregation, fellowship seemed to be about gossiping about who hadn't shown up, and so far everyone had ignored tall, slender, sexy, and oh-please-God-let-gaydar-be-for-real. The guy's build and longish golden brown hair had caught Silver's— well, back then the audience would have known him as Jordan—eye during the service, but when the new church member bent to pick up the sugar packet he'd dropped, the sweetest ass Silver had seen not on a porn site had him eager to be polite and sociable, like his mother was always nagging him to be.

"You look a little lost," Jordan said as he held up a plate of hideously dry cookies from the bargain bins at Stop 'n' Save. He knew where they'd come from. His parents might be loaded, but God forbid they actually spend any of it.

The man's smile was even more devastating than the sight of his ass in tight khakis had been. He placed a hand over his heart in a sign of exaggerated shock. "You mean, New Hope Church isn't a convention hall for fans of *Star Wars: Episode IV*?"

It surprised a laugh from Jordan, brought it bubbling up through all the cynicism that kept him safe in hostile environments. Tall and Sexy was the first person to make the same connection since Jordan's parents had dragged him to this church. "Do you really think you've got the midi-chlorians for so dangerous a place, Padawan?"

"Blasphemy," the guy said.

The word shut down all Jordan's amusement. So this guy was just like the rest of them. Then he grinned so broadly his eyes turned to slits, and Jordan would have sworn there was a CGI twinkle in one of them.

"Do not speak of *Episodes I* through *III* in my presence." The man held out a hand. "Zeb Harris."

Jordan shook it, dazzled by the impossible twinkle. No sunlight made it to the basement. He had to be hallucinating. Heat flashed where their palms met. Yes. This was it. Like a movie, but for real. Smiling back, he said, "Not even *Episode III?*"

"Maybe I can give that one a pass just for you. I saw you sing. Your voice is amazing."

Nothing about how he managed to hit deep notes when he was so obviously young or skinny. Jordan winked and licked his lips the way he'd practiced in the mirror. "Lung capacity."

Zeb flushed and swallowed. For the first time, Jordan made a heartfelt prayer of gratitude. Hell, yes. Zeb Harris was gay and interested.

"So, um, I'd love to talk more *Star Wars* with you." *Damn, Jordan, why don't you just ask if he wants to see your action figures?*

"Jordan," his mother summoned. He turned instinctively.

When he turned back, Zeb was still smiling. "Jordan, huh?" Zeb's voice was warm, like his hand had been.

"Like the river." Jordan sighed. "Um—my parents haven't quite—come to terms with—" It didn't matter how carefully he whispered it, dropping the word *gay* in the church basement would echo like a gong. He gestured between them, hoping Zeb would understand.

Zeb nodded. "Mine either. Fortunately, they're in Ohio."

"Oh. So, maybe we could meet for coffee sometime?"

Zeb's feet didn't move, but suddenly there was a distance between them. "Jordan," he began, and four years in the future, a guy in a jail cell remembered everything about how hearing his name like that had felt.

Jordan knew what the problem was. "I'm"—*eighteen* would sound too dead-on—"nineteen. I know I look younger. Get that all the time. Guess it's better than looking older, right? I live with my parents because I'm going to Pleasant Valley Community College, trying to save money to go to a bigger school. No point starting out in debt, right?" *Stop babbling, Jordan.*

A pencil and the edge of a mini memo book stuck out of Zeb's pants pocket. Without stopping to think, Jordan grabbed them. Zeb pulled away, then relaxed.

"I have to write stuff down or I forget it." The shy smile on Zeb's face made him look younger than Jordan's real age. Not like age was a big deal. But the guy couldn't be more than twenty or twenty-one himself.

"Don't forget this." Jordan wrote down his email and cell number. "I'll bring an ID next time." Taking a deep breath, Jordan stuffed the notebook back into Zeb's pocket, letting his pinky stretch out toward the fly, barely brushing it. Maybe it was only the thought of what was under there, but the impression of heat sizzled right up Jordan's arm. Without looking at Zeb's face, Jordan sprinted to where his parents waited impatiently.

Here and now, under the courthouse or police station or wherever this hole was, Silver felt that same warmth—though not the remembered heat. Despite the constant reminder of "No touching," Zeb had moved his foot until his ankle pressed into Silver's from behind. The flashback had mellowed him enough to return the pressure, but now he jerked away. The shackles clanked and chimed like an alarm. Since everyone was staring at him already, he did the chain-gang shuffle toward the bars, and a guard met his eyes.

"What?" It was the one who'd called him Blondie.

"Someone is supposed to be bringing me my prescription. How will I know when he gets here?"

Silver didn't think it was possible for the guy to look more disgusted, but he managed with an exaggerated shake of his head. "Must be true what they say about blonds. No way we're giving you something someone brings in. Should have told the booking officer."

"He didn't ask." The film in his head replayed the smiling but serious expression of the woman at the clinic. "I have to take it every day at the same time. It's really important."

"I'll put a word in. Get the paperwork started." The helpless, pathetic tack had been the right one for the guard. He sighed. "What's it for?"

Silver didn't have to fake embarrassment. On top of everything else, he was a fucking cliché. He lowered his eyes. "What do you think?"

The guard snorted. "Shoulda figured. Yeah, we get a lot of that. They know how to handle it."

Silver should have been past the shame brought on by the guard's sneer. How could something like that have power when Silver had spread his ass for a camera so close it was almost in him? Turned out he had a bottomless pit of shame, especially when he became conscious of Zeb's watchful attention.

An hour ago he'd been determined to hurl every bit of the last three years at Zeb, make him gag on that first bitter load Silver had swallowed to earn a ride from Morgantown to Shrewsbury, only to get turned away by the man who said he loved him. Wanted to fill Zeb's gut with the fear of trying to find an unlocked car to sleep in, an abandoned building that hadn't been taken over by a gang. Then to burn him with the shame of trading his ass or mouth for the hope of someplace safe and warm.

Now he didn't want Zeb to find out about any of it. Least of all about the last nail in Jordan Samuel Barnett's coffin. He shuffled back to the bench.

"What was that about?" Zeb murmured.

"I'm hungry. I asked when they were going to feed us." Other than the lies and omissions to keep his age a secret back then, Silver had never lied to Zeb. Now it came as easily as it did with the rest of the world.

"What did he say?"

"When they get around to it." Rather than wonder how long it would take before Zeb got curious again and asked questions Silver didn't know if he had the energy to make up answers to, he said, "So, Haiti, huh?"

"Went with a mission group to rebuild a school. Stayed to teach."

"What was it like?"

Zeb shrugged and brought an end to the conversation. He could lecture, for sure—Silver knew more than he wanted to about how important math was for the real world—but when it came to personal stuff, Zeb was a much better listener than a talker. Back then it had been awesome.

First it had been the dizzying warmth every time he thought *I have a boyfriend.* The tingle of secret knowledge: *I'm going over to my boyfriend's tonight.* The kissing and touching were awesome, and an orgasm with someone else's hand on his dick was the most amazing thing ever. Until it was someone's mouth. But by then it wasn't only having a boyfriend, even one he couldn't tell anyone about. It was Zeb.

Zeb listened. He paid attention. And kept track of stuff in his little notebook. Which wasn't always good, considering how sometimes the truth had to get a bit twisted in order to keep up the *I'm nineteen* lie. But everything Silver felt, and everything he told Zeb about those feelings—that had been real.

Around two thirty, two more unlucky bastards ended up in the tank. They tried socializing, but when no amount of prodding would get anyone to answer their "What are you in for?" questions, they sat and muttered to each other on the bench opposite.

Silver watched the hands move on the mesh-covered institutional clock. Everything on cop shows had been specific with numbers. Time of death calculated to the instant. When was the Baltimore PD going to join the digital age?

"I'll keep an eye out if you want to catch some sleep," Zeb said after the new guys had stopped trying to organize a group share.

"I'm usually up most nights anyway."

"Oh." Zeb's slow nod had Silver pressing his lips together in frustration.

"I work in a restaurant that stays open late." He was up to thirty legit hours a week. Since he'd started waiting tables at With Relish, he earned enough to pay for the room on Tyson Street.

Zeb was silent.

Silver bit his lips against swearing it wasn't a lie. "I'm good if you want to rest," he said instead. He doubted Zeb would be any help if shit got started—not that Silver was a badass fighter. He had stayed alive this long by not being where trouble happened. He just hoped Zeb was snoring whenever these pricks got their shit together enough to bring him his meds. Though he doubted Zeb would sleep through someone yelling *Who here's got HIV?*

Zeb didn't snore, but his eyes closed eventually. At some point during the night, the meth head passed out with his face on the toilet.

By morning no one had shown up with meds, but at 8:17, the guard called them up one at a time for breakfast. There was a tiny bottle of no-name water and a plastic-wrapped sandwich, which was either made with rubbery cheese or rubbery egg.

It was hard since the chains didn't let his hands get above his temples, but Silver found the best thing to do with breakfast was to stuff it behind his head to cushion it as he leaned against the wall. More comfortable, and he'd still have it in case anyone did show up with meds.

Despite advice from the new inmates, Zeb bit into his.

Nine thirty was when Silver always took his meds. An hour couldn't make much difference, or even a day, he told himself, but by eleven he was starting to freak out. Another twenty-four hours of this? And then if he couldn't make bail, if he got convicted, how long? How long would he be waiting for the clock to move? He was pretty sure no amount of trying to squeeze a prison sentence into a montage would keep him from suffering every minute of a year locked up. Any more than it had saved him when they'd shoved him into the Reflection Room back at Camp Path to Screwed Now That Your Parents Know You're Queer.

Silver was staring so hard at the clock, when the guard banged on the cell door, he jumped. His meds?

"Hey, you. Jesus." The guard nodded at Zeb.

Six inches between them, but Silver still felt the sudden tension in Zeb. "That's you, Harris," the guard added when Zeb didn't move.

"Where am I going?" Zeb asked.

"Judge is here. You too, Blondie."

Silver controlled any outward show of relief, but knowing he wasn't going to get left behind was the first good thing to happen since Zeb charged out of his car last night. Once they were out of the cell, the guards went in and shook the meth head until he staggered out to join them.

Their destination was another cell and more waiting. Being shuffled around like this reminded Silver of a trip to Disney World back when he was fourteen. Just when you thought it was the end of the line, it was another room. Though he didn't think this was designed to entertain the people caught in the system.

There was only one small bench in the new cage and no toilet. They'd barely been in there for a minute when a black guy in a uniform so crisp and freshly cleaned Silver could still smell the starch from the ironing said, "Zebadiah Harris?"

Silver fought the absurd desire to grab Zeb's hand and beg to go with him. Curling sharp nails into his palms, Silver mocked himself. A few hours around Zeb was all it took to forget three and a half years of surviving alone.

Zeb stood, turning to face Silver. "I'll see—"

"Just go."

"Can I call someone?"

Silver shook his head. If Eli couldn't bring his meds, what could anyone do? Alarm snapped Silver's head up like a yank on a collar.

"Don't. Don't call—" He swallowed. "—them." He was pleading, a weakness that was dangerous here, but he couldn't change it. He'd rather be in jail than ask his parents for help. Not that they'd bother.

Zeb nodded.

The guard led Zeb away. *Have a nice life. Or not.* Silver choked the words back. He was afraid it would come out more pathetic than sarcastic, and he wasn't going to add to his humiliation. After the clinking of Zeb's shackles faded under the sounds of the other prisoners shifting around, Silver plastered his most determined go-away glare on his face, pressed his spine more tightly against the wall, and wished he could disappear.

He didn't know how much time passed before a guard said, "Blondie, your lawyer's here."

Lawyer?

Eli had come through big-time.

The room the guard sent Silver to was small, with just enough space for the table divided by a mesh screen. Silver's eyes widened in surprise as he took in the guy on the other side. The watch on the lawyer's wrist wasn't a Rolex, but his loafers were Gucci and his suit was Hugo Boss, and Eli's sugar daddy setup was looking pretty damned sweet if he could swing someone like this.

"Silver? Is that the name you prefer, Mr. Barnett?" The lawyer pulled out a chair on his side of the table.

"Yeah, I mean yes." Silver started to slump into his chair, then straightened. This guy could be his ticket out of here.

"You were a little difficult to track down, given the different aliases. I wanted to be sure I had the correct individual."

"You're really here for me?" The watch might not be a Rolex, but it was worth five large, easy. The wedding ring was solid, not fancy. Platinum.

"My name is Kevin Millhouse, and I have been hired to represent you, yes."

"By Eli?"

Millhouse shook his head. "But Mr. Montgomery wanted me to assure you there is no need for you to concern yourself with reimbursement."

Montgomery. Silver's hands remembered the smooth feel of a Tiffany blue box. Expensive shoes and expensive jeans. Eyes that seemed to see some-thing they liked when they met Silver's. A friendly smile. Gavin Montgomery had been a surprise guest at Silver's fake birthday party. Gavin had come to Silver's rescue then, too, when Marco's car wouldn't start.

Silver nodded, neck tight.

"Now, the prostitution charge has been dismissed, but the assistant district attorney is going forward with the fraud charge. Although Mr. Montgomery has of-fered to post bail, they could hold you unless you can demonstrate evidence of a permanent address."

"I have a room on Tyson Street," Silver said. "It's paid through next week."

"Yes, but that is exactly the sort of accommoda-tion the court might find too transient to secure your release. Is there another address? Family? Friends?"

Silver guessed Gavin's angel of mercy gig didn't go as far as giving a street kid a place to live, not like Silver could blame the guy after Gavin had gone this far.

"No. No family. My friend Eli. If you ask, he'd say I live with them." Eli could handle things with Quinn.

"And who is part of 'them'?" The lawyer took out a notepad.

"Just him and his boyfriend. Quinn is pretty…" Silver tried to think of a way to describe him. He didn't dislike the guy, exactly. "…tight-assed," he finished.

The lawyer gave a hint of a smile. "'Tight-assed' is precisely what the court is looking for. I'll see what I can do. Is there another option? Other friends?"

Marco's older brother was still on parole, and most of the other guys Silver knew well enough to hit up for so much as a cigarette were either hustling or still modeling in the clothing-optional, full-penetration way.

Silver shook his head.

"We'll work with what we have, then." Millhouse closed his briefcase and stood up. "They should be ready for you in the courtroom very soon. I'll see you there."

SILVER HAD half convinced himself the whole conversation with the lawyer was a product of his imagination, an add-on scene born out of insanity-provoking boredom. The shock of relief at the sight of the expensively dressed man from Silver's not-a-fantasy waiting for him in the courtroom washed the strength from Silver's knees. As he shuffled in, his eyes picked up a quick wave and landed on Eli, who flashed what was for him a subtle thumbs-up. Silver took another deep breath. Maybe this was going to be okay.

The breath got caught in his throat when he saw who else was waiting for him, squashed in between Quinn and the asshole cop in the second row. Zeb hadn't left. And Silver couldn't decide if that made everything better or worse. They couldn't mention his HIV status in the courtroom, right? Or say anything about his porn-star past?

Silver tried not to wince when the judge said his name. "Jordan Samuel Barnett."

They went through who everyone was. The judge and the assistant district attorney both looked annoyed and strict, like stressed-out teachers at state-exam time. Silver's lawyer was still smooth and relaxed, so he hoped that meant they were already ahead. He wished he had on something besides his club clothes. His Fresh Cream tank probably wasn't scoring any points.

After the judge said her bit about possession of a fraudulent document and Silver had said *not guilty*, the other lawyer shot him the kind of disgusted look he would have expected if he'd been in English class dressed like this and said, "We request no bail, Your Honor. Forged government identification and no legal residence."

The judge asked, "Is there any evidence of Mr. Barnett obtaining property or goods through this fraudulent identification?"

"Not at present, Your Honor." The accusing lawyer acted like it killed him to admit that.

"Your Honor, to address that concern, Mr. Barnett has found a stable residence with close friends and is able to post a bond for his release."

"Is there any proof of this stable residence with friends? Or am I to take Mr. Barnett's word for it?"

Mr. Millhouse turned around. "Mr. Maloney?" Quinn stood up.

Mr. Millhouse faced the judge. "Mr. Maloney is a former officer in the US Navy and a public school teacher in Baltimore County. He is also a homeowner in Mount Washington."

The judge nodded. "Mr. Maloney, can you confirm that Mr. Barnett is staying with you?"

"Yes, Your Honor."

"In what capacity?"

"As a friend."

The judge scrutinized their row. "Bail is set at fifteen thousand. Cash or bond."

Trying not to look like the idea of that much money had made his knees wobble again, Silver glanced toward Mr. Millhouse, but the lawyer's reassuring smile said they had gotten what they wanted.

ALTHOUGH SILVER was perfectly fine slipping right on out of the courthouse and possibly the state of Maryland, it would be interesting to see if anyone would be waiting for him. He was pretty sure now that he'd made Gavin cough out fifteen large, he and his cop boyfriend would be ready to wash their hands of him. Maybe he'd be able to mail the money back someday. It was chump change to a guy as rich as Montgomery, and Silver figured by leaving, he'd save the guy money in the end. A lawyer like Millhouse would cost more than fifteen thousand to keep working on Silver's case. He'd stick around until no one was paying much attention and then maybe try the West Coast. Do movies again until he could get a decent job. Right now all he wanted was a shower. The one at Tyson Street might be crap, but it was wet and usually lukewarm.

Zeb was the first person Silver saw when he came into the lobby. Though Eli was right up in Silver's face as soon as he cleared the hall, his gaze locked with those warm, gold-brown-green eyes. All Zeb did was nod with an almost smile and then the bastard was gone. Was there some point Silver was supposed to get? Was Zeb too good to stick around now, like he hadn't just been in jail with Silver all night?

"Here." Eli shoved a plastic baggie with pills in it at him. "There's a fountain right down there. Or do you need a soda? Do they bother your stomach? I heard they can bother your stomach."

"Christ, Eli, keep it down." Silver glanced around. "Trying not to tell the whole damned world about it, thanks." He snatched the bag and slammed into the men's room. Eli followed; of course he did.

Plucking a pill out of the bag, Silver swallowed it dry. It got stuck, so he gulped some from the faucet. And then he got a look at Eli's guilty face in the mirror.

"What? Jesus fucking Christ, I told you not to say anything to anyone about it." Silver spun away and pressed his back into a wall, wishing he could hide in a stall and not have to deal with all this shit.

"The cops wouldn't let me bring you the pills, and you said you might be there until Monday and that you had to have them every day, and I couldn't get in to see you, so I started to freak out—"

"Who. Knows?" Silver ground the words out past the puke rising in his throat. He needed to figure out the extent of the damage and then get the hell out of here.

"I wouldn't have told anyone if I didn't need to. But I didn't know what to do, so I told Quinn, and he said he'd ask Jamie what we should do because Jamie's a cop—" Eli barely paused for breath. "—and then, well, Gavin—we needed someone who could actually do something, get someone out of bed on a Sunday. It was the only thing I could do to make sure you were being taken care of."

The list was too much to take. Silver shoved away from the wall, banged into the stall, and heaved up the inside of his stomach. Not that there was anything in it besides the pill and the water. And the bile making his guts spasm over and over again. It made his eyes water, and that pissed him off more.

"Silver? Do you need something? Should I—"

Silver wiped the back of his hand across his mouth. "I'm fucking fine. I'm HIV positive. I'm not going to drop dead in the bathroom from puking." That redheaded cop was a total fucking gossip queen. Silver might as well have put the info on Grindr. It was a good thing he'd already decided to go to LA. When he'd gotten a grip on his insides again, he made it out to the sink and rinsed his mouth. "Does *he* know?" He'd rather every queer in the city know than one in particular.

Fingers gripping the sides of the sink for support, he watched Eli in the mirror. Eli had easy-to-read tells when he was lying or exaggerating. Right now his face squinched in confusion—or constipation.

"That guy? Zebekiah or whatever? I don't think anyone would have told him. Why would they? And why give a shit what he thinks, since he's why you ended up getting arrested?" Eli's eyes went wide. "He didn't give it to you?"

"No."

"Good. Then I don't have to beat the shit out of him." Eli wasn't kidding, but that didn't mean Silver was going to forgive him for spreading his business everywhere. "He's gone anyway, so that's good. How do you know him?"

"Just an ex. Bad breakup." Silver splashed water on his face.

"Seriously small world. Oh my God. You should have seen it when we both got a phone call at 2:00

a.m. As soon as Quinn told me who was on the other end of *his* phone call , I knew that self-righteous prig was why you left the party...."

Eli's ramble faded under the whine of the air dryer. Silver bent to try to get it to blow across his face. Stupid place was too cheap for a piece-of-shit paper towel.

When the air whimpered to a stop, Eli was still going strong. "...I mean, you and I go way back, so no question about it. And now that you...." Eli made some kind of gesture with his hand.

Silver thought about drowning Eli out with another blast of air, but it was already stifling in this tiny room. And Silver was pretty sure he knew the whole hand-waving stuff meant Silver was all delicate and in need of help now because he was positive, but he said anyway, "Now that I what?"

"That attitude is the thanks I get for getting your skinny ass out of jail?"

"Actually, I think it's Gavin who gets the thanks. I'll get right on that. Catch you later, Eli. Thanks for bringing me these." Silver waved the bag with two pills still in it before stuffing it back into his pocket. He'd get one to stay down later. But before he could get through the door, he banged into Quinn coming in. "He's all yours. I'm heading out."

"I don't think so." Quinn didn't move.

A quick glance at Eli showed he didn't know what the bug up his Daddy's ass was. Silver took a step back. "What the fuck?"

"I told the judge you were living with me."

"Okay," Silver agreed warily. "Thanks for that. Appreciate it."

Jamie and Gavin crowded in behind Quinn. There was more wiggle room on a westbound Metro at 5:05.

Jamie leaned back against the door. "My boy-friend just put fifteen grand plus lawyer fees on you showing up for your court date."

"Thank you." Silver didn't have to fake that gratitude. He gave Gavin his best choir-boy-who-could-be-tempted smile. "If there's anything I can do for you, you know how to get in touch."

Gavin's lips quirked briefly.

"Therefore," Quinn said, and how Eli put up with all that toppy-Daddy shit, Silver had no idea, "you will be staying with me until the court date."

"The fuck I will." Silver eyed the window, which of course had fucking bars on the outside. "If your boy toy isn't doing it for you anymore, don't look at me."

"Maybe he could stay—" Gavin began.

"No, he couldn't," Jamie said quickly.

Someone pushed at the door from the other side, and Jamie slammed it back. "Cleaning. Go upstairs."

Eli stepped toward Quinn. "Be serious. What are you going to do, lock him in?"

"This was your idea, Eli. I'm not going to lie to the court."

"You can't make me live with you, for fuck's sake." Silver's muscles still burned with the need to run, hide anywhere, but short of squeezing down through one of the gigantic cracks in the uneven black-and-white floor tiles, he was trapped.

"No, but he can tell them you don't have an established place of residence, and they can decide to revoke bail." That was Jamie, and Silver didn't doubt this shit was all his idea so his boyfriend didn't lose his fucking money. Like he couldn't afford it.

"Good food. Nice bed. It's a haul down to the restaurant and bars, but it's not all bad." Eli's awkward shrug told Silver he was on his own. Again.

"No bars. He's twenty." Jamie didn't have to sound so fucking gleeful about it.

They couldn't watch him all the time. Silver would get his emergency bag after work one night and not go back. As for now, "Fuck all of you very much. Assholes."

Chapter Four

ON MONDAY afternoon, Silver slipped through the kitchen. Eli stood at the stove, stirring something. All he needed was a fucking apron. Domesticated in the extreme.

Silver swatted him on the ass. "See ya, Mom. I'm going to work."

Lightning fast, Eli grabbed Silver's hand. "That just gets funnier every time you say it. What are you in such a hurry for?"

"Gotta take the bus to work."

"No, you don't."

"Okay, I put up with the rest of your Daddy's control freak-out, but I'm not going to skip work or lose this job." He had to hang on to every penny if he was going to get out to LA and not have to turn tricks in an alley to get a place to sleep.

Eli dragged him toward the front door. "No, I mean you don't have to take the bus." A horn beeped as Eli flung open the door.

Silver stared at the car with that fucking red-haired cop driving, arm impatiently waving. "You've got to be fucking kidding me."

"C'mon, kid. I start wanting a cigarette when I've gotta wait like this," Jamie yelled.

"Quinn and I will pick you up at eleven, after your shift." Eli gave him a little shove.

Not that Silver wanted to ride the goddamned bus everywhere, but this was fucking humiliating. "It's an undercover-cop car."

"I guess," Eli said without any sympathy. "Jamie's truck is getting restored someplace. He and Gavin had an accident."

"Why couldn't Gavin drive me?" Silver heard the whine in his voice and snapped his jaw shut. Though that car of Gavin's was sweet. He'd do more than whine for a ride in it.

"I don't know. Jamie offered. Maybe you should ask him." Eli gave Silver a more forceful shove toward the door.

"You drag me up here and now you're pushing me out? Make up your mind."

For once Eli didn't have anything else to say, only nudged him forward and out the door. Silver thought about running in the opposite direction of the way the car was aimed, but the bastard would probably radio for another cop to pick him up.

He leaned in the open window. "Do I have to ride in the back?"

"Nope." Jamie pointed, and Silver went around to the passenger door and dropped himself inside.

"So what's this now, house arrest?" Eli had said to ask, so Silver was asking.

Jamie ignored that for a minute, cruising down the block before swinging a right to head back around to the main road. Silver hated the way he drove, with an arrogant attitude that he owned the goddamned road and everyone could get the fuck out of his way.

"I'm going to lay some shit out for you. You don't have to like it. I don't care one way or another, but this is just facts. I don't know what happened in your life, but I get that you were fucked over. Welcome to the planet, kid. Some people get more than their share of shit, and they deal and try not to fuck things up for anyone else."

Silver tried to squeeze in a word when Jamie took a breath. "I didn't ask—"

"I'm still talking."

Silver glared out at the strip malls and gas stations rolling past his window. Jamie could talk. Apparently without breathing much. Didn't mean Silver had to listen.

"So you didn't ask," Jamie went on. "But now other people are involved. People give a fuck about your future, even if you don't. And one of those people is someone I don't want to see hurt."

"And the fifteen thou means nothing, right?" Silver sneered.

"Does to me." Jamie coughed a dry laugh. "But for God knows what reason, Gavin actually cares what happens to you. And that means so do I now. Here's what you need to know. You will not be running off anywhere. You will be there on your court date. If I get a call saying you're unaccounted for, I will come find you. Trust me on that."

The way Jamie's voice held no temper, no inflection at all, let Silver know exactly how fucked he was if he tried to head to LA.

"So, what, I get to rot in jail for a year for a fake ID?"

"If you didn't commit any credit card fraud, Gavin's lawyer says you should be off with a fine and community service, assuming he can't get the whole thing dropped. Did you use the ID to steal stuff?"

For the first time since he'd gotten into the car, Silver felt Jamie's stare digging at the back of his head. Silver snapped around. "No. I didn't steal anything. Only sold what was mine. And trust me, I paid plenty for the ID."

Jamie grunted. "Okay, then. We're clear on you sticking close. Because you will not be happy if I have to come after you."

"Christ, you're an arrogant asshole. You have serious control issues."

"Didn't seem to bother you when you chased my ass around the club last December."

Silver shook his head. "Smug too. I had my reasons, dickhead."

Jamie's gaze fixed on him for only an instant before he looked back at the street, but Silver felt like it was the first time Jamie actually saw a person there instead of a problem he needed to solve.

"Yeah? What's that?"

"In addition to you being a giant tool—notice I didn't say having one"—the guy had enough attitude already—"you talk a lot."

"What do you mean?"

"You run your mouth." Silver watched Jamie's jaw drop open with some satisfaction. "You gossip like some high school chick about who you've done."

"Hope you weren't looking for any kind of recommendation, kid, because you sucked. And not in the good way."

Silver folded his arms over his chest and leaned into the corner. "I can wait while your stupid cop brain catches up."

Jamie swerved the car off into a spot in front of a hydrant. "Why would you want me to—? Why the fuck—?"

As funny as the cop's little freak-out was, Silver wanted the conversation over. "Guess you don't watch much porn."

"Prefer living it, thanks." His smug arrogance settled back around him like armor.

"Right. So you didn't know who I was. Swear you were about the only guy in Baltimore who didn't. And who didn't think because I'd done it on camera I'd do it for them."

Again Silver was on the other end of that look, the one that said Jamie was suddenly taking this seriously. This time it didn't shift away, since they were idling at the curb.

"I was fucking sick of it. I'd rather someone spread the word that I couldn't suck water through a straw in real life." Silver wouldn't go as far as saying it was worth it, but when Jamie's surprised confusion became a nod of grudging respect, Silver felt a little pride.

And then it was gone. Jamie swung the car away from the curb, and after another dry cough that might have been a laugh, he said, "Glad I could help. Slobberjaws." There was a long pause as he barreled down the street before slowing a bit. "Did you know you were positive then?"

"No. I got the news right before Christmas."

Jamie nodded. "Do you know who—?"

"Does it fucking matter now? If I didn't get it shooting bareback videos, I got it from a boyfriend. And I don't need to know if you think I was stupid to risk it."

"The one from yesterday? And the party you ran out on two weeks ago—in case you think I was too stupid to notice that too?"

"No. Zeb—" How could it be weird to say that name when he'd doodled it in his notebook all the time? "He was a long time ago." *A really long time ago*, Silver said in his head. And though he knew they'd both been virgins, they'd been careful.

Jamie didn't say anything else until he was blocking traffic in front of With Relish. "One last thing you need to know. Eli went all kinds of cut-a-bitch crazy on your long-time-ago ex in the lobby for landing you in jail. Quinn couldn't hold him. I had to step in before the kid ended up in jail too."

"So?"

"So, like I said. You got people who care. So don't go throwing yourself some epic pity party."

Silver shrugged and pushed open the door.

Jamie grabbed his arm. "And remember, Blondie, you're not going anywhere but back to Mount Washington."

"Fine." Silver shook free, climbed out, and slammed the door shut. "Go tell your boyfriend his money is safe."

Silver slipped through the alley to the back of the restaurant. The fuck if he needed advice from some overbearing asshole who'd fucked his way into the sweetest setup ever. Stupid dick didn't even have to work for money anymore. Like Eli. Though Eli's setup in the suburbs wasn't quite the kind of thing Gavin Montgomery could bankroll. It was easy to go around handing out advice when everything was going your way.

WORK SUCKED.

It was one of those half-dead nights that made everyone pissy, including the cook. There wasn't enough traffic to make time go by fast, and tips were pathetic. Even though there were only two servers on, Silver got shafted the most because he was the newest. Definitely the kind of scene that needed to be montaged, with something like a Goo Goo Dolls song for background. As he pushed the specifics out of his head, he realized there wasn't anything different about work today. It was him.

When he'd started working as a waiter, he'd felt as if he'd actually achieved something. A real job. One even people like Thomas and Cheryl Barnett could have been told about—assuming he ever spoke to them again. The job hadn't changed. But seeing Zeb had dragged up the memory of what a stupid, naïve kid named Jordan had wanted. The idea that if he tried and worked hard, he could have his dreams. Now what had seemed like a decent job was only a reminder of how dead everything to do with Jordan was.

Around eight, Eli's old boss Nate came in with his boyfriend. Eli'd been so hung up on Nate, Silver had sworn the three of them were going to do some kind of poly thing before Eli moved in with Quinn. Silver rolled his eyes and went to get their usual order of KZ sodas. Plunking the bottles and glasses down at their table, he asked, "So what are you supposed to be, spies? Did Eli send you?"

Nate peered through his Harry Potter glasses at Silver like he was some kind of bug, but the boyfriend, Kellan, said, "Huh? Eli? Is he okay?"

"Eli's fine." *And I'm good too, thanks for asking,* Silver added to himself. Pasting on a smile, he channeled the preppy queen group leader at Path to Glory. "Eli's swell. What can I get you?"

Kellan looked up intently—probably still worried about Eli—but Nate bitched, "A menu would be nice for a start."

"What do you need one for? You always get the same thing," Kellan said, earning his boyfriend's bitchy attention.

"True." Nate's eyes narrowed. "Make it two veggie burgers, Philly toppings, no cheese."

Kellan flicked some of the sweat from his bottle at Nate. "If I gotta have veggie, I'm getting cheese on mine. And fries."

Nate nodded, like Kellan needed his permission or something to order his own food. As Silver went back to put the order in, he wondered if they did that

same stuff Eli and Quinn did. Christ, it had been loud
last night. Even with earplugs.

Silver's only other table at the moment was a guy
writing something on his computer while drinking
coffee. He'd inherited him when his shift started, but
as Lisa had informed him, the guy had already paid
and given her a shitty tip for taking up the booth for
an hour. Then she'd been ranting about how she'd told
Ben this would happen when they gave free Wi-Fi access, and Silver had tuned her out. He stepped out of
the beverage station with the coffee carafe and ran into
Kellan.

"Don't mind Nate. Bad day at work."

Since Silver had spent Saturday night in jail and
had been driven to work in a police car, he thought he
won the whole "bad day" contest. But he was curious.
"So he gets to order your food?"

Kellan shrugged. "I like veggie burgers, but don't
tell Nate." He winked. "Of course, I like 'em better
with bacon."

After flashing a grin and then tapping Silver on
the shoulder with a fist, Kellan strode back to his table. Silver refilled Wi-Fi-mooching-computer-guy's
coffee and went into the kitchen to ask if they'd slide
a piece of bacon onto Kellan's burger. He did not get
the whole having-to-sacrifice-something-you-liked-
to-please-someone-you-liked-fucking. What the hell
difference did it make to Nate what Kellan ate?

The one time Silver had bothered to try to please
someone with food....

A ripple dissolve threatened a candlelit flashback.
No matter how Silver tried to push it away, he couldn't
completely block out what had happened after Zeb

mentioned that he missed his mom's beef stroganoff. Nothing stopped his brain from replaying the laughter and love on Zeb's face when presented with the resulting gluey paste studded with blackened strips of meat.

A table of rowdy women landed in Silver's section, and the need to concentrate on six special orders and four separate checks was enough to blot out the chance of further flashbacks. When he brought the bacon-augmented veggie burger and the sanctimoniously boring one over to Kellan and Nate, the resulting laughter and bitchery made Silver almost too entertained to be pissed when Eli and Quinn showed up an hour early, acting like they just wanted some loaded fries instead of being there to make sure Silver didn't sneak off.

THE NEXT morning Silver spent lounging on the couch, poking around on the tablet Eli had given him after he'd chased Silver out of the spare bedroom. One of the walls in that room was taken up by Eli's computer and graphics stuff, and apparently Eli did more than cook and put out, since he claimed he had to do some work.

Silver couldn't really complain, since the couch was comfy and they had streaming services so he could watch pretty much anything. At first it was fun to catch up on the last three seasons of *Ice Road Truckers*, but that got old fast. Silver didn't have another shift at With Relish until Thursday.

He went into the bedroom and flopped on the bed. "I feel like a freaking virgin trapped in a tower."

Eli snorted. "Rapunzel, Rapunzel." He spun around in his desk chair. "You may have the blond locks, but I think you're past the expiration date on virginity."

Crunching his abs, Silver curled up enough to see the computer screen, then jerked to his feet for a closer look. It was a black-and-white picture of one of the ships in the harbor in the pouring rain, and somehow Eli had made it look like there was another layer of water on it. Like if you touched it, your fingers would get wet. Everywhere there were shadows and light that made the picture look 3-D. All of it black-and-white except for a splash of neon reflected on the water.

"Fuck, Eli."

Eli studied Silver's face, then smiled. "Thanks. It's for a show. In an art gallery."

"Fancy shit." Silver flung himself back onto the bed. "So this is you now? Quinn's boy toy slash housewife who makes pretty pictures to keep from dying of boredom."

"Yeah." Eli's grin was huge. "Isn't it awesome?"

"I guess. If you like that kind of thing." Silver smoothed a lump in the cover he'd thrown over the unmade bed. "You do really like that kind of thing? I heard him the other night. Hitting you."

"Spanking me, you mean?" Eli bounced onto the bed next to him. "I fucking love it. I can come just from that and a little friction. Have you ever tried it?"

Silver smoothed the blanket out again. Eli knew about the hustling. The winter they'd met, neither of them had been doing too well. But Silver hadn't told Eli about the web stuff. Might as well. "Kind of." He poked around on the tablet and handed it over. "Here."

Eli took it, and his eyes got comically wide. "Holy shit."

"I did lots of live subscription web stuff. This is out everywhere."

Eli stared back down at the tablet. "Oh my God. Is that Papa Grande?"

"Yeah."

"He is so fucking hot. I can't believe I never saw this, and now I can't ever jerk off to it. Ow. Those are some swats." Eli winced.

"People paid to keep it going. And they also gave a free six-month membership to someone who could predict how long I could take it before I'd break."

Eli turned the tablet facedown on the bed. "I didn't know."

Silver shrugged. "I didn't tell you. It was after the shelter. We'd lost touch."

"You never said why you took off like that."

"I was still underage. Was afraid with the social workers and shit that they'd find me."

Eli was smart enough not to ask who *they* were. Eli always had a half a dozen insults ready to go when he mentioned his asshole parents, but Silver's weren't worth the effort.

Eli smoothed the same lump under the cover and then met Silver's eyes. "Was it better than hustling?"

"Better in some ways, worse in others. Got fucking sore sometimes."

Eli rolled his eyes. "Seems like cake by comparison. At least there's furniture—and a director to keep an eye on things."

"Yeah? You try getting drilled by a dick that size for six hours while they adjust the cameras." But for the most part, Eli was right. It had felt safer. That first winter wasn't anything Silver wanted to relive. Eli either. Silver leaned back until he was propped up on his elbows. "Does Quinn know? About you tricking?"

Eli stretched out on his back and folded his hands across his stomach. "As much as he can?"

"What the fuck does that mean?"

"It means I told him. But I don't know how much he gets it. How much anyone else can. Any time it comes up, he gets super protective. Which is sweet, kind of, but I don't want to be packaged in bubble wrap in order to leave the house, you know?"

Silver didn't know. No one had ever really given a shit about protecting him.

Controlling him, yeah.

When he'd been with Zeb, things had gone like they had the night in the cell. Silver having to look out for himself while Zeb floated around in his flower-child, Jesus-loves-you bubble. How the hell had Zeb managed two years in Haiti? Only in private did Silver ever get to see the real Zeb. The one with the wry smile and the absurd sense of humor.

Silver rolled onto his side, careful not to touch Eli. Didn't matter. Eli didn't get the concept of boundaries. He reached over and shoved Silver.

"So how come you're not loaded, Mr. Porn Star?"

"Pretty twinks who'll fuck on camera aren't hard to find. I had to do the spanking and bareback stuff to make much. And it was hard to hang on to without a bank account."

Eli shot off the bed. "Bareback?"

Silver had known the explosion was coming. Figured now was as good a time as any.

He gave Mr. Safe-Sex Lectures a bored look.

"Is that where you got it?"

"Which? Gonorrhea or HIV?"

"My God—"

"Save it, Eli. I'm not stupid. And there's no guarantee it was the modeling." Silver's mouth quirked in a half smile as Eli responded to the euphemism with a predictable echo of modeling and flinging his hands over his head. "I did have two boyfriends."

"And you weren't safe with them?"

"Come off it. Don't tell me you aren't getting bred by Daddy every night."

Eli stopped flailing and folded his arms defensively across his chest. "We waited. And got tested."

"How poster-child perfect of you." Silver rolled off the far edge of the bed and started for the door.

"Silver, wait." Eli caught his wrist. Not roughly, not anything Silver couldn't yank free of, but if he was going to get an apology, he'd stick around for it.

But Eli pushed him onto the bed. "You are a serious mess, my friend."

"Fuck you."

What was it with everyone thinking they could give Silver the tough-love lecture? First that fucking cop, and now Eli? Bad enough he had to stay here, but he didn't need the lectures on top of it. If he couldn't leave, he could sure as fuck check out. He picked up the earbuds he'd been using, but before he could take the tablet and turn his back, Eli yanked the cord out of the tablet.

"Why didn't you say something?" Eli demanded.

"To who?"

"Me, dickhead."

Silver shrugged. "You didn't owe me anything. Why was any of it your problem?"

"I thought we were friends."

"So?" Silver whipped the cord out of Eli's hands. "That entitles you to hear about all my problems?"

"No, that entitles you to tell me about them. And me to help you if I can."

"By help you mean I get whisked away to Boringland with you and Quinn?" Silver rolled his eyes.

Eli shook his head. "I mean you could have been safe."

Chapter Five

SAFE. FOR the rest of the day Silver turned that word over and over in his head. What the fuck did Eli mean by safe? Usually when it came out of his mouth, it was as a pair, one word. *Safesex.* But Silver didn't think that was all Eli meant this time. What? Safe like they'd been in the shelter, barely off the freezing street, surrounded by drunks? Safe like Eli was, trapped here in suburbia, cooking and cleaning like a good little housewife? Or safe like they'd offered at the clinic, under the supervision of case managers and social workers crawling into every bit of his life?

He hated this feeling. Eli acted like there was some kind of simple answer that Silver couldn't see, when he'd been trying everything to keep himself safe.

The sound of the front door opening had Silver ready to retreat to his room in case Quinn launched

into his own version of the your-life-sucks-and-it's-
your-own-fault speech. But when their paths intersect-
ed in the hall, Silver saw Quinn had brought home a
nice *safe* target for Silver's anger.

He stood in front of Zeb. "So what are you supposed to be? My gentleman caller? Is he on the ap-
proved list, Daddy?"

Before Quinn could answer, Eli came out of the
kitchen. With a sneer in Zeb's direction, Eli got up in
his boyfriend's face. "Did it follow you home? I've
told you to wipe your feet before you come in."

Quinn put his hands on Eli's shoulders. "He's a
friend. And he's a guest." Quinn's calm was usually
a nice contrast to Eli's flail over everything, but right
now it got on what was left of Silver's nerves. Quinn
started to back Eli into the kitchen. "And he's here to
apologize." Quinn looked back for a second and raised
his brows in Silver's direction.

Nice for someone to ask permission in running
his life. Silver rolled his eyes and said, "Fine," mostly
for Eli and Quinn's benefit.

Zeb, looking earnest and so damned sure his *sorry* would fix everything, provided a perfect opportunity to cut him to pieces, let him know nothing would
ever be all right. Because there was no fix for what had
happened after that night. But instead, Silver's toes
curled and gripped inside his sneakers, and he found
himself fighting the urge to back away, swallowing the
words to send Zeb out of his life for good this time.

"Jordan—or should I call you Silver like your
friends do?"

It didn't matter. Because Silver wouldn't let Zeb
be around long enough to let it matter.

Silver shrugged. "Jordan's fine." *Silver* sounded weird coming from Zeb. As long as it wasn't *Jordie*—Silver blocked the memory of the way Zeb had whispered it, voice full of awe.

"It suits you, though. Silver. With your hair and eyes."

As if Silver didn't know what he looked like. White-blond hair and gray eyes, thin and tall. One of the tweakers he'd met when he first landed in the city had given him the name. He'd liked it enough to keep it.

He couldn't keep his feet still anymore, so he let them take him into the living room, plopped in a chair, and swung his feet up so he could press and flex them against the coffee table.

Zeb took the couch. "I owe you an apology."

Well, that was the fucking understatement of the decade. "Yeah? What for?"

"Getting you in trouble."

It sounded like someone from church talking about a girl who was pregnant. Silver arched his brows.

"Getting you arrested. I should have listened to you the other night. Seeing you—I didn't think. I only wanted to know you were okay."

The *other* night he should have listened? The *other* night he wanted to know if Silver was okay? Last Saturday was the only night he was going to apologize for?

Silver's tongue was thick enough to choke him. It was the only excuse for the fact that none of the words were making it out of his mouth.

Zeb went on, "If your friends hadn't stepped in—I want you to know, I would have done anything to get you bailed out. I was praying I could get enough from selling my car, but your friend Jamie said they had it covered."

"He's Quinn's friend." That pathetic protest was what Silver came up with? Every reason in the world to tell Zeb what he could do with his lame-ass apology, and Silver whined something about the cop not being his friend. *Pathetic* didn't begin to cover it.

Zeb's smile showed off one dimple and crinkled his eyes. "Arguing with you would be a lousy way to apologize, but I think he is your friend too. You have good friends. Great friends. Though I'm not surprised."

"What's that supposed to mean?"

"I've always seen something amazing in you, Jordan. Like a light to draw me in."

The last little piece of bullshit from Zeb's sanctimonious mouth finally shook something loose. Silver snorted in disgust. "Drawn to wanting to fuck me, maybe."

"That's not true." Zeb's protest was instantaneous, but Silver caught the quick glance aimed at his crotch.

Sitting down or not, Silver knew how to show off. He shifted his weight and crossed one leg so the ankle rested at his knee, lowering his lashes and giving Zeb a shy smile.

Zeb blinked.

"Or"—Silver hardened his voice—"wanting to fuck me over."

Zeb squared his shoulders, and his cheek lost its dimple as his jaw tightened, though his voice was soft. "I'm so sorry, Jordan. For everything that happened."

It wasn't really an apology. He said it the way people said *I'm sorry* when you had a bad day. Or at funerals. Not the way you should say it when you were the one who tripped the guy into the grave.

But maybe Zeb would be sorry. If there was something he wanted, counted on like Silver had needed Zeb back then, maybe he'd feel what it was like when he couldn't have it.

Zeb still had an itch he figured Silver could scratch; the look had been plain enough. Wouldn't take much until the guy was gagging for it. And then Silver could dish out a little payback. Nothing like what he'd been through standing outside Zeb's apartment, needing to check with a hand on his stomach to be sure his guts hadn't actually been ripped out.

"Yeah. Thanks." Silver gave Zeb a smile like that half-assed nothing of an apology made the sun shine bright. "So, you want to stay for dinner?"

OVER ELI'S dinner of enchiladas, rice, and salad, Silver tried to study Zeb as if he were a guy Silver planned to pick up. After all, he used to do it to stay fed, so it shouldn't be too hard.

When was the last time he'd fucked anyone just for fun? Jason? No, Jason had been fun, and things had been good, but their relationship had been as much about getting to stay in Jason's gorgeous apartment as Jason himself. The boyfriend before him. Austin. Neither of them had had much of anything, and it had been all about having a good time. Silver had sometimes found himself wondering when the drama would kick in, but it didn't, even when Austin said he'd gotten the job offer of his dreams and moved to Charlotte— never suggesting Silver come with him. Following the announcement, it was two weeks of almost constant

fucking and then a *Been fun. Have a nice life.* Silver
had texted after he got the positive test, but the *Not
Austin's number anymore* was a dead end.

In the middle of his musings, he realized things
had gone quiet, except every time Eli put a dish down,
there was a loud *thunk*.

Silver glanced over at Zeb, but all the lines he
might have used tasted blander than water. Zeb wasn't
a trick. He wasn't Jason or Austin or anyone else.
There was too much history, and it was hard to keep
the image of Zeb cutting into his enchilada at Quinn's
dining room table from mixing with the funny, sexy,
shy man Silver had fallen for four years ago. No matter how much concentration he poured into hating this
Zeb, someone whose rejection had hurt him more than
any of the shit that happened afterward, having Zeb
here made it impossible to forget that this was also
someone who'd once loved him.

After another noisy meeting between Eli's water
glass and the table, Silver went with a question he actually wanted the answer to. He glanced at Zeb. "How
did you meet Quinn?"

"Last summer we were both working at a camp in
Pennsylvania for children with cancer."

Sounded like Zeb all right. Good deeds. The Zen
bubble he always seemed to float around in was a little more drawn in, like he'd toned down some of the
eagerness, and along with it the way he'd taken everything as a new way to experience the world.

Quinn paused with a fork to his lips. "When I
heard a teacher in the district was retiring at winter
break, I got in touch with Zeb about the position."

"So you ended up back here." Silver wrapped things up, nodding at Zeb.

Zeb's smile at Silver held the dimple plus a shared secret and history Silver had to ignore before his brain exploded all over Eli's pastel tablecloth. "Well, this isn't exactly New Freedom, is it?"

"New Freedom?" Eli's voice went high. "Fuck me, that sounds like a cult. Wait." He stabbed his fork at Silver, eyes wide under the black bangs. "Were you in a cult?"

"No. It's a small town right over the border on the Pennsylvania side," Zeb said.

"Fucking felt like a cult growing up there." Silver rolled his eyes at Eli.

"Uh-huh." Eli pushed his chair back. Coming to stand behind Silver, he said, "Gimme a hand in the kitchen," and yanked on Silver's collar until he could get strangled or get up.

Eli's height forced him to shift his grip from Silver's collar to a belt loop to finish propelling him into the kitchen. A sudden twist and release spun Silver into the counter next to the stove.

"What the fuck is going on? You call me from jail and tell me that guy's the reason, and now I'm fucking feeding him enchiladas?"

Silver settled his T-shirt back onto his shoulders with a shrug. "He apologized for everything. It was just some ex-boyfriend drama."

"Really?" Eli's brows arched under his bangs. "Even Quinn's ex-boyfriend drama didn't land anyone in jail."

"At least not yet." Quinn's voice rumbled from the archway as he joined them in the kitchen. "Guys, the man out there isn't an idiot, and the walls aren't soundproofed."

Silver rolled his eyes. "Tell me about it."

"Silver"—Quinn looked him in the eye—"if there's a reason you don't want this guy around, tell me, and I'll respect that. But he sounded sincere about wanting to apologize, and my gut tells me he's a good guy."

Eli's cough sounded exactly like the word "Peter." Quinn hipped Eli into silence.

"Thanks. I can handle it. I'll go talk to him." Silver went back through the archway to find Zeb pushing away from the table.

Again, Silver's brain froze trying to figure out which Zeb he was talking to, the one he'd loved or the one who'd turned him away.

"I'm sorry to have made everyone uncomfortable, so I'm going to go. I appreciate you hearing me out, Jordan."

Well, this was fucked. How was he supposed to execute his plan when he couldn't keep the guy around for dinner? Silver realized he liked this self-assured version of Zeb. It seemed as if the more priggish, self-righteous part of him had grown into a guy who didn't have to draw attention to doing the right thing.

"I'll walk you out." Silver managed to keep from crossing his arms over his chest. Zeb gave him a sharp look, like the offer was a surprise.

Without any talking, the trip to the car was full of sounds Silver usually wouldn't have heard. Maybe it was the humidity in the air that made the front door opening and closing so thick, the brush of Zeb's loafers and slap of Silver's bare feet echo off the cement walk.

As soon as Zeb started the car, the window whined down. Silver went around to the driver's side, only to watch Zeb slide his seat belt into the buckle as he said, "They care about you. A lot."

"At least somebody does."

"Jordan."

If his name had been spoken in that patient, scolding tone Zeb had always used when Silver bitched about life in New Freedom, Silver would have backed away. But there was a note in his name, a pleading completely unlike Zeb's sexy begging in bed, and it sure didn't fit with his new confidence.

"What?" Silver waited.

"I wish—I *hope* maybe sometime we could be friends again."

Silver's throat was too tight to answer.

"Quinn has my number if you decide you want to talk. Any time."

Silver nodded and backed away.

AFTER FINALLY falling asleep around 2:00 a.m., Silver woke up with morning wood that just did not quit. He lay there and glared at the ceiling, picturing maggots and roaches and everything disgusting he could come up with, and the blood still pounded until his balls ached. He'd like to blame Zeb for it, but a request to be friends again sometime was not exactly the stuff wet dreams were made of.

For longer than Silver wanted to think about, popping a boner had become nothing more than an annoying body function to take care of. More in line with feeding his growling stomach than taking a dump, but still not worth the fuss. Hell, scratching an actual hard-to-reach itch had become more satisfying.

He listened before he staggered into the bathroom. He got an earful of Eli and Quinn at night—he didn't need to catch an eyeful in the morning. Squinting at the dim outlines in the bathroom, Silver realized it wasn't full light yet. Fuck. He didn't know what time Quinn had to roll out to make it to work, but Silver remembered that back in his day, high school had started way too fucking early.

Still, it didn't take much friction to drain his balls when it got like this, and the shower beat any other option for ease of clean up. After washing his hair, he cupped his balls in a slick hand. It had been while he was doing porn that something switched off. Everything still functioned, but it was like he didn't care if it did.

And then after the positive test, he couldn't stop thinking about it. Right when he was about to come, he'd think about all those spiky-looking cells from the pamphlet, the virus gathering in his nuts, ready to launch. Half the time he'd get there and the thought would freeze him, lock his balls in some kind of vise until he managed a pathetic kind of sputtering shot. He knew it was only his imagination. Knew the pills kept his viral load low. But it was the same with a tiny cut. Thinking about how what came out of him was potentially lethal made him think of movie aliens with acid for blood. Not exactly a mood enhancement.

Not enough of a mood killer either—his biology didn't care how fucked-up his brain was. His dick was still hard, pulsing with blood, his balls heavy and full.

He put more shower gel on his hand and gripped the shaft, sliding it down. The skin wasn't completely tight. He wrapped his fingers in a band around the base, wondering if that would help calm things down. One of the guys he did a shoot with had said he sometimes flicked his cock hard with his finger or a rubber band to back off coming too soon. But that sounded like it hurt way too much.

With a sigh he gave in, stroking fast enough to move things along. Thumb across the head, catching the bump under with the crook of his index finger. Nothing fancy, just scratching the itch so he could get back to sleep. It felt good. But it used to feel amazing.

Like—

And he was barely seventeen again, that first time, dick sliding into Zeb, the unbelievable heat and pressure. It had felt so fucking good, so amazing to have his cock inside Zeb, everything inside Silver seemed to be hot and tight too. His brain shorted out, and his lame mouth said, "God, Zeb, I'm inside you."

Watching Zeb, the way he licked lips all dark and wet from kissing, feeling the ripple and squeeze of those muscles, the prickle of hair on Zeb's ass against Silver's balls, it made him have to thrust. And though Zeb's face screwed up in a grimace, he grabbed on to Silver's ass and pulled him in deeper. Took him all the way inside.

Two more thrusts, and the look on Zeb's face became one of surprise. He grunted, tipping his hips up farther. "Jordie, fuck me."

And that had been it. Over in a flash, as quick and sudden as lightning, he was at the peak and hanging there so sweet and perfect he never wanted to come down. But he did, hips slamming against Zeb, dick pumping over and over as his balls emptied.

In Eli and Quinn's shower, Silver bit his free hand to keep the groan inside as he jerked and shot against the wall, body shaking with the echoes of pleasure. Despite the fact that his first time topping wasn't going to be winning him any adult movie award nominations, it had always been his favorite jerk-off session. It had gotten him through lots of bad times, first at camp, no matter how many times he had to pray to be delivered from unclean behavior—and those fuckers went through his trash for evidence of spunk-filled tissues—but even after, after the night when Zeb had treated Silver like he was a piece of DNA-soaked trash.

Silver stretched his jaw and pulled his hand free, glancing at the teeth marks in his hand. No scary infected blood, only dents.

He angled the showerhead to rinse his jizz off the tiles, then got a bleach wipe from under the sink and wiped down the wall. He was going to stagger off to his room, but then he thought about the tub. He knew—but it didn't seem to matter what he knew or had had explained to him in one of those skin-crawling counseling sessions at the clinic.

He found the cleaner under the sink and sprinkled it over the tub. When the door banged open later, Silver was scrubbing the toilet. Quinn loomed over him. "What are you doing?" He rubbed his face.

Silver figured he probably ought to be more freaked out by the fact that he and Eli's boyfriend were both naked in the bathroom at the same time, but he was more embarrassed by what he was doing.

"I'm cleaning."

"At oh five forty?"

"I was awake."

Quinn scrubbed at his jaw some more. "I've got to get ready for work."

"Yup." Silver scrambled to his feet, glad to not be eye level with Quinn's dick anymore. "I'll just—" He shoved the brush into its stand. "Uh, have a good day." He sprinted back to bed, jammed the earphones in, and put a pillow over his head.

WHEN ELI yanked off the pillow and pulled the buds out of Silver's ears, it was bright in the room.

"I'm sleeping, Eli." He had been. At least he thought so. It had been like he blinked and Eli was there.

"It's almost eleven."

"So?" Silver reached for the pillow.

Eli flung it out of reach. "So aren't you late taking your pill?"

"Fuck." Silver flung the sheet off and put his feet down. If he was back on Tyson Street, this wouldn't have happened. He'd never have slept this long on that skinny mattress, never have been comfortable enough to jerk off in the shower.

I'm happy you've decided to begin the medication, but I want to make sure you understand the commitment, Silver. If you don't follow the regimen, you'll be creating serious problems for yourself in terms of managing the condition.

Silver had assured the counselor that he could handle eating a meal and taking a pill at the same time every day, even if he wasn't going to take them up on the offer of housing where he'd have to put up with inspections and other kinds of intrusions. He'd been doing pretty good. The pill he'd puked up Sunday had been the first one he missed in the two months since he'd started.

Eli took the pillow with him as he went to his desk. "I kept some french toast warm in the oven, or you can nuke a waffle from the freezer."

Silver bit back a comment about not needing a mother, since the evidence wasn't on his side this morning. He stood up and stretched.

Eli dropped the pillow on the chair and headed for the door. "And you might want to put on some kind of pants. I don't think there's any furniture in the house we haven't fucked on."

After Eli's breezy exit line, Silver snatched his pillow off the chair and grabbed his briefs.

Eli hadn't gone as far as setting a place for Silver at the kitchen table, but as he carried his french toast and coffee in hand, Silver still approached it warily. No way would Eli be satisfied with Silver's quick *I'm over it. Everything's fine* explanation in the kitchen last night.

Silver lowered his plate to the table as quietly as if he were around someone nursing a hangover. Eli continued to flick through stuff on the tablet, a cup of coffee next to his elbow.

"Syrup?" Eli offered without looking up.

"Sure."

"It's in the fridge." Eli flashed a grin like it was a brilliant joke.

"Thanks." Silver rolled his eyes as he got up. But at least Eli wasn't fixated on digging. It had been easier having him as a friend when Silver could just say he had someplace else to be and escape any inquisitions. "Cream?" he asked Eli, while he had the fridge open.

"No thanks. Had some already," Eli purred. "Fresh and full of protein."

"Yeah, whatever. Aren't you the lucky bitch?" Silver sank back into the chair and saturated his french toast with the syrup.

Eli put the tablet down. "If you want to get laid while you're staying here, you can bring him back—"

"Not fucking likely."

"I know it's embarrassingly suburban." Eli waved a hand, then hid behind his coffee mug.

"No, I mean, I'm not likely to want to get laid while I'm here." Or for the foreseeable future. "And I like the house, Eli. You're lucky."

That threw Eli off his stride. "Uh, thanks." The mug hit the table with a *thunk*. "Quinn told me you were cleaning the bathroom this morning."

Silver cut his french toast into pea-sized pieces and swirled trails through the syrup.

"You don't have to do that." Eli talked to the top of Silver's head. "That kind of casual contact doesn't spread—"

"I know. I got the pamphlet and got an A in health class, so you can save the public service announcement. I couldn't sleep."

"Is that a side effect of the reverse transcriptase inhibitor?"

Silver couldn't have rattled the information off so easily, even if it was his med. The doctor at the clinic had talked about NNRTIs and NRTIs and antiretrovirals. Silver had thought this pill sounded best because it was a combo and he only had to take it once a day. But he had read the warnings on the side. "Yeah."

"Sorry. Did they give you anything for that?"

Silver shook his head. "I figured I was lucky to get this. It's not like I have insurance, you know."

"Me either. Though if Quinn and I got married…." Eli trailed off, then hid behind his mug again.

Silver stabbed another piece of sticky bread. The Eli Silver had met in the shelter would mock the hell out of the Eli sitting across the table. "Got your gown picked out?"

"You know I love to dress for an occasion. Speaking of occasions, it's time for a special one."

"What?" Silver used his last piece of bread to mop up as much syrup from the plate as he could.

"The one where you tell me what the fuck was up last night with you and—" Eli's lips pursed. He seemed to be having trouble coming up with one of his labels for Zeb.

"Saint Zebadiah?"

"Right. Him. Though I will say he's rocking the whole bad-boy-Jesus look with the scruff."

"Nothing." Silver should have known he wouldn't be able to escape the questions.

"Don't 'nothing' me."

"What are you going to do?" Silver sneered. "Kick me out? Please?"

Eli tapped his chin in consideration.

For a second there wasn't enough air, that last chunk of sticky breakfast clinging to his throat. He resisted the urge to wipe his hands against his thighs.

This was the problem with living soft. Too easy to get used to it again.

"Oh, I've got worse tortures in mind." Eli narrowed his eyes. "I'll send you bowling with Quinn."

"Oh please. Anything but that." Silver held up his hands in surrender. "Hey, did you really go all psycho on Zeb in the courthouse lobby for me?" It was kind of cool to think that Eli would, plus getting him to talk about himself would equal total derailment of his questions.

"Did he say that?" Eli got all indignant.

"Nah, Jamie told me. Only he said 'cut-a-bitch crazy.'"

Eli huffed. "Well, all I knew was what you told me on the phone. And don't think I couldn't take him."

Silver didn't doubt it. He'd seen Eli in action once. He was small but fearless, and he went right for the nuts. Silver relied on a shove or a trip and the speed in his long legs.

"And don't do that," Eli said.

"What?"

"Distract me."

Silver sighed. "What are you so hot to know for, anyway?"

"This may be Quinn's house, but if there's a reason that guy shouldn't be hanging around you, I want to know it."

"Fine."

Eli eyed Silver with one brow arched in suspicion. "You could start with how we go from you freaking out and leaving your own birthday party—yes, I figured that part out—to get away from him, and after one night in jail later, everything is peachy keen."

"Did you really just say 'peachy keen'?" Silver doubled the raise on his own brows.

"Don't change the subject again."

"Someone's been taking toppy lessons from Daddy."

Eli didn't bite. He stared and let the silence stretch between them.

Silver could have played that game too, folded his arms and waited, but Eli was better as an ally. The story would have to be edited. No way would Eli—at least not cut-a-bitch-crazy Eli—let Zeb hang around if the whole disaster came out.

"Zeb and I used to—" *God help me, Jordan. Do you know how much I love you?* "He's an ex," Silver finished, and leaned back to balance the chair on two legs.

"Yeah, I got that much. From when? Quinn said he's been in Haiti for two years and just got back last summer."

"I guess. I wouldn't know. It was back when I was living at home."

"That's the way to work it." Eli offered a fist bump Silver ignored. "I'm not the only one who goes for older men."

"He's still a lot younger than Quinn." Which wasn't the only difference.

"So, was hooking up with him how your parents found out?"

"Yeah." Now was the time for careful work in the editing room. "Before they knew, they actually liked me hanging out with him. Thought it was a bible study group."

"But you were studying him in the biblical sense."
Eli chuckled at his own joke.

Silver checked frame by frame, looking for places
to cut. Even after his parents had left New Hope for
a different—less liberal, according to them—church,
they'd been thrilled at all the interest Silver showed in
staying with the old congregation instead of fighting
them every Sunday. And when he'd announced he was
doing a bible study group with one of the youth leaders, they'd praised Jesus up and down.

All Silver had to do was a quick internet search
for a couple of verses and interpretations and he could
be out until 11:30 two nights a week. That had always
been the worst part once they'd started making lo—
fucking. Having to get out of bed and dress, a long
good-night kiss at the door before the drive home.
Most of his friends wished they could find someone
to bang regularly. Silver dreamed of a time when he
could spend the night in his lover's arms.

Silver examined his younger self with disgust.
Poor pathetic sap. No wonder he'd been so fucked.
He never should have opened his mouth. Shown Zeb's
picture to his best friend. Maybe then nothing would
have happened. It had taken a whole lot of *if*s to get to
the place where everything went to hell.

If Zeb hadn't gotten a job filling in for a teacher on maternity leave over on the middle school side
of the campus. If Marissa hadn't wanted to go over
to that spot in the woods to sneak a cigarette during
lunch. If Zeb wasn't such a good teacher that he had
his seventh graders outside to do some practical geometry, measuring shadows. And mostly if Marissa
hadn't said loud enough for the other two girls with

them to hear, "Mary's donkey balls, Jordan. Isn't that your boyfriend?"

Marissa wouldn't have deliberately screwed him over. But once it was out—

To Eli, Silver said, "I'd just turned seventeen, and my parents threatened to have him put in jail. That was one of the reasons I agreed to go to that place I told you about."

"But if you were seventeen—shit, the laws in Pennsylvania suck. How does anybody get laid?"

"I heard them talking with a lawyer. It was because two weeks before we got busted, Zeb got a job in my school district. Made it different, even though he wasn't teaching me." Silver made a disgusted sound. "I should have known they wouldn't go through with it. Too much public exposure of their queer son."

Eli cupped his chin in his hands and leaned forward. "So, after the hot-for-teacher drama, what then?"

"You know the rest." Or as much as Silver was willing to tell. "That place was worse than a prison. After I managed my jailbreak, I hitched back home. They didn't care what that place was like. It was that or the streets. You know what I picked. It was Baltimore or Philly, and I figured Baltimore was warmer. It was closer."

"No, what happened with Zeb?"

"He wasn't there when I got back." That much was true. At least not the Zeb that Jordan Samuel Barnett had been in love with. "I don't know if he quit or got fired. I didn't know how to find him again."

"Oh my God, you guys are like Romeo and… Julio." Eli's eyes were wide with sympathy. "But wait.

Why did you skip out when you figured that was him coming to the party?"

Yeah. What about that? Lying was extra easy when most of it was true. "I'd managed to get a note to a friend to give to him after I got shipped off so he'd know where I was, what had happened. But the other night I found out he never got it."

"Totally Romeo and Julio. And you never saw him again until he jumped out of the car Saturday night?"

"Nope."

Eli sighed and dragged his coffee cup across the table. "That's pretty fucking epic. Even better than Kellan and Nate."

"An epic disaster, yeah."

"Do you still love him?"

Silver jerked his head up from where he had doo-dled a *Z* in the syrup on his dish.

Scratching it out with force, he said, "When did I ever say I did?"

"You were seventeen. Of course you were in love."

Not at first. At first he'd just been horny and Zeb had been cute. And funny. After that, yeah, so maybe the earth did move and Silver's stomach flipped over from nothing but a wink of one of those warm hazel eyes.

"So?" Silver challenged.

"So do you still feel about him the way you did before?"

There hadn't been any of those feelings when he saw Zeb this time. No earth moving or stomach flip-ping or horniness. So why was it so important to get back at Zeb? If Silver didn't care, it should have been easy to say *Fuck off and get out of my life*. And if he still cared, he wouldn't be coming up with a way to hurt Zeb.

It wasn't as if the plan was to destroy his life. Just give him a little taste of what it had felt to be turned away like that. To want something, to believe in it so much that you convinced yourself it was real, only to have it taken away. Silver only knew he couldn't let it go. So what was another lie to Eli if it got Zeb free access to the house?

Of course, the way Eli was looking right now, kind of dreamy and misty-eyed like he wanted to take Silver's hand and squeeze it sympathetically, Eli would be doing everything he could to spin this as his "epic" love story. That might come in handy.

He was also looking like he was waiting for Silver's answer, and instead of taking his hand, Eli jabbed Silver's arm with a finger. "Do you still love him?"

"I don't know." Silver shrugged. "It's been a long time." To his surprise, it was the absolute truth.

Chapter Six

THE AIR was hot and sticky and as disgusting as a trick's unwashed ball sac. Which was normal for Baltimore in late May. Silver was helping Eli carry plates and shit out to the patio table. Which was abnormal when there was a nice air-conditioned kitchen right behind them.

"Cook and eat. Outside. On purpose. Like ten thousand years of progress never happened," Silver complained as he put the stack of stuff down. "Benjamin Franklin would totally curse you out."

"Look at you, all history-knowing. Wait until I tell Quinn." Eli peeled a piece of hair off his face.

"Don't get excited. If a guy's face is on money, I know who he is."

"Apparently cooking outside is required for man points." Eli tipped his head toward Silver and jerked his chin at the grill, where Quinn and Jamie were standing.

"And apparently," Quinn said as he strode over, "someone went a little crazy in the outdoor living area of the Home Depot, and I said if we bought it, we were using it." He draped an arm around Eli's shoulders.

"That was in March. When I had all these lustful feelings for spring. Now I'm over it. And hot." He shoved Quinn's arm away.

"And cranky." Quinn's hand landed on Eli's ass with a light tap and squeeze.

Silver rolled his eyes. One look at Eli and it was obvious all his protesting about suburbia was complete crap. He loved this setup, just as much as he loved having a Daddy. Everything about the way he carried out his tray full of burgers and ketchup and relish and cheese and buns and pickles and pasta salad showed how much he loved having a house—home to take care of for his man. Probably would have been perfectly content as a fifties housewife.

Jamie stomped over, knocking back some of his Red Dog beer. "Be sure to stick to soda, kid. Wouldn't want to have to bust Quinn for serving to someone underage."

"Wow. That was a dazzling example of wit. Did you spend all day thinking it up?" Silver grabbed Jamie's beer and stole a sip. "Uh-oh. Now you'll have to bust yourself."

"Hey." Jamie snatched the bottle back and glared.

Oh shit. Sometimes it was so easy to forget. Forget that Silver had something inside him that scared other people. Scared himself when he thought about it.

Jamie glanced down at his beer, then brought the bottle to his lips and knocked it back again.

"Smart-assed kid." He flicked a nail against Silver's knuckle.

Silver tried not to make his exhale audible. "Ow. Hey, isn't that abusing someone underage?"

"Yeah, nice try."

Quinn went back to the grill, and Eli carried over the plate of burgers. Nothing veggie, so Nate wasn't coming, but even assuming Jamie and Quinn ate two each, there were too many.

Silver sank into one of the chairs. "Where's your better half? And I mean 'better' in every sense of the word."

"Gavin," Jamie said with emphasis as he sat opposite, "is not half of anything. We're not joined at the hip. But he was invited, and he'll be here after he takes care of some stuff."

"Uh-huh." Silver couldn't blame Gavin if he was already doing his best to avoid spending time around Jamie's annoying ass. "So what do you call him, then?"

"Usually I call him Gavin. It being his name and all." Jamie picked at his beer label.

"He's not your boyfriend?"

"Why, you looking for a date?"

"No." And fuck no. But Jamie would probably think Silver was disrespecting Gavin if he said it aloud, and that was far from true. "Just asking. You're kind of touchy about it." This was the most fun Silver had had in weeks. "Did you ask him to marry you and he turned you down, gold digger?"

"I liked you better when you were just some brat at the club who couldn't give a decent blow job." Jamie made a disgusted sound and swung out of the chair.

When Gavin walked down the driveway a few minutes later, he greeted Jamie with a kiss. It went quick, but Silver could tell it would have been longer and deeper without the audience. He could always tell. Truth was in the body language, the way a couple became more than two guys standing near each other. Though they weren't looking at each other or touching, there was something in the way they held themselves, like there was a magnetic field between them so they were pulled to each other, even if neither of them moved. Something porn with a plot never managed to show, why "Real-Life Lovers" porn sold well. No matter what guys said about only wanting to get off, they still craved the fantasy of a connection deeper than skin.

Quinn saluted Gavin with a grill spatula, and Eli offered a full-body hug before going back inside the house. From Silver's point of view, sprawled in the nicely cushioned patio chair, it was like watching a movie—or a really boring reality show. Real House-husbands of Baltimore. The cliché was complete when Eli came out of the house with a glass of red wine and handed it off to Gavin.

"It's from the bottle you gave us at the party. I made sure to let it breathe," Eli said.

"Thank you." Gavin nodded as he took the glass. Except for the Gucci loafers, he wasn't dressed much differently from Jamie, cargo shorts and a short-sleeved collared shirt. What set him apart was the crispness of it, the way it seemed like a photo shoot was about to start any second, complete with a fan to capture the flow of Gavin's hair from his face as he posed with a hand on his hip. Perfect and rich, he ought to be more out of place in Eli's slice-of-suburbia backyard than Silver. But it was clear who didn't belong. And it wasn't Gavin or Eli, with his goth hair and waving, gesturing hands.

Silver breathed in the sizzle and smoke of the grease from the grill, a smell from his childhood. Not that there were barbeques in his backyard. No, that wouldn't have fit the image Dr. and Mrs. Thomas Barnett were so careful to create. But at friends' houses, and at church, back when church felt more like a fun place to do an art project or sing and act out stories with other kids, instead of a lecture on why he was destined for hell.

Gavin made his way to the table and chose the folding chair that didn't match the rest of the set.

"I don't think I've thanked you for saving my ass." Silver wiped a hand on his shorts before offering it to Gavin. It wasn't like Silver was nervous; it was still hot as fuck. Even the outsides of his elbows were sweating.

Gavin shook hands, but his shoulders lifted in an apologetic shrug. "Glad I could help."

And that could have been it. A few standard phrases, the expected thing. Gavin didn't seem to be any more interested in prolonging the conversation than Silver. He'd probably only come over here to be polite. Like he had when he gave Silver that outrageous present at Eli's party, a silver money clip from Tiffany's.

One of the few things Silver owned worth hanging on to.

It wasn't good to rock the boat. Gavin seemed mellow enough, but there was no way to be sure he wouldn't decide to stop paying the lawyer or pull the bail if Silver pissed him off. Or maybe his goodwill only went as far as Jamie's interest, which was due to Quinn, which was due to Eli. Maybe it was better to not make anyone think too hard about why they had decided to give a shit whether or not Silver rotted in jail.

He'd approach with extreme caution. "Can I ask you something?"

"You did." Gavin's slight smile was polite, though his answer was smartassed. No wonder he could tolerate hanging with that arrogant asshole cop.

"I mean...." Maybe Silver should drop it, but Gavin nodded like he was telling Silver to go on.

"Why are you helping me?"

"Because I can."

Yeah, no shit. But what did it mean, and what— "Like what do you expect from me? You gotta know I can't ever pay you back."

Anyone else and he'd be sure he knew what kind of payback a guy would expect, even if what Silver needed was only a place to crash and some food. But the way Gavin had looked at him the night when Eli threw him a birthday party—it wasn't the kind of interest or attention Silver was used to seeing on a man.

Gavin's finger stroked the bowl on his wineglass for a bit before he answered. "Maybe I'm helping you because I hope you'll learn something it took me years to figure out."

When Gavin didn't go on, Silver prompted, "What's that?"

"Sometimes people simply like you. They offer kindness and friendship, even if you didn't do anything to earn it."

"Yeah. And then when you learn to count on it, they fuck you over."

Gavin smiled, but his eyes were flat. "Yes, that, unfortunately, is also part of the equation. But somehow I doubt you need any help in learning that."

Gavin wasn't staring or doing anything else creepy, but Silver still felt uncomfortable. He had the feeling there wasn't much Gavin didn't see through, that the lies Silver could spin so easily to friends and assholes alike would raise a red flag along with Gavin's eyebrow as he said whatever people like him said instead of *You are so full of shit*.

The only other person who had seemed so aware of who Silver really was had been Zeb. And even then, his knowing had been based on one lie after another to maintain the first one he'd told him about his age.

"Hey, Silver, you want cheese on yours?" Quinn called from near the grill, providing a perfect opportunity for escape.

"Yeah. You ready for the rolls?" Silver would happily trade Gavin's too-perceptive sympathy for Eli's overt nagging.

"Sure," Quinn said.

As Silver crossed the whole four-yard space of lawn and handed Quinn the package of Goldman's buns, Eli was saying, "And the next time they saw each other was Saturday night, when Zeb got lost going home from the bar."

"Guy needs a GPS to find his way to the head in his own house," Quinn muttered.

Jamie was the only one who noticed that Silver was standing there. "Maybe you should have let the guy tell his own story, Eli."

"Hey." Eli waved and grinned exaggeratedly, then shrugged. "Sorry. It just slipped out."

"That's what he said," Jamie said, and both he and Quinn burst out laughing.

"Sorry." And this time Eli did sound sorry. "Honestly. When Jamie's around, it's like they're both twelve years old." As the laughter faded, Eli turned his head toward Silver. "You know, thinking about it, why didn't Zeb ever try to find you?"

"Let's save a small bit of consideration for what it was like for Zeb to find out he'd been screwing a high schooler." Quinn shuddered like it was the most repulsive thing ever, like *he* wasn't fucking someone half his age.

But Jamie called bullshit. "Hey, you got a taste for fresh chicken, you gotta learn to check the date on the package. Did you bother?"

Eli chuckled. "Oh, he did. I showed him an ID."

"I told him I was nineteen," Silver mumbled. Then he glanced at Quinn. "And Zeb was only twenty-two when we met."

"Still, you were, what, sixteen?" Jamie asked.

Silver glanced away. Maybe he'd have been better off with Gavin. He might see through bullshit, but he didn't act all judgmental.

Quinn started sliding the burgers onto a plate. They'd taken two steps away from the grill when Eli poked Silver's biceps. Hard.

"That wasn't your actual birthday. On your license. The one I threw you a party for."

Silver shook his head.

"When is it really?" Eli asked.

"August."

"Well, don't think you're getting another one." With that pronouncement, Eli flounced his ass onto a chair.

"Or more presents." Jamie flicked some of the sweat from his fresh beer at Silver. It was nice and cool.

"By the way, I won a hundred twenty on those scratch-offs you gave me." In reality, Silver had been surprised to win ten dollars, but he figured the inflated amount would piss Jamie off.

Instead, Jamie grinned and dropped a hand on Gavin's shoulder. "Told you my present might be worth almost as much as yours."

"Almost." Gavin smiled. With Jamie behind him, Gavin had to know the guy couldn't see his face, but still the smile was so much more than the polite attention shown in the ones Gavin gave Silver.

The ache was so sharp and sudden, Silver first thought it was the heat, the stifling air burning into the lining of his lungs.

It wasn't the heat. It was almost jealousy, because Silver wanted Gavin to smile like that at him. But he knew the feeling wasn't about Gavin; it was about him and Jamie. Not as if Gavin wasn't totally hot. If Silver still wanted to fuck as much as he wanted to breathe, he would pay Gavin for a chance to suck him off.

No, what hurt was what the smile meant. If someone who was as much of a complete asshole as Jamie could get such a smile out of Gavin, it was enough to make Silver want to believe in some bible verse he'd drawn a picture for in Sunday school. *Love forgets mistakes.*

To believe maybe there'd be someone, someday, who'd do that for him. Look at him like he mattered, the way Zeb used to. Someone who'd make Silver give him the smile that forgave everything.

After the food was distributed, Gavin asked, "Are you excited about your exhibition, Eli?"

"You seriously have to ask? I'm totally freaking out. Thank you so much for introducing me to your friend at the gallery."

Gavin did his shrug thing again, like he wasn't some kind of fairy godmother waving around the money wand. "My friend thinks he's the one who will be grateful. He expects you'll sell very well with the limited run of prints."

"You're all coming to the opening, right?" Eli gave them a peeking-from-under-his-bangs look. Effective on Quinn, maybe, but it made Silver cover his face in disgust.

"If I don't have to work," Jamie answered quickly, then added in a mutter to Gavin, "How come when you get involved it means uncomfortable suits?"

"It's artsy. You can get away with skipping a tie," Eli said. Gavin nodded, and Jamie's habitual scowl faded slightly.

Eli and Gavin started talking more artsy details while Quinn and Jamie talked about a bunch of guys Silver didn't know. Which was fine. Silver had had enough attention on him. A little peace was a nice change. He washed down his burger with iced tea and figured in another five minutes he could go inside and stop sweating.

The conversations faded, and Gavin cleared his throat. "Silver, I spoke to the lawyer today."

Ah. A setup. All the stuff about having a cook-out today because Jamie had to work Memorial Day weekend was a cover so there was a good crowd for the latest intervention.

"Okay," Silver answered cautiously. It couldn't be really bad news, or Gavin wouldn't have given that speech about learning people could be nice without you blowing them or whatever.

"They're working out a plea to avoid any jail time, but he feels the judge would be more inclined to look favorably at it if you were working on a GED."

Gavin used a lot of pretty words, but Silver cut through it. School or jail.

Even conscious of how far out on a limb these people had already gone for him, Silver didn't remember a whole lot of difference in terms of boredom between sitting in class or sitting in a cell. "I don't want to take adult-ed classes with a bunch of losers."

Jamie snorted. Silver glared. Gavin said, "Perhaps a tutor."

"Quinn's a teacher. Couldn't Quinn tutor him?" Eli offered.

"Uh." Quinn didn't sound particularly enthused about that.

"Zeb could," Silver put in.

Gavin's gaze felt like it went right through Silver's brain and picked out all the ideas attached to what he'd hoped was an innocent-sounding suggestion.

Eli's look was suspicious, but for a different reason. "We're talking actual studying this time, Silver. Not the fun kind."

"Yeah, I got it." Silver sighed. "Look, he said he was sorry for getting me arrested, and he'd do

anything to fix it." He avoided Gavin's eyes. Eli's be-
lief in the whole epic-love thing should help. "Please,
Mom, we'll work here at the house where you can
keep an eye on us." It wasn't as if Silver's plans involved actually having sex with Zeb, only making him
want it. Want what they'd had so he could know what
it felt like to lose it.

"Will you ask the lawyer about that, Gavin?" Eli
ignored the rest of it.

"I will. The sooner things are official, the better,"
Gavin agreed.

"I can call him." Silver hoped his smile didn't
look as fake as it felt. "You've got his number, right,
Quinn?"

WITH EVERYONE grabbing something, it didn't
take as long to get stuff back into the house as it had
taken Eli and Silver to haul everything out. He wished
he'd have that kind of help when he worked lunch
tomorrow. But when Silver went back for the stuff
that had been left by the grill, he was surprised to see
Gavin wiping off the table.

"Is this weird for you? Doing a maid's job?"

Gavin gave Silver a look like he was trying to figure out if Silver was serious. "Amazingly enough, I've
applied a damp cloth to a flat surface in order to clean
it a few other times in my life."

The guy was touchy. If Silver had that kind of
money, he'd never do his own cleaning. He'd hire
someone to follow him around that he could hand
shit to. The touchiness could be Jamie getting under
Gavin's skin. Like that wasn't bound to happen sooner
rather than later.

Or maybe there was a problem with communication. Though they were both sarcastic, Gavin was a lot quieter. They'd both be happier if one of them said something.

And Silver owed Gavin. Giving him the 411 on his boyfriend's issues was the least Silver could do.

"You really like him? Jamie?" Silver asked.

Gavin straightened immediately. "Ah—"

Silver held up his hands. "Relax. I'm not hitting on you." Though that car was something. "Unless…?" He let it trail off hopefully.

"No." Gavin's voice was firm.

"So. Do you?"

A tiny smile teased the corners of Gavin's mouth. "I do."

"Well, maybe you need to tell him that. He seems kind of weird about the idea of you guys being a couple."

"Does he?" Gavin sounded like that was something to be amused by rather than a problem.

"Christ. I just said that." What the hell was the point of trying to help people? Silver grabbed the spatula and tongs Eli had sent him out for and stomped back into the house.

Jamie was doing the dishes, and Silver was only too glad to dump the utensils into the soapy sink so the water sloshed.

"Thanks for the shower, brat."

"You're welcome."

"Teenagers," Jamie said in disgust. "Reminds me. How's your buddy's car? He get a new solenoid?"

"Yeah, I think," Silver muttered, guilt knotting the muscles of his spine until he felt himself shrinking.

When Eli had thrown Silver a birthday party, Silver had wheedled a ride out of Marco. But when they left, the car wouldn't start until Jamie did something involving sneering, snarling, and sparks in the engine. Predictably, Marco's control-freak older brother had acted like it was Marco's fault that the piece-of-shit car had something wrong with it when they got it back, leaving Marco carless for weeks. Marco had sent a bunch of texts lately, but Silver hadn't answered.

He tapped out a quick *How're you doing?* text to Marco.

"You think?" Jamie asked. "You guys seemed tight enough at the party."

What the hell planet was Jamie on that he thought Silver and Marco were tight? He probably only worried about Silver hitting on Gavin. "Seriously? Are you giving me boyfriend advice when you don't even know if you've got one?"

"Suit yourself." Jamie turned sharply. "The fuck do I know is right," he muttered under his breath.

Silver remembered he was trying to do Gavin a solid and pushed away the irritation brought on by heat and guilt about blowing Marco off and by being in the same room with Jamie.

Silver found a dish towel in a drawer and took a glass off the counter. "You guys are good."

"Huh?" Jamie snapped his head back around.

"I watched. He's really into you."

Jamie's eyes narrowed with suspicion.

Putting the glass away in a cabinet, Silver reached for another one to dry. "Maybe you should have like a relationship talk. Like 'where do you see this going' or whatever?"

"Yeah. No." Jamie let the soapy water drain out of the sink. His voice wasn't as gruff as it usually was when he said, "So, your buddy. He got an issue with you being positive?"

"None of his business. He's just a friend."

"Still. Must be hard."

Silver shrugged. He didn't plan on fucking anyone anytime soon. If he did, he'd worry about it then.

Marco's pissed-off answer of *Why? Need a ride somewhere?* came back two hours later while Silver was tucked up in a chair, headphones on as he poked around on the tablet and tried to ignore Quinn and Eli on the couch. They weren't fucking or making out. That would have been easier to deal with. They weren't cuddling, exactly. Quinn was reading a book, and Eli was watching something on Bravo that had to do with clothes.

But they were touching in little ways. Quinn's arm along the back of the couch by Eli's shoulders, Eli running a hand along Quinn's thigh or through his hair every once in a while. It was disgusting. Not the casual affection between them, but Silver's reaction. The way he was wrestling with a great big messy, hungry ball of envy. Hiding behind the headphones and tablet wasn't working anymore, couldn't keep him from driving his nails into his palms because he wanted someone to touch him like that, in a way that didn't mean anything while it still meant everything.

He pushed to his feet. "I'm going to bed."

"Good night." Quinn glanced up and blinked as if his eyes were refocusing.

Eli offered a smile. "Night. Don't forget to call Zeb tomorrow. About tutoring." He added with an eyebrow waggle.

Silver shut himself in his room and sprawled on the bed. Could he get more pathetic? Cowering in his room at nine thirty. He hadn't been to bed as early as nine thirty since middle school.

Rolling onto his stomach, he pulled out his phone and texted Marco back. *Sorry been out of touch. Got busted. Just got out.* Funny how it was close to the truth. His lying muscles would get all flabby if he kept sticking so close to the truth.

Marco's answer was immediate this time. *Busted?*

For a guy who lived in a part of the city that made Silver nervous, Marco could be hella naive.

Cops picked me up. Fake ID.

Puñeta! Fucking pendejos. You okay?

Marco also loved drama. And any chance to be seen as more badass than he was. If he really wanted to stir up shit, he could tell his extremely scary older brother about having a taste for dick, but Marco wasn't that stupid.

Fine. Laying low. That was an understatement right now.

Want to go out?

No, Silver did not. When he'd hit the bed, he'd realized he was tired. The idea of actually falling asleep and staying that way was a sweet promise. If Marco's car didn't work, it was three bus transfers to meet him on West Eager Street—and then the same crap back up, assuming there were buses running. No one had told him he couldn't go out. Jamie's warning had only extended to skipping out on bail, not being chained up in Mount Washington.

And even if this soft bed in a nice house was just an illusion of safety that Silver shouldn't learn to count on, it was good enough for right now.

Silver propped himself up on one elbow. *Can't. No ID. Don't want to get picked up again.*

No club. Party. Carro bien.

Silver was hesitant to rely on Marco's description of the car as fine. *Laying low.*

Aguafiestas.

Silver wasn't sure if that was a spell-check disaster or a description of the party being wet, so he sent a question mark back.

Rain on the party. Always. Marco sent a pouting emoticon. *No go alone.*

Silver sighed. He felt like a giant wet blanket, all right. Supposing Gavin's lawyer got him off, Silver couldn't hide out in Eli's spare bedroom for the rest of his life.

He tapped out his answer. *OK.*

Chapter Seven

As soon as they stepped off the elevator, Silver smelled disaster. It wasn't only the burnt-carpet reek of a meth pipe and some overly pungent sex. There was an overlying reek that raised the hackles on the back of his neck.

If it wouldn't have been a cliché of epic proportions, he would have leaned down and muttered *I have a bad feeling about this* in Marco's ear. Silver knew all his friend could see was the gleaming chrome and modernist leather and steel Bauhaus furniture of the loft space, but Silver had been raised by snobs, and it only took a quick glance to tell that Mies van der Rohe and Lilly Reich hadn't been anywhere near the rent-by-the-week living room set. And the clothes were trying a little too hard.

Going to so much effort to sustain a lie was warning enough. When a guy with a rug barely covering his balding scalp threw an arm around each of them and claimed, "I didn't know Heaven delivered, but you are the answer to my prayers," Silver figured even Marco would have seen enough to start backing for the door.

Instead, Marco ducked and patted the guy's arm. "My prayer is to have a Cuba libre. You can help me?" Marco batted his thick-lashed eyes.

Silver rolled his as the guy went to get Marco's drink. "What the fuck? Did you look at him? You liked him pinching your ass?"

"Free drinks, *cuate*. Not all of them can look like that, *sí*?"

"Get your own rum and Coke." Silver pointed at the bar.

"Aw yeah." Marco's accent disappeared under a perfect imitation of a Chesapeake drawl.

Silver grabbed his arm. "If you put it down, get a fresh one, and don't drink anything someone hands you."

Marco shook him off. "You are not my brother. *O mi novio.* Am 'just your ride.'" He gave Silver a shove. "*Vete a la chingada.*"

Silver wanted to follow him, but the pain and longing that shook Marco's voice when he said Silver wasn't his boyfriend kept Silver glued to that spot. He couldn't be. Not only for Marco, but anyone right now. In fact, Silver couldn't imagine a scenario where he didn't end up dying alone. And per Marco's instructions, Silver would be glad to fuck himself rather than look as pathetic as that future made him feel.

He hoped his expression was more aloof than worried as he leaned against a support beam near the bar. He caught glimpses of Marco's curly black hair, but his friend was too short to keep a close watch on

in the dim light. The next time he spotted him, there
was cloud of smoke around Marco's head, but after
an initial burst of anxiety, Silver realized it was only a
blunt between Marco's lips.

Weed didn't worry Silver; the idea of a crystal
pipe in Marco's hands did. And not just because Marco would be too fucked-up to drive him home. Silver
had seen enough tweaked-out hustlers; he didn't want
to see Marco dropping down that hole. It had never
held any allure for Silver. His life was fucked enough
without dragging drug addiction into it.

For all Marco's pretended hood-rat bad-assery,
his overbearing brother had seen to it that Marco was
about as streetwise as Silver had been when he got off
the Greyhound down on Haines Street.

Rather than dealing with a come-on from a guy
way older than Quinn and nowhere near as hot, Silver took out his phone and pretended to text. When he
realized it had been a good fifteen minutes since he'd
caught a glimpse of Marco, Silver was tapping at the
keyboard for real.

Despite the streaming ambient music in the main
area, Silver would have heard Marco's antique-car-
horn text tone if he was there. His phone was never off.

Silver searched around every partial wall, finding
two not-Marco twinks getting felt up—and down—by
some creepy guys. On the back deck, Silver spotted
a thick neck and gunmetal brush cut above a yellow
polo collar. Party like this, that could only be Todd
Pike, the producer from the spanking website. Knowing that guy was here doubled the urgency to grab
Marco and get the fuck out of here.

When no one answered a pounding on the bathroom door, Silver dug out an old hotel room key he kept in his wallet and used it to push in the cheap door lock.

Marco's jeans were falling around his hips, shirt up around his neck, as the douchebag who'd greeted them when they walked in licked his way down Marco's chest.

"Hey, sorry. Gotta take a dump. Like, now." Silver reached for Marco.

Toupee guy scrambled to his feet. "Get the fuck out."

"Sure, okay. I'll just do it in the kitchen sink. I think that's what someone else did. Smells like it."

"What the hell?" The guy yanked his own pants over his hips and charged out of the bathroom.

Marco blinked, eyes unfocused as Silver grabbed his arm and shook him. "We have to go. Now."

Marco pulled free. "No. You run out on the party alone this time. Some *hijo de puta* ex-*novio* make you cry again? *Vete a la mierda.*" Marco shoved Silver toward the door. "I wanna get laid."

"Do you want to be raped?"

"Not rape when I want it." Marco draped himself on Silver's side, planting a wet kiss on his neck.

Like Marco was able to know what he wanted now. Sometimes his brother Timo's protectiveness did more to risk Marco than it did keep him safe. Silver was sure Marco's sisters weren't innocent enough to take drinks from skeezy guys.

Silver peeled Marco off but kept a grip on his shoulder, tipping his chin up to study his face. "What did he give you?"

"Rum. Amigo make Cuba libre *estupendo*. Not taste the diet."

"I bet. That's the same asshole who grabbed our asses when we got off the elevator. You want to fuck him?"

"He is... nice."

"He's a...." Silver searched for one of Marco's favorite insults. "...*pendejo*." Silver dragged Marco out of the bathroom. "Look around. Fifteen minutes ago, was there anyone here remotely hot?"

"Mmmm. I get to pick?" Marco cuddled up against Silver's side.

Jesus. Even fresh out of New Freedom, Silver hadn't been this stupid. "Marco. He drugged you. You ever hear of a roofie?"

Marco looked at him blankly.

Senorita Kaminski's Spanish class had never covered date rape drugs on a vocab sheet. Maybe she saved it for senior year.

"Liquid X," Silver explained. Marco smiled. "*Sí. Bueno.*"

"No. It's bad. Gimme your keys. I'll take you home."

"No. *Arrecho.*" Marco wrapped his arms around a support post.

"Huh?" Senorita Kaminski should have spent more time on the slang and less on the conjugations. Sure as fuck would have come in handy right about now.

"*Arrecho*," Marco whined. "Need to come. *Necesito que me agarres.*" The grind of his hips against the beam was all the context Silver needed for translation.

Fear and desperation were tying knots in Silver's intestines. He could make it out of here no problem, but he couldn't leave Marco.

Silver placed a soft kiss behind Marco's ear. "Okay. You come with me." Kissing him again, Silver fished Marco's keys from his jeans. "And I'll blow you when we get there."

"*¿De veras?*"

"Yup." Silver threaded him through a few predators lurking near the door.

One of them was Pike. He might have been a bottom-feeder, but he had charm, and even sober, Marco might fall for a play.

"Behave now," Silver murmured when Marco winked at the *Bad Boys Real Tears* producer. Pike might decide Marco would rather be here. And Silver didn't know if he could fix that mess.

Marco came to a halt, eyeing the stretch of yellow polyester across Pike's shoulders. "*¿Tu prometes?*" He demanded of Silver. "*Bésame.*"

Silver made not-kissing an art form in his hustling days. Kissing still felt more intimate than sex. Avoiding it hadn't been difficult. That wasn't what they wanted his mouth for. Hating himself, he turned Marco's face toward him and kissed him.

Marco's tongue drew his in, hungry, desperate. Silver doled out calculated encouragement, firm pressure, a few sweeps of his tongue between Marco's lips, and a hand stroking his back.

At last, Marco giggled and relaxed. "*Vamonos.*" He grabbed Silver's hand and pulled him toward the elevator.

Marco was still handsy in the car, but as they got closer to the address Silver remembered from their last fucked-up car trip, he subsided. When Silver stopped the car on the street in front of the row house, Marco was snoring. He'd probably be safe enough in the locked car—his brother would come out looking for him in a few minutes—but Silver couldn't leave him like that. Even if Marco started yammering about the blow job Silver supposedly owed him.

He came around to the passenger side and tried to shake Marco awake. The way Marco's head flopped set off a three-alarm fire under Silver's rib cage. He lightly slapped Marco's face.

"Hey, c'mon. I don't want to have to go get your brother. I don't even know which is the right house."

Marco's eyes moved under his lids but didn't open.

Silver bounced on the balls of his feet, the timer in his head ticking down toward disaster. "Marco." He leaned in and whispered in Marco's ear, letting his lips and breath tease the skin. "I'm going to get off without you if you don't wake up."

"Mmmm." Marco made that purring sound again, hand wrapping around Silver's neck. "Silverrrrr. *Argénteo.*" Marco's fingers played with the hair that covered the collar of Silver's shirt.

The skin there prickled in warning, but he couldn't extract himself in time. A rough arm yanked him back.

"What the hell are you doing to him? *Puto.*"

It wasn't the first time Silver had been called a whore, and he was glad the accompanying shove moved him out of range of the gob of spit Marco's brother aimed at him.

"No, Timo," Marco whined. What followed was some extremely rapid exchange of Spanish that Silver only caught a few words of. Unfortunately, one of those words was *novio*. And Silver had a feeling that he was being labeled the boyfriend in question. Whore yes, boyfriend no.

Timo spun around, anger and disgust twisting his face, and Silver remembered Marco telling him that Timo was still on parole.

Well, Marco was out of the car now. Silver was done. He put his hands up and took another step back.

"I'm not his, uh, *novio*. I swear. I just drove him home." Marco leaned against his brother. "Not drunk. Drugs." Silver took another hasty step back, hoping Marco's dead weight would slow Timo down if he decided to eliminate the blond part of his problem. He wouldn't drop his brother onto the sidewalk, would he?

"I didn't drug him. He was drinking soda. At a party. Someone put something in it. I saw he was messed up so I got him home safe."

"He safed me. *Mi novio argénteo.*"

"Not his boyfriend," Silver repeated when it seemed like Timo was thinking that dropping his queer brother to the cement so he could beat the fuck out of the guy who'd corrupted him was a good plan. "He's only fucked-up. He'll be fine in the morning." Christ, and he'd thought his own coming out had been a shitstorm.

"No," Marco said, and there followed another stream of Spanish and English, and of course the one thing Silver heard as loud as a fart in church was "blow job."

At least that focused all Timo's attention on Marco again. A female came out of one of the doors and joined in. Curtains were twitching. An audience. Timo couldn't hurt Marco now, Silver told himself as he backed away.

He was getting ready to kick it into another gear when Timo yelled in barely accented, perfectly understandable English. "Hey, you. Not-his-boyfriend. I see you around him again, I'll kill you."

"Got it," Silver said and took off.

By the time he stopped running, all he knew was he was in a neighborhood where cabs didn't go. A blow job would have been so much easier.

Chapter Eight

HE CHECKED a street sign to get his bearings but was still lost. Worse, stranded and lost. His phone was a burner. No GPS. He had no idea what buses ran 24-7 on this side of town. Assuming he could figure out where on the east side he was after his blind sprint away from Marco's scary older brother, Silver could head back to Midtown and get the Pimlico bus. That ran all night. He'd slept on it once or twice. Walking the ten miles back up to Quinn's place would take till long past dawn.

Silver's hand pressed on his phone. When he'd announced he was going out, Eli hadn't tried to stop him, only said to call if he needed anything.

But Eli didn't drive. So that meant Quinn would be the one who'd have to come down here. Although it had been Quinn's idea to make Silver live way the fuck out in Mount Washington, he had come through big-time and didn't deserve a 2:00 a.m. call when he had to work the next morning.

For a minute Silver pictured Gavin rolling up in that sleek night-black car, beckoning him inside. But even if that happened, the reality would be Silver crammed in the back while he listened to Jamie bitch and moan the whole ride.

Not that Silver had Gavin's number.

Silver had someone else's, though. After dinner, Eli had nagged about calling Zeb. That had been about the tutoring. But if anyone was responsible for Silver needing a ride to Mount Washington instead of being able to head back to his room on Tyson, it was Zeb. If Zeb hadn't been such a moron last Saturday night, none of this would have happened.

It was a long shot anyway. Zeb wouldn't even pick up. He slept like the dead. But standing here like an ass wasn't going to get Silver to a bed anytime soon.

"Hello?" Zeb's sleep-rough voice curled deep in Silver's gut. But Zeb sounded alert, and it only took three rings.

"It's me, Sil—Jordan."

"Jordan? What's wrong? Are you all right?"

Three years ago, Silver would have given anything to hear that much concern in Zeb's voice. Obviously Silver wasn't all right, but what came out was, "Yeah. I'm fine, at the moment."

"At the moment. What does that mean? Did you get arrested again?"

"No. I wouldn't have gotten arrested then, if—" Silver swallowed. This had been a bad idea. He didn't want Zeb to know this Jordan, the one who in less than three hours managed to seriously fuck with a friend's head, get his life threatened, and end up stranded in gang territory at 2:00 a.m. "No, I didn't get arrested."

"Jordan, you wouldn't have called unless something had happened."

Why was it so hard to ask Zeb for this? He owed Silver so much more than a lousy ride. But it wouldn't come out.

"You know how the other night, before you left, you said...."

"I said I hoped maybe we could be friends again."

"Yeah."

"You didn't call me at two in the morning to talk about that."

"No."

"You're scared. I can hear it in your voice. What happened?"

Scared? He'd been scared all the time when he first got to the city. But then it became like white noise, a constant hum, so normal he couldn't get worked up over it. What was the big deal if some other horrible shit happened?

To be scared now, there had to be something he was afraid of losing. What had he started to give a shit about to make the feeling surge back? He heard the rapid breath in his voice, too, now that Zeb mentioned it.

"My ride got wasted, and I'm stranded in the city."

"I'll be there as fast as I can."

Silver hadn't even had to ask. He listened to rustling noises, Zeb getting out of bed, putting on clothes.

"I think I'm in Linwood, maybe Ellwood Park." Silver had never been on Noble Street before, and he sure as fuck didn't ever want to be on it again.

"You're in a park?"

"No. The neighborhood." *Shit.* Silver remembered Quinn saying something about Zeb getting lost a lot. "I can help you with directions." *I hope.*

"I'll be okay if you can give me an address. After, well, after getting lost on Saturday, I decided I needed a GPS."

An address. Okay. Silver could probably manage to come up with one. "Good. So—" A low-slung car with blacked-out windows slowed, pacing him as he walked. "Shit," he whispered. "Just a sec."

He and the car were at an intersection. He crossed behind the car and held his breath as it turned right. As soon as it did, he sprinted off in the other direction, eventually wedging himself in a slot between two garages that opened onto the street. It took some wrestling to get the phone back up to his ear.

"Jordan. Jordan? Are you all right? Can you hear me?"

"I'm okay." And he sort of knew where he was now. The cross street had a familiar name.

In his usual hoodie and jeans, Silver was better at blending in, being just another kid on the street. But over here on the Eastside, dressed in his tight party clothes, he looked like a skinny blond white boy from the suburbs trying to buy weed in the hood. And that was trouble.

There was a main drag a few blocks up, bound to be places lit up, maybe something would be open. "Does your GPS do intersections?"

"Let me check." Zeb was in the car already? Yes. Silver heard the engine, tires humming on pavement. Not only in the car, but driving. Zeb had never moved that fast in his life.

Zeb was back on the line. "It does. I'm headed toward I-83, right?"

"Okay. Put in Pulaski Highway and North Highland Ave. I'm headed there." Silver peered out through the space toward the street. A car went by, usual speed, nothing that set off alarms. He twisted a little as he prepared to edge back out, scraping an elbow raw on the bricks. It smelled like something had died in this slot; definitely something was peeing here regularly. He waited for Zeb to tell him he was on his way.

"I've got it. It says, shit, it's going to take me at least twenty-five minutes to get there."

"You swore." Silver felt about eight years old when the words left his mouth, but he was so shocked he couldn't stop it. Zeb's curses had been limited to some *Oh God*'s when he was coming and an occasional *fuck* in reference to the actual activity.

Zeb ignored the idiocy. "I'll be there as fast as I can."

"See you then."

"Jordan, wait. Don't hang up."

"Lost already?" Silver tried to keep the exasperation out of his voice.

"No." A pause and the sound of Zeb swallowing. Then his voice was back, thicker. "I'm scared."

This time there was no hiding Silver's frustration, even if Zeb said *hell with it* and went back to bed. "For fuck's sake, you're in a moving car. You'll be fine."

"No." Zeb's voice didn't carry any answering irritation. Only an emotion strong enough to leave his
voice thick, rough. "I'm scared for you. Keep talking."

The same warmth that had curled around his
stomach at the sound of Zeb's fresh-from-sleep voice
spread through Silver's chest. "You know, talking on
the phone while driving is illegal in Maryland."

Zeb's laugh almost made Silver forget where he
was, trapped with the smells and blood trickling from
his elbow.

"Thanks to your friend, I've got a clean record
now. I'll take the risk."

Forgetting where he was could be dangerous. Silver needed all his attention on his surroundings.

"I don't have enough minutes. I'll call when I get
to the intersection." Silver ended the call before he
gave in to the temptation to make Zeb laugh again.

Oops. Thanks, by the way, he mumbled at the
dead air before sliding the phone in his pocket and
wriggling free.

SILVER'S ASS had barely landed in the Pontiac's
passenger seat when Zeb blurted, "You're bleeding.
What happened?"

Silver looked down at his elbow. It had slowed
to a seep, but yeah, it was a mess. "It's fine. Scraped
it on a wall." The trip north a couple of blocks had
been uneventful. Silver had moved fast and kept his
head down, and he'd found an open minimart in a strip
mall.

"There's a first aid kit under your seat."

Silver reached down and found the plastic bin.
Homemade and so loaded Silver noticed a suture kit

and tourniquet. Zeb hadn't been so Boy Scout prepared back then. He'd been all OCD about keeping
track of things in his little notebook, but this had-
his-shit-together-in-a-crisis Zeb was a guy Silver had
never seen before. Maybe living in Haiti had a bigger
effect than he'd thought.

"Thanks." He gritted his teeth and used an alcohol pad to clean the spot. It wasn't too bad—until it
was—and he hissed.

"We could stop and get some water."

"Not if you don't leave this parking lot."

"Seat belt."

Silver wanted his answer to sting with sarcasm,
but Zeb's response was so him, a laugh slipped out.
"You'll break the law to talk on the phone, but I have
to wear a seat belt?"

"I trust my driving. Not everyone else's."

Silver pulled the belt across with a sigh so loud he
almost missed Zeb's soft "I want you safe."

There was that word again. How did everyone
come to believe they knew what was best for Silver?

"We're still sitting here," he pointed out.

"Where am I taking you?"

Was Zeb asking if Silver wanted to come home
with him? He had to squeeze the pad hard against
his scrape so the pain would shut away the idea of
climbing into Zeb's bed. The most horrible part was
realizing the longing wasn't centered in Silver's dick,
but higher. Something hollow right below his ribs,
like the constant gnaw of hunger he remembered from
when he'd been living on the street. The thought of
being pressed up close to Zeb's skin, the familiar arms
around him, the brush of hair against his neck. The

idea hurt worse than when Silver had smelled fried food back then. Because there was no way he was ever going to be able to feed this rumble of want.

"Oh. Back to Quinn's. I'm still staying with them."

Zeb nodded and tapped on the screen stuck to the dashboard.

Despite the lack of a question, Silver found himself saying, "I just went out. It wasn't—I didn't run away or anything." He almost bit his lip to avoid the rush of explanations. *I had permission.* He didn't need permission. He was an adult—had been on his own since seventeen. "I could have called Quinn, but he's already done so much."

"He's a good person. He and Eli both."

Silver heard an unspoken comparison in Zeb's words. As if the persons in this car didn't measure up. Did Zeb expect Silver to gush gratitude about the ride so Zeb could feel like a good person?

"I met Eli a few years ago. He's really loyal to his friends."

"I noticed." Zeb's dry humor reminded Silver of Jamie's description of the courthouse lobby.

Silver found himself smiling. "I wouldn't fuck with him. He fights dirty."

"Never tell me the odds." Zeb's Han Solo quote made the emptiness ache again, this time for the taste of popcorn and the DVD of *The Empire Strikes Back* playing on Zeb's TV, Silver's head in Zeb's lap, Zeb's fingers playing with Silver's hair.

"He might be the size of an Ewok, but he's more like Boba Fett."

"I'll keep it in mind."

Which reminded Silver of Eli's dogged bounty hunter intensity. He'd be sure to ask if Silver had said something about tutoring him for the GED.

Silver rubbed his hands along his jeans. "My lawyer"—the word felt weird in his mouth, especially since the guy was Gavin's lawyer—"said I should be able to show the judge I'm working to get a GED."

"You didn't finish school?" Zeb made it sound like an unheard-of crime.

The tone snapped something inside Silver, and it came pouring out. "For fuck's sake, don't you listen? Ever? After you shut the door in my face, I got what cash I could from *friends*, which you obviously weren't, and took a bus to Baltimore. There wasn't exactly time while I was homeless to do The Littlest Hustler Goes to School. Though it might have been the title of one of the pornos I did. I can't keep track of them all." He clenched his teeth together to stop the words. He hadn't meant to tell Zeb about it like that. If at all. It didn't fit the plan. But being around Zeb made it too easy to forget there'd ever been a need to lock himself away.

Silver had lost control of more than his voice. He realized he'd shut his eyes, zeroing in on how much it had hurt. The door slammed in his face. He felt pressure on his body. Imagining himself watching the movie again, he looked down and saw the two of them in a Burger King parking lot, and Silver had wrapped his arms around himself as he curled up against the car door.

When Zeb spoke, it forced away the detachment, dragged Silver back into his body, but the close-up

view didn't help Silver figure out the expression on
Zeb's face as he said, "I didn't know. I'm sorry."

At least he sounded like he meant it this time,
voice quiet and measured. Then a sharper, "God, I'm
so sorry."

Silver didn't know whether he should be relieved
or disappointed Zeb didn't make any effort to reach
over, offer comfort or apology in a touch.

"Drive. Before we end up in jail again."

They merged onto the interstate, and the heavy
silence in the car, the rush of sound, and hum of tires
made Silver suddenly so tired he shivered with it.

Zeb cranked off the AC. The loss of cold air made
Silver sleepier. He could just let it go. Take the loser
adult-ed classes. Never see Zeb again. It would be easier. But why should anything be easy on Zeb?

It wasn't until they'd turned onto Quinn's street
that Silver threw it all out there. "I said the stuff about
the GED because I needed to review the stuff before
the test and thought you could help with the math
part."

"You want me to help you study for it?"

It had been exactly what the fuck Silver had just
said. He nodded.

Under the streetlight, Zeb's smile was soft and
real. "Thank you. I'd like to help. Very much."

When Silver got inside, the house was quiet. He
stood in the hall with the silence beating against his
ears. His plan was working, but anger pounded in his
blood, rushing to fill that silence in his head. No matter how hard he tried, he couldn't slip away to watch
from a cool distance. He didn't want to care whether
it was good or bad that Eli didn't bother to see if he'd

made it back. Or Zeb finally seeming to get how much he'd fucked up that night. And more than anything, he didn't want to give a shit about the last smile on Zeb's face.

WHEN SILVER went in to work lunch the next morning, he found out Travis had quit and Lisa was on forced bed rest until she dropped her baby. He'd been promoted to full-time waitstaff, which meant a hell of a lot more hours and no breaks. His next day off came after working sixty hours in four days. But he had more in his pocket in tips than he'd had after some of his porn work, and only his feet hurt. That Tuesday he woke up, ate, and took his pill before crashing again.

Eli shook him awake in the afternoon-hot room to tell him Zeb was there with a freaky large pile of books. Silver couldn't remember his dreams, but he felt like he was still in one.

"Books?" Silver swung his feet onto the floor and squinted at them. They'd been sore. He wiggled his toes. Better.

"Don't you have a study date?" Eli said, and everything crashed back to reality.

"Right." Studying with slash seducing Zeb. Silver pissed and washed up, brushed the fuzz off his teeth, then disgusted himself by spending a good two minutes trying to figure out what to wear. Most of his clothes fell into either a fuck-me or fuck-off category. Nothing middle-of-the-road. He went with a tank top and his one pair of shorts. The fact that it was ninety degrees out should make it less obviously a let's-fuck and more about the heat.

His bare feet skidded on the wood floor of the dining room when he saw Eli hadn't been kidding about the size of the book pile. Worse, the pile was made up of thin books. The kind of thing they'd called workbooks in school.

Yeah, maybe he'd get around to taking his GED, but he hadn't planned to do much actual studying with Zeb.

"We can go into the living room. It's more comfortable." Shit. That sounded like a majorly corny come-on.

Zeb's smile was friendly, but Silver could tell Zeb was in teacher mode. "Comfortable but hard to get work done."

The ominous pile of books was in the middle of the table, next to a couple of nectarines. Silver snatched up one and slid into a seat alongside Zeb, right as Eli came in.

"Thanks, Mom." Silver waved the nectarine.

"Don't thank me." Eli held his hands up, palms out.

Zeb murmured, "I thought they'd be a good snack."

A quick flush in Silver's cheeks surprised him. As much of a surprise as Zeb remembering nectarines were Silver's favorite. He bit into it, juice running down his chin. A good one for early season. He started to wipe his mouth on the back of his hand, remembered he was supposed to be seducing a guy, and licked up the juice instead, cleaning off his chin with a thumb he then sucked in the most obscene way he could manage.

"Are you staying for dinner?" Eli asked Zeb. "Quinn's at the gym, so we probably won't eat until seven."

"Um…." Zeb's eyes were fixed on Silver's mouth, throat working as he tried to answer Eli. "No." Zeb looked away with an effort Silver found encouraging. "Thank you, though."

Eli went into the kitchen and came out with a napkin he handed to Silver, along with an accompanying eye roll. Standing behind Zeb, Eli mouthed *Study* at Silver before disappearing again.

Zeb's gaze shifted everywhere but back at Silver's face. "I know you specifically mentioned math, but these booklets cover all the parts of the test. I thought we'd start with a pretest and see where you'd need help. I covered pretty much everything when I was teaching in Haiti." Zeb pulled the top workbook from the pile and opened it.

Silver knew Zeb was all about the good deeds, and he was a dedicated teacher, but he really couldn't imagine him in Haiti. "Did you like it there?"

Zeb paused in consideration, as if the question was as confusing as the uses of the freaking semicolon in the sixth question in the grammar section. He rubbed his shoulder for a minute. "I loved the teaching. I wanted to finish what I'd started."

"Why didn't you?"

"I got malaria."

"But I thought—didn't you get shots?"

Zeb nodded. "And we were on a daily dose of a prophylactic, but they ran out for a while."

"So, that's something you always have, then, right?"

Zeb tipped his head, brows arched as if he was wondering why Silver would care about that. Yeah, Silver wanted payback, but he'd never have wanted

Zeb to get sick. Not with something that lived inside him forever. "Yes," Zeb said finally. "Mine is drug resistant."

"That sucks." The next few exam questions were easy. All he had to do was think about how someone with a stick up his ass talked, and that was the right answer. But the silence was uncomfortable.

"So, how were the guys in Haiti?"

Zeb leaned back in his chair. "Stop stalling." But his face didn't match the sternness of his words.

"I'm not. Look." Silver spun the workbook around so Zeb could see there was only one question left in the first part. After circling the right answer, Silver said, "I answered those. You gonna answer mine?"

"There weren't any," Zeb said as he scanned the booklet.

"Not a single male human in Haiti? That's got to cut down on overpopulation."

"I wasn't there for—it wasn't safe. Their culture is different."

Silver knew plenty of otherwise-straight guys who'd do gay for pay or take any hole they could to get off. Guys couldn't be much different in other countries.

"How long were you there?"

"Twenty months."

Silver might not be interested in bumping bits with anyone right now. But twenty months was a long time to go without. The next question mattered for his plan, but the way his voice hit a snag on the way out meant it mattered more than he wanted it to. "How 'bout now?"

"Now what?" Zeb set Silver up with the next part of his pretest.

"Are you with someone now, or making up for lost time?"

Zeb rubbed the bridge of his nose. "Jordan, I'm not sure that's something we should talk about."

"You said you wanted to be friends again. I'm going to go with a yes for your answer, then." And look. This section was on reading comprehension, otherwise known as reading between the lines. Silver should get a bonus point for already getting one right. What kind of guy would Zeb be dating? Some nerdy guy in glasses with sweater-vests, who'd take Zeb out for coffee. As if some guy in a sweater-vest could give Zeb the long, hard dicking Silver knew Zeb loved.

"You would be wrong."

"Huh?" Silver hadn't written anything down yet.

"In your assumption. I'm not seeing anyone now."

"Okay." Damn right, because Mr. Imaginary Sweater-Vest didn't give him what he needed. Silver hid his smile in his nectarine as he went through questions ranging from stupidly easy to brainteaser, but he knew this wouldn't be a part of the test he was going to have problems with.

"Social studies," Zeb announced as he flipped open the workbook to the next section.

This was going to be the boring part, the hard part. But it didn't have to be. Because this wasn't really about studying for a test, Silver reminded himself. He moved like he was getting closer to the table but dragged his knee along Zeb's thigh. Until then, he'd forgotten they were both wearing shorts. Right away, the prickle and tease of hair on Zeb's leg dragged against Silver's, making a nice rash of tingling goose bumps pop up. He shifted back, and Zeb answered the pressure, warm calf against his.

Simple pleasure in the touch of skin. It didn't wake up his cock, didn't feel like an approach he needed to decide how to respond to. Just there. And nice.

He knew he was getting a lot more questions wrong in this part, and not only so Zeb would have to keep tutoring him. It was too lame to care about. Same with the science part, big words and people's names attached to theories Silver was supposed to remember after all these years.

When he started on the math part, he asked Zeb to give him a quick refresher on the formulas. A couple of hints on some base-times-height and distance-divided-by-rate and solving-for-x, and the rest of it seemed to bubble up from the back of his head. After the last two parts, it felt good to get stuff right again.

"It's all coming back to me now." He pressed against Zeb's leg, and swear to God he only meant it in a friendly way that time, a thanks-for-the-help way. And there was no double meaning in what he'd said.

But Zeb glanced over, a regretful smile on his lips and a look in his eyes showing he knew what game Silver was playing.

His cheeks burned. He could not be blushing. He had done porn. How the fuck could he be going this red in the face over something as simple as rubbing his calf on Zeb's?

Zeb's lashes lowered as he wet a thumb to turn a page in the book he was using. Silver remembered that expression so well. The slightly embarrassed look when Silver got a little affectionate—usually more than a little—in a too-public place. The not-now shake of his head had always been followed by Zeb shooting over a glance that promised all Silver could handle when they were alone. But this time Zeb's gaze stayed on the workbook, and his leg inched carefully away from Silver's.

Silver wanted to grab his face, kiss him, force the understanding that this thing between them couldn't be brushed away with an apology and some tutoring help. He wanted to remind him how it had been, Zeb clinging, his fingers digging in hard anywhere on Silver he could reach, hungry for more. Wanted Zeb to look at him the way he used to, like Silver was sharing something amazing and precious with him. Something Zeb could only find with him.

Silver saw himself kissing a whimper out of Zeb's throat. Biting out a moan from his jaw. Then he'd turn Zeb around, yank down his pants, and bend him over the table. Shove inside him, spit and skin, fuck him right on that smooth polished surface where Eli played host, make the books fly everywhere as Zeb tried to find a way to hold on against the slam of Silver's cock. And when he was done, he'd let—

"Are you finished?" Zeb asked.

Silver swallowed. No. This wasn't going to be finished for a while yet. "Got a few more." Silver turned to the side to keep the tension in his shorts from becoming obvious. He hurried through the last page and slid it back. Probably could have done better, but his concentration was still busy fucking Zeb into next week.

Zeb flipped through the pretest. "Good. You'll need some extra practice with science and social studies, but—"

"Homework? Seriously?"

"But," Zeb went on, "you're in great shape. You should be ready to take the exam at the August test session."

August was two months away. Silver couldn't remember the last time he'd had plans so far ahead. Assuming they didn't throw his ass in jail, he supposed he could take the test. A little surge of pride reminded him Zeb had said he was in great shape. So school was lame. Didn't mean Silver didn't have a brain.

Zeb pulled out a workbook labeled GED Science. "I got you these books for practice, and I'll come help as often as I can before I leave."

"Leave? For what?" Silver's pulse throbbed in his ears, drowning out most of Zeb's explanation. He was leaving? He'd just moved here.

With the angry rush of sound, Silver only picked up a few words.

"Camp where I met Quinn last summer. Kids with cancer. Plenty of time for review."

"When?" That one word was all he was sure he could manage to say clearly.

Zeb seemed like he had to force himself to do it, but he met Silver's gaze steadily. His voice was calm, but at least he didn't act like it didn't matter. "A little less than a month. I have to leave on June 20."

Chapter Nine

GOD, THE workbooks were so fucking boring.

Since Zeb had dropped his bombshell and wandered in his oblivious Zen cloud out the door yesterday, Silver had tried to look at the science book ten times. If there was a time limit for getting Zeb panting and desperate, he'd have to need less actual academic interaction. He'd skimmed to the part about sexual reproduction, but it was mostly about plants, and he didn't see how he could use that to turn on anyone who wasn't a florist.

The house was too quiet. Eli was off on a photo shoot with Nate, so that distraction was off the table. Not getting any texts from Marco suggested that he'd lost custody of his phone, which wouldn't be the first time. Timo treated him like he was twelve instead of someone going to college. Every time Silver thought of texting him, he worried that he'd be making things worse.

The sound of Nate's scooter made Silver ridiculously glad Eli was back, even if he had to put up with Nate's attitude.

He hauled the science workbook onto his lap again, opened it, and muttered, "Hey," when Eli came in.

"Hey." Eli's answer was distracted. Come to think of it, Eli hadn't even bothered to ask how the lesson had gone yesterday.

Silver thought he'd find Eli in the kitchen, but it was empty. He poured himself an iced tea, and when Eli did show, he looked startled and unhappy to find Silver there.

What had he done?

Supposing Eli didn't kick him out, Silver didn't want to stay if he was causing problems. He pictured Quinn at the table last night. He hadn't seemed any different. And they'd gone to bed early. Silver had stayed up with the TV blaring to drown anything out.

Still, Silver moving in like this had been too much to dump on even a mellow boyfriend. Silver hadn't exactly been pleasant about it, and it had to be a drag for Quinn. He hoped Jamie wouldn't take moving someplace else as Silver ignoring police orders. He'd still make his court date. He owed them all that much.

Silver didn't know what the fuck to say. He'd never needed to come up with anything to start a conversation with Eli. It was eerie him being so quiet, looking everywhere but at Silver.

Eli took two bites out of a container of potato salad and then shoved the fork back in and stared at it.

"Something wrong?" Silver asked.

"No. I'm fine."

"I meant the potato salad. Is it bad?"

Eli shook the hair off his face. "It's fine too."

"Okay." Everything was fine. Except that it wasn't.

"I really don't know how to say this, so I'm just going to."

"Okay," Silver said again as he started mentally packing. Maybe he could store the GED workbooks here until he found a place. The room on Tyson Street was gone, since it had only been paid through Friday. He had a little money now, but not having ID to use was the big problem.

Eli spoke so fast the words ran together. "Does it freak you out when you hear Quinn spank me?"

"Huh?" Silver blinked.

Eli waved his hand. "Is hearing the spanking a trigger thing? Because of your coerced consent."

Silver had been so sure this was a don't-let-the-door-hit-you-on-the-way-out speech that it took him a few seconds to backtrack through what Eli was saying. Coerced consent and triggers? That had Nate written all over it.

"Jesus, Eli, did you have to tell Nate?"

"It's not a secret. The vids."

"No, but why didn't you ask me instead of dragging his pretentious ass into it?"

Eli hid under his bangs. "It kind of came up. We were doing a shoot downtown, and Nate was bitching about how the cops are using carrying a condom as grounds for a prostitution charge for any woman. And

I've been worried that hearing us was maybe reminding you of—"

"Enough." Christ, Silver was glad Eli had gotten over his crush on Nate. It had killed him to try to pay attention to interpreting everything Nate said or did. But he really didn't need Nate thinking he was some poor exploited piece of ass.

"Listen to this, and you can tell Nate the exact same thing. I consented. To all of it. No one made me. No one came after me. I answered the ads and I knew what the deal was and I signed off on forms."

"Illegally."

"It doesn't fucking matter. I knew what I was doing. I could have stayed at the shelter with you."

"But your parents?"

"They probably never even looked for me. So it's fine, Eli. You guys can fuck however you want, your Daddy can beat your ass purple every night if that's what gets you off, but would you please talk to me next time before getting your sainted ex-whatever involved?"

Eli laughed.

Silver was so not in the mood. "What?"

"You realize that's what you called your ex? Saint Zebadiah? No wonder Nate gets on your nerves."

Yeah, it was a laugh riot. Except Nate saw what was wrong in the world and used that to look down on everyone. Zeb wanted to fix it. As long as when what was wrong wasn't underage and at his door in the middle of the night.

"Hey, I forgot." Now that all was spanky-free in his world, Eli was back to himself. "How did your lesson go yesterday?"

"It was fucking peachy. Now I gotta go study."

SILVER DIDN'T do anything the next few days but go to work and drag himself through that lame science book. Living in Mount Washington with Quinn and Eli was easy on the budget. Sometimes he didn't have to take the bus, though he could have done without the ride in Jamie's cop car when he worked late that one night. If he didn't end up in jail, he'd have enough money for a place that wanted a security deposit. Gavin's lawyer was working on how he was going to get ID in his real name.

Since the lawyer had told him the easiest way was to ask his parents for his birth certificate, Silver didn't like thinking about that too much. He'd thought about saying no, that he didn't have any idea where they were, but he also really didn't want to go to jail. Bile burned his throat as he spat out the names, address, and numbers, including old Thomas's office number.

At least he didn't have to contact them.

When he'd texted Zeb about some more GED practice, they'd set up a meeting at the Pimlico Branch Library before Silver went in to work on Monday. Not great for seduction, but a cool break during the ninety-minute bus ride.

Silver dropped the science book in front of where Zeb sat at one of the tables. Ignoring the way he was trying to get Silver in the seat opposite using the power of the Force, Silver dragged over a chair from another table and sat beside Zeb.

"Guess you decided to skip facing Eli today. He threaten your nuts?"

"No. In fact, I was surprised when he called to invite me to the opening of his gallery exhibition on Thursday."

"Yeah, he's pretty pumped about it. He's probably called everyone in his contacts. Just saying."

Zeb nodded. "Right. Are you going?"

Silver hoped like hell he still had that night off. Eli would have a cow, a cat, and a litter of cow-kittens if anyone missed it, but Silver had a job he didn't want to lose. "If I don't have to work."

"Speaking of work." Zeb opened the science review book.

So they were all business today? Zeb was full of praise for everything Silver had worked on, but it was from that safe teacher distance. Like Zeb had never groaned and glanced back over his shoulder, begging Silver to fuck him harder.

The jump-cut flashback had an annoying effect on Silver's concentration. His stupidly exact memory skipped through dozens of moments: his first taste of a man's mouth, his skin, his cock. The first surprising shift in muscles when the cock inside him stopped burning and felt like it belonged there.

Adjusting the fit of his black slacks around the heaviness of an unwanted semi, he tried to get his attention back on the lame workbook, since that was all Zeb cared about.

It was a short reading passage and questions on cross-species imprinting. Baby ducks following humans like they were their momma ducks. Was that all it had been? All those feelings, nothing more than that Zeb had been the first cute, available guy in Silver's life? He'd sexually imprinted?

If that's all it had been, then why was what he wanted most right now a hug? A big solid Zeb hug, the kind that felt like there was nothing in the world but the two of them, Zeb's breath easy and slow, his heart strong and solid against Silver's chest. A kiss wouldn't be bad either. Fuck, any kind of attention he couldn't have gotten from a well-meaning guidance counselor. Something that proved what they'd been to each other.

Maybe that was the reason behind meeting in the library, the arrangement of the chairs so none of them were on Zeb's side of the table. Maybe he wasn't all serenely immune to the fact that it probably wouldn't take much more than a hug as a reminder of what they'd been so very good at before.

Silver might not have liked studying science, but he knew how to test a hypothesis. The next couple questions were on chemistry. Stuff about covalents and electrons did not stick in his head. It wasn't faking to lean closer and shove the book over the top of the one Zeb was reading, working one arm in between Zeb's to point out the issue.

"I can't get this shit to make sense for me."

The contact was only in two spots. Knees, though they were both in slacks, and the inside of their arms where they met over the book, also shielded by a layer of cloth. Still, tension flooded into Zeb's muscles, and the sun-bronzed hair on his forearm prickled and stood on end. That wasn't very teacher-like.

The final data in the experiment was when, after a long breath, Zeb said, "Just a second."

He extracted himself gently but completely, then stood before walking over to the reference desk. When he came back with some scrap paper, he sat on the opposite side of the table.

Yup. Experiment supports hypothesis: Zeb was avoiding contact. Too bad Silver couldn't quite set

up an experiment to prove why, though slipping off
his shoe and curling his foot over Zeb's junk ought to
have a measurable effect.

"Okay." Zeb started to draw a circle. "Now an oxygen molecule—"

"Wait." Silver put his hand over the circle. "That's
what's in the book, and the circles just look like Mick-
ey Mouse's head to me."

"Okay." Zeb reached into his pockets and spilled
out a bunch of change. "This quarter is the oxygen
nucleus. Eight is the atomic number so…."

Silver had done a foot-job customer once. A re-
peater, so he must have gotten it right. He slipped off
the back end of the black Chuck he wore for work. It
might be entertaining to watch Zeb's face as he got
hard right here in the Pimlico Branch Public Library.

*Just when you thought it was safe to sit back at
the study table….*

There were a lot more coins now. Circles of pennies around the quarter and two nickels. Silver wiggled
his toes in his shoe and flexed the sole while Zeb went
on talking. "So when the water molecule forms, the
hydrogen electrons attach on the ring of oxygen electrons." He replaced four of the pennies with dimes.
"See? But there are still eight oxygen electrons."

Silver could see now how to answer that next
bunch of questions, yeah. But it was still what-the-
fuck-was-the-point stupid. "I see that with three more
bucks you can trade your water molecule for a cup of
coffee at Starbucks."

Zeb's brow lowered. "Well, molecules do tend
to be—"

"Relax. I got it. Thanks." Silver couldn't figure out why he wanted to try to make Zeb feel better. He wasn't the one stuck learning high school shit out of a lame book instead of having it all done with years ago. But Silver found himself saying, "You're pretty good at this." Because it *was* easier to see with the money to move around rather than the lame circles in the book.

Zeb smiled. There was something besides the potential for a foot job to be said for sitting across from each other. Silver got to watch the way Zeb's smile crinkled and sparked in his gold-green-brown eyes. Lots of gold today. Silver used to try to figure out if it was mood or the background colors that made the color shift so much. He'd never been completely sure it was based on how Zeb felt, but gold was a good sign. It had been around a lot back then. And Silver had come to think of it as happy in the Zeb's-eyes-as-a-mood-ring game.

Silver finished up the last few chemistry questions, then stretched his arms over his head and behind his chair.

Zeb leaned back, his legs encroaching on Silver's side of the table. Did that mean teacher mode was done?

"What are your plans, Jordan?"

He didn't think Zeb meant the seduction plans, though he wasn't sure Zeb didn't see through the tutoring excuse to implement them. And then Silver remembered. "You mean after you head off to summer camp?"

"I mean for your future. The rest of the life that's ahead of you."

Assuming his meds worked and he stayed out of Linwood and didn't get bashed or killed in jail. Those scary things almost bubbled out of his mouth despite the tight clench of his jaw. He could barely think past the next few hours, and Zeb expected a plan for life?

"Why? You worried you might be surfing for porn someday and end up having to relive a night with me?"

"No, that's not what I mean."

Was it anger overriding Zeb's patient tone? Good.

"Oh, I forgot. You probably don't watch porn. Guess you'll be safe from me for good once June 20 rolls around."

Zeb glanced away, like he could find patience somewhere over by the reference desk. And he did, because the anger was gone when he said, "You could work with kids."

"Are you fucking nuts?" Silver heard his words echo and lowered his voice. "First, I hate kids. Second, with my history no one would let me anywhere near kids. And third, thank God, because I hate the little shits."

Zeb sat up, confusion drawing his brows together, chasing the gold from his eyes. "But you were great with the kids at Sunday school."

"I was trying to impress you."

"It worked." Zeb swallowed, but his eyes held Silver's. That color, the darkest one, brown with a hint of green. Either Zeb was turned on or really pissed off. From the way he was leaning forward across the table, Silver was going with choice A, circling it, and putting it on his answer sheet.

"Jordan—"

Silver's phone went off. He thought about ignoring it, but Zeb was already back on the other side of the table, a nonspecific smile on his face, nodding like the phone ringing was something he'd personally arranged at that moment.

Silver glanced at the number. "It's the lawyer guy. I have to take it." But if it was bad news, he didn't want to have to worry about what his face looked like in front of Zeb. "'Scuse me." Silver pushed away from the table.

Based on the disapproving looks from the librarians, Silver decided he'd better take it all the way outside. They got through the greetings right as Silver hit the outside wall of heat.

"Silver, I'm afraid there's been a slight hitch in acquiring the identification documents from your parents."

Big fucking surprise. "But we can still get my birth certificate from the county where I was born, right?"

"Ah. Apparently the Monongalia County Clerk is on a fishing trip and will not return until Wednesday."

Silver heard the rustle of paper and the tap of a keyboard, pictured the flash of gold from the cufflinks under the expensive suit jacket.

There was irritation in the polished-sounding voice. "And Monongalia County has yet to join even the twentieth century. No one else is empowered to authenticate the document."

Without his birth certificate, he had no proof he was now using his legal name. He couldn't register to take the GED or open a bank account. All the things the lawyer said they'd need to show the judge. And the court date was only two weeks away. He was seriously screwed. Again.

"Is there any other way to get my birth certificate?"

"There is a potential remedy. I realize it's a less-than-desirable outcome, but I spoke with your father's attorney. He says your father will release the documents only to you, in person."

"Can he do that?"

"I'm afraid he can. They are in his possession. Even if we could legally compel him to provide them, that would take additional time."

"Right." Which left him with saying *Fuck you, Thomas Barnett* and probably going to jail, or finding a way to haul ass up to New Freedom. Once he had the papers, he could still tell him to fuck off in person. He did some quick calculating. He could take the bus on his day off, assuming Thomas would give him an appointment. He started walking back into the library. The librarians could just chill about his phone call; he needed a bus schedule. "I can make it up on Thursday."

"I'll get back to you as soon as I have more information."

Silver yanked the 83 commuter bus schedule out of the rack and stuffed the phone back in his pocket. Now he'd probably miss Eli's opening. Not that Silver really gave a shit about the art, but it was a big deal to Eli, and Silver owed him. A lot more than just showing up at a gallery.

He flopped back down in his chair and yanked the book as close as he could, propping up his forehead on his fists to hide his face as he tried to make the marks on the page turn into words. They didn't, so he dug his knuckles into his closed eyes until he saw bright patches of purple and blue against the black.

The touch was so light, he thought it had to be a brush of air at first. A stroke through his hair. But then there was another, tingling his scalp. Then firmer. A caress. Comfort.

Zeb was petting his hair in the middle of the library? Silver sat up. "Don't go losing your job."

Zeb yanked his hand back as if he'd been burned. "Bad news?"

"Wow. You must be psychic or something. I guess we don't have much time left. I gotta catch the bus." He shoved the book into his backpack.

Zeb put his hand over Silver's on top of the canvas. "Jordan. Are you going back to jail?"

Silver glanced down at Zeb's hand, and he pulled it back. "Not yet."

"You don't have to leave now. I'll drive you in."

"I'm not exactly in the mood to concentrate on anything."

"I'll still drive you."

Silver didn't care about the lame plan to get his revenge anymore. It felt like nothing he did mattered. Everything he'd been through, and he still wound up being jerked around by his father. Right now all he wanted was to get away from the other half of why he'd sworn he'd never go anywhere near New Freedom again.

"Why?" he demanded. "You think a couple of rides and some GED tutoring will make up for everything?"

Zeb looked at Silver with an infuriating calm. "I think we both know there's nothing I can do that will ever make up for what happened."

Damn right. "So what the fuck difference does it make if I take the bus?"

"Because it's ninety-four outside, my car has air-conditioning, and I hope you'll tell me what happened."

Silver would have sworn when he left the library he was headed across the street to the bus stop, but he found himself next to the passenger door of Zeb's Pontiac. His Chucks were sticking to the blacktop.

After Zeb popped the locks, Silver slung himself in and waited for the even greater blast of heat in the car to blow out the open windows as the AC took over. It wasn't until the second light that Zeb said "Watch your fingers" and rolled up the windows. "How's your elbow, by the way?"

Silver glanced down as if he could see it through the black sleeve of his work shirt and the gauze he carefully taped down after his shower.

"It's okay."

He dug the tie out of his backpack and put it over his head. The air felt good, and he leaned his face into it, let it lift his hair. Which reminded him of Zeb playing with his hair in the library. He sat back. Zeb not asking him about the phone call was just as annoying as if he'd nagged.

And more effective.

"I need to have proof of my legal name before my court date. We're having trouble getting my birth certificate from the county where I was born, and my father will only hand over the official copy and my social security card if I show up in person."

Zeb nodded, but Silver saw his hands tighten on the steering wheel. It had to be scorching his palms. Silver couldn't even rest his forearm against the door panel.

"When is your next day off?"

"Don't worry. I'm going to do it. One night in jail was enough." *I hope.*

"When?"

Okay. Nagging was definitely more annoying. "Thursday. That okay with you?" That shut him up for a while.

"You'll have to make a left up here on West Mulberry," Silver pointed out.

Traffic on Mulberry was stuck at every light. Silver wanted to get out and push the car. Pedestrians cut in front of them, ignoring the crosswalks—which was pretty much what Silver did all the time, but trapped in the car with Zeb with what felt like all their baggage plus Silver's parents watching from the back seat, it was enough to make him want to scream.

"I'll get out at the next light. Charles Street is one-way in the wrong direction."

"I'll take a personal day and drive you up Thursday," Zeb said as if Silver hadn't just told him how desperate he was to not be in this car anymore.

"You need more get-out-of-hell-free points? How about this? I forgive you. There. It's all fine. I'm sure Jesus is fine with it too." Silver reached for the door. Which was locked. He forced down a sharp breath. Zeb hadn't done it on purpose; Silver had heard the doors lock automatically as they left the library lot. But it took his last bit of self-control not to start kicking at it to make it open. He'd think after surviving that night in jail, he'd be over that locked-in panic attack. Every locked door wasn't the one on the Reflection Room at Path to Glory.

"I want to do it." Zeb pulled the car over into a spot right under a "No Stopping or Standing Tow Zone" sign. For a guy who used to be so intent about doing the right thing, he sure bent a lot of laws.

"You don't have to do it."

Zeb released the door lock. "Actually, I think I do."

Silver climbed out. "I told you, I don't need you to."

Zeb's voice was calm, but there was a determination in it that made the hair on the back of Silver's neck stand up.

"I didn't say I was doing it for you."

Chapter Ten

WHATEVER THE fuck Zeb had meant by "not do-ing it for you," the only reason Silver dropped his ass into the passenger seat of Zeb's Pontiac two days later was because of Eli, and Silver said that immediately.

"I don't know what you plan to get out of the trip, but whatever it is, we need to be on our way back by five thirty."

Thomas Barnett had dictated a four-thirty ap-pointment. Silver owed it to Eli to be at that opening. Not only was Eli the reason Silver got to walk around free in a space bigger than a jail cell, he couldn't stand to imagine the sad puppy eyes if he missed it.

"Understood. My business won't take long."

"Why are we leaving so early, then?" Silver dragged the seat belt across to the buckle.

"I didn't think you'd want to risk being late."

It was true Silver hated to give Thomas any reason to go back on the deal, but not having a car didn't mean he was also lacking a brain. "I don't." And because Zeb had spoken in that irritatingly reasonable teacher voice he'd been using lately, Silver tacked on, "But don't think because you're helping me with the GED you need to plan out the rest of my business. I've been living on my own for years." *Thanks to three of the people whose faces I have to see today.* Shoving the seat back as far as it would go, he slipped off his Chucks and put his bare feet up on the dash, knees bent close to his face.

As the GPS dictated their trip to I-83, Zeb said in a voice about as full of life as the computer's, "Have I mentioned that I don't trust other people's driving?"

"Yup. Wearing my seat belt."

"Have you considered what could happen if we were in an accident?"

Silver glanced around at the cars and trucks whizzing by as they squeezed into the early rush hour traffic on the interstate and shrugged. "Probably get creamed. And not in the fun way," he added with a leer.

"Riding with your legs like that is more dangerous."

"Oh, I seem to remember you liking a ride with my legs up around my shoulders once or twice—or was that around your shoulders?" Silver turned to see how Zeb took that.

Instead of the flush of heat and gulping swallow Silver had been counting on, he found a jaw clenched tight enough that a muscle jumped in a spasmodic tic.

"You won't be up to your usual running away if both your legs end up amputated."

Silver stared down at his knees. "I'd have crawled. To get away from that camp. To stay me." He glared back at Zeb. "And who the fuck are you to talk about running? Haiti, seriously?"

"I called."

"Yeah, on my eighteenth birthday." Silver rolled his eyes.

"No. I tried calling a few days after you showed up that night. When I couldn't reach you that way, I checked some of the places I thought you might be."

Silver had already been on his way to Baltimore. Not that it would have fixed anything, but he was curious. Zeb sounded like that had meant something to him. Tipping his head to get more than a side view, he asked, "How hard did you look?"

Zeb glanced over, then back at the road before he let out a long breath, blunt fingers stretching and then regripping the steering wheel. "I'd had to resign. I got to keep my teaching certification because they didn't press charges. But only because I met their requirements. Ten years in prison is a long time, Jordan."

If Zeb had lived long enough to serve it. Silver pictured him trying to calmly intervene in a knife fight. The theater in his head expanded to IMAX size in time for him to watch the blade go into Zeb's gut, perfectly capturing both the spread of dark blood on prison orange and the pained confusion on Zeb's face. The AC blasting in the car was suddenly a little too effective as the hair all over Silver's body stood on end.

"Actually, it wouldn't have been that long," Zeb said dryly. "Sex offenders don't have a long lifespan in prison."

Zeb's wry sense of humor had popped up at some of the weirdest times and had always been something Silver loved about him. But with that scene playing out in his head, he couldn't laugh. And he couldn't control a shiver.

Zeb reached out and turned down the AC. "I'm not trying to boss you around. I just don't want you to get hurt."

"Everybody hurts."

Zeb sighed. "Michael Stipe aside, it doesn't mean I can't care about you."

In his best Alec Guinness imitation, Silver intoned, "You cannot escape your destiny."

Zeb gave him a wry smile. "Thanks for the insight, Obi-Wan, but I was talking about your feet on the dashboard."

"Oh." Silver glanced at his feet, then dropped them into the footwell on top of his Chucks.

The next couple of miles were quiet but nowhere near as awkward as when Silver had first gotten in the car. Until one phrase started to repeat itself in his head. Zeb had called himself a sex offender. Like he was a pedophile or something. That was nuts. Silver might have been sixteen, but if anybody was the offender, he was. He'd pushed things as fast as he could, though Zeb had put the brakes on penetration for the first nine weeks and three days.

Cinematic memory or not, Silver wasn't likely to forget losing his virginity. Or when he'd lost it the other way two days later.

On the subject of sex and laws telling you how to have it, Silver had another question, considering they were talking now and they were still five miles from

New Freedom. "If you were so freaked out about being arrested as a sex offender, how come you wouldn't back down that night with the cops?"

There was the reaction he'd been looking for earlier, the flush and the thick swallows. But not for the right reason.

After a pause Zeb said, "When I saw you that night, I lost it. I couldn't think about anything else. I didn't think about anything else."

"Anything else but what?"

"You." Zeb's tongue moistened his lips. "I had to make sure you were all right."

"And you thought getting arrested was a good way to do that?"

"Behold my master plan."

Silver had missed that smile. Not the warm and friendly one Zeb gave to everyone. No, this was from the real guy, the one who didn't throw sunshine around like some kind of happy bubble. The one with the crooked grin.

Zeb shot a look over to the passenger seat. "Worked, though, didn't it?"

"How the fuck do you call getting arrested a success?"

"I found out how you were."

Silver snorted and folded his arms. "I didn't tell you shit while we were in jail."

"But I know now." Zeb did his smile again, then reached over to lightly shove Silver's knee. "And you are all right."

All of the easiness between them disappeared as soon as they took the exit. It was still two miles from town, and another two to the shiny new development

near the golf course where Silver had lived between
the ages of thirteen and seventeen plus two months.
His breath sped up, and no matter how hard he tried,
he couldn't make the transition out of himself and into
that wide-angle lens. If he were shooting the scene,
he'd use some kind of effect to make everything look
washed-out and pale. But everything was bright under the June sun. Even the cows on the outlying farms
gleamed like they were freshly washed. An unnatural
freaky land where everyone was white and straight
and knew each other's business. Eli was right. It was
a fucking cult.

It was a miracle the shit hadn't hit the fan before
when Zeb got the job at the local school. If Zeb hadn't
lived almost all the way up in York, Silver would never have been able to pull off lying so long.

"The coffeehouse closed," Zeb said as he took the
left off Front Street.

"Yes, I can see that." Silver hated the mockery
in his own voice. Hated everything about how he felt
right then. Because it felt like it had before. Before
Zeb and a sweet six months of someone who saw
who Jordan Barnett really was and said he loved him
anyway.

Before had meant constantly failing to live up
to whatever it was Thomas and Cheryl expected in a
son. Where earning a B in a hard class was practically
failing. Or making the second-team doubles in tennis
wasn't any better than being cut. Then listening to the
talk of perversion and disgusting deviants, knowing it
was about him, though he wouldn't dare say it out loud.

Silver wiped his hands on the work pants he'd
worn instead of jeans—as if he really gave a shit what

they thought of his clothes. As soon as he had his birth certificate and social security card, he'd never have to even say their names again.

As Zeb passed the last few close-together houses, his jaw did the tight-tic thing, knuckles showing bone-white on the steering wheel. Was he mad because Silver had been such a shit? The coffeehouse, their first date, trading a few details while the electricity built between them so they left half-filled cups to check out how the *Star Wars* DVDs looked on Zeb's new hi-def TV. The DVDs never made it out of the box. They didn't get as far as Silver wanted, but far enough to let him know he'd wanted more.

Silver pulled at the knees of his slacks to loosen the crotch. "Did you ever wonder what would have happened if we'd met when we—if I was older?"

"No."

Ouch.

Okay. Silver wanted to say he couldn't blame him, but of course he did. It had been something Silver had liked to tell himself some nights when he couldn't find a place to sleep. Nights when he felt like he was a short doze away from freezing to death. Nights when he'd suck or fuck anyone to keep warm, to have a place to sack out for a few hours. He'd walk and walk and believe Zeb hadn't turned *him* away. Hadn't told Silver to never come show his face again. That Silver's age had been the only thing keeping them apart.

Silver was staring hard at the edges of the golf course as the GPS ordered them to turn left, but he felt Zeb's gaze and looked back to face him.

"I don't have to." Zeb's voice didn't give Silver a clue about whether that was good or bad.

Zeb stopped the car right before the Appleblossom Road cul-de-sac. "Do you want me to come with you?"

"I think that probably won't help me get the stuff I need. But thanks."

Zeb nodded.

"You can go take care of whatever you needed to do. I'll meet you back here." Silver climbed out of the car, trying to unhunch his shoulders as he stood next to the manicured lawn.

"My stuff won't take long," Zeb said.

Silver didn't look back while he walked past the first three houses, but he didn't hear the car pull away either. Maybe because there was other stuff going on. Kids whizzing by on bikes. Cars pulling into their drives, doors slamming as people came home from work. He felt people looking at him, someone walking in a neighborhood devoted to wheels. Did they recognize him, remember him? The tall, pretty blond boy who'd kept to himself. Would they stare more when he went to the front door and rang the bell? He could go around back, take the key out of the fake rock, and let himself in through the garage. Had they kept his car? The one he'd earned for keeping straight As through sophomore year. Funny to learn it wasn't his, though he'd worked part-time at the golf course to contribute to insurance and pay for gas. The phone wasn't his. The computer.

The clothes or anything else in his bedroom. At seventeen, he hadn't owned a damned thing if his parents said he didn't.

The front door, then, since this wasn't his house anymore. His hand shook when he pushed the bell, so he shoved them both in his back pockets. They had all the power. Everything he'd done since he left had been so no one could dictate to him again, and now he was back begging at their door. He felt less shame about having been a hustler. If he was fucked over then, it was on his own terms. He'd made the choice. And he dealt with what consequences there were.

His father answered the door. "Come in and sit down."

Silver stepped in and aside so his father could shut the door. The grim lines in the lightly golf-tanned face were probably what a patient got when Dr. Barnett was about to deliver the bad news about melanoma. As his father moved toward the sitting room, Silver realized he was now taller than his father, enough to look down on the light brown wavy hair and see the gray roots.

If Silver was in for a lecture, he'd take it, but only if he got what he needed in exchange. "Are you going to give me what I came for?"

"I said I would."

Yeah, but he'd also said *You're my son and I'll always love you* and *This is for your own good* when he'd sent Silver off to Camp Path to Glory. Silver wasn't dumb enough to take people's word for it anymore. The tweaker who'd named him Silver had taught him that. *Always get the money up front.*

With an exaggerated sigh more drama queen than even Eli could pull off, Silver's father went to the mantel and held up a manila folder, then used it to point to a chair in the sitting room. After a quick glance to see that his school pictures were conspicuously absent from the mantel, Silver focused on the folder that didn't leave his father's hand. Silver sat on the edge of the chair. The golfing tan was darker on his father's forearms, tough sale for a dermatologist, or maybe the years were catching up to him.

His father sat, crossing one khaki-panted leg over the other and opening the folder on his lap so Silver could see what was in it. It didn't look like what he'd expected. The blue social security card he recognized, and his license, but not the paper that looked like a form covered with boxes. It wasn't anything like the framed certificate he remembered seeing in his father's home office, the one with the scrollwork and gold paint and tiny inked footprint declaring the birth of Jordan Samuel Barnett on August 4 at 2:35 p.m.

Silver ran a quick film in his head, him overpowering his father, yanking away the folder, and running to the entrance of the development, down the highway to catch Zeb, get himself the fuck out of here. A couple of weeks ago, he might have done something so stupid.

Now he played the film out to the unavoidable ending: the cops picking him up at the gallery, Eli and Gavin and Zeb shaking their heads in disgust for having wasted so much on Silver, who would always fuck up, never be worth it.

"Where's…." he rejected a couple of choice words before settling on "your wife?"

"Your mother," Thomas corrected sharply, "is upstairs resting. She has a migraine."

Silver nodded, curling his tongue back against his palate to stop the words that would demand his father accept some reality. *Migraine* was the unchallenged

cover for his mother working her way through her second bottle of wine.

Silver knew he should probably wait his father
out. Speaking first put Silver in the weaker position,
but he only wanted to leave. It had been made clear
three years ago this wasn't his home, and it sure as hell
wasn't his life anymore.

"Why am I here?"

His father skirted the question. "Impressive
representation you have. My own attorney recognized the name of the firm." He scrutinized Silver's
less-than-impressive, washed-out-to-dullness black
slacks and thrift-store shirt.

Silver ignored the how-can-you-afford-that-law-
yer question his father didn't ask aloud. "Thanks." So
maybe it was sarcastic gratitude, but given how much
anger Silver was sitting on, he figured he was doing
the best he could.

"Exactly how are you supporting yourself?"

Score one for me. He'd made his father say it out
loud. "I'm working."

"Without your social security card?"

Silver studied his father. He was desperate to
know the worst, believed the worst—though the worst
in Silver's father's mind would be Silver living with
some sugar daddy. His father had no idea what the
worst really was.

"Something you want to ask?" Silver leaned back
in the uncomfortably rigid chair.

Who'd have thought the old man cared?

His father's gaze broke away, shifting to the side.
Silver wanted to pump his fist in triumph.

"I've only ever wanted the best for you, son."

"Your definition of it."

"Can you honestly tell me you have been living a life that would make me proud? Yourself proud? One that pleases the sight of the Lord?"

"You obviously have the answer all figured out." There wasn't any point in getting into it with his father if it was going to turn into a battle over religion. Nothing he could say to win that fight.

"So you agree."

"I didn't say that. Maybe I haven't always been proud of what I've had to do, but I'm not the one who threw a seventeen-year-old on the street." Silver heard his voice rise and had to grip the chair arms to keep from following it out of the chair.

"Don't be so dramatic. We sent you to people who could help."

"Help me? They were helping some kids to kill themselves."

His father waved that off. "Some children are already too disturbed to save."

"I'm not disturbed. I'm gay."

And there was the disgust Silver knew so well.

"No one is homosexual, Jordan. It isn't something a person can be. People are molested or confused or led into that behavior. As you were."

Silver wanted to laugh. "By Z—" He froze. Zeb was out there, in New Freedom. And even if his rejection had been the biggest betrayal of all, Silver couldn't pay him back by putting his name in the head of a close-minded bigot like the one in front of him. He took a deep breath and rose to his feet. "May I please have the folder?"

He could fake politeness with the right words but couldn't do anything about the way anger scraped his voice raw.

His father stood, the folder in both hands, his brow furrowed but his eyes open, as if he really meant what he said. "I'm offering you a chance to get your life back. You could go to college. Whatever situation you've found yourself in, you can change. You can be forgiven."

For half a second, Silver thought maybe his father wasn't hopeless. Maybe he wanted to be the dad Silver remembered before they'd moved here from West Virginia. Before they'd bought this big house and everything changed.

But that invitation was only extended to an imaginary straight version of his son. "No, thanks."

"You could spare a thought for your mother's health."

"Her health? There's nothing wrong with her a few weeks in rehab couldn't fix." In a blur, his father backhanded him across the face.

Silver's ears rang and blood filled his mouth. Controlling the urge to spit it back, he swallowed the coppery mess and worked his jaw for a minute, glancing down at the papers that had dropped when his father lashed out. "That's a new tactic. Watch what I learned in Sunday school." He turned his other cheek toward his father. "Go ahead. I can take it."

The old man trembled, then shoved his hands in his pockets.

"I'll just take these, then." Silver bent and scooped the papers back into the folder.

His father stood silent, fists clearly visible in the pockets of his khakis, weathered cheeks flushed.

"Guess what, Dad?" Silver put as much disgust in that word as he could. "I was a whore. Sold my ass on the street. And I hated myself for it." His lip was still bleeding, and he wiped it on the back of his hand, almost a smile stretching the hot, swelling skin as he remembered Zeb and his first aid kit. Ready to drive Silver's sorry, bleeding self out of danger. "But I'd rather have lived like that than let you try to change me. Or make me ashamed enough to lie."

Silver strode into the foyer to find his mother coming down the stairs, a tight grip on the railing, her body rigid as she tried to look sober. She'd been faking it so long, she was pretty good at it.

Now she faked a pleasant complaint. "My head is pounding and you're shouting."

Silver would have suggested she lay off the merlot, but he really didn't care anymore.

"Have a thought for your soul, Jordan." His father had come up behind him.

"Did you talk to him, Thomas? Honey, we only want you to be with us in heaven. With Nana and Grandpa and Ginger. You can be. We can fix it."

Silver would rather take another backhand from his father than this faked softness from his mother. Emotional blackmail only worked if he gave a shit.

"Your church says dogs don't go to heaven, remember?" Silver did. Every bit of being twelve and having to put Ginger to sleep, consoling himself with the idea of Ginger running around up there waiting to come bouncing up to meet him when he died. He talked about it so much, his parents brought him in to talk to Pastor Stu, who had calmly but emphatically explained animals didn't have souls and couldn't go to heaven. Silver had responded that he would rather go to hell then himself.

Come to think of it, that was how he felt about it if he was going to be stuck with Cheryl and Thomas for eternity too.

Silver opened the door to permanent escape.

"The door is always open if you want to change." Thomas's voice was so kind and calm, you'd never know he'd just split his son's lip.

Silver stepped over the threshold. "On this side, it's closed." He pulled the door shut behind him.

Chapter Eleven

ZEB'S PONTIAC was in front of the next house down. Silver raised the folder to shadow the mark he could feel swelling the right side of his face as he hurried down the walk. He wasn't sure why he didn't want Zeb to see it. The bleeding had stopped, so Silver didn't have to worry about his contaminated blood getting anywhere. And being backhanded meant the bruise faced away from Zeb. Maybe it didn't look as bad as it felt.

"Did you get everything you needed?" Zeb asked as Silver settled himself in the passenger seat.

And then some. Silver poked with his tongue at the fat part inside his mouth, then opened the folder to double-check. The thing that had looked like a form with boxes was his certified birth certificate. Then there was the social security card, and best of all, his license, still valid.

It was totally worth a split lip.

"Yeah. I'm good." Silver grabbed for the seat belt and latched himself in. In a few minutes, he'd be done with New Freedom for good. Bonus, they'd even be back in plenty of time for Eli's show opening.

"I'm glad." Zeb popped open his door. "I'll only be a few minutes. I'll leave it running for the AC."

Zeb was already at the bottom of the walk before Silver's brain caught up to what his eyes were telling him. Fuck. What the hell did Zeb want with them?

By the time Silver had wrestled free of the seat belt and shut off the car, Zeb was at the door. Despite a breathless sprint, Silver didn't make it to the stoop until the show was already in progress.

"—still perverting my son?" His father's face was pale under the golfing tan, his voice a low, furious whisper, a stabbing finger an inch from Zeb's chest.

"Using his innocent love of God to lead him into sodomy." Cheryl clutched the doorjamb and her pearls with equal intensity. Probably so she didn't face-plant on the welcome mat. "I trusted you, a child molester, to shepherd my only son."

Silver wanted to share the embarrassing absurdity of her posturing with Zeb. But Zeb wasn't making eye contact. With anyone. Shoulders hunched and head down, he was just taking it.

"Call the police, Cheryl." Thomas puffed himself up, chest out, head back. "We'll send this pedophile to jail like we should have then."

Even then Zeb didn't say anything.

This might have been a good prank on one of those hidden camera reality shows, but as real life, it sucked.

"You can't have him arrested. I'm twenty fucking years old." Silver got in front of Zeb.

"Watch your language in front of your mother." His father jabbed a hand like a knife against Silver's chest.

"Or you'll hit me again? You know what? Call the cops. I'm pressing charges for assault."

That got Zeb's attention. An audible intake of breath and a gentle turn of Silver's head. "Jordan." Zeb's whisper sounded pained, like he was the one who'd been hit.

Silver pulled free. "Did it leave a nice mark? That'll look good in the paper and online, Dr. Barnett. Maybe my impressive representation could hook me up with a personal-injury lawsuit."

Cheryl's hand went from her throat to her husband's shoulder. The squeeze looked painful. Maybe her perfect manicure pierced the skin, because Thomas deflated like a popped balloon.

How had these people ever had any power over him? Why had he cared what they thought of him? "And I can't wait for the trial so everyone in town can hear exactly what filthy sodomizing I did. Every detail of cocksucking and ass—"

"Enough." His father pushed Silver into Zeb, and they both fell off the stoop. "Get out. Just get out."

"No cops?" Silver smiled, flashing his teeth.

Zeb grabbed Silver's wrist and pulled, but it was over. The door shut, and it was only the two of them trampling the landscaping.

Silver waved at the lady neighbor on the left who was pretending to do something to her dogwood as she eavesdropped.

Zeb reached for Silver's cheek. "Are you all right?"

"It's fine." He knocked the hand away. "I've had worse."

"He's hit you before? I should have come with you."

"Because that went so well." Silver wanted to know why the hell Zeb had bothered with his parents even now, but he wasn't giving Dogwood Lady any more free drama. That's what HBO was for. "Not that I give a shit about any of these assholes, but let's get the fuck out of here."

Zeb nodded, lips white and bloodless. A quick tremor echoed up Silver's arm as he pressed the keys into Zeb's palm.

"You okay?"

"Yes." Zeb turned away.

The air in the car was so thick Silver couldn't find words to fit his questions. Right before they got back on 83, Zeb swung the car off into Polson's Auto and Tires, bouncing and scraping over the rutted dirt and gravel. No matter how hard Silver stomped, there was no brake pedal on his side of the car, but he didn't stop trying until they jerked to a stop a few feet from the trees bordering the lot.

Zeb shoved open his door and staggered into the brush before hunching over, hands on his thighs. Silver pushed his own door open and followed cautiously. Carsick? But Zeb hadn't puked. He was only sucking wind.

Silver put a hand on Zeb's shoulder. The skin shuddered, his whole body vibrating. "Zeb? You okay?"

A long noisy exhale and another deep breath.

Shaking and hot. "Is it malaria, a relapse?" So maybe he'd looked it up, what could happen long-term after the initial infection.

Zeb let out another breath and then stood straight, though he didn't turn around.

Silver felt ridiculous with his hand resting on Zeb's shoulder, so he yanked it back.

"No. I'm fine. I'm sorry."

"Yeah. No. This is not fine."

He knew Zeb. There may have been some changes, but the three years in between now and then couldn't change knowing the shifting colors of his eyes, the quirks of his smiles, what tension and complete relaxation looked like on every part of his body.

But Silver had never seen Zeb like this. And with Zeb not looking at him, Silver didn't know what to do.

If Zeb wouldn't turn around, Silver would go to where his face was. He stepped around him, pants catching on sticks and leaves. He tore free and stood squarely in front of him.

Zeb was rubbing his shoulder and upper arm. Silver hadn't gripped him hard, hadn't bled on him. What was that about?

Zeb tried that patient, distant smile. "I'll be okay in a minute. Sorry," he said again. "You can go back to the car. I'll still get us back in time."

"The fuck you will."

The smile froze for a second then resumed its curve. "Excuse me?"

"You may not trust other drivers, but I don't trust you to get me back in one piece right now. Christ, you're still shaking."

Zeb gripped his arm more tightly, pain rippling his forehead, making his eyes into slits.

"Did you get hurt when you pulled off the road?"

"No." Zeb turned like he was going to go back to the car.

Silver got around in front of him to block his path. "What the hell was that all about, you talking to my parents?"

Zeb's dark gaze lasered in on the place on Silver's cheek where it felt thick and hot.

A shake of Zeb's head and he started forward.

"What does that mean?" Silver caught Zeb's wrist.

"It means it's none of your business, Jordan."

Silver stared back, digging behind that pleasant mask Zeb seemed to wear so much more now than he ever used to. The one that made everyone think he was a sanctimonious prig. He'd almost convinced Silver that fun Zeb was gone, except for the drive up in the car. That crooked smile. The slanted humor in his eyes.

Silver wasn't giving up. He pictured Zeb on the stoop, taking that abuse from his parents, letting them call him names and—

"Holy fuck. You believe it."

Zeb's fingers tightened on his arm. "What?"

"You think you deserve it? Is that why you wanted to come? So you could let them nail you to a cross?"

"Don't talk like that."

Silver controlled the urge to roll his eyes. "Okay. Then tell me why."

"I owed them an apology."

"For what?" Silver couldn't stop disgust from filling his voice.

The pain on Zeb's face made Silver furious. He wanted to stomp off to the car, let Zeb roast in his own stupid self-made hell. He couldn't really buy all that crap.

"You didn't—pervert me. I came after you. God, I'd have jumped your bones a lot sooner than you let me."

Zeb shook his head.

"For fuck's sake, you're not a pedophile."

"No?" At last there was that cynical half smile, but it was all wrong.

"No." Silver put as much force as he could into the word.

Zeb's hands landed on Silver's shoulders as if he'd shake him, then slid down in almost a caress before gripping his biceps. His eyes were so dark they could have been black. "I knew you lied about your age. I don't know when I knew it. I didn't want to."

Zeb glanced away for a minute. When he looked back, his eyes were wet. "I pretended to believe you, but deep down, I knew. I wanted you so much. God help me. I wanted you anyway. I'd never wanted anything as much as I wanted you. Never. And I ruined your life."

Silver wanted to chase that look off Zeb's face. Send it somewhere Silver would never have to see it again. The corner of his mouth lifted. "So… I made your dick hard, huh?"

Zeb squeezed once then let him go. "It was wrong."

"Didn't feel wrong to me. Or—" The sudden thought made the earth drop away from Silver's feet.

He wished Zeb was still holding on. Because there was this huge ragged hole between what Silver had always thought and what Zeb was saying. And maybe the real reason Zeb wouldn't help that night was echoing in Silver's ears. "Or were you only pretending when you said you loved me too?"

"No. I swear to God, no, Jordan. I'd never pretend—about that."

"So what's the big deal? You were only, what, twenty-two?"

"It was wrong," Zeb repeated.

"Think about it. Was there ever so much as a single second where it seemed like I didn't know exactly what I was doing and what I wanted?"

Zeb might have been the one with a little experience, but Silver had led every step of the way.

"Wait a minute. Is that why you made us wait until my birthday before we actually fucked?"

Zeb glanced down. "I hoped it meant you were eighteen."

"What the fuck is so magic about a day on the calendar? It had nothing to do with you and me. I mean, seriously, did I suddenly taste older?"

"Jordan." But it was muffled when Zeb buried his face in his hands.

"You've been thinking that all this time? That you corrupted me? Ruined my life?"

Zeb looked up. "Didn't I? I just didn't know how much." His thumb grazed Silver's sore cheek. "I've done so much worse than this."

Silver caught Zeb's wrist again and dragged him closer. He didn't resist, but he didn't respond as Silver tucked a long wavy strand of warm brown hair behind

an ear and dragged his own thumb across the hint of
scruff on Zeb's chin.

"I always knew you had one hell of a god complex, heavy on the martyr side, with this hair and chin
fuzz." Silver shook Zeb's trapped arm. "But could you
get over yourself for a second? You can't take credit
for everything."

"I should have helped you that night when you
came to me."

"Yeah. You should have." Silver dropped Zeb's
arm and let out a big sigh. "And maybe I should have
tried to figure something else out." He moved his other arm to rest on Zeb's neck. "It sucked, all right. But
you weren't responsible for all of it." The muscles under his palm relaxed. Almost without his permission,
Silver's fingers rubbed the skin under Zeb's hair. Fragile barrier over hard muscle and bone. Vulnerable soft
skin Silver had licked the sweat from, sucked his mark
into as their bodies crashed together. Zeb hadn't been
the only one full of a desperate wanting back then.

But Silver's wanting days were behind him.
Stilling his fingers, he tipped Zeb's head until their
foreheads almost touched. "Besides—" Silver felt an
odd trace of laughter in his throat. "—if I let you take
all the credit for that, I'd have to let you take credit
for things getting a lot better since you popped back
up. And God knows I don't need to feed into your
complex."

Zeb gave a short laugh like the one Silver was
holding back. "'Better' like getting arrested?"

Silver shrugged. "Weirdly enough."

The shrug moved his head enough to brush Zeb's,
and that was all it took. Zeb's arms wrapped around

him, and Silver found himself hugging back. At first it felt like any other hug from a guy he wasn't planning on having sex with—which in Silver's world boiled down to a hug from Eli. Only holding Zeb didn't require hunching over, and Zeb didn't squeeze the breath out of a guy like Eli did.

They shared an exhale, and it wasn't a friendly hug anymore. It wasn't suddenly about sex, but a gradual awareness of what their bodies had been to each other, the physical part of them jumping ahead of where their heads were. A little sway, a shift of pressure, and Silver's face found that space in the crook of Zeb's neck. Soft curls and the smell of his shampoo and skin and sweat. Home. Home the way the house on Appleblossom Road had never been. Something that had been missing dropped back into place with a *click* Silver felt all over his body. There was no need to run to or away from anything. Because he'd always belonged right here.

He wanted to stay right here forever.

"I'm sorry. God, I'm so sorry, Jordan."

Until Zeb opened his stupid mouth and reminded them both why it couldn't be that easy. The brief connection dissolved faster than paper in a storm drain. Should have known it could never stand up to any pressure.

Silver shifted his weight back onto his own feet and patted at Zeb's back. "It's okay."

But when something that right could be broken again so quickly, he wasn't sure anything ever would be.

THERE MUST have been some sporting or concert thing going on in the city, because there was enough traffic going their way to make Zeb need to concentrate. At least that's what Silver told himself as the silence stretched on and on in the car.

As the exit for Quinn's house came up, Zeb blurted, "Does the lawyer think having legal ID will make sure you don't go to jail?"

"It's more to show I'm following rules now. Besides, I needed it to sign up for the GED. The whole thing hinges on whether I used the other ID for illegal activities."

"Like buying alcohol?"

Silver snorted. "Not really my thing. I don't trust most people enough to be drunk around them—and I don't do drugs. No. They're looking to see if I signed up for any credit cards or stuff like that."

Zeb nodded, like that solved that problem. It was nice to know Zeb didn't believe Silver would steal stuff, but the guy was still kind of clueless sometimes.

"I didn't, but someone else could have, using that name. I bought the ID, but it didn't exactly come with a warranty."

Stopped at a light, Zeb shot him a questioning glance. "Why risk it?"

It had gotten him the side income of porn faster since he didn't have to wait until he was legal, but that wasn't why he'd been willing to pay. "I was afraid my parents would find me and drag me off to that camp. They weren't even looking." Silver swallowed back shame, staring at the artwork on the produce truck ahead of them at the light.

"From the way your cheek looks, that probably wasn't a bad thing."

Silver could handle a lot more pain than a slap on his cheek. And anything was better than the solitary room at Path to Glory.

He glanced over at Zeb as they accelerated away from the light.

"I'll drive you to the gallery. What time do you want me to pick you up?"

They rounded the corner onto Rockspring Road. Quinn's old-man Buick was still in the drive. Zeb's Pontiac was marginally cooler. Red and newer. And not a Buick. Of course, he'd rather be rolling up in Gavin's Bentley. That wasn't a choice, and he'd already used enough of Zeb's gas.

"Don't need a ride. Quinn's still here."

"Right." Zeb's response was almost too quiet to hear.

Silver popped open the door as soon as the car stopped. Weighed against the drama of the past hour, having his own ID barely balanced out, but a thank-you was probably the expected thing. He leaned back down to offer one, and Zeb gave him a crooked smile. "Be sure to tell Eli where that bruise came from. I don't have a cup to wear under my pants tonight."

Silver felt a smile tickle his own mouth, but it hurt to slide the muscles all the way up. "I promise."

Folder tucked under his arm, he was only a step into the hall when Eli grabbed his forearms.

"Oh my God, you have to help me. Quinn is hovering, and it's driving me nuts."

Silver peered around Eli to see Quinn sitting on the couch in his suit, remote in his hand as he faced the TV. Quinn glanced over, brows arching. Silver shook off the question and tipped his head toward Eli. Quinn shrugged and folded his arms across his chest.

Eli tightened his grip and gave a shove. "Stop talking over my head. It drives me fucking insane."

Silver was betting that was a really short trip right now. "I think—"

"Oh my God, what happened to your face?"

"A lovely parting gift from my father."

"That son of a bitch." Eli dragged Silver into the kitchen. "Did you put any ice on it?"

"It's fine."

Eli opened the freezer, took out a bag of peas, and slapped it in Silver's free hand.

"You look like a street punk."

"I am one." Silver bit off the *So were you before Daddy showed up*. Because Eli hadn't been. He'd had jobs and an actual apartment with decent plumbing. It hadn't just been Quinn riding to the rescue.

And now Eli had art for sale in a gallery. And a house. And a steady, though tight-assed and boring, boyfriend. Silver had... his birth certificate. He put the folder on the table. Whoever thought he'd be jealous of Eli?

But he was. And so angry he wanted to take off. Cut all these ties to people who reminded him what he would never have.

Eli stared at him like he was trying to see to the back of Silver's eyes, then pushed the hand holding the peas toward his face. "Put it on."

Silver sighed. "Okay."

"I could probably tone that down with a little makeup. Maybe bring out your eyes more too."

"No."

"Everything okay?" Quinn came to the doorway.

"Will you fucking back off for five seconds?" Eli snarled.

Quinn looked like he'd been sucker punched and vanished from the doorway.

"I need a shower," Silver said, though he sounded like he was eating marbles with the bag on his face.

"We have to leave in thirty-eight minutes."

"I think I can manage that." Silver pulled the bag down. "You know, Quinn might be a little stressed with all the attention on you."

Silver had never seen Quinn look anything worse than constipated, but he thought Eli would buy it.

"You mean he's jealous?"

Silver shrugged. Quinn was proud, not jealous, and Eli was insane. But Silver could manage one good deed today. "I think if you showed him some attention, he'd be able to relax and let you alone."

"Like?"

"Go into the living room, pop open his fly, and blow the fuck out of him. You'll—he'll relax and everything will be better."

Eli gave Silver a squinty look.

"Trust me."

Eli laughed. "Maybe I will. Keep the ice on for a few minutes before you shower." He winked. "And don't come down till I call you."

Chapter Twelve

WHEN SILVER got out of the shower, he found a new shirt on his bed, laid out next to his tight dark blue party jeans. It was lightweight, white and gray-blue checkered pattern, except the plain white collar and cuffs. He thought about complaining about not needing Mommy Eli to pick out his clothes, but damn, he liked that shirt.

Eli came in while Silver was shrugging into the shirt. "You were bitching about not having anything to wear."

Eli himself was dressed in something a hell of a lot brighter than the black-on-black he'd been wearing at the door. Turquoise slacks, tight as skin, a denim shirt with a denim bow tie, and a bright yellow jacket. It should have caused immediate bleeding of the eyes, but on him, it worked.

"So, things a little less tense?" Silver buttoned up the shirt.

Eli grinned. "Yeah. I got that excess tension all over my other clothes. Then Quinn reminded me I'd be happier in what I'd first planned to wear, and everything is peachy keen once more."

He rolled up Silver's sleeves in neat cuffs to the elbow, then buttoned the shirt at the collar.

"Thought I wouldn't need a tie."

"You don't. It's perfect just like that. Of course, if you'd told me you were going to get punched, I would have tried to color coordinate with the bruise."

"Thanks." Silver shoved away Eli's hand when he tried to push hair onto Silver's face to hide the mark. "Tonight is all about you, Eli. No one is going to look at my face."

No one would have looked twice on the bus, but wandering around the Arbuton Gallery ninety minutes later, people looked. And stared. Some of them tipped their heads and openly studied his face as if he were some kind of performance art. Guess violence was something they were only used to seeing in a *representative form*, as he'd heard one guy go on about while staring at some other artist's picture that appeared to have gone through a shredder.

Feeling too much like an exhibit, Silver made his way into the reception area and winced when he got a look at himself in the glass walls. In the past two hours, the bruise on his cheek had deepened to a dark violet-red, complete with individual marks to show where the knuckles had hit. He wished he'd taken Eli up on the offer to try a little makeup. Having pale skin

that marked so quickly had been an advantage shooting spanking videos, but right now it sucked.

He glanced back around into the gallery. He'd
been really excited to see the Sold tags on two of Eli's
things, then almost shit himself when he saw how
much they cost. Jesus, he wished he'd been able to
make that much for one porn shoot.

Gavin stood next to Eli. Quinn was talking to
some straight couple. And Nate and Kellan had just
come in and were headed for Eli. That was reason
enough to stay out of the gallery. Silver liked Kellan,
but he didn't feel like dealing with Nate's condescend-
ing pity about triggers and consent or whatever the
fuck he'd told Eli. How could Zeb have not made it
yet? He had GPS now, so it wasn't like he could get
lost. Waiters were bringing out appetizer trays and tot-
ing champagne around already.

A guy in a nice suit with an open collar showing a tanned throat gave Silver a slow once-over, then
tipped his champagne glass toward him. Silver did his
own quick evaluation. Money, but with that sharply
chiseled face and the hint of hard muscles under the
shirt, this wasn't a guy who needed to pay for it—at
least not for sex. The way he tossed back that champagne suggested he was bored enough to want more
expensive entertainment.

With a wave of confidence rolling out before
him, he approached, snagging two fresh glasses from
a passing waiter. It wasn't until both hands were oc-
cupied that Silver noticed the cane, sleek and slender,
now clamped under one arm.

The man offered one glass with something like
a little bow. "David Beauchamp. You have to tell me

who dared put that mark on your very pretty face so that I can turn his into minced hash."

Silver let a half smile form on his lips as he gave David Beauchamp a closer inspection. Despite a few calluses on the palm of the hand holding out the champagne glass, Beauchamp wasn't a fighter.

"We can't risk *your* pretty face on that, can we?"

Beauchamp laughed. "Good comeback. That surely deserves a toast."

"No thanks."

Jamie was sure to be lurking around somewhere, and Silver didn't want a scene over underage drinking.

"You're going to make me drink alone?" Beauchamp played the disappointment exactly right, hugging the edge of serious and teasing.

"I'm guessing that doesn't hold you back much."

Beauchamp laughed again. "I can't strike out completely. Please tell me you're here by yourself."

"No."

The guy shot him a look of disbelief, light blue eyes wide with fake hurt.

"I'm here with a friend who has stuff in the show. And his boyfriend."

Beauchamp grinned, and Silver knew why the guy had such confidence. It was the kind of grin that could carry you into stuff you really knew better than to get involved in.

"Then my evening is definitely improving." Beauchamp finished off one of the champagnes and rested a free hand on Silver's shoulder. A light enough touch that it didn't have to mean anything, except for the caressing thumb he felt through the thin cotton shirt.

It was fun to be flirted with by someone who didn't want anything but… fun. Silver edged back just enough to signal Beauchamp to lay off a bit. Though maybe it would be nice for Zeb to see Silver wasn't so broken and repulsive that a hot rich guy wouldn't hit on him.

"Beach. How are you doing?" The familiar voice had Silver turning fast.

"Go fuck yourself, my friend." Beauchamp's voice was perfectly pleasant. "I'm busy."

"Silver, nice to see you." Gavin turned to him, looking gorgeous in package-hugging slacks and a thin green silk shirt that did the same for his torso. He was so wasted on that stompy little cop.

"Hey." Silver moved so he was between them, between two hot guys who were both focused on him, wishing Zeb would show up at that exact moment.

"Silver?" Beauchamp tilted his head like he was mocking the name.

"Beach?" Silver said with the same emphasis.

Beauchamp laughed again. "I really like him, Gavin. We should take him out."

"So do I. Which is why we won't." Gavin plucked the extra champagne glass from Beach's hand.

"Or because Sergeant Boyfriend won't like it."

Silver watched them. He'd figured Beach was rich, but he didn't know that he was Gavin kind of rich. Silver might owe Gavin big-time, but it didn't mean Silver had to take orders.

"So, Beach, what do you drive?"

"Hmm. What do you say we let you do all the driving?" Beach's gaze paid careful attention to Silver's crotch.

Gavin gestured at Silver's cheek with a champagne flute. "What happened to you?"

Silver didn't really want to go all pity party in front of Beach, so he sketched it as roughly as he could. "I had to go back home for my birth certificate. My father decided to give me a little something extra."

"Fathers, huh?" Beach said, shaking his head like assholes as birth parents was a minor inconvenience.

Gavin had glanced down as Silver spoke; now he raised his eyes, and the look in them gave Silver a chill. "No. Not like us." He said to Beach, "Silver's father threw him out when he was a teenager. He's been on his own since."

"The *since* moves us to legal territory, though, right?" Beach gave them both that grin and brushed against Silver's arm.

Gavin glared. "Two words, Beach." He leaned in to mutter, "Fort Carroll."

"All right. You're going to use that against me forever, aren't you?" Beach raised a palm and champagne glass in wide-eyed surrender, as if Gavin had just threatened his balls. "Sorry, Silver. Your loss."

"Did you get what you needed?" Gavin asked Silver.

"Yup. For all I care, Dr. and Mrs. Barnett can rot in hell. I never need to talk to them again."

Beach's joking manner fell away. "Doctor? What kind?"

"Dermatologist," Silver said, wondering what the fuck that had to do with anything.

"Where's his practice?"

It sounded like Beach knew old Thomas. But a guy with Beach's money wouldn't have to go to some little minihospital in Shrewsbury to get a mole examined.

"It's in some clinic. Mid Coast Health."

"Really." Beach's eyes lit up. "Be a shame if the good doctor found himself locked out of his own office."

"What?"

"I own it." Beach shrugged. "Own a bunch of health care corporations. Even if I can't break his current lease, there's a lot an administrator can do to make him wish I had."

Maybe Silver didn't like the idea of people trying to run his life—which had seemed to be the most popular job opening in Baltimore since he'd called Eli from jail. But Gavin's anger and concern, plus the offer from some random guy to ruin Silver's asshole father, felt kind of good. Felt like belonging somewhere. Like those few seconds with Zeb earlier, it felt like home.

"Thanks, but I'm all right. Got all I need from him."

"And a little more." Gavin's voice was tight.

"Little more what?" Jamie barged in, manhandling his champagne flute like it was a beer bottle. He glanced over at Beach. "Well, if it isn't my favorite asshole."

Beach put a hand over his heart as if he were gravely wounded. "Sergeant Boyfriend."

"I thought I was your favorite asshole," Gavin murmured. For a second there was silence, but Silver felt a flash of heat just from watching them look at each other.

"Uh." A flush stained Jamie's cheeks almost as red as his hair.

Seeing Jamie get so very owned made Silver forget his cheek until his smile hurt.

"Well, yeah." Jamie was back to himself. "Here, brat, hang on to these." He passed Silver his champagne flute and the one plucked from Gavin's hand. "Let's go talk about that." He tugged Gavin away.

Beach tucked a hand into his pocket in a not completely subtle effort to rearrange his gear. "My my, that was enough electricity to—did he growl?"

Silver wasn't sure where that low vibration had come from. It was like one of the polarization bonds he'd read about in the science book.

"Well, damn. Now I really need to get laid. And as it's been made perfectly clear that you, sweet thing, are off-limits, I'm going to have to settle for something else." Beach's gaze shifted to a woman in a short black dress. More specifically, the way it clung to her ass. "Any port in a storm." He winked and strolled away, the swagger completely hiding his slight limp.

Silver searched for a place to dump the champagne glasses, but the waiters all seemed to have vanished. And of course, having a table or something to put stuff on would ruin whatever vibe the windowed walls and chrome floor was trying to create.

"Thought that wasn't your thing." Zeb stood in front of him, arms crossed in so much righteous indignation it strained the seams on his sport coat.

Which was a shame, because he looked pretty cute with the sleeves rolled up over tan forearms. The full, soft mouth would have added to the cute, if it wasn't pinched in a frown.

Silver flicked his gaze at the champagne glasses in his hands, then pushed them both out at Zeb. "Here. Save me from myself."

Zeb was startled, but his hands shot out to grab the glasses.

Too late, Silver thought he should have dumped the champagne on Zeb's head. "You know what? After today, I am so completely over having anyone tell me who I am or who I'm supposed to be. Fuck. Off."

He crossed the reception room and pushed open the door that took him out onto a wraparound balcony overlooking the harbor. He wasn't alone there—other people had snuck out to enjoy a cigarette in the heavy air. As he moved along the railing and rounded a corner, he half expected to trip over Jamie and Gavin interlocking some body parts, but eventually he found a spot to be alone. Mostly because the view was blocked by some other building. It was almost a perfect hideaway, except for the glass wall behind him. Thunder rumbled, first only a vibration, then loud enough to get people's attention.

Good. The rain should drive everyone else inside, though Silver hoped people stuck around long enough to drink and buy more of Eli's pictures.

The storm blew up fast. From partly cloudy to early sunset in minutes. The wind lifted his hair, sweeping cocktail napkins off the balcony to spin away into the street four stories down. It was a great place to watch people from, see them hurry into buildings or cars, though the trash was more interesting. The wind kept picking up plastic bags and sending them up like kites.

He didn't have to worry about where he'd sleep or if the roof on Tyson Street had a new leak. And for a few minutes, he didn't have to worry about whether he was living up or down to people's expectations. When lightning backlit a cloud to the south, he glanced down at the metal railing and decided not to worry about that either.

He leaned forward against it as the first hard drops of rain fell, letting them sting against his sore right cheek.

"Hey." Zeb's voice.

With almost anyone else, Silver would have turned and put his back against the railing, feeling safer facing a person head-on. But if Zeb was going to hurt him some more, Silver would just as soon not let Zeb see his face.

"Hey," Silver offered in answer.

Zeb put his hands on the railing to Silver's right. Lightning flashed, and Zeb's fingers tapped off the seconds till the thunder. He raised his hands for a second, then settled them again. Maybe his righteousness exempted him from lightning strikes.

The hands flexed and gripped the railing. That scar hadn't been there before, the ragged one extending from the webbing next to his pinky, over the next knuckle, and then over the back of his hand. And his left index finger was missing a little piece. On his right hand, two of the fingers had swollen knuckles, and the tips leaned, like they'd been broken and taped together.

Silver remembered the skin smooth and straight, the tips and nails teasing the inside of his thighs, palm sliding across his belly, a grip on his hips to hold him flat as he tried to buck up into a hot, wet mouth. The way those hands had trembled, half pushing him away on the first thrust inside Zeb's body.

Maybe it wasn't his eyes but Zeb's hands that showed what he was feeling. Right now they were hesitant, stalling, opening and closing on the top rail, tapping lightly.

"I shouldn't have jumped to conclusions," Zeb said at last. "It's been a long day. A lot of emotions raked over." He gave a rueful laugh. "I'm not perfect."

Silver leaned sideways to face him. "Surprised you can admit it."

"You know that better than anyone." Zeb's hand made it halfway to Silver's face and fell away, but his eyes stayed focused on Silver's. "I thank God I got this chance to see you again. To apologize. And I thank you for hearing me out. I guess anything else is a little too much to expect."

Zeb glanced away.

The rain sliced sideways, and Silver wiped it away from his cheek and ear and eye. "What does that mean?"

"If you want, I'm gone. I'll find a job somewhere else. Let you get on with your life in peace. You won't ever have to see me again."

"Did I say I wanted that?"

"Not in words. Specifically."

"You expected a nice-to-see-you-again blow job?"

"Of course not." Zeb's eyes were dark, but there was very little light coming from behind the glass at this end of the balcony. Only the flicker of a fake candle on a table barely as wide as one of the miniquiches the waiters had handed out. Maybe the dim light was what made the lines around his mouth so stern.

"Though was there some other message I was supposed to be receiving based on the way you acted when being tutored?"

The heat in Silver's cheeks should have turned the rain to steam. He shifted back to face the street. "Must be losing my touch."

"I wouldn't say that."

Silver didn't need to look to see Zeb's wry smile. "Jordan."

No smile in Zeb's voice now. It was the voice that had sent him away. Silver watched the tiny river in the gutter and waited him out.

"Do you want me out of your life?" Zeb said flatly.

Silver spun to face him. "No. I don't want that."

"What do you want?"

He had to decide now? What if it was the same thing he'd wanted at sixteen? Zeb. Zeb and a house and a dog. To be able to touch Zeb in public and not have to worry. To know when he had a nightmare, he could roll over into Zeb's warm body. What if Silver spilled his guts with everything he wanted and Zeb laughed? Or worse, shook his head patiently and explained that he might have loved Jordan then, but he could never love who Jordan was now?

He couldn't say any of it out loud. "I don't know."

Zeb nodded, then leaned in for a kiss, but Silver could tell it was headed for his cheek. He tipped his head so their mouths connected instead.

At first Zeb froze and then kissed him, steady pressure, gentle movement. The electricity tingling under Silver's skin should have been enough to call a lightning bolt right to them.

Zeb's hand cupped Silver's cheek carefully, and their heads tilted in unison. Like the memory of how they did this couldn't be erased in years and distance and scars. Silver pulled Zeb's lip between his own, tasted rain and then Zeb. Felt the hint of his tongue as the kiss got hotter, wetter. Zeb's thumb moved, pressing and then jolting away from his bruise.

His lip. It could start bleeding again. Silver stayed in that kiss for another second, a few more moments to imprint that memory, and then backed away.

Zeb let out a long breath. When he spoke, his voice was rough. "When you figure it out, you know where I am."

Then he was gone.

Chapter Thirteen

SILVER HADN'T realized that the Sold stickers on Eli's stuff meant the whole run of prints had sold out. It didn't take a math genius to realize that Eli was swimming in cash. As they made their way out to Quinn's car, Silver ducked down so he could bump shoulders with Eli.

"Holy fuck, Eli. You got it made. Your Daddy will have to roll on his back and take it now."

Quinn made a sound like a pissed-off bull as Eli laughed.

"Not exactly. The gallery gets a big percentage of sales. No one would even know about my stuff if it wasn't here."

"They know about it now." Damn. Why hadn't Silver been born artistic? The only thing he could do was sing well enough to not have people beg him to stop.

"They do. And Henry wants me for another photography show in January." As they crossed a side
street, Eli teased, "How 'bout it, Quinn? Ready for a
little extra income?"

Quinn spun around, and the intent expression on
his face, even in the dark, yanked on Silver's guts and
gave them a hard, mean twist of jealousy.

Grabbing Eli, Quinn lifted him off the pavement, hugging him tightly. "I am so goddamned
proud of you."

Silver's throat squeezed. Like he was going to
cry. Which was about as lame as it got. He didn't think
Quinn was hot. And Silver was definitely not looking
for a toppy Daddy in bed. So why did he want what
Eli had?

The want was a live thing inside, chewing on
Silver's guts. He had to look away, take a few steps
toward the Buick, and rest his hands on the metal of
the roof.

Since that kiss with Zeb, Silver hadn't felt right in
his skin—and worse, didn't know if it was a good or
bad thing. Did the kiss mean something new? Something besides hurling all his anger and hurt into the
space where Zeb used to be? That had been about as
successful as landing punches on a ghost. Nothing but
missed swings and bleeding knuckles.

The interaction hadn't been imaginary this time.
A real kiss. Zeb live and in the warm, nice-smelling
flesh. But with the way Zeb had kissed Silver, maybe
it was Zeb seeing ghosts.

Because Zeb had kissed him like Silver was still
Jordan. Still young and learning how to do it. Jordan

was dead and buried. And Silver didn't have much to offer in his place.

"Are you getting in or going to keep mooning over the clouds?" Eli nudged him.

Silver jumped. He hadn't even heard them approach, hadn't noticed Quinn unlocking the car. Stupid. And dangerous.

"Quinn was all set to invite everyone to meet us at With Relish, and I said how would that be fun for you, so we're going to Angelo's in Little Italy."

Silver wondered if he was supposed to say something—*thanks* or *yeah, that would suck on my day off*—but Eli went on.

"I called Zeb, too, since I didn't see him around when we were wrapping up."

Silver's stomach did the kind of dip that would have echoed to his knees if he were standing instead of belting himself into Quinn's back seat.

"Sorry." Eli's monologue continued. "I had to leave a voicemail. Do you want to try him?"

Another one of those dips, this time more solid with disappointment. Christ. Maybe Jordan wasn't as gone as Silver thought. He still could do the quick mood shift like a fucking teenager.

"No. It's fine."

At the restaurant, Eli's version of *everyone* turned out to be the usual suspects. Nate and Kellan and Jamie and Gavin. The last pair might not have been out on the balcony, but they'd found someplace to get busy. Silver knew freshly fucked when he saw it. And smelled it. He wasn't the only one rolling his eyes at Jamie's smug grin. Quinn did a little head-shake thing that only made Jamie smugger.

Was there such a thing as a seventh wheel? Maybe the waitress would bring over a booster seat, since Silver felt like Eli and Quinn's sorry-we-couldn't-get-a-sitter baby baggage.

His phone rang, and Silver shoved himself away from where he was wedged between Jamie and Quinn. Not knowing what to say to Zeb was preferable to being stuck at the table.

It wasn't Zeb. It was Marco.

"Timo is keeping my phone because he thinks I will call you, and I couldn't remember your number forever—but in calculus class today, something hit—" Marco made a sound like a blast from an ion cannon. "—and I remembered and borrowed a phone on break."

Eli could take monologuing lessons from Marco.

"Uh-huh," Silver contributed when Marco ran down. Damn, they had classes that kept you so late they took breaks at nine at night? That sucked.

"So?"

"So what?"

"What should I do about Timo? He said he'd give me my phone back when classes started, and now he won't."

"I don't know. He scares me."

"*Pendejo.* Fuck him."

"No thanks. He told me if he saw me with you, he'd kill me."

"Timo never goes anywhere." Marco sighed. "*Me aburro.*"

"Huh?" Without Marco's face and gestures, translation was harder.

"I'm bored." Marco rolled the *r* like he had in *aburro*. "I want to go out and have fun."

Silver missed dancing at the Arena, but not the rest of the hassles involved in what used to be fun— creepy guys, long lines, wondering if his luck would run out and he'd get jumped on the way home. Marco wouldn't be nineteen until September, and his fake ID only passed in the dark.

"Hang out with guys from your class."

"*Petardos*. Nerds."

Whereas Marco's presence in calculus made him cool. Silver rolled his eyes.

"I can't really go anywhere. I have my court date in two weeks. I can't risk getting in any trouble."

"You're still staying up there with your friends? Eli and his *papi*?"

"Yeah. The cops"—Jamie was a cop, right?— "and the judge said I had to stay with them."

"But they're gay. And *papi* is hot. You have it good."

"Well, there's no parties and no three-ways going on. All I do is go to work." *And the tutoring with Zeb, let's not forget that part.*

"But they don't make you feel wrong." No whine, simply stated as fact.

Silver heard the desperate need all the same. Remembered the hunger, the way it left him raw and empty. The yearning for one voice to tell him he wasn't deviant, bad, a perversion. He'd have gone crazy in high school if he hadn't had Marissa to talk to.

As if the sudden sympathy came through in the sound of Silver's breathing, Marco pressed, "One night. Saturday. Somehow I'll get a car."

"I have to work four to midnight."

"I don't care. I have to go somewhere that isn't the library or school or church."

Saturday. When Silver had hoped he might meet up with Zeb for tutoring and then see what happened from there. Which reminded Silver it hadn't only been the promise of sex to make him count down the hours to being with Zeb again. Back in New Freedom, Zeb's tiny studio apartment had been a safe place to be themselves.

"Okay. If you can get a car, come up at around noon."

"I will. If I trade babysitting that night, my sister's husband will give me a car."

"Just don't get in any trouble."

And please don't get me in any, Silver added to himself after he shut off his phone.

SILVER JERKED out of sleep with an erection like the goddamned Eiffel Tower between his legs. He didn't have to wonder where the fuck it had come from. That dream.

It had taken him back to the restaurant. Only in his dream, Zeb had shown up. Silver could have done without the audience and the judgy commentary from Nate and Jamie, but he hadn't cared when Zeb had slid under the table. His tongue. His mouth. Jesus.

His dick was so hard it hurt. Legs trembling with it. No way he'd make it to the bathroom. The tissues on Eli's desk would have to be cleanup enough. But damn, he couldn't move. No strength in his legs. All of it in that granite spike. He spit in his hand, worked it in with the precome, and stroked.

Fuck. He'd thought when it turned back on, it would be nice and slow. He'd see a hot guy, and there'd be a nice, prickly warmth like stepping into the shower. And it would grow from there.

Not this. Not a flip of a switch and the coming-out-of-his-skin desperation like he'd had at fourteen, needing to jerk off to a jeans commercial because they talked about the fit of the crotch.

His hand wasn't enough. Wasn't anything like his dream. He wanted to—had to—fuck his dick into Zeb's throat, drive it into his ass, feel that hot pulse of wet flesh. The convulsive pressure, the friction taking him higher until he spilled sticky and wet inside Zeb's body.

Silver shuddered, hips bucking as he shot onto his stomach, imagined painting Zeb with it, his chest, his nipples, his face, and that pathetic patch of beard.

As the spasms slowed, faded until Silver was just stroking slowly, he remembered why it couldn't happen like his fantasy. He might not need to rush off and wash the sheets with bleach, but he wasn't going to be pumping come into anyone. Ever again.

But somehow, the thought of Zeb looking up at him, mouth around Silver's latex-covered cock, was enough to give his stomach another hard rock of want. Yeah. He could manage that. Run out for some condoms, ask Zeb if they could squeeze in a little tutoring tomorrow before Silver had to go in to work.

He wiped up with the tissues, trying not to think why Eli would need tissues at his desk.

As Silver climbed back into bed, he picked up his phone, clicking to his last text exchange with Zeb.

Got Eli's voicemail. Do you want me to come?

He had and he hadn't.

He'd wanted to see Zeb again, see if that kiss had been something Silver built up in his head to be bigger than it was. But not with the audience. He and Zeb had enough shit between them without dragging everyone else's issues into the mix.

Silver had wimped out on his answer. *Going to be leaving soon.* Now he sent *What time do you get out of work tomorrow?*

It was almost 3:00 a.m. If Zeb sent an answer in the morning, maybe they'd be able to work something out. Waiting didn't seem possible. Any more possible than sleep right now. Every cell in Silver's body buzzed with energy. This was nothing like the zombie wakefulness he chalked up to side effects from his pill.

When his phone buzzed with a call, he almost dropped it in surprise. "Is everything okay?" Zeb asked immediately.

"Yeah. I'm fine. Um. Sorry I woke you."

"I wasn't asleep."

"Lying is a sin, you know."

"I'm not lying. I've been up for a while." Zeb's voice had a note of something when he said *up*. Something touching the edge of a dirty pun.

"Well, vengeance isn't the only thing it's a sin to take into your own hands either."

Zeb laughed, the sound so warm Silver felt it wrap around him, like they could almost slide under the sheets right there to take care of things together.

"Though I might have done that earlier," Silver added.

"Yeah?" Zeb's sex voice. Rough. Urgent. So completely unlike him and only him at the same time.

There was an invitation in that *yeah*. One Silver wished his dick wasn't too sore to accept. Apparently abstinence was better than Viagra. But for the first time in his life, he didn't take the direct path. His voice betrayed him with a small hitch, but he stuck to his plan. "What time does school get over?"

"They're setting up for commencement. It's a half day."

Was it possible that things were actually going to go Silver's way for once? "I—uh—have to be at work by four, but I was hoping…." He was just as nervous as he'd been that first time, asking if Zeb wanted to talk about the *Star Wars* movies, only this time so much more was at stake. And Zeb didn't offer any help, the bastard. "We could meet and go over the social studies part of the test?"

"Sure." Pleasant, but with none of the teasing edge that had made Silver's cock ache as blood tried to fill it again.

"Um, could we meet at your house?" Silver wanted to kick himself for the breathlessness in the question. He sounded like Marco, for fuck's sake.

"I'll pick you up at noon."

Chapter Fourteen

"I NEED a drink." Silver pushed away from Zeb's small kitchen table.

Silver couldn't believe this. They were actually looking at the social studies workbook. Like the kiss and the conversation last night hadn't happened. As if Silver had really wanted to talk about what a bunch of dead guys did and why the fuck anyone would care.

"Help yourself. Glasses are in the cabinet to the left of the sink. Grab anything you want from the fridge." Zeb stayed plastered to his seat with the workbook in front of him.

Okay, so Silver had set things up to go exactly like this. Sort of. He'd wimped out on the phone, gone to something a bit more subtle than *Let's go to your place and fuck.* Because until last night, he'd never felt like he had so much of himself on the line if he asked that question.

And dammit, now he couldn't figure out if fucking was ever going to be on the table—literally was fine with Silver—next to the lame-ass workbook. He'd been pretty sure Zeb was flirting last night, that the kiss had been more than hey-nice-to-see-ya. But Zeb had been the one to end it all last time, and Silver needed something more obvious to be sure they were on the same page.

Silver took out a plain glass from the cabinet. The restaurant got fancier stuff for a quarter a pop. Nothing special on the glass, not even an indented base. Like Zeb's apartment. Not dirty or rundown, it just wasn't anything. Beige walls, beige carpet. The kind of place you rent when you don't plan to be there long.

Oh.

"So how long does the summer camp run?"

"Six weeks. Plenty of time before school starts again."

"You're going to stick around here then?"

Zeb's back stiffened. After a moment, he turned to look at Silver. "Unless I hear otherwise. From the school district. Or from you."

Silver shook his head. Realizing he'd been pathetically eager, he added, "Live where you want. When do you get to hear if you still have a job?"

"They can decide not to renew my contract right on up until school starts in August."

"That sucks."

"It's all part of the fun of summer as a teacher. No pay and no job security."

"All that and brat kids too? Why would anyone do it?"

Zeb did that half-smile thing. "I guess it's one of those things you just know is right for you."

The expression on his face was hard to read—or maybe Silver was afraid to read it. He opened the fridge—orange juice, cranberry juice, a pitcher of iced tea. After nudging the door shut, he filled his glass from the tap and took a couple swallows before looking over at Zeb. He'd turned back to the table, and he could have been examining the workbook, but Silver didn't think it held Zeb's attention. There was something about the way he sat, spine straight, shoulder blades drawn together. Like he was waiting for something.

Silver hadn't waited at all the first go-round. The moment they'd been alone in Zeb's apartment, sixteen-year-old Silver's hand was on Zeb's shoulder, pulling him toward that first kiss.

This wariness was all on Silver. He was the one who'd made it about studying. Said he didn't know what he wanted. Because he was afraid of rejection. He'd offered sex a hundred times for money, but asking for this left him paralyzed, staring at Zeb's tense back.

If he said no, how could it be worse than that night when Silver had begged for Zeb's help, begged him to run away, leave all the bigots behind and be together? Silver had survived that. So he could risk this.

He put his hands on Zeb's shoulders, slid them over the surface of his dress shirt, warm, smooth fabric over hard, tight skin. Silver pushed his hands lower, fingertips leading as his palms settled over Zeb's pecs, feeling the nipples swell. Pressing against Zeb's back, Silver rested his chin on Zeb's shoulder and listened to his breathing speed up.

"What question were we on?" Silver used his hands to apply circular pressure to the muscles under his palms.

Zeb leaned back, head dropping to Silver's shoulder.

Silver turned his head so his lips brushed Zeb's ear. "I missed your answer. Could you repeat it?"

A shudder went through the body under his palms. Blood pulsed slow and sweet in Silver's balls, his dick.

"We only have three questions left. Shouldn't we get this done?" Zeb murmured, but there was a trace of laughter in his husky voice.

Silver smiled against the prickle of Zeb's cheek. "Can't you think of anything—anyone—else who should get done?" Silver's hands glided lower, over Zeb's stomach, until the fingers brushed the waistband of his trousers.

Zeb's hands landed over Silver's, holding him there, leaving them both on that edge. "God, Silver, you're killing me."

Silver froze then took a step back, hands retreating to Zeb's shoulders. "What did you call me?"

Zeb turned around. The hurt and confusion on his face smoothed out, a slow smile replacing it. "Silver," he said, as if he was playing it back in his head.

Silver tipped his head. Waited.

Zeb stood and wrapped an arm around Silver's waist. "I called you Silver. It suits you. And if you're willing to let go of the past, I am too."

With the other hand behind Silver's neck, Zeb kissed him. Mouth in gentle, careful motion, soothing the still-sore spot.

Just wet enough to make the glide smooth, tingling. The heat in the three spots where Zeb touched him spread the flush through Silver's body, sending a welcome surge of blood to his cock.

Yes. All systems armed and ready to fire. It took all Silver's self-control not to pump his fist in triumph.

Zeb's tongue teased at the corner of Silver's mouth. He wished he could grab Zeb and kiss him, really kiss him, drive their mouths together until they were sharing every oxygen atom with its eight penny electrons. But though the mark was less swollen today, a rough, deep kiss could split the healing tear.

Goddamn Thomas Barnett to hell.

Silver pulled his mouth back but held on to Zeb's head. There were so many other places Silver could put his lips, his tongue.

He licked a line along Zeb's jaw, felt the reaction in the squeeze of Zeb's arms, the stutter of his breath. Silver wanted, needed to feel more. Grabbing Zeb's hips, Silver jerked them together. The pressure of Zeb's cock on Silver's was better than anything Silver had managed with his hand the past six months put together. It could only get sweeter when he cupped Zeb's ass to grind them against each other.

God, had Zeb's ass always been that hard and muscular? Because even Silver's hi-def memory hadn't been doing it justice.

He got a better grip, stepped closer, and they stumbled into the table.

The table was good. It was steady. That could work. Right as he was about to try to lift Zeb onto it, Zeb stopped panting in Silver's ear long enough to mutter, "Bedroom. Ten feet away."

Silver let Zeb steer, stumbling backward toward the promised flat surface, which was good news for knees that couldn't make up their minds between folding from a case of the wobbles or bending to get Silver's face up close and personal with Zeb's cock.

As Zeb pushed, Silver found a bed behind him and started trying to work on the buttons of Zeb's shirt. Zeb reached for Silver's. It didn't work out like of one of those romantic moments in a movie when the camera swung around the couple slowly undressing each other. It was a mess.

Their arms and fingers kept getting tangled and twisted, and slow wasn't on the menu. Silver wondered if it was because he was afraid Zeb would change his mind. And maybe Zeb was afraid of the same thing, because after a harsh breath, Zeb leaned back. "How about—?"

Silver caught one of Zeb's hands and smiled. "You do you and I do me?"

"Yeah."

"But I'm gonna watch." Silver unbuttoned his cuffs and freed himself by yanking the shirt over his head.

Zeb's hands had been at his belt, and now they dropped away. "You are not helping." He laughed.

Silver stood up and shucked off his slacks, boxer briefs, and socks in one quick motion before sprawling back on the bed.

"Still not helping." Zeb's gaze was hot, lingering on Silver's chest before dropping lower.

"Too bad. If you want some of this—" Startled by the sting of a tiny missile on his chest, Silver broke off. Another shirt button flew past.

Zeb finished tearing off his shirt, buttons pinging the bed and floor. He shoved his pants down and threw himself forward, like one extra step would mean too much more time apart. He landed on the mattress between Silver's spread legs, mouth dropping kisses on Silver's chest.

"I never stopped wanting you. Never. It's killed me. Every minute of being with you and not touching you." Zeb's lips and stubble tingled across Silver's stomach. "God, I want you."

"I'm here." Silver tried to pull Zeb up higher, see his face, feel the hard skin of his dick rub on Silver's, know they were both ready for this.

Zeb resisted, mouth moving lower. "Need this. Need you in my mouth."

God yes. The heat and the soft, wet kiss on the base of his dick, the vibration of Zeb's groan, and the wet tease of his tongue on the shaft.

The bare shaft of Silver's dick.

Shit. "Wait. Condom." Zeb lifted his head.

Those eyes, Zeb's eyes looking up at him, the silky curls of his hair sweeping Silver's thighs. He wanted to say fuck it and drag Zeb's head back down but couldn't.

"For this?" Zeb's tongue teased a line up Silver's groin.

Things got white and fuzzy for a second. Then the wet lap on his balls made him lean up on his elbows, remembering something really important despite the ache of wanting to forget everything but that mouth.

"Yeah. Because—" Everything he'd been about to say evaporated in the sudden desert dryness of his mouth.

How could he have forgotten? Zeb didn't know.

Silver's friends knew. And when Zeb shifted into that category, somehow in Silver's mind, Zeb knew.

But that was only Silver lying to himself. More than anything, Zeb didn't know because Silver hadn't wanted to have to tell him.

Until now, there hadn't been a reason.

But it wasn't that easy to say with Zeb's hands on him, his breath teasing the skin of Silver's dick, even if it had wilted under all the thoughts crowding into his head. His thighs burned where Zeb's fingers rested.

"Is everything okay?" Zeb's eyes were soft with concern.

This wasn't something Silver could lie about. "No." And there wouldn't ever be an easy way to say it. "I'm HIV positive."

Chapter Fifteen

ZEB'S HEAD disappeared.

Silver pushed himself to sitting and found Zeb hunched over, kneeling on the floor. Silver's stomach churned in the way that threatened to spew if he opened his mouth, but he couldn't stand that echoing silence. He leaned to hook his briefs out of his pile of clothes. "Yeah. Okay, then. I'm going to head out."

"No." Zeb snapped it with an anger Silver couldn't remember hearing from him before. "You're going to wait."

Silver tucked his briefs against his junk and waited.

Zeb's voice was less angry but still full of emotion as he said, "I realize I'm not in a position to ask you for anything, but could you please give me a second to digest what you said?"

"What the hell does that mean? Not in a position to ask? Just ask whatever the fuck you want to ask." Like there was some big mystery how he got it. As if the only possible response to Silver telling someone he was positive was *Who gave it to you?*

"I didn't mean it like that." Zeb buried his face in his hands. "God, I'm so sorry."

Silver took advantage of the freak-out to haul up the briefs and find his slacks. "It's fine. You don't want m—to have sex with me now. It's cool. No need to apologize."

Zeb looked up, pushing his hair away from his face. "No? Not even for sending you away that night so that—"

Silver finished zipping his fly and slapped a hand against his thigh in frustration. "Shit. I thought we were past this."

"How do I get past—? I thought you were okay and now—"

What the fuck was it with people and that vague wave gesture? You couldn't catch HIV by saying it. And it wasn't like Silver was likely to forget.

"I am okay. I'm HIV positive. I don't have AIDS. I take a pill and have to get my blood checked once a month."

Zeb was still on his knees, sunk back on his bare ass, pants around his ankles. It should have been ridiculous. But the bastard managed to pull off looking sexy and annoying at the same time.

"I'm so sorry," he said again.

Silver had had enough. They had been close enough to touch the amazing feeling that was the two of them together, and if it wasn't going to work this time, he wasn't going to let Zeb walk because of some lame sense of responsibility.

Silver reached down and yanked Zeb to his feet. "No, you fucking don't. You don't get to take credit for this. You're not God. You only look like him."

Zeb put his hand on Silver's unbruised cheek. "Jord—Silver."

"Shut up."

Zeb tried to pull his hand free, but Silver held it there.

"Shut up and listen," Silver said. "Why did you go to Haiti?"

"To help build a school and to teach."

"Bull. Shit."

Zeb jerked his hand free. "What's the point of doing this now?"

Silver's hand started to reach for Zeb's face, to hold him so he couldn't hide behind averted glances and fake smiles. But he wouldn't force it. If they were going to make this happen, make something honest, it could only be because they both wanted it.

"You said when I figured out what I wanted, I should tell you."

Zeb nodded, lips a thin line.

"Well, I did. Now I'm trying to figure out if I can have it."

Zeb smiled. Not the fake one or the twisted one. But a small one. Like for once he didn't have the right answer for how to act. Leaning in, he kissed Silver, just long enough to make him remember why this was so damned important.

"Yeah." Silver sighed. "Okay. That much we've got. But it's going to take a little more this time around. Hard truths. Why did you go to Haiti?"

Zeb glanced down. "Because…." He drew the word out, then a long inhale before the rest of the words came out in a rush. "I knew it was wrong. You—God, you were sixteen. The guilt of it."

"So with your logic, I'm the reason you got malaria."

"That's insane."

"So is you feeling responsible for me being positive." Silver shrugged. "You knew the risks when you went to a tropical country with no health care."

Zeb looked like he was about to argue, so Silver said, "And if I decided to have sex with guys without a condom, I knew the risk. It was my choice, and I sure as fuck am not watching you nail yourself to another cross over it."

When Zeb moved toward him, Silver met him. Holding him tight, being held. Silver rested his head on Zeb's shoulder. "I was so angry. At them. At you. At the whole fucking world. So I did some stupid stuff."

This was easier than face-to-face. Easier to hear when Zeb said, "I was mad at you too. Enough to do my own share of stupid. And I'm sorry."

Silver lifted his head. "No more sorries. I don't want then, I want now. I could go to jail. For a year." No matter how much Gavin's lawyer cost, that was another hard truth Silver hadn't been ready for. And now the idea of it made him cold right down to having ice for bone marrow. "And if that's going to happen, I don't want to spend the year thinking about what could have been happening if I wasn't so goddamned pissed off."

Zeb laughed, and it wasn't so cold anymore. Warmth spread out from where Zeb's hands pressed Silver tight in the hug. "And I thought you were precocious at sixteen."

"Yeah, well, it turns out that kind of precocious only gets you so far." Silver tried to laugh, but it was more than half sigh.

Zeb held Silver's face between his hands and kissed him. Lips parted, more pressure and heat and urgency this time. Silver opened his mouth and flicked an invitation with his tongue. They both groaned with the first wet contact, the taste and heat of each other's mouth.

It wasn't only the kiss that was different. Getting turned on was different too. Instead of his dick sending sparks out, this feeling curled out from his belly, waking up his cock, yeah, but rippling up and down his spine and legs and even his arms. Zeb groaned again, a sweet vibration on Silver's lips, hands sliding down, shoulders, back, until they cupped Silver's ass.

A twinge of pain in his lip as Zeb deepened the kiss made Silver pull back. "Can we start over?" Zeb whispered into the space between their mouths.

"My lip."

Zeb released him. "Sorry."

"Not that. I'm afraid it's going to start bleeding again."

"Oh." Then Zeb's eyes opened wider. "Oh."

"Yeah."

Zeb's tongue made a shifting protrusion around lips and cheeks. "I don't have any cuts in my mouth." He wrapped his arms around Silver's waist and smiled. Not the fake smile, but the one that let Silver see Zeb wasn't completely sure of himself. "I'm ready if you are."

Because he didn't want any misunderstanding, Silver grabbed Zeb's wrist and brought his hand to where Silver's dick pulsed, then moved it off before he could enjoy the sensation of a hand not his own there for the first time in months. "Ready, yeah. I want to." God, he wanted to. Before he forgot how to do it. And to find out if it was as good as he remembered with Zeb. "But I'm going to be all responsible for a minute and say no."

Zeb's smile disappeared for a second before being replaced by a brighter one. "No?"

"I don't want it to be because you think you have to prove something." Silver shrugged.

"Nice to know what you think of me." Zeb had kicked out of his pants, so when he dragged Silver's hand forward, there wasn't any barrier to the proof of Zeb's interest. Silver's fingers barely brushed the satiny skin of Zeb's shaft before Zeb released him.

"Does that feel like I'm only trying to prove something?"

He bit back the impulse to ask when Zeb *wasn't* trying to prove something. "The first thing you said after I told you I was positive was that you needed time to 'digest' it. And I think you should."

"Do I get a say in this?"

"Sure." Silver sat on the bed and scooped his shirt off the floor. "You digest it and then let me know."

Zeb pushed him backward onto the mattress, pinning his shoulders flat. His eyes had never looked more intense—except maybe with a dick up his ass. "Don't you pull this self-righteous crap on me. I invented it."

"I think your crown of thorns is safe enough."

"Finding out you're positive was a shock. I admit it."

When Zeb paused, time froze with him. The next thing he said was either going to be something Silver could live with or something that would kill any chance of making this work. They were too close to the edge, one way or another. The tension was worse than the ache of straining to come when he'd pushed it back too many times, waiting for the director's call.

This pain came from higher up, his ribs shrinking, strangling his lungs, his heart. When Zeb's gaze softened, Silver knew it was over. Being positive was the final stroke that killed off whatever Zeb had felt for Jordan, those feelings impossible to transfer to Silver. He wanted to slap a hand over Zeb's mouth, put it off for a few more seconds.

"Jordan."

Yup, bad news.

Zeb's lips pressed together, and he made a tiny shake of his head as he corrected himself. "Silver, I could take between now and doomsday to think about it, and it wouldn't make a difference. I want to be with you. Any way. Every way."

Silver played the words back in his head, hoping they burned a permanent loop in his brain.

The cramp in his chest eased, a deep breath bringing everything back into balance.

He fought a smile then gave up. "Get off me, then. Gotta get my pants off."

Zeb grinned and rolled off. Silver ditched his slacks and briefs, taking a second to hang them and his shirt off the doorknob so they'd be less of a disaster at work.

Climbing back on the bed, he dragged Zeb under him. "Okay. But we're not fucking until I think you're ready."

"Seriously?"

Silver nodded. "Payback's a bitch, huh?"

"I was an asshole."

It was still a shock to hear Zeb say anything like that, more the language than admitting his fault, though it did sound more sincere than his usual martyrdom.

"I wouldn't go that far. A moron, maybe."

"I remember it didn't slow us down much." Zeb's hands stroked down Silver's back, gliding over his ass, fingers grazing the crease.

"No," Silver agreed as Zeb's grip lifted him forward so their dicks dragged against each other. Slow rhythm, heat growing, skin tightening, cocks swelling harder, hotter. Silky friction tingling from his slit to his balls. Silver arched, pumped his hips, eyes closed, concentrating on the reawakened sensations chasing around inside. The dizzying flash along his cock, the solid build of excitement sparking his balls. And when he opened his eyes, it was Zeb there with him, straining up into another kiss.

Silver welcomed Zeb's tongue back inside, slipping his own deep, and somehow even after three years that taste was familiar. Satisfaction and renewed craving tangled up in their bodies and mouths as they moved together.

They were both panting when they broke for breath. Zeb's hand stroked through Silver's hair, eyes fixed on his face. "It's you. Really you."

He knew what Zeb meant. Dreams had taken Silver back to this more than once. Left him bitter, aching, and absolutely empty when he woke. "Yeah."

Zeb's fingers sifted through Silver's hair again. "I missed you."

Silver had had this. Pleasure and hunger, for fun as much as necessity. Most of the time it had felt the same, but the difference happened when it was over. Right now there was a huge difference.

"Me too."

And that had been long enough without kissing him, without the tingling stroke of tongues and the hard friction between them.

It wasn't all perfect, rough with only a little precome to ease the scrape, but the idea of stopping—of separating—was way worse. He resented the need to catch his breath, that he couldn't just drink it out of Zeb's lungs. Nothing would be enough; not even Silver's cock inside Zeb could be enough when what he wanted was to melt into him, taste him, breathe him, cover him with sweat and come. Fuse completely at the bone.

Except when they did have to gasp and drag in fresh air, Silver got to watch Zeb. Watch pleasure shape his eyes and mouth, color his cheeks and throat. See the reflected hunger that sent them back into another kiss.

Zeb arched up harder, harsh gasps breaking from his throat. Tension slammed into Silver's balls, coiling at the base of his spine. Warning and promise. He'd been locked in a chastity cage for years, and no way could he hold back anymore. A question screamed in the back of his brain. Was this safe? What was the risk in his come on the head of Zeb's dick? The flood drowned out everything but an ability to gasp a warning.

"Shit. I'm gonna—"

Zeb shifted them so as Silver's muscles locked into those beautiful spasms, his cock pumped onto Zeb's stomach and chest. Zeb nipped at Silver's jaw, his lips, making that sensation roll on until he collapsed, dropping his forehead onto Zeb's.

An easy motion tipped them onto their sides and let Silver slide a hand between them to get a good grip on Zeb's dick. The familiar groan against Silver's shoulder reminded him he knew exactly what Zeb wanted. Tight, a hard tight strip on the shaft. Silver knew what Zeb liked whispered in his ear too.

"Come for me." Silver took Zeb's earlobe between his teeth.

The sound would have been at home on a barrel-chested bear, deep and rough, vibrating from Zeb's slim chest. Zeb's hips jerked, the first shot landing on Silver's shoulder, the rest mixing with the jizz already sticking them together.

After a long, shuddering breath, Zeb pulled Silver closer. This was what he had missed. Welded together, sticky, sweaty, and smelling like sex. Bodies still shaking, hearts slowing.

But instead of being able to relax into it, Silver found himself wondering if this was okay. If Zeb wanted Silver's unsafe spunk drying on him. If the hugging after was only Zeb's determination to prove that things hadn't changed.

If Silver could turn off his damned brain, it would be nice to drift to sleep like this. His phone alarm would beep when he had to leave for work. Except it was way the fuck over in his pants.

Zeb kissed his forehead. "What time do you have to be at work?"

"We've got time." Silver didn't want to let go, so he wiped the hair from his face using Zeb's shoulder.

"Not enough. Not for everything I want to do with you."

Silver's stomach made a painful flip, half fear, half longing. It couldn't be real. Not lying here plastered with come and not Zeb saying stuff Silver wouldn't even have come up with in a dream.

"I could pick you up tonight. You could stay with me."

That was something Silver *had* dreamed. More than once. But he hadn't imagined Zeb would sound so desperate for a yes.

"I could, but I have to go back in the morning to get my pill." And if that wasn't mood killer enough, he knew Marco would be early. "And then I have plans before work tomorrow."

"Oh." Zeb didn't release him, but his embrace grew slack. "So."

That was a weird shift in tone. Silver leaned back enough to prop his head up on a cocked elbow. "What?"

Zeb swallowed, throat bobbing in a way that made Silver's tongue want to go along for the ride. "Who was that guy?"

"What guy?"

"The one last night at the gallery. In the nice suit. The one who gave you champagne."

Well, Jamie had handed it to him, and he hadn't been wearing a nice suit. And Zeb had met Jamie, whose red hair and asshole attitude tended to leave an impression. Not Jamie.

"Beach? He's Gavin's friend. That's about all I know about him." Silver felt his lip start to curl and sucked it in to hide the smile, which hurt. "And the plans tomorrow, that's a friend thing too, not a date."

"Good."

Silver couldn't help the smile this time. He couldn't remember the last time anyone had bothered to care. It probably would have been Zeb, back then, but Silver had been too caught up in having a boyfriend to even think about cheating on him.

"You think you should have something to say about that?" He peered down, enjoying Zeb's attempt at hiding how much he did want a say in it.

"I understand if you don't think it's my business."

"I didn't say it wasn't." Silver stroked his free hand down Zeb's chest. Slender, yeah, but hard. Definition in his pecs and abs. Not pumped for bulk like a gym rat, but like someone who put the muscles to use. Teaching didn't need heavy lifting. Did Zeb like sports? There was so much Silver didn't know about him. They'd been busy learning other things about each other then.

"Maybe we should take it slow." Zeb's breath hitched.

That wasn't the answer Silver wanted to hear. "How slow?"

He licked a line down Zeb's breastbone, tasted sweaty skin and their come mixed together. Moving to a nipple, Silver tongued it, then teased it with his teeth. Zeb's hand fell heavy on Silver's head, then petted, sifting through his hair, as the heartbeat under Silver's mouth pounded faster.

He glanced up at Zeb's flushed face, watched his tongue poke out and smooth his parted lips. "Well?"

"It's hard to think when you're doing that."

Silver rolled on his back. "Okay. Didn't think the question required that many brain cells to answer."

He should have kept going, taken the soft cock into his mouth and let it lengthen and stiffen until he couldn't hold it just in his mouth, had to open his throat to fit it all inside where it was wet and warm. He had plenty of practice with older guys who needed serious work to get off. Pushing Zeb to the limit of his recovery time wouldn't be hard at all. Then he wouldn't be lying here with that hollow feeling, wondering what Zeb wanted. When a guy's cock was in your mouth, you always knew what he wanted.

Zeb rolled onto Silver. "I'm not sure you asked the right question."

"I don't feel like playing some teacher game."

"I'm not playing any kind of game."

Silver didn't want to meet Zeb's gaze. Because if he was hiding what was really going on, Silver didn't want to know. "Just tell me what the fuck you want from me."

"Whatever you want to give me."

That was completely unhelpful. And all their rolling around had put Silver right at the edge of the bed. There was no place left to go except the floor. Why couldn't this be easier? Suck or fuck, come, and then holding each other was nice. Right now, the list of guys Silver was looking to do that with was one name long: Zebadiah Harris.

"Yeah, right, you're not playing a game. Then stop with the riddles, or is there some lesson from Proverbs you're trying to get to?"

"Silver, what's wrong? What happened?"

"Nothing. It's fine. I got off, you got off."

Zeb put his hand on Silver's jaw and turned him so they were face-to-face. "And that's all it was?"

Closing his eyes would be pathetic and childish, but Silver was still tempted. He tried to make his face blank. "That's what I'm trying to find out."

"It was more than sex to me." Zeb's mouth curled up at the corner. "Not that the sex wasn't absolutely amazing."

Silver shrugged. "I'm a professional."

Zeb's fingers tightened on Silver's jaw, though they steered clear of the bruise. "Was that all it was for you?"

"No." And the hoarseness in Silver's voice, the way he sounded close to tears, was humiliating, but he didn't struggle to get free.

"Can I see you again?"

"I only work until two on Sunday. Fuck. I forgot." It had sounded like an awesome plan when he'd been invited. Gavin taking them out on his yacht. Silver, on an actual fucking yacht.

"Another not-a-date?"

"It's a group thing." Silver remembered the invitation. *In celebration of your success, Eli. You're also welcome, Silver. As is a friend, if you'd like to bring one.*

At the time Silver had been glad Gavin at least knew how much it sucked to be a third/fifth/seventh wheel, but Silver hadn't been sure about things with Zeb, so there hadn't been any additions to the guest list. But since Gavin had offered, it would be fine if Zeb wanted to come. Assuming that was the kind of "see you again" thing he had in mind.

"You could come too," Silver said.

"I wouldn't want to make people uncomfortable."

"It's just my friends." Sounded weird to say *my friends* and know they were. Good friends who'd be there for him. Even weirder to know his friends included Gavin Montgomery. And grudgingly, Jamie Donnigan. "Quinn likes you. And Eli—I edited the past pretty heavily when I explained how things went."

"As much as I'm glad my testicles will be spared his wrath, I don't want you to lie to your friend."

"I didn't lie."

Was it always going to hurt? The way Zeb looked at him when he said *lie*?

"I left a lot of stuff out," Silver said. "But if you don't want to go, that's fine. We could get together after. Just us." He cupped Zeb's junk to be sure that part of the invitation was clear.

"Could we do both?"

"I guess."

"So it's a date." Zeb gave him the self-mocking half smile. Like he knew how weird the word was.

It might have been hard to make that word fit with the way Silver knew his life was, but Zeb's real smile could trick anyone into thinking it was exactly right.

Chapter Sixteen

THE SIGHT of the red Pontiac had Silver sighing in relief when he finally made it out the back door at With Relish at one thirty Saturday morning. When a big table had come in fifteen minutes before closing, he'd shot Zeb a text telling him not to bother picking him up because he didn't know how late he'd be. No matter how many laser stares of doom Silver sent their way, that table was determined to eat every last particle of food on their plates and tell every last story five times. Only the kitchen closing and the restaurant's inability to sell alcohol after one had finally sent them looking for some other place to get drunk. At least they'd left a decent tip.

But as Silver approached the car, he found himself hesitating before opening the passenger door. Things had been fine when Zeb waved goodbye ten hours ago. But that was ten hours for Zeb to think about what having sex with a positive Silver meant. Ten hours to regret the whole thing.

Of course he'd still pick Silver up. Zeb's sense of responsibility wouldn't let him go back on a promise. But Silver didn't want to be a responsibility. And he sure didn't want that to be why they were having sex.

"Hey." He slid in, dragging the seat belt over immediately and starting an apology and an explanation of his endless last-minute table.

"I didn't mind. I was reading." Zeb jerked his thumb at the back seat, where a small tablet reader rested in its case.

"For fun or work?"

"A little of both." Zeb's quick glance at Silver's face made him wonder if any of the reading had been about HIV. Silver could tell Zeb where to get all the best pamphlets.

The monotonous voice of the GPS guided them toward the interstate. Silver heard something about North Charles Street and then the car wasn't moving and Zeb was stroking his hair.

"Uh. Sorry." Silver peeled his head off the window, blinked, and checked his mouth for drool. He shook his head and glanced out the window to see Eli and Quinn's house. Something cold squirmed in his stomach. "Thought I was spending the night with you."

"You're exhausted. You need sleep."

Silver had caught a look at himself at around eleven. His eyes were a little sunken and bleary-looking. He hadn't slept much the night before. There'd been the waking up to jerk off and then trying to imagine what was going to happen when they got to Zeb's apartment.

"Could sleep at your place. Just sleep, I mean."

"No. We couldn't." Zeb's voice wasn't sex rough or seductive, completely matter-of-fact, but his words were a sharp, sweet shot of excitement to Silver's dick. He had to stop himself from shivering.

And then he looked over, looked closely at Zeb for the first time since getting in the car, and the hunger there had Silver lunging across the seat to kiss him. Zeb met him halfway, their lips pushing together hard over teeth, the slick rub of Zeb's tongue sending another jolt to Silver's cock.

As Zeb's hand moved up Silver's thigh, he let out a gasp, and then a groan of desperation when Zeb only unlatched Silver's seat belt.

Pulling away, Zeb whispered, "Get some sleep. I'll see you Sunday."

MARCO SHOWED up at eleven thirty the next morning, driving a car that Silver was surprised didn't have ten cops trailing behind it as it ventured into very suburban Mount Washington. A Firebird rode on fat tires with toxic-green custom rims, black frame two inches from the pavement.

Yeah, it cut into time Silver would rather spend reintroducing his happy parts to Zeb's happy parts, but Silver was glad to see Marco. A couple hours of Marco's combination of cannot-be-real innocence and ability to skewer some dickhead with one ingenuous comment was something Silver found himself looking forward to as Marco pulled the car to the curb in front of Quinn's house.

"Nice ride," Silver managed with a straight face.

Instead of the kind of comment he'd usually get, about how the colors matched the inside of his Tía Raquel's oven, Marco frowned, glanced over his shoulder at the car, then shrugged. "Got me up here."

"Where do you want to go?" Silver asked.

Marco shrugged again. "Can we hang out here? Do your friends mind?"

"No, it's fine."

"What happened to your face?" Marco sounded horrified. And a little nervous.

According to the mirror, it looked a hell of a lot better today, but there was still a three-knuckle bruise above the right corner of Silver's lip. He didn't feel like getting into it all again. And Marco had enough of his own disapproval shit going on with his brother.

"Accident. At work."

Quinn was in the dining room, dealing with a gigantic pile of papers he had to grade, and Eli was tearing through his closet, trying to find something yacht-worthy for tomorrow. Even if they did mind, Silver didn't think either of them would notice Marco.

In the hall Marco asked, "You can have all-night guests?" He waggled his eyebrows.

"Yeah, I guess."

Quinn stood in the dining room archway. "Uh, Silver, how old is he?"

"Nineteen, *papi*." How Marco managed to make that sound like a purr without any *r*'s in the word Silver had no idea.

"He'll be nineteen in three months," Silver corrected. "He goes to Baltimore City Community College."

"Does he have real ID to prove he's eighteen?" Quinn asked.

"*Sí, papi.*"

Eli appeared on the stairs. "Enough with the *papi*-ing. His name is Quinn."

Marco turned to Eli. "Your *novio* is very hot."

"Thank you." Eli crossed the hall in front of Marco to stand next to Quinn.

Quinn put his arms around Eli and gave him a long, wet kiss, but that probably only made Marco more interested. "Don't worry. I took French and Greek." Quinn laughed. "Lucky for you." He gave Eli another quick kiss.

"You said the Greek alphabet backward when we met." Eli sounded like he was trying to figure Quinn out.

All Silver knew about language stuff was he was glad there wasn't a foreign language part to the GED.

"Do they teach you nothing of our culture and history before they turn you loose on the queer world?" Quinn glared at each of them. "Google it." He went back into the dining room muttering about the death of gay history.

Eli had his phone out immediately, but then glanced up. "Do you guys want anything?"

Silver looked at Marco, who shook his head. "We're just going to hang out. Don't worry. We won't touch your computer."

As Silver hit the top of the stairs, he heard Eli laugh. "God, Quinn. Even you and Jamie weren't born then. Gimme some active Greek, Daddy."

Silver was not going back downstairs for at least an hour. He had a terrible mental image of something involving yogurt.

As soon as they were in the room, Marco dropped onto Silver's—the guest—bed. The only other chair was the one at Eli's desk, and Silver didn't want to be tempted to poke around on the computer, so he stretched out as far from Marco as the bed's geography allowed.

"This is better than your other room."

The bathrooms at the Arena were better than Silver's room on Tyson Street, but at least he'd known it was his. Feeling sure Eli wasn't going to toss him on the street without any warning was different than knowing it. And even if he didn't wear out his welcome before the court date, the judge could lock him up.

Silver ran a hand across the comforter, tracing the stitching holding the stuffing in its neat bumps. It was a plain blue stripe, solid navy on the other side. Not something he'd have noticed in the old days. A bedcover was only something to hide dirty clothes or a spooge stain. The first winter on his own, any extra layer between him and the freezing cold would have been heaven. Back on Tyson he'd had a ripped sleeping bag with a broken zipper he'd found outside a day care. Five dollars of laundromat later, it stopped smelling like pee.

His fingernail caught in the wire stitching and pulled up a loop. He tugged and pressed it down, but it sprang back up. Jail or no, Silver couldn't sponge off his friends forever. He smoothed the spot out again.

Marco glanced up and scooted over. "It's bigger than the room I've got at Timo's." He settled his head on Silver's stomach. "Everything is bigger here." He leered, eyeing Silver's crotch.

He was willing to take some of the blame for that. Patting down the pull in the comforter might have been seen as some kind of invitation.

He tried to nudge Marco to a less sensitive spot without being too obvious about it. "Do you want to go do something? You said you were bored."

"Just this is nice." Marco rolled his head so he could see Silver's face. "Being here is a nice break from Timo's lectures. 'Your grandparents didn't save all the money to send you here so you could turn *maricón.*'" Marco imitated his brother's deeper voice, then rolled his eyes. "And they didn't save all their money to send him here to boost cars and end up in juvie either."

Silver smiled. "Did you tell him that?"

Marco nodded.

Brave fucker. Silver wouldn't have dared.

"*Pendejo* took my phone." Marco reached up and touched the bruise on Silver's cheek with a gentle finger. "Did you tell someone something to get this?"

"No. It was an accident."

"At work. Riiight, hon." Marco mimicked a native speaker's sarcastic drawl.

"Doesn't matter. Sorry Timo found out."

"He had already guessed. Always '*pato*,' '*mariquita*,' and 'Walk like a man, Marco.'"

"That sucks." Silver didn't have to put up with that kind of crap anymore. And up until the end, his parents didn't have any real evidence.

"If I made more money, I could try to find a room like yours. But I'd have to quit school to work."

The thought of Marco on his own in a place like Tyson Street was terrifying. Marco, who didn't even know enough to watch his drink at a party. Silver might have spent his late teens getting fucked, but at least he knew what was happening. Had chosen to go down that path.

"Don't do that. Get your degree first. Maybe you could get a scholarship to another school."

"That's so long—so far—away. I can't keep waiting to have my life."

Silver got that. Hell yeah, did he get that, but Marco couldn't make the same choices. He didn't deserve it—not like Silver had deserved it—but Marco wasn't ready to face some of those decisions.

"Maybe I should get arrested," Marco said. "It was good for you."

"If you don't count the jail part of it."

"You won't go to jail." Marco's confidence didn't do anything to keep Silver from picturing June 16 on the calendar circled in red with the following days all blacked out. He wondered if people in jail made those hash marks on the wall like they did in movies. That night, he'd only seen the usual graffiti.

Marco sighed, and his head moved on Silver's waist, really damned close to a dick that had just remembered how fucking awesome sex with another guy was. Maybe it would be better to risk being scarred for life by someone's Greek yogurt kink than to be stuck in his room with a horny teenager.

"We could watch a movie downstairs. They've got a couple of streaming services to pick from."

"I think they're fucking." Marco's head shifted again, and Silver swore Marco's hair was starting to brush against Silver's cock.

Down, he thought. Silver might not think of his friend like that, but Marco was still another guy. A cute, desperate guy. Who wanted him, Silver. Not Jordan. Not Branden Woods from the porn vids.

"Can you hear them, at night, when they do it? Like porn?" Marco's cheek moved less than an inch from where things were getting very tingly.

Silver definitely wouldn't call it. Awkward was the first thing that came to mind.

"It would make me *arrecho*. Horny."

"Breathing makes you horny, Marco."

"*Sí*. It's true." Marco nodded, and Silver's dick got another little shot of *hey, how you doin'*. God, it would be really easy to give in to this. Not only the rush of sex, but the extra throb of heat from how much Marco wanted this.

Which was why things had to stop right now. "Marco—"

Too late. Marco rolled, his face, breath, *mouth* right there, heat and humidity on Silver's way-too-interested dick. "You don't have to do it to me back. I want to. Want to do it to—with you, *argénteo*."

"No." Silver said it as softly and gently as he could.

"Why not? *Tu verga*—your cock—is getting big. You're horny too. And you don't have a *novio*—boyfriend."

It was true they hadn't quite worked out the details, the conversation going everywhere but a definition of what they were doing now. But even if Zeb weren't part of the decision, the answer still had to be no. Silver couldn't be that person for Marco.

A weight, bitter and burning like acid, dropped into Silver's gut. Had it been like this for Zeb—shit, was it still like this for Zeb? Could the overwhelming intensity of someone wanting you so badly be pressure enough to shift your feelings? Maybe that was all they'd had. Not this epic love story Silver had spun for Eli, one even Silver had believed. If he could convince himself—a born cynic—maybe he'd convinced Zeb of the whole thing too. It would have been a hell of a lot harder to say no to Marco back in New Freedom.

Before Marco could take Silver's silence for agreement, Silver put a hand on Marco's cheek and eased out from under him, stroking his hair for an instant and then letting go.

"I kind of do have a—I'm seeing someone."

"Oh." Marco's thick lashes dropped over his eyes.

But that was the easy way out. Silver had to make him understand. "You're really cute. But, I can't—I don't think of you like that."

"Oh." This time the word was sucked in, like an exclamation of pain. Marco sat up and slid off the bed.

Silver tried to salvage things. "I don't think of Quinn like that either." He shrugged. "It's just when you—you'll know what I mean when—" finishing his sentence with *when you start having sex* was not going to score any points with Marco right now. "Think about it. You don't want to fuck every guy you see, do you?"

"Only the hot ones. But I am *cute*. Not hot enough to fuck."

"That's not what I meant, Marco."

"I know what you meant. I'm cute enough to be your ride, but not your *novio*—boyfriend." He spat the correction like a curse.

"Marco." It wasn't much help, repeating his name. But Silver didn't know what else to say.

Eli would know the right thing. Zeb too, probably. Hell, even Jamie—the asshole—wouldn't have fucked things up this much.

"You're my friend." Which guaranteed Silver would be winning the Lamest Thing to Say award for the year, no matter how much backtracking he did to avoid the nomination.

"Well, I don't need friends. And I get more than enough advice from Timo. If you need a ride somewhere, *vete la chingada. No me llame.*" Marco paused, straightened, then enunciated with only a tiny trace of accent. "Fuck. Your. Self. But don't call me."

He took off.

It wasn't only guilt that made Silver ignore the threat of witnessing active yogurt to chase Marco down the stairs. It was a sudden fear that Marco was serious about staying the hell out of Silver's life.

"C'mon, Marco. Wait a second."

Silver caught his breath more from emotion than exertion when Marco stopped and waited with his hands spread flat on the roof of the Firebird.

"Why?"

"I'm an asshole. I'm sorry."

"Yes, you are."

"Can I try to apologize? Explain?"

Marco kept the car between them, studying him for a second.

"If I didn't want to fix things, would I have chased you out here?" Silver asked.

"How do I know anything? You've been playing me the whole time."

Marco had a point there. But until a few weeks ago, Silver had been playing everyone, including himself.

Silver tipped his head toward the front steps of the house.

Moving like a deer ready to bolt, Marco crossed the sidewalk and perched next to Silver on the cement stairs. One thing Silver would miss if Marco rightly decided to tell him to fuck off was the way Marco always seemed to know when to fill the space between them with distracting chatter or comfortable silence. Right now, in the tight press of Marco's lips, Silver saw him waiting for any reason to go flying back to the car.

"I've really been an asshole."

"You said that already."

Yeah, well, Silver was still waiting for some inspiration to strike.

"You've been a better friend than I deserve." Silver started off in Zeb script.

Marco snorted.

The whole martyr thing didn't really sell it for Silver either. He tried to imagine what Eli would say. "Upstairs. You saw I was hard. I was. You made me hard."

Marco sat up straighter. "I did."

"And I was scared."

"Because of your… boyfriend?"

"No." God, honesty sucked. Was it really worth it? Silver thought of how many times Marco had made him laugh. How he had always been there when Silver called. And how much Silver had taken it for granted. "I was scared because of how much you reminded me of me."

Silver wondered if he made the same expression when he was trying to figure out Marco's shifts between Spanish and English slang.

"I remembered what it was like, how crazy I was to get laid. And I did some really stupid things."

"I remind you of you being stupid? Not much of an apology."

"I never told you what I was doing before I got the job at the restaurant. I was a whore. I had to have sex with a lot of guys who weren't hot at all."

"And me offering to suck you makes you think of that?" Marco looked even more hurt.

"No. If I didn't have a—if I wasn't seeing someone—I probably would have let you." A smile twisted Silver's mouth. "And it would have been wrong for another reason."

"Because you would only be pretending? I know you don't really want to be *mi nov*—my boyfriend. I understand that. But I want. I think about dicks all the time."

Silver let a thin laugh past his throat. "I remember that feeling. But I got scared for another reason, and it's why you need to be really careful."

Marco rolled his eyes. "Oh, Timo lectures all the time about AIDS."

Silver stared down at the edge of the bottom step. It had started to crumble at the corner. "I'm positive."

"I know. It's the first thing everyone thinks about being gay. Wait. You weren't only agreeing. You did not mean—Silver?"

"I'm HIV positive."

Marco grabbed at Silver's hand. "*¿De veras?*"

Silver nodded.

"I'm so sorry."

Silver shrugged.

"Who you are seeing? Is he too?"

"No. We're being careful. Going slow."

"You would've told me before I—?"

"Of course. But that's why—" Silver needed Marco to really understand. "I know what you're going through. My parents didn't like that I was gay. And I didn't have anyplace to go. So I had to do whatever I could. You can't ever know if someone is positive. I know Timo is a prick, but you're going to school and you're going to have a good job. Don't let being horny fuck all that up. I get scared when I think of something bad happening to you."

Marco bumped Silver's shoulder. "If you couldn't be *mi novio*, why couldn't *you* have been *mi hermano*—brother?"

"I think Eli and Quinn should be done getting freaky. Wanna come in and watch a movie with me?"

"Can it be something where Channing Tatum takes off his shirt?"

Silver was pretty sure it happened in all that guy's movies. "That can be arranged."

He left Marco on the couch with the remotes and peered cautiously into the kitchen before slipping in to nuke some popcorn.

Eli came in behind him. "I heard some doors slamming. Everything okay?"

Silver shrugged.

"You knew he had a crush on you, right?"

"I did. I guess somehow I forgot how that can be. But I think it's cool now. Would you mind if he stayed for dinner? He's living with his brother and has our kind of family issues." Silver jerked his thumb between himself and Eli.

"That sucks out loud."

The microwave beeped. Silver reached in and shook out the bag. "I worry he'll end up running away and doing something stupid."

Eli's eyes got big and wide. "Gee. I wonder if there's anyone around who could warn him of the dangers in that."

"Fuck you." Silver shoulder-checked Eli against the counter. Eli laughed.

"So if I can't be a good influence, I'll have to be a horrible example?" Silver pulled down a couple glasses to fill with iced tea.

"Something like that."

Silver slammed in some ice then stared at the glasses. "I told him I was positive. Hoped it'd slow him down a little."

He wasn't looking, but he felt Eli's nod. "Did you tell Zeb?"

"Yeah."

"And?"

"We're working through it. Taking it slow."

"Sounds like fun." Eli's sarcasm put a lilt in his voice.

Even if the answer scarred him for life, Silver's curiosity got the better of him. "So what the fuck was all that Greek stuff about?"

"Oh. Old-school gay code. Like back in the seventies and eighties. For saying what you were into. French or Greek, oral or anal, active or passive for top or bottom. Like I can't tell in five seconds with a guy. Usually." Eli tipped his head. "You're hard to read, though."

Silver put his hands on the counter, bracketing Eli's hips, and stared at his face, from his lips to his eyes. "Am I?"

Eli's lashes dipped, and a laugh stuttered in his throat. "Not right now, no."

Silver peeled away and smiled.

"Jesus. Where have you been hiding that?" Eli made an exaggerated fanning motion.

"Wasn't up to me for a while."

"Damn. If you didn't have company, I'd drag you with me to the discount racks and find you something to make Zeb lose his shit when he sees you on the dock tomorrow."

The hell with going slow. Silver pulled out his wallet and handed Eli thirty bucks. "There's my budget. Knock yourself out."

Chapter Seventeen

AT THE marina the next afternoon, Silver wouldn't go so far as to say Zeb lost his shit, but the next time Silver heard the scrape and creak of boats against a dock and smelled marine diesel, he'd be playing back that look of hunger in Zeb's eyes, the way his tongue darted out to wet his lips. Satisfaction surged hot and sweet.

Eli had worked magic in the bargain racks on Silver's thirty bucks, offering proof in a receipt and three seventy-eight in change. It hadn't seemed as if it was much in the bag, but with Eli wielding double-sided fabric tape, the bright blue tank top clung to every inch of Silver's torso, and an overshirt made Silver's biceps look like Channing Tatum's. Cargo shorts hugged his ass.

A look like the one in Zeb's eyes would usually prompt Silver to do something to frame his cock.

Which, after the dreams he'd had last night, he was desperate to get up Zeb's ass in short order.

Instead, Silver had the unfamiliar sensation he could only label as shyness. Now that he had what he wanted, he didn't know what he wanted to do with it.

It was all Marco's fault. That was where the doubt came from. Knowing how close Silver had been to giving in when drowning in someone else's want. Doubt had dug in deep, as persistent as wood at age fourteen.

Or sixteen.

Was that what Silver had done to Zeb, pushed so hard he couldn't say no? Was he still doing it?

A boat shining so white it hurt his eyes swung broadside to the dock. Gavin waved from the stern as it was piloted backward into the slip.

It was another one of those moments Silver wanted to freeze. Lock down all the possibilities while they were still all good before anything got said or done to change the way things felt. But the dock shifted under his feet, and Zeb stood next to him.

"Is that shirt painted on you?"

Silver shifted his shoulders. "Feels like it." He shot a glance Zeb's way. Clean-scraped jaw, a hint of sandalwood stronger than the oily backwash bubbling up from the boat's motor. A scent so familiar it eased some of the unfamiliar shyness. Funny that Zeb had never changed his aftershave. No reason to, just because Silver used whatever was around. "You shaved."

Zeb glanced down. "The principal will be happy."

Gavin had a line in his hands as he stood over the letters naming the boat the *Carpe Diem*. Jamie drove a boat as arrogantly and as smoothly as he drove his cop car, swinging it into the narrow berth without ever touching the sides of the slip.

It wasn't as big as Silver had been expecting, something that slept twenty and needed a launch to get out to, but another couple could join them before it would feel crowded.

When he stepped forward and helped Gavin with the cleat hitch, Gavin favored Silver with one of those almost smiles, and he found himself blushing. He put a hand up to his eyes as if shielding them from the sun.

"You're a handy guy," Zeb said in Silver's ear.

"Handsy too." Silver tried to pass it off with a leer.

"I didn't know you knew your way around boats."

"Sue me. In addition to *Star Wars*, I went through a hard-core Johnny Depp/Orlando Bloom pirate... thing."

It had been a full-blown kink. Jack teaching Will what two men could or couldn't do on a boat and then Will turning the tables, putting Jack on his knees.

"Thing, huh?" Zeb murmured as Eli and Quinn stepped aboard.

"A kink, okay?"

"Hmmm." Zeb shouldn't have been close enough for Silver to feel the sound vibrate against his skin, but it did, tingling in all the best places. "And here we are. On a boat."

"With four other people," Silver reminded him.

"You coming aboard?" Big surprise, Jamie was acting like he owned the damned boat.

Gavin urged Zeb toward the steps. "Silver and I will cast off."

Jamie held out his hand to Zeb. "Help you aboard? Uh, sorry, forgot your name, buddy."

Silver doubted that. Jamie didn't forget much, so he was offering a mild Jamie-style insult. But whether it was general assholishness or something particular about Zeb, Silver couldn't tell.

Gavin unwrapped the cleat as Silver climbed the stairs over the gunwale. He knew Gavin didn't actually need help, but as he swung up over the gunwale himself, he passed the line and Silver retied it on the boat's cleat.

"Where'd you pick that up?" Gavin watched Silver secure the line.

"Uh. Movies and a summer at camp."

Gavin frowned. "The conversion camp Eli told us about?"

"No." A choked laugh came out along with the answer, surprising Silver. Bitter as the laugh was, he didn't ever expect he'd have managed any amusement at the thought of Path to Glory.

Gavin's gaze shifted to where Jamie was gesturing from next to the wheel. "He looks better with the close shave."

For a second, Silver thought Gavin was talking about Jamie, but that didn't make sense.

Gavin meant Zeb. All this interest in Silver's love—sex—life was starting to drive home the fact that despite every effort to keep ties to a minimum, he'd acquired friends. He couldn't pin the interest on Gavin or even Quinn's financial investment anymore. And it didn't feel creepy. It was kind of nice. If a little weird.

"Yeah," Silver agreed. "The bad-boy-Jesus thing only gets him so far."

"I would imagine it could be challenging getting it up for a mythic philosopher martyred in the early days of the Common Era."

Silver laughed, and the corners of Gavin's eyes crinkled.

With a chin jerk to indicate the redhead acting all proprietary about Gavin's yacht, Silver said, "He wears a cross and a saint medal. How do you guys handle that?"

Gavin regarded Silver steadily as the *Carpe Diem*'s engines churned the bay beneath their feet. Under Gavin's appraisal, Silver's tongue stuck like glue to the roof of his mouth. He didn't know if Gavin knew Silver had had his boyfriend's dick in his mouth. He didn't want to be the bearer of bad news—however lacking in passion those fifteen minutes had been. He and Jamie hadn't moved more clothing than strictly necessary, and it hadn't been when Silver had spotted the religious stuff.

He pried his tongue free. "I've noticed it on him. Is it a problem between you, you not being a believer?"

Gavin shook his head. "I've never had a problem with other people's superstitions provided they don't use them to harm others." His voice got hard there, and Silver wondered what—whose—superstitions had fucked with someone Gavin cared about. "Do you think Zeb's beliefs will be a problem for you?"

Silver hadn't had much time to think of the future. There was so much else, so much other baggage that still needed to be unpacked. The whole religion thing hadn't made a ripple in Silver's consciousness until now.

"I don't know."

Zeb hadn't cared about Silver's cynical attitude back then, but that was before Path to Glory, before just mentioning a Bible verse could get Silver twitching. He knew it wasn't only words to Zeb, or superstition. And Silver wasn't planning on changing his attitude anytime soon.

Gavin had waited patiently for Silver to expand on his lame answer. "It hasn't come up. There's been so much else to deal with."

"I heard. And I suspect there may have been more tragedy involved than was in the romantic fiction that reached my ears."

"Kind of." As the boat picked up speed, Silver hauled out a tried-and-true deflection. "Do you mind that I invited him?"

"I told you it was fine to bring a guest. I suspected we might be seeing him. Or perhaps your friend with the charming accent and car troubles."

Marco would love this. Silver could picture him looking all around with wide eyes. "Maybe. If there's a next time." Silver tried to not make it sound like a request by looking at the deck instead of Gavin.

"I would very much like for there to be a next time." Gavin tapped Silver's shoulder.

"Thanks." Since Silver wanted as many yacht trips as he could get, keeping drama to a minimum would probably help. He got the idea Jamie was the possessive kind. "Your boyfriend keeps cranking his head to stare at us."

"So he is, but I have great faith in his ability not to run us aground."

Silver didn't think anyone would ever have great faith in his ability to keep himself dry and fed for a month. He headed for Zeb, but Gavin's soft call made Silver turn back.

"Silver, I certainly can't claim any expertise in relationships, given that I am new to navigating one myself. But I am learning that should you find yourself in one, not only do they require some effort at negotiation, the rewards are worth it." Gavin went up to the bridge to stand behind Jamie.

Eli was tucked between Quinn's legs on a couch-like bench, leaning back against his chest, Quinn's hand straying to the exposed flesh over Eli's waistband. Zeb was in a seat near a sink and bar. Wondering if he was pissed at having been left alone made Silver's stomach tighten as he sank into a seat opposite.

Being on a yacht was awesome and not something Silver had ever pictured in any coming attraction. But it did make you have to deal with the other people on board. No escape if something went sour. What had seemed hot in fantasies was not so much in practice.

"Something wrong?" Zeb asked.

"No. It's fine. Great."

Zeb put a hand across the small table between them, the arch in his brows saying he didn't buy it.

Silver let his hand drop on Zeb's for a split second. "What wouldn't be great? Did you miss the part where we're on a yacht?"

"Surrounded by water."

"Are you aquaphobic?" Silver was damned pleased he pulled the word out of his head. He'd once studied the whole list of them for some school project. Ranidaphobia and gephyrophobia were his. Some nightmares had swarms of frogs trapping him on a bridge. He didn't know why the stupid stuff felt worse than the truly horrifying things that had happened. He should be more afraid of fifty-year-old guys with bad comb-overs and an aversion to hygiene.

"No." Zeb opened his palm in invitation. Silver's hand was too damp to take him up on it.

"For someone who has a boat kink, you seem tense in the not-fun way," Zeb added.

"It was pirates."

A boat wasn't the same as a bridge. Silver wasn't trapped; they were going somewhere. And he was pretty sure the gleaming chrome and light varnished wood and white pleather didn't hide any tadpole colonies.

As subtly as he could, he dried his hands on his cargo shorts. He'd felt so badass on the dock, making Zeb's tongue hang out, the day full of sun and promise. Should have known it wouldn't last.

They approached a big bridge. At the wheel, Gavin wrapped himself around Jamie from behind. God knew what Eli and Quinn were up to behind them. Eli didn't exactly seem to have boundaries with that kind of stuff.

Silver slid his hand into Zeb's as the bridge made a high roof overhead. Zeb curled their fingers into an interlocking spiral, a double fist resting on the table.

"You missed the grand tour. But I could be persuaded to recreate it privately," Zeb offered.

Silver cranked his head to see what looked like a door for hobbits that must have led below the deck. "How private?" He rubbed his thumb across the top of their fists. It would take the edge off and piss off Jamie, so bonus points there.

Zeb smiled and used their grip to lever himself up and around the table to share Silver's side. "Galley, couches, and if people can manage in airplane bathrooms…."

"That desperate, huh? Coming off a long dry spell?"

Zeb let go of Silver's hand, cupping his face in both palms, then pressing their foreheads together. The scent of sandalwood was stronger now, making Silver's heart rate tick up.

"Why would I be desperate?" Zeb whispered against his mouth. "Side by side all those times and not able to touch you? You teasing me over those workbooks. Do you even need help for that test?"

Silver put his arms around Zeb's neck. "Kind of. But I was starting to think you didn't notice my other suggestions."

"I noticed."

"Why didn't you do something?"

"I wasn't going to make the same mistake twice."

Silver slumped back in the seat. He dragged his arms with him, a sharp burn on skin that had become glued together with sweat and spray from the water.

Zeb rubbed his neck with a wince. "Not like that. Hey." Zeb put a hand on Silver's thigh to keep him on the cushion. As if there was someplace he could run to on the boat. "You'd asked for help. I didn't want to take advantage of—"

"Me?"

"The situation."

"You think something could happen if I didn't want it? For the last time, I made my own choices. I was plenty old enough to know who I wanted to fuck."

Rather than get pissed off and frustrated back, Zeb smiled. "Am I allowed to be glad it was me?"

Sometimes Zeb's earnestness made Silver want to shake him. But right then, it was kind of adorable. "I'll allow it." Silver's lips curled hard enough to hurt.

They faced into the rush of air as the boat sped farther south into the bay. Zeb's hand found its way under both Silver's shirts in the back and teased with a brush of rough-edged skin along his spine. They'd never had this before. Anywhere but in the sanctuary of Zeb's apartment, they'd had to keep a frozen distance, their stiffness probably drawing more attention than an occasional touch would have.

Which was why it must have been alien to have Zeb keep up the tingling-but-soothing brush of skin on skin. No, it felt strange because Silver had never had any kind of casual touch like this. Specific sexual touches, yes, designed with a purpose. Even with Austin or Jason, the post-fucking hugs or kisses had been nothing more than part of the process.

These endless circles and lines left Silver hypnotized as they bounced along the waves. Which was good, because if he wasn't lulled into a zone, he might have been scared by how happy he felt.

When he opened his eyes, the sun was hitting his face from a different direction.

Shit. At the rate he kept falling asleep on Zeb, Silver should be ready for a senior home. "Sorry." He straightened from the lean against Zeb.

Zeb pulled him back down. "I liked it." His lips brushed Silver's ear. "Remember how we used to wish we could spend the night together? I like finally getting to watch you sleep."

Zeb's words sent a jolt of heat low into Silver's belly, but not to his dick and balls, even though it was definitely the sexiest thing anyone had said to him in forever.

He glanced around. Jamie was piloting them into a small cove lined with wind-flattened grass and trees. There was absolutely no one else in sight, but it wasn't the farmland he'd grown up around. Only white-tipped waves on the other side. The water was a beautiful blue Silver never saw in the harbor. It was like having been taken to another planet.

Gavin came out of the hobbit hole. Behind him, Silver glimpsed more gleaming chrome and wood and a nice flat-panel TV screen set in the wall.

Gavin had to duck, but the way it opened meant he wasn't exactly crawling. Eli followed him out, and the doorway was a perfect size for him. Eli had a tray with fruit and bread and cheese and meat. Gavin held dark wine bottles.

"For our celebration I have a lovely toasted walnut and honeyed orange Krug Grande Cuvée Brut and what I am assured is an equally lovely nonalcoholic sparkling wine from California." Gavin placed the bottles near a sink and pulled champagne glasses from the cabinet beneath.

Silver was appreciative Gavin had brought the N/A for him and pissed as fuck it was necessary because of some stupid rule only Jamie seemed to give a shit about. He bet Krug was a better champagne than Cristal or whatever people thought was swanky. His parents had probably never had anything so good. And Silver was missing his chance.

"Nonalcoholic for me," Jamie called back from the cockpit. "I'm driving."

"God, doesn't he always?" Eli plopped the big tray on the table in front of Zeb and Silver. "Seriously, can we say overcompensation?"

"Now you know that's not so, hon," Jamie drawled back.

Eli raised his hands as if surrendering to Gavin. "All innocent, I swear. And I meant for your height, Officer Donnigan."

Gavin looked bemused.

"So, Gavin, come on. I gotta know. Does he always… drive?" Eli smirked.

A hint of a smile twitched the corner of Gavin's lips. "I would never kiss and tell."

"Which means he doesn't. Yes." Eli made a fist pump of triumph. "Nobody's that much of a toppy bastard unless he's secretly dying for a dick up his ass." Eli bounced into the cockpit to better torment Jamie.

Served the arrogant prick right.

"I'll take the N/A too," Quinn said, stepping forward to the main part of the deck. "Feeling a little dehydrated."

If you didn't pop a load in your boyfriend every two hours, maybe your mouth wouldn't be so dry. Silver kept his lips pressed together to keep the words from spilling out. What had Austin said? *The definition of promiscuous is anyone having more sex than you.*

Eli coughed in an attention-seeking way as he skipped back toward the table and flashed his grin along with plenty of skin above his waistband.

Silver knew they'd been up to something back there.

"Filthy bastards." Jamie joined them. He swung a hand toward Eli's ass but changed direction at the last second so it landed on his upper back, hard enough to send him stumbling against the tray. It had a railing around the edges to keep things from sliding.

"We're at anchor," Jamie told Gavin.

"I am so having champagne." Eli picked up a glass.

"I'll stick with the nonalcoholic," Zeb said, all noble. And stupid.

Silver pushed his sneaker into Zeb's instep. "Go ahead. Have a glass."

Zeb did a little tilt of his head to go with the look he gave Silver. Like he would believe Zeb would be all rebellious and hand off his glass. There were other ways of getting a taste. Silver stared back at Zeb's lips until he gave an almost imperceptible nod.

To everyone who wasn't Eli.

"Oh my God, he's going to drink it off his lips. You guys are so fucking cute."

Silver lov—liked Eli. A lot. But sometimes he could see why Quinn kept his dick stuffed in him as often as possible.

Gavin handed off the fake stuff to Jamie and worked on the darker, bigger bottle with the gold on the label.

Eli leaned over the table to mutter in Silver's ear. "When I saw him take it out of the fridge down there, I tried to look up the price online, but I couldn't get a signal. If you want some later, take mine. No one will give a shit."

There was no big pop and spray from either bottle, only a hiss and something like smoke. But as Gavin took Eli's glass and tipped it to meet the bottle, the gold bubbles rushed out with barely any effort.

He took the glass full of paler stuff from Jamie, who nodded at him like it was some serious moment.

When they all had a glass, Gavin said, "I would like to propose a toast to Charm City's most sought-after new artist. May your success be the first of many." He raised his glass. Eli clinked his with Quinn, and they all drank. Silver's tasted like fuzzy grape juice, but Eli's and Zeb's eyes both widened at their first sip.

"I need to sell enough to be able to buy more of this." Eli laughed. "Thank you."

"To Eli's new career." Quinn raised his glass. Swinging his arm around Eli's neck, he rubbed their cheeks together. "I'm so proud of you."

"Eli's new career," everyone echoed. Including Silver.

He sipped, but he didn't taste anything. His ears got hot. And it was as if his clothes had disappeared and he was standing there naked. Not naked in the fun way, or even in the businesslike way of shooting a vid and standing around naked while people moved lights and brought the camera an inch from your asshole. But like those dreams in middle school and high school where he was naked and everyone was laughing because they all knew.

His friends had careers. Silver waited tables while waiting to find out if he was going to jail. He hadn't graduated from high school. Shit, he half hoped the judge locked him up before everyone found out just how much nothing he really was.

After Eli's third glass of champagne, Quinn broke out his Daddy voice to urge Eli to eat something, and while everyone was stuffing their faces, Silver slipped around the cabin to lie on the cushions covering the long bow. The late-afternoon sun baked the open space, but Silver stretched out on his stomach and let the heat sink into his back and ass muscles, while his belly relaxed on the giant heating pad of waterproof cushion.

His head faced the tip of the bow, but he sensed someone moving behind him. Despite knowing it couldn't be a threat, his muscles tensed, though he didn't roll over. It couldn't be Zeb—as much as Silver wished it was. Zeb had been trapped listening to Eli tell some story. Eli buzzed on expensive champagne wasn't much different from Eli sober, except that he had an even bigger disregard for personal space. No way was Zeb escaping unless he dumped Eli on his ass.

From the slit of his eyes he noticed leather deck shoes. They were almost like the ones Zeb had on, except they weren't. Not with the tiny green-and-red tag that meant they cost twenty-five times more.

"According to the catalog the Sunseeker company dutifully sends me each year, we should only be lounging here if we are blond and in bikinis," Gavin said.

Silver rolled onto his side. "I can manage half that requirement."

"And far more attractive than anyone in a bikini I've ever seen." Gavin held out a glass and recrossed his legs as he lounged. "I tasted the nonalcoholic and it's a disgrace. I apologize."

Silver took it and sipped. He didn't know what to expect other than fizz, so the creaminess startled him. He couldn't describe all the different flavors, but right then he decided he definitely had expensive tastes. Too bad he couldn't even afford a bottle of store-brand water most of the time. No point getting used to that.

He passed it back. "Aren't you afraid your boyfriend will go all pissed-off cop?"

"No. Though Jamie's bristling can be fun to encourage at times. I believe you enjoy yanking his chain as well."

Silver peered down at the cushions and stuck his finger onto one of the sunken buttons as Gavin kept talking.

"It's a passion and intensity I admire. Like Eli's. It's hard not to want to see it brought to the surface."

Silver had barely gotten around to believing Gavin liked him. Now it seemed like he was pointing out exactly what Silver lacked. As if he didn't already know.

"It's not the same for people like us."

Whoa. Did Gavin just compare himself to Silver?

Gavin held up the champagne and took a sip. "It's harder for us to find something that stirs our passions."

Silver couldn't help the glance at Gavin's crotch.

"Not that one, necessarily." Gavin's laugh was short but sweet. Satisfying to know Silver could amuse a guy like Gavin.

"But when we do find something important to us, it burns just as brightly. Even though we may not show it like they do." Gavin paused.

This was the place where Silver was supposed to say something equally profound. Or at least agree. But he didn't want to agree. The only thing he'd ever

wanted with the kind of passion he saw Jamie and Eli
fling at everything was Zeb. And that was a hell of a
thing to stick a guy with. Like the way Marco expected Silver to have all the answers.

Maybe that was what Gavin was trying to warn
him about. That until Silver had a thing of his own, it
wouldn't work with Zeb.

Gavin had gone silent, and there was only so
much poking Silver could do to the button.

"I guess." He wasn't trying to be a sullen brat
about it.

"Is Zeb one of the ones with that intensity?"

Silver shook his head. Zeb could get all wound up
about teaching or anything else he knew a lot about.
But it wasn't like the way Eli and Jamie were. And
not all snotty know-it-all like Nate. Zeb was committed. If he went into something, he went all the way.
Which was why that door slammed in Silver's face
was something he'd never seen coming. Funny that as
razor-sharp as the memory was, it didn't cut as deeply
as it used to.

"He's more steady. Like Quinn."

Gavin nodded. He'd been leaning back on his
hands with his Gucci-clad feet toward the bow, but
now he sat forward, cross-legged. The stem of the
glass was still between his fingers. When he noticed it,
he swung it over the rail, an arc of pale gold catching
the sun splashing into the water. There had to have
been thirty or forty dollars left of champagne, now
mixed in with fish pee.

"I am sorry you didn't care for the champagne or
the sparkling juice. I could break into Jamie's not-so-
secret stash of KZ sodas. Or I have Pellegrino."

Was that Gavin's passion? Hosting parties and smoothing things over? He'd only been sitting here talking because he felt bad Silver didn't like the drinks? How pathetic could he get? Silver had actually thought Gavin was trying to tell him something deep. Just in time he stopped himself from blurting out a refusal.

"Thanks. That sounds good."

When Gavin moved, Silver stopped him.

"You don't have to get up. One thing I can definitely handle is carrying stuff out from a kitchen." Where maybe Silver could also manage a few minutes alone. Quinn and Jamie were in the cockpit, pointing at the board full of screens. Eli and Zeb were in the stern, Eli dropping pieces of bread over the side while some fish knocked each other senseless trying to get it.

Silver ducked down through the hatch. Holy shit. This would be a pricey apartment.

He couldn't imagine what it cost to have this kind of setup on a boat.

A couch faced a plasma TV screen, and he caught a glimpse of a double bed through another door. He wasn't sure if he was about to open the door to the head or the fridge, but he picked right. Tiled shower stall, sink with a mirror, and a toilet.

He made use of it, washed his hands, and then dropped the lid to sit and catch a few minutes of peace. Before getting arrested, he'd been surrounded by people all the time and felt completely alone. Now it was nice to have a few friends who cared, but this much interaction was fucking exhausting.

He shouldn't have locked himself away. Too much time to think right now wasn't good. Eight days until his court date. Four days after that and Zeb would be gone.

If Silver wasn't in jail, he would be—well, wasn't that the million-dollar question?

And he'd used up all his lifelines. And probably his alone time.

Hesitant steps tapped on the wooden stairs. Bingo.

"Silver?"

Zeb. A twist of the funky center lock and the door swung in. Moving around it didn't feel too seductive, but Silver figured he didn't need to work it too hard. Zeb had followed him down here. And there was one thing Silver was even better at than carrying food out of kitchens.

He found a good lean on the open doorframe, despite the wide lip that he guessed made it watertight.

"Yeah?"

Zeb started a smile but lost it when he swallowed. Silver remembered he had permission to touch and trailed a finger over the bob in his throat, down to the open collar of Zeb's shirt.

Zeb took a deep breath. "I was going to ask if you were okay, but it wasn't why I came down." His gaze dropped to watch Silver's hand slide fully under the collar to disappear around to the back of Zeb's neck. "I'd hoped you came down here so we could be alone for—"

Silver yanked him forward and, dammit, forgot about the three-inch-high lip separating their feet. Zeb tumbled into him.

Silver caught a sink edge to the ass and a towel bar to the back but wrapped his arms around Zeb and managed to keep them on their feet.

Zeb started laughing, and Silver couldn't help it spilling out of his own mouth as he shut the door and twisted the lock.

"Guess we're alone now." Zeb waggled his eyebrows. Silver had to sit on the toilet seat to get his breath.

Oh yeah. He was fucking awesome at seduction.

It hadn't been the plan, but laughing felt good. Not that he hadn't had fun sex with other guys, but no one had ever seemed to set him off like Zeb. And since they'd both pretty much been learning their way around back then, there had been some funny moments. Like learning why you should never put tingling lube on your dick.

Zeb braced himself with a hand against the glass shower door as he wound down. "Part of your pirate kink?"

Silver stood. "Consider yourself my prisoner." He'd meant it as a joke. Not anything kinky.

But Zeb leaned back against the tiny space of wall, eyes dark green, chin tilted to the side to expose his woodsy-smelling neck, and Silver couldn't remember what was so funny.

He dove in, cheek gliding over freshly shaved skin, inhaling Zeb in deep breaths, tasting his sweat in the skin under his ear.

Zeb groaned with the first touch of tongue on his skin, and Silver couldn't wait to hear what sounds he'd get when his tongue got to the really interesting places.

Grabbing at Silver's shirt, Zeb shoved the tank top up as far as he could get it. "Off. Soon as I saw you on the dock I've been wanting this off."

Silver leaned back enough to peel off the shirt and tank, then in to kiss Zeb.

His mouth opened, and Silver drove his tongue in, slid it along the winey taste of Zeb's, then lost himself in the way their mouths worked together. The way the intensity went to his head, the frustration with the pathetic need to stop for fresh oxygen.

Zeb's palms stroked up and down Silver's back, firm, solid. When they shifted for a breath, Silver got his fingers between them to pop the button on Zeb's fly.

The weight of Zeb's hands on Silver's shoulders stopped him right as he eased the zipper clear of the bulge.

He met Zeb's gaze, the eyes almost black, a narrow rim of green around the wide pupil. "Is this okay? Did you think about it?" *And decide not to have sex with a guy who's positive?* was the part of the question Silver couldn't make himself say out loud.

"I did." Zeb blinked, then his lashes hid his eyes as he glanced down. "Spent all morning in church thinking about it." When he looked back at Silver, there was the familiar twist in the corner of Zeb's mouth. "Had to keep a hymnal on my lap."

The heat and pressure of his palms slid down over Silver's pecs.

"Yeah." Zeb's thumbs brushed Silver's nipples. They weren't super sensitive, but his cock appreciated the contact just fine. "Thought about this. And this." One hand shifted lower, thumb petting through the hair right below Silver's navel. "In church." Zeb leaned in for a kiss and then shook his head. "During the sermon. Then you show up looking like that."

The last bit was swallowed up by Silver's mouth because they were kissing again. Bodies held only far enough apart to let hands get to the flesh that made groans echo in the tiny space. Silver wrapped his palm around Zeb's dick, a charge rushing to his own cock at the satiny weight of it, the throb of blood under the skin. Silver raised his head to probe the inside of his lips with his tongue. If that hard kissing hadn't reopened the split, Zeb's dick wouldn't. At least that's what the want pulsing inside told Silver.

He was about to hit his knees when he realized sitting on the toilet lid would be a whole hell of a lot easier.

"I stopped on my way home from church. To buy condoms." Zeb's pause made the blood pump harder in Silver's cock. "And lube."

"Is it wrong how fucking hot it is that you stopped for that on the way home from church?"

"I'm the one who was thinking about it when I should have been listening to the sermon." Zeb's voice was rough. "So no. Or yes. God, Silver, I don't care."

Silver dropped onto the convenient seat and met Zeb's cock eye to eye. Silver hadn't had much opportunity to make comparisons back in New Freedom. But he'd seen enough by now to appreciate what Zeb had. The thick ridge that made the head look like a big button, the way the shaft got a little thicker in the middle. The skin a healthy red, pubes neat, sac soft and heavy below. Silver's mouth watered. He wanted to swallow him whole.

A clear drop welled from the slit, and he licked it. Then stopped. "Condom?"

Zeb made a strangled, cut-off sound, but Silver was pretty sure it was "Oh fuck."

Zeb's dick bumped against Silver's lips. He avoided the crown and moved his mouth down the shaft, full intent kisses, tasting salt-sex-man.

"You jerked off." He made sure the words vibrated against the tight skin.

Zeb made that strangled sound again. Definitely *oh fuck*. "Had to. Or I'd've come in my pants when I saw you—uhn—the marina. Please."

Silver used his tongue on the underside. Tracing the vein from root to tip.

"Please." It wasn't a whine but no less desperate, and Silver had to spare a hand to make room in his pants for his own needy dick.

He fished a condom out of the side pocket of his cargo shorts, tearing the wrapper with his teeth before going back to lick every inch of Zeb's shaft. This Silver knew how to do. Hell, he was really damned good at it. And if he could rock Zeb's world back then, all this experience should be good for sending him into orbit.

Silver pulled the condom out.

"We're okay without it." Zeb's breathing was uneven, but Silver understood every word.

Still, he hesitated.

"Your mouth is healed, right?"

Silver made a jerk of a nod. He wanted this, nothing between them, like he'd wanted their clothes to melt away, their bodies to melt into each other. They couldn't fuck raw, but maybe they could have this. Zeb's hands landed on Silver's head, dick right at his lips. He waited for the rough tug forward, waited to be dragged onto a cock until it filled his throat. But fingers sifted through his hair, and a thumb brushed gently across his unbruised cheek. Because this wasn't every other guy, it was Zeb.

"I want to feel you. Please."

Silver parted his lips and sank down. Zeb made a sigh like it held every bit of air in his lungs, showing the relief he might have after hearing the apocalypse was canceled. The hand on Silver's head cradled his neck, steady support instead of pressure.

Not a hand keeping him there like Zeb thought Silver would stop, and not tickling soft like he was too fragile. But like he mattered. Wasn't just a wet hole.

Silver pulled back enough to circle the thick ridge at the crown with his tongue, leaving only the tip in his mouth, then went down to the base, swallowing, holding Zeb deep.

His fingers gripped Silver's neck but didn't push, didn't grind into Silver's nose.

Silver rocked back and forth to make his throat tighten and squeeze around the head.

Zeb grunted as if he were the one who couldn't get a breath. One hand rubbed the base of Silver's skull, the other combed through his hair in time to the *ohGodohGodohGodohGod* bursting from Zeb's lips.

Silver's left eye watered. Not from choking, but from the hand in his hair. He'd gotten used to guys wanting to play with it, but it had never been right. He'd gone so far as to buzz most of it off at one point because it bothered him. How wrong, how different it was.

He'd missed this more than anything. Zeb's fingers in his hair. The way he'd stroke it sometimes like he didn't know he was doing it.

Silver forgot everything he knew about getting a guy off fast and hard. He clung to Zeb's hips, and Zeb's hand slid through his hair. It wasn't Silver giving a blow job; it was them doing something together. A steady bob at their pace. Silver flicked his tongue not for effect but for a taste, sucked for the silky press on his palate, for the sound Zeb made when Silver swallowed around him.

He didn't need the verbal warning when Zeb gasped. "I'm—" Silver felt it in the grip on his hair, the shake and shudder in Zeb's legs, and the throb of the vein against his lips. Silver wanted Zeb's orgasm as deep inside as he could get it and took him down to the root, Zeb's cock gliding on the thick come that coated Silver's tongue and throat from the very first blast.

When Zeb's hips stilled, Silver swallowed and drew off slowly, keeping the tiled floor pristine.

Zeb's fingers made circles against Silver's scalp as they both caught their breaths.

Zeb's thumb pressed into the corner of Silver's mouth, wiping something away.

Silver's stomach dropped straight down into the water below them, and he scrambled to his feet, turning to look in the mirror.

"What's wrong?"

He ignored Zeb in favor of getting an inch from the glass and examining every inch of his lip, inside and out.

"It's okay." Zeb wrapped his arms around Silver from behind, leaning over his shoulder so both their faces stared back from the mirror. "See?"

What Silver saw was his mouth swollen and his eyes wide with fear. Zeb was the opposite, happy and relaxed—which, yeah, Silver had something to do with, so yay on him for that.

Silver nodded. Zeb kissed his neck, his shoulder, a soft trace of lips, leaving a buzzing path on the skin, one hand spread wide on Silver's stomach.

His dick had wilted in that moment of panic, but the kisses, the ones under his ear with a hint of tongue and teeth—added to the way Zeb's fingers were petting along the trail of hair—reversed the blood flow. By the time Zeb's fingers were skating toward the waistband, Silver's cock was stretching up to say hi. He tucked his abs and rocked his hips to force the meeting, getting Zeb's knuckles to barely graze the head.

As he slid his hand between shorts and dick, Zeb's groan vibrated against the wet skin on Silver's neck. Silver had an appreciation for the calluses and new strength he'd seen in Zeb's fingers as they wrapped around the shaft.

"You feel so good." Zeb's nose made the trip up from collarbone to ear this time, along with a tickling amount of breath. "Smell so good."

Silver couldn't come up with a word at first, but as Zeb repeated that motion, it hit him. Nuzzling. Like snuggling squared. One arm holding him against Zeb's chest, the shivery goodness of Zeb's face in his neck, and the sweet pull of Zeb's hand on his cock. Silver wanted to stay right here. Let the warmth build to heat, then explode into fire as they rocked together.

He'd closed his eyes as Zeb started to stroke but snuck a look at them in the mirror. Zeb's soft hair was part of what tickled Silver's shoulder, Zeb's palm resting on Silver's chest over his heart.

Silver knew what he looked like having sex. Hard not to when there were videos loose online, gifs and screen caps. But his face looked different in the mirror. He'd say older, or fuller—blame Eli's cooking—but it was relaxed, which was kind of weird considering he hadn't come yet. Maybe he was used to holding back, to stopping and starting, but that wasn't it. It was knowing how safe it felt, knowing there wasn't some script he had to follow, that whatever happened, he wouldn't get this wrong.

"Mmm. My turn. I can't wait to taste you." Zeb stepped away to pull Silver's shorts and boxer briefs down, one hand working the shaft as Zeb turned Silver around.

With the sudden aching hollow in Silver's gut, only Zeb's hand kept Silver's dick from shriveling up. Why couldn't they have kept going the way they were? When Zeb said that kind of stuff, Silver kept wondering if Zeb was trying to prove something, like how okay he was with Silver being positive. He hadn't worn a condom since those few months with Zeb in New Freedom. What if he couldn't stay hard with one on? What if he hated it?

The alternative was just as scary. Zeb sucking him may be a really hard way to transmit, but what if?

"What's wrong?" Zeb's brow was so wrinkled in concern Silver had to rub his thumb across it to smooth out the bumps.

Zeb smiled, but Silver thought it probably wasn't a real one. "You want to do something else?"

Even if the smile was fake, Zeb's voice was husky as he leaned in and cupped Silver's face. "I could be *up* for it." There was the real Zeb smile.

The accompanying tighter grip, the way his thumb rubbed just the right spot under the head of Silver's cock, made his eyelids drop and his breath catch.

"What do you want?" Zeb blew the hot words into Silver's ear. "I want to give it to you."

What Silver wanted could fill a terabyte. But mostly what he wanted right then was to pin Zeb against the wall and fuck him through it.

Frustration burned at the base of Silver's skull. Now that all the other stuff was getting better between them, there was this virus. The thing inside him that was so tiny and so fucking big at the same time.

Before he could put his hand up to ease that tension, Zeb's fingers were there, rubbing, soothing, sifting through Silver's hair. "Just tell me, Silver."

If he said anything, too much would come out. How much he wanted to change what had happened. And that was never going to be possible.

Zeb pulled him in close, so that Silver's forehead rested on Zeb's shoulder. His hand moved from those long strokes on the shaft to palm the head and then tighter, tugging Silver back out of his head and into his body.

Zeb's fingers and hand must have had a long memory, because that alternating pressure was making everything tight and loose inside at the same time. Silver's hands landed on Zeb's ass, and he squeezed.

Zeb's hips bucked against him. "Okay."

"But like before." Silver's voice came out a whisper. "Remember? When you wouldn't let us?"

Zeb leaned back, eyes narrowed for an instant before widening as he nodded and smiled. He reached into his pocket and handed Silver a small bottle of lube before turning around and bracing his hands on the wall under the mirror. He kept his legs pressed tightly together.

Silver slicked his cock before kicking out of the rest of his clothes and wrapping an arm around Zeb's waist, the other across his chest to steady them. Aiming at the cross of ass and thighs, Silver pressed his cock forward.

A little too cool at first, air-conditioned skin, but as he pushed harder, friction and Zeb's body heat took over. The head drove into Zeb's balls, and he clamped one hand over Silver's.

"Okay?" Silver asked.

"Yeah." Zeb clenched his muscles, warm snug flesh, the extra friction of hair teasing sensation from every bit of Silver's cock.

He tangled his fingers with Zeb's, then arched back and drove in, sliding in the grip of his thighs, hips slamming into his ass at the bottom of the stroke. Zeb's muscles got impossibly tight, tighter than a fist as Silver fucked into Zeb's balls again and again.

In the mirror, Silver watched Zeb's face. His eyes were closed. Above his neck everything was relaxed, but the grip on Silver's fingers and cock told him Zeb was definitely paying attention.

Silver grunted as Zeb timed a squeeze perfectly, and Zeb's eyes shot open, a smile meeting Silver's gaze.

Close. Everything so close in the tiny room, Zeb's ass rubbing the base of Silver's cock as he shoved in, all that wet texture on every inch, and the rough grip of muscles fighting his strokes.

It built fast. Rearing up inside his balls with only a few seconds of warning. He had to bite down on Zeb's shoulder to keep the shout from echoing back up to the Inner Harbor as he shuddered, pumping hard and hot and long onto Zeb's balls.

Silver peeled his mouth—and teeth—off Zeb's shoulder with a wince of regret. "Sorry."

Watching Silver in the mirror, Zeb brought the tangle of their hands from his belly to his balls and dragged their fingers through slippery come.

"That was hotter than I remember."

"Me too." Because it was. Zeb didn't seem to be in any hurry to get Silver's contaminated jizz off him. Even better, Zeb didn't have that righteous pinch around his mouth that would have meant he was proving a point.

Movement rocked him against Zeb, sending them almost nose-first into the mirror. Now that Silver could think again, he realized his legs weren't only shaking from a good hard come.

"We're moving?"

Zeb's wry smile flashed in the mirror. "Maybe I'm just that good."

Silver tugged his slippery hand loose. "When did that start?"

"Right before you came."

"Did anybody—uh—knock?"

"Nope." Zeb tossed him a guest towel from the rack.

"Ha. I bet Jamie's pissed."

Zeb's brow got all bumpy again. "You think he will be?"

"I fucking hope so."

Chapter Eighteen

THE SUN left a blinding path on the water to the portside as they bounced through the wakes of other boats heading back up the bay toward the Inner Harbor. With no buildings blocking the way, the heat and light scalded the side of Silver's face even as a cool spray misted over them.

The only thing more conspicuous than the sunset was the complete lack of reaction from Jamie. He hadn't glanced their way or so much as mumbled anything since Silver and Zeb came out from below deck.

Maybe Gavin had threatened to never blow him again.

Eli rolled his eyes. "You could have at least brought up what you *said* you went down to get."

Gavin followed Eli through the hatch. With Jamie nothing but a solid back in the captain's chair, Quinn nodded at Silver and said, "Well, if they're not back up in two minutes, I'm going after them."

Gavin toted two bottles of KZ and a Pellegrino when he came up. Eli carried more cheese and bread. "I'm hungry."

"Maybe if you hadn't fed the rest of the bread to the fish and brought over every seagull on the Eastern Shore, you wouldn't be," Quinn complained but wrapped an arm around Eli anyway.

They were at the table where Zeb and Silver had sat on the way out. Silver wanted to see what it felt like to ride at speed on the bow cushion but wasn't interested in setting Jamie off by being in his view. And it was nice here, alone in the stern, Zeb warm on one side and the sun on the other.

As they neared the marina dock, Jamie came aft. "Gimme a hand tying up, Silver."

Zeb put his hand on Silver's thigh, a question, an offer, but Silver shook his head.

Whatever shit Jamie had to say, Silver could handle it.

When Jamie handed off the line, Silver stepped down onto the dock, looped the bowline around, and made a cleat knot. He looked up to see Jamie staring down.

"Nice job, kid."

That couldn't be all. Not from Jamie.

Jamie leaned farther over the rail. "Hope he got the deluxe treatment."

Silver put on his best get-the-trick pout. "Yeah. *He* did."

Jamie barked a laugh and stepped back from the stern.

It was twilight as they headed back to the parking lot. A shiver caught Silver by surprise.

"Did you get sunburned?" Zeb asked.

Silver pressed on his cheeks and nose. "I don't think so. I had on sunblock." It wasn't a burn. It was leaving behind the warmth, the security of an afternoon on Gavin's boat. The farther away they went, the more Silver remembered that his life was anything but settled in a sipping-champagne-on-a-yacht kind of way.

"Do you want to come back to my apartment with me?" Zeb nodded at where his Pontiac was a row away from Quinn's Buick.

"I can't guarantee I'm good for much but sleep." Even as Silver said it, a yawn split his jaw.

"Duly noted." Zeb cupped the back of Silver's neck.

An itch between Silver's shoulder blades reminded him they weren't on the yacht or even in relatively gay-friendly Mount Vernon.

"Behave, boys. Remember it's a school night." Eli's teasing let Silver twist away.

"We'll just do what you would. Only better." Then Silver remembered. Zeb would have to bring him home before he went to work. "Hey, what time do you have to be at work tomorrow?"

Quinn beeped the locks on the Buick. "Teachers have to report by seven thirty-five."

"You'd have to bring me all the way back to Mount Washington at six thirty."

Zeb laughed. "You make it sound like a fate worse than death."

"As I remember, you really like your sleep."

"Some things change." Zeb shrugged.

"For Chri—crying out loud, there's an easy solution. Zeb sleeps at our house and we drive in tomorrow together." Quinn so had a head start on the crotchety-old-man routine. But it was a nice offer.

"I need some stuff from my apartment."

"We have lots of lube." Eli's voice was full of bright innocence.

"I think he meant like a tie and pants, Eli. I'll go with you." Silver took a step toward Zeb's car.

"You'll fuck and fall asleep and end up with the hassles of morning commuting." Quinn's hand on Silver's shoulder pulled him back. "Evaluations are coming up. I want you to keep your job." Quinn directed that at Zeb. "And I promised the judge you were staying with me," he said to Silver.

Silver was about to sneer a *Seriously?* but the look on Quinn's face changed his mind.

He did take it seriously.

As Silver buckled himself in the back seat, he let out a quick laugh.

"What?" Eli turned to face him.

"I'm wondering if Quinn's going to make him sleep on the couch."

In the car, Silver had been so drowsy he'd doubted if he'd still be awake when Zeb got there. Now, curled up in the squishy chair in Quinn's living room Silver had adopted as his space, Christmas anticipation and test-failure dread battled it out for control in his stomach. Either way, he was worried about keeping down the PB&J he'd scarfed when they came in.

Spending the night with Zeb was straight out of Silver's dreams at sixteen. But that might as well have been a lifetime ago.

Maybe he should go upstairs and see how his dick felt about a layer of latex. Then at least he would be spared embarrassment if they got there. After the last three years, he'd thought he didn't have any shame left. Turned out it was because of the absence of the one person who could make him this self-conscious.

A car came down the street, and Silver turned to look through the front window. "Awww. He's so cute. It's like it's his first date." Eli flung his head onto Quinn's lap with an exaggerated sigh.

"Awww. Shut the fuck up." Silver matched Eli's singsong tone.

Silver didn't have a sibling. Never met his "godless" cousins from New York. Casting Eli and Quinn as Mom and Dad was too bizarre outside of mockery, but Silver had to wonder what it might have been like if his parents weren't assholes. If he'd been somewhere like he saw online, where same-sex couples went to the prom and got voted cutest couple and everyone acted like it was perfectly fine. Maybe that kind of shit happened in Massachusetts, but it didn't happen in New Freedom, Pennsylvania.

He still wouldn't have been able to bring Zeb home—at least not for a night. He thought about Quinn's tight-assed view of his responsibility to the judge and had no doubt if Silver were sixteen, there'd be no men in his bed.

"You ever been on a date, smartass?" Silver glanced over at Eli.

Eli sat up and made a zip-lips motion.

"I know of one," Quinn said.

"Yeah. That about sums up my history." Eli's vow of silence lasted all of a tenth of a second.

"And?" Silver asked.

"He never went home," Quinn said in the same flat tone.

"Seriously?"

Eli smirked.

"Lesbian." Silver sneered.

"Excuse me?" Eli cupped his dick.

Quinn put an arm around him. "What does a lesbian bring on the second date?"

Eli tipped his head up at Quinn.

"A U-Haul." To Silver, Quinn added, "It actually took him a few trips on the bus to get most of his stuff up here."

"For which you are eternally grateful, asshole." Eli straddled him.

Quinn's repetition started out robotic. "For which I am eternally—unf—"

The doorbell rang and spared Silver witnessing whatever game they were about to get started as he escaped into the hall and opened the door. Only to get smacked with a paralyzing wave of unaccustomed shyness when Zeb stepped in, clothes on a hanger over one shoulder, a soft laptop case slung over the other one. "Hi."

"Hi." After that he was stumped for a minute, since it was as far as he'd gotten in planning what to say. For fuck's sake, he wasn't a virgin, not by a long shot, and this wasn't their damned wedding night. At least Zeb's stuff gave Silver something to do. "I'll hang that up for you."

Zeb handed over the hanger, and Silver headed upstairs. He had it hooked over the bar in the closet in record time, but Zeb was at the door when Silver turned around.

Zeb put his computer bag on the floor under the desk. "Thanks. Is that where the magic happens?"

"Huh?" Silver looked at the bed. *Not a virgin. Not a wedding night.* Only—what had Marco called it?— an all-night guest.

"Eli's photography. The digital work he does." Zeb pointed at the NASA-like screens Eli had.

Silver was pretty sure the screens multiplied while he was sleeping. "Yeah. That's his setup. You want a drink? Water? Iced tea?" He tried to move past Zeb.

Zeb put a hand up across the doorframe. "I want you."

Silver stopped. Looked at Zeb. His serious eyes, his familiar face, the trace of a day's stubble on his chin and jaw.

Lowering his arm, Zeb went on, "I know you said you were tired. We don't have to do anything. But I came here to be with you."

Silver started to answer, then nodded. But he didn't exactly know what he'd agreed to. If they were wound up, hungry for each other, he'd know how to do this. But this, being so careful with each other, it was hard. He didn't want to be the one to fuck things up.

Zeb leaned forward and kissed him, firm deliberate pressure. The crazy anxiousness in Silver's head went quiet. Zeb knew where they were going. That made one of them.

Lifting his head, he asked, "Do you need to take a pill before bed?"

"No."

"Go brush your teeth. You taste like peanut butter."

Silver grinned. "You're a freak. How does anyone not like peanut butter?" Zeb was under the covers when Silver got back and closed the door.

"You're not brushing your teeth?" Silver tossed his shirts and shorts on the desk chair. Sometimes he stripped the boxer briefs too. Not tonight.

Zeb blew a *ha* at Silver as he climbed in the bed. "I got all minty fresh and ready at my apartment. I should have asked. Do you have a side you like to sleep on?"

Silver saved himself from stupidly blurting *My stomach* as his brain caught up. Side of the bed, Zeb meant. Anytime Silver had slept with a guy—really slept in the unconscious sense—they'd just ended up wherever they were when they were done fucking.

"No. I don't care." Jealousy stung, left an itch no amount of reason could quiet. Silver settled on his back. "Do you?"

"I've never had any reason to get used to one."

"Okay." Irrational or not, Silver liked the answer.

Although it was only a bit after ten, if he were alone, he'd probably be in bed. The nights he didn't work, he was tired enough to crash early. He reached over to switch off the lamp, and when he settled back, found Zeb wrapped around him. Warm, bare skin against his back, Zeb's arm over Silver's waist, a kiss on his shoulder. They fit, equal heights lining them up. It felt nice. He could deal with being the little spoon.

He put his hand over Zeb's, fingers tracing the scars. It was a part of Zeb Silver knew nothing about.

He rubbed the oddly smooth part where a piece was missing from the outside of the index finger.

"What happened?"

"Improper use of a machete."

Silver reared up and spun around. "Someone—"

"Me. I was the one with a machete. Trying to cut something I was holding on to at the time. Bad decision."

Silver settled back down and lifted Zeb's hand, tracing the ragged one from pinky all the way across his hand.

"Torn on a nail. And yes, I'd had a tetanus shot."

Silver pulled the other hand out from where it was under Zeb's head and pillow.

Without the question, Zeb said, "Crushed. Concrete block. They're a little hard to bend in rainy weather, but I can still write. And make enough of a fist for other purposes."

Silver couldn't really see Zeb's wry smile but heard it in his voice. Normally he'd dive right into the opportunity for dirty jokes, but he didn't feel like it now. "I thought you were teaching."

"And helping to build the school. And houses and churches. Where I was, if there were four walls and a roof, it was a luxury. Tents were the best accommodations."

"Why did you stay?"

"I liked teaching kids who really wanted to learn. Not that it isn't fun trying to trick bored tenth graders into liking geometry. But the kids there, they had to go through so much to get to school, they wanted to be there."

Silver remembered Gavin talking about passion. This was Zeb's. And Silver had almost cost him the chance to ever do it again. "Sorry you didn't get to stay until you were ready to leave."

"I'm not. Things happen for a reason."

Before Silver could roll his eyes about God having a plan that included Silver being HIV positive, Zeb said, "I know that's not something you're interested in talking about, so call it fate or whatever, but I'm glad we got the chance to see each other, put all that behind us."

"It wasn't all bad." Silver's voice came out as a whisper.

"No. Definitely not."

Silver found Zeb's mouth in the dark, kissed the smile there. Kept on kissing him because if Silver stopped, he was afraid the hard lump he was swallowing around would turn into actual tears, and that would ruin everything.

Zeb's lips opened, and Silver fell into the feeling of how right it was when their tongues slid past each other. Every time they kissed it felt like the first time, like he had found something he'd always needed. He held on to the sides of Zeb's face to keep him there, because the way things worked in Silver's world, there was no telling how long he'd get to have this.

Zeb wrapped his arms around Silver and rolled him under, Zeb's weight so perfectly balanced on Silver they fit together like puzzle pieces.

And tired or not, there was definitely the potential for interlocking pieces if Zeb kept rubbing against Silver like that.

"Want you." Zeb's words were so close to Silver's mouth it was like they were his own. "Want to suck you. Please."

Silver bucked his hips, dick on board despite Silver's big head being slow to follow.

Zeb's lips and tongue shifted under Silver's chin, down his neck, onto his breastbone.

"Pull off," he warned.

"I will." Zeb was already kissing his way onto Silver's belly.

He lifted his hips to help Zeb tug off the boxer briefs Silver should have ditched with the rest of his clothes, and then Zeb's mouth was there, tight around the tip, hot and wet and a flicking tongue.

Silver'd had better, more practiced blow jobs. But that didn't matter when Zeb's silky hair brushed his thighs, when it was the shine of Zeb's eyes meeting Silver's as he stared down.

Zeb might not have learned every trick, but with one hand cupping and lifting Silver's balls and the other on the shaft matching the bob of Zeb's head, Silver thought those tricks were overrated. A holy-fuck intensity was just fine. He wanted Zeb's tongue to rub the head like that forever, until the pressure from the roof of his mouth felt even better. Back and forth between the sensations with hard friction on the shaft.

Silver's neck arched, head flung over the pillow, hands dropping to Zeb's hair as the sensation built, an arc toward the sky, a long swing up as the pleasure spiked in his balls. They tightened, and Zeb's hand fell away. A drop of tension on the return swing, and then it rushed back in, stronger, bigger. Flooding into his cock, buzzing, rushing with his blood.

He pushed deeper into the wet heat, surprising a gasp and a hum from Zeb's lips, and he hit the edge. With a frantic shove at Zeb's head, he spat, "Off. Oh fuck, off."

Zeb moved, and Silver's hips bucked, and if he didn't hit the ceiling with the first shot, it sure as hell felt like it. He grabbed his cock to finish it, pulling out a rope that hit his shoulder, and then, shit, two more on his belly.

Zeb's hair tickled the insides of Silver's thighs, head resting on Silver's hip.

Silver let out a long breath. "Fuck." He didn't know if he'd ever come so hard before.

Zeb dragged a finger through the puddle on Silver's stomach and put a soft, wet kiss on his hipbone.

Everything in him wanted to drag Zeb up like a blanket and sink into sleep, but he really should offer reciprocation.

He took another deep breath of the come-sweat smell of them and shifted into motion. His ankle slid through a cooling wet spot.

Guess he knew where the hand on his balls had gone off to. "Yeah?"

"Didn't think I'd want to after double action today, but when you made that sound… things got urgent."

Silver didn't remember making a sound, but after swallowing, he realized his throat hurt. "Oh shit." Eli would rag on him forever.

"I really thought tonight we could just sleep." There was an apology in Zeb's tone.

A blow job before bed was not the kind of thing that should require an apology.

Silver rubbed a thumb across Zeb's mouth. "How do you like to sleep?" The mouth under Silver's thumb curved.

"On my back."

"Perfect." Silver rolled to the far edge of the bed to make room for Zeb to shift out of the wet spot. As soon as he was settled, Silver crawled up onto his chest and tangled their legs together.

Zeb sighed. "I should shower."

"It's down the hall," Silver said through a yawn.

"Are you going to let me up?"

"Wasn't planning on it."

"Good." Zeb wrapped his arms around Silver.

Gray light met Silver's eyes when he opened them. Despite the hard surface of Zeb's chest and the dried come sticking their chests together, Silver hadn't woken once during the night. Now Zeb's fingers slipped through Silver's hair, and even the nudge of his bladder wasn't enough to keep him from drifting back to sleep.

Until his pillow heaved a sigh. "Gotta shower."

"Yeah, you do. You reek of sex." Silver hitched his arm tighter around Zeb's ribs. The rumble under Silver's head warned him of the laugh before it gusted across his ear.

"You really aren't helpful at all."

"If that means I can sleep here for a few more minutes, it's good."

The stroke of Zeb's hand sent tingles down Silver's spine, spreading out like warmth to his fingers and toes.

"Do you have a shift today?"

"No."

Again, he could hear the change in Zeb's mood, the gathering of air in his chest as he hesitated.

Silver lifted his head. "What?"

"I wondered if you wanted to maybe go out to-night. To a movie?"

Silver lowered his head again and worked his hand to reach the base of Zeb's spine. "Or we could just have sex."

Because after months of being uninterested, suddenly it was on his brain every minute. If his dick wasn't sore enough to register a protest, he'd have started grinding against Zeb the minute they woke up.

"I'd like that too." Zeb squeezed him. "I know it might sound stupid, but it's something I wished we could have done before. And I know how much you love movies."

Silver did. But money to waste on a movie hadn't exactly been part of his financial situation for the last couple of years.

"I don't know about you," Zeb murmured, "but no matter how much I want to again right now, my dick needs a few more hours off."

Silver laughed. "A movie is good."

"I'll see you here when I get out."

It was probably good Silver had fallen back asleep by the time Zeb got back from the shower, or Silver might have tried to see if wanting was stronger than the ouch-not-now. But he got up on his own for breakfast and his pill, which turned out to be good because Eli seemed really distracted.

Not sad, but for Eli, quiet. Like he had a lot to think about. Since Eli usually thought things through out loud, the quiet was deafening. It wasn't as if Silver had wanted Eli to tease about Zeb, but this felt off.

Eli puttered around the kitchen while Silver shoveled in some cereal. Now he handed over a mug of coffee and winced as he sat down in a kitchen chair.

"Jesus fuck, Eli. Did Quinn go too far?" Silver was on his feet before he realized it, adrenaline not particular about details like Quinn being off at work, and Silver and Eli both living in Quinn's house.

The wide-eyed expression on Eli's face was more reassuring than his words. "No. Not at all." He shifted, grimaced, and then grinned. "You know I love it."

Silver sat back down with a grunt. He didn't get it. But who was he to judge it? Still didn't explain why Eli was so weird this morning.

"What were you going to do?" Eli raised his coffee mug. "Go punch him in the mouth?"

"I don't know," Silver admitted.

"I can take care of myself, thanks."

But Eli put the mug back down without drinking any, and Silver had to ask, "Then what's going on?"

"We did have a… thing. About you."

"Me?" Quinn was the one who'd been so adamant about Silver not sleeping over at Zeb's. So that must mean it was Eli's nerves Silver was getting on. "I'll be out of here before you finish your coffee."

"Sit down." Eli snapping at a guy was a lot more intimidating than Silver would have imagined. "Where were you going to go, Zeb's?"

Silver hadn't considered it. Back into the city was all he knew. The idea of being where he wasn't wanted tore a scab off a wound he didn't even know he had. He shrugged.

"I like having you here. I'm still not used to all this time to myself. Quinn likes you here, because he knows I have someone to talk to."

"So what's the issue?"

"You know how yesterday Quinn said I moved in after one date?"

"Yeah." Silver drank some of his coffee. He wasn't in the mood for it black but didn't want to interrupt Eli to go to the fridge.

"It was true. And we got to talking about what was the big deal if you wanted to stay at Zeb's, and after Quinn did his duty-and-honor shit about the judge, he said it wouldn't be good."

What the hell was that about? "I thought he liked Zeb."

"He does. Says he's a really good teacher."

Maybe Silver wasn't good enough for Zeb? Silver wouldn't bother pointing that out to Eli, he'd probably get all defensive. "So what's Quinn's issue, then?"

"I don't know. He just gave me the don't-worry-your-pretty-head look that pisses me off and—" Eli cut himself off.

Silver wasn't sure if he should ask. If he wanted to hear what Eli was trying not to say.

"And?" But it seemed like the least he could do if his being around was fucking up what the awesome thing Eli had going here.

"And if it wouldn't be good for you to move in with Zeb when you don't have anyplace else to live and you've known each other for years, maybe me being here with Quinn…." That time Eli let it trail away.

"No. No way. You—the way he looks at you? And he is fucking lucky to have you."

"Damn right he is." But there was something in his voice to suggest Eli didn't quite believe his own words.

"Here's what we're going to do. Go downtown, buy you something to wear, and when you look hotter than even you usually do, you'll ask him right out if you being here isn't the best thing that ever happened to him."

"You know, that's kind of a good plan." Eli gulped down some coffee.

"I know," Silver said.

"And here I thought you were the one who made stupid, impulsive decisions."

"Thanks a fucking lot."

Chapter Nineteen

SILVER PEERED through the glass-fronted cabinets at the ice cream containers. The battle between curiosity and disgust was making the decision hard.

Eli nudged him. "Get the strawberry-basil. Ooo, no, the lavender-Earl Grey tea."

Feeling guilty about being the cause of whatever kind of thing Eli and Quinn had had, Silver had suggested a treat after Eli was done picking through his favorite secondhand-clothing store. He didn't expect a place like Take Your Licks.

"It's so awesome," Eli had said as he dragged Silver to the counter.

"Blue crab ice cream?"

"It's Bawlmer, hon," Eli had said as he eagerly accepted samples of combinations that should never have existed.

Silver declined Eli's spoon sharing and kept staring at the demented blends. On the *Just Vanilla, We Promise* was a neon orange tag labeling it *For Wimps*. Silver wasn't ready for blue crab, but that was too much of a dare to ignore.

"Chipotle chocolate," he told the girl behind the counter.

"Damn," Eli said, "I've already had that one."

Sometimes Eli took the notion of sharing a little too far. He hemmed and hawed for a few minutes before deciding on Old Bay-caramel-bacon.

Silver paid an insane price for two cones, and Eli tugged him toward a plate-sized table and chairs made out of wire.

"It's too hot to eat ice cream outside."

The chairs were about as uncomfortable as they looked, but Silver spun it around to straddle it, and that was better.

"Mmmm." Eli licked the cream off his lips and pushed his waffle cone toward Silver. "Want some?"

"I'd rather blow a syphilitic wino."

"Not much money in that."

"No, thank fuck." Silver shuddered.

"How's yours?" Eli went back to giving enthusiastic head to his unnatural mix of ingredients.

The inside of Silver's mouth was on fire, but the chocolate was rich and intense. He kind of loved it.

"Not bad."

Eli's sneaker thudded into Silver's bare shin. "Ow."

Eli didn't miss one deep lick of his cone. "What are you going to do?"

Silver stopped rubbing his shin and looked at Eli. Knowing what Eli was asking and knowing how to answer him were two different things. And it made his brain go back to chasing its tail over what Quinn had meant about it not being good for Silver to move in with Zeb—as if he'd been planning on it. Maybe Quinn had been referring to Zeb leaving for two months.

Stalling, he lapped at the spicy chocolate, broke off a piece of the waffle cone, and chewed. Sweet and still crunchy, it was perfect with the burn on his tongue.

Eli paused, ice cream at his lips, looking at Silver through thick dark bangs. It was one hell of a sexy look. But it was ice cream, not a dick. And it was Eli, so Silver was relatively immune, if not completely unaffected.

"I mean, since there's not a lot of money in the syphilitic-wino clientele." Eli sucked on his cone. "Not that you can't stay with us for a while, even after you see the judge."

"After I see the judge, I might be staying in jail, Eli."

Eli flapped his hand like that was impossible.

"I know Gavin got me a good lawyer, and I owe you both for that, but it doesn't mean I'm not going to jail."

"'Kay, but suppose you don't." Eli dropped that part of the argument. "You can stay with us. And no matter what the bug up Quinn's ass is about it, I can tell Zeb would be happy to let you stay with him."

They were barely at the point where they didn't keep using the past to carve big slices in each other. "Except Zeb's not going to be here much longer."

"What?" Eli's hand slapped down on the table. "Where's he going? If Quinn knew—"

"Save the drama, please. Your eight-dollar ice cream cone will melt. Zeb is going back to work at that camp where he met Quinn. I assume your Daddy is staying home to tuck you into bed every night."

Eli's cheeks flushed, and he shifted on the chair. Whatever kind of tucking-in had gone on last night, it must have been one hell of a time.

"He's leaving the Friday after my court date. I don't even know if he's keeping his apartment. Guess Quinn wins this round. I won't be moving in with Zeb."

"Bastard. I hate having to tell Quinn he's right." Eli pouted. "And how could Zeb just leave after all you guys have been through?"

"I don't know what the fuck's going to happen with Zeb, but if I don't go to jail, I'm hoping to get an apartment closer to the restaurant. I can manage a security deposit off what I've saved since I went full-time there. Course the lawyer says I've got to tell 'em my real social and start paying taxes and not get paid under the table."

"How's that going to go over?"

"The owner's kind of a stoner-hippy type, so if I tell him I was in witness protection, he'd probably buy it."

Eli snorted into his puke-colored Old Bay-caramel-bacon ice cream. Spit could only be an improvement.

"Manager'll be pissed. But right now he barely has bodies to cover the shifts, so he won't fire my ass. And you've got ice cream all over your nose."

Eli licked as much as he could before giving in and using the skimpy napkin wrapped around the cone.

"Not one of your sexier moments, my friend."

"Good thing there was only a friend around to see it, then." Eli stuck out his tongue.

"Don't be pissed at Quinn. He had a point about Zeb. So don't think it has anything to do with you guys. Me and Zeb—there's a lot of past shit involved. And there isn't with you two. 'Sides, when you think of it, I owe Quinn a blow job or two for letting me crash in his house. You have to make good for me." Silver stuffed the rest of his cone into his mouth. "If you can."

THERE MIGHT be too much past shit to know where he and Zeb were going, but things inside Silver still did a happy skip at the sight of the Pontiac next to the curb in front of Quinn's house. They'd timed it perfectly to get back right at four.

It had been a hot, thirsty walk from the bus stop with the chipotle chocolate burning in Silver's mouth. He'd have a big glass of iced tea, and then he'd see if the leftover chilies would sizzle Zeb's tongue. But as they got closer, Silver noticed two things that were seriously going to fuck up his plans.

Zeb wasn't in his car. Silver had forgotten Zeb and Quinn had gone into school together. And Marco sat on Quinn's front steps, an overstuffed backpack next to him.

"Hey." Marco jumped to his feet as Silver and Eli came closer. "Eli, I hope you don't mind I sat on the steps while waiting for Silver." To Silver, Marco added, "I wanted to hang out, but when I went to the restaurant, I found out it was your day off. Lucky for me, huh?"

Marco sucked at faking casual. The knot of oh-shit that had started in Silver's stomach when he saw the backpack got fatter, more tangled.

He cut to the chase. "What happened?"

Marco slumped back on the stairs like someone had cut off his legs. "I can't. I can't be there anymore. It—he makes me hate everything. Hate myself."

Eli took a seat on the step under Marco's. "Your brother?"

"He made me go to the priest. He told the priest to fix me."

"Did he? The priest, I mean."

Marco and Eli both snapped their heads up to look at Silver with almost identical expressions of irritation.

Then Marco smiled. "No. But he was very nice. The priest, I mean. And cute." Marco winked.

"What are you doing here, Marco?" Silver asked.

"'Kay. I loved being here for dinner. You don't know how much. Like heaven to sit and eat and not get sick with the yelling. When I went back, it was so much worse. You and Eli made out okay. So I thought you would know what I should do."

"Marco, Silver and I didn't have a choice." Eli said it more nicely than Silver would have put it.

"And we lived on the street for a while. I told you about being a hust—whore."

"Oh." Marco's inquisitive look at Eli went unanswered.

Eli tapped Marco's thigh. "Did your brother tell you you couldn't live there anymore?"

"No. But—" Marco's eyes widened. "*Mierda.*"

Silver spun around. He'd have known they were in deep shit without Marco's curse.

There couldn't be two cars with those toxic-green rims, even in East Baltimore. "Jesus, Marco. Does he have a LoJack on you?"

Marco patted his jeans like he was taking that seriously and then said, "*Soy un tonto.* The GPS, I used it in Ernesto's car. I didn't think to erase it."

The fact that the black Firebird had to park two doors down to avoid driveways and a fire hydrant didn't give Silver much time to plan.

"Never mind." Marco picked up his backpack. "I'll go with him. I'm sorry. I'll call you when I can."

Eli put his hand on Marco's shoulder. "Wait."

Marco's brother slammed the passenger door and started charging up the sidewalk. "Timo?" Eli muttered.

"Yup."

Timo wasn't much taller than Marco but a hell of a lot more thickly muscled. Premature gray bristled at the temples and in the stubble standing at attention on his angrily jutting jaw. But with Eli and the house behind them, they could handle Timo. The serious worry was the other guy, who looked like professional muscle. Since he'd been driving the car, Silver hoped he was Marco's brother-in-law Ernesto and not a hit man.

Without talking it out, Silver and Eli had taken a position in front of Marco on Quinn's yard.

Timo raced up, finger stabbing at Silver's chest. "You. I told you if you came around him again, I'd kill you."

"He came to us," Eli said.

"I don't care who came to who. Marco, get in the car. These boys aren't your friends. They only want to make you like them. *Maricónes.*"

"Seriously? Faggot is the best you got?" Eli rolled his eyes. "'Cause I've never heard that before."

Silver snuck a look around Timo at who he was guessing was Ernesto. He was about a yard back, looking like he'd rather be getting a root canal than standing there. It didn't mean he wouldn't wade in if it came to swinging. And if Eli kept baiting Timo, it would. There was a vein throbbing in his temple that might be one extra corpuscle away from an aneurysm.

"Marco, I told you to get in the car, or I swear—" Timo tried to go around them on Silver's side. When Silver moved to keep Marco behind him, that was the trigger. Timo shoved Silver out of the way.

Silver didn't know when he had decided, but no fucking way was this guy taking Marco anywhere. Silver locked his hand into a fist as he regained his balance. But before he could swing, there was an arm, then a body between them.

Zeb.

Timo let loose a stream of Spanish Silver couldn't follow. But Zeb did. Silver had forgotten Zeb had spent his junior year of high school as a foreign exchange student in Argentina.

When Silver's ears caught up, he whispered a translation to Eli. "Zeb asked if Marco was eighteen. Timo says Marco is, but he's too young to know and is something—something about the internet." So much for Silver's straight As in Spanish.

Marco leaned in. "Timo thinks I got crushes on boys from watching TV shows on the internet." He made a disgusted face. "Now they are arguing about religion."

"Good luck winning that round with Zeb," Silver told them.

Marco nodded. "Zeb can quote a lot of the Bible."

He was relieved when it went back to screaming rather than swinging. Although now that Quinn had joined them and stood next to Ernesto, Silver liked their odds if things got physical again.

"Marco, *chico*, what did Father Rossi tell you?" Timo had gone from demanding to cajoling.

"That God made me and He loves me." Marco grinned. Silver tried not to laugh.

The vein in Timo's temple bulged. "What did he say about homosexuals?" His accent got thicker on the last word.

"He said loving others is what God wants but any kind of sex before marriage was a sin, and I should carry a rosary and say my prayers if I start thinking about sex."

"See?" Timo threw his hand heavenward, as if he could get God to help make a point on his behalf.

Marco blinked then held his eyes wide open in innocence. "Is that what happens when your *nov*—girl-friend Tessa comes over and you go in the bedroom and close the door? You say the rosary together? I've never heard it like that."

"That's different." The words came from behind Timo's clenched teeth.

"How?" Eli's teeth were bared.

Silver relaxed his fist, swallowing back not acid frustration but a warm burst of pride. Theirs was the winning side for once.

Marco pressed the advantage. "Because a pussy is better than an ass?"

"Because, God, Marco, because that's how you make babies. That's why it's different. If that happens, I'll marry Tessa."

"Blow jobs don't make babies," Marco said. "Doesn't she suck—?"

"*No más.*" Timo spit at their feet. "That's it. You come home with us right now or—" Before Silver could stop him, Timo grabbed Marco by the arm and was hauling him forward.

Marco dug in his heels, twisting, tearing at Timo's grip until he was free.

"There is no or." Timo's voice was flat. "You have no choice."

"That's not true." Quinn's voice was calm, but the rumble of it got Timo's attention. Zeb stood next to Marco. "Do you want to go back with your brother?"

Marco shook his head.

"*Eso es estúpido. Chico*, where will you stay?"

Quinn looked Marco in the eye. "You can stay here until you decide."

"Quinn?" Eli sucked in the name on a gasp.

"So you can fuck him too? Pimp Daddy doesn't have enough boy whores?" Timo snarled at Quinn.

Marco's gaze flicked from Quinn to Timo and back to Silver.

He wanted to tell Marco to be safe. Silver just didn't know what the safest choice was. He couldn't imagine Marco managing to live with Timo after this, and Quinn and Eli would try to help—but Silver had thought he'd be safe with Zeb.

Marco backed away from Timo.

"You do this and you have no home, you understand?" Timo shook a finger in Marco's face. "No family. Nothing."

Marco turned away. Silver saw the shine of tears on his eyes. "*Sí. No tengo familia.*"

"Don't think your sisters will help you because you are the baby. When I tell them what you are, they won't want you around their children."

Marco stumbled, and Silver caught him, hugging him close. "It's okay."

"I knew you were the one who did this to him." Timo glared at Silver over Marco's head.

Marco's arms went around Silver's waist, and Silver hung on to him, staring Timo down.

"You made your choice, *chico.*"

Timo turned around and started back for Ernesto's car. Marco squeezed Silver harder.

Eli tapped Silver on the back. "Take him into the house."

Silver walked Marco up the steps. He was crying, but silently, which bothered Silver a lot more than if Marco had been ranting.

He stopped in the foyer, unsure, Marco's arm still clinging like a tentacle to Silver's waist.

"You want a drink—water or something?" Marco shook his head.

Eli came in, Marco's backpack over one shoulder. Silver met his gaze over Marco's head.

They're gone, Eli mouthed, then jerked his chin in the direction of the stairs. "C'mon up to my room." Silver urged Marco toward the stairs.

At the top, Marco rubbed his face with the hand not twisted into Silver's shirt. "*¿El baño?*"

Silver steered him toward the bathroom. "I'm not holding it for you, though." Marco gave him a weak smile.

As soon as the door shut behind Marco, Silver's text alert went off. Eli.

Don't leave him alone.

Yeah. I'm not a total asshole, thanks, Silver sent back. He hoped Eli didn't mean in the bathroom. After Silver heard the toilet flush, he knocked and the door swung open.

Marco was washing his face. "Sorry. I'm sorry. I am a—*el pato*, a pussy."

"No, you're not." Silver went into the linen closet across the hall for a towel. "You stood up to him. That takes guts."

Marco's knuckles showed white where he gripped the washcloth. "I couldn't—it was too much, every day. But I didn't think—"

"Yeah." Silver had known his parents weren't going to like it. He just hadn't known they'd rather see him dead. "I don't think anybody does."

"After my parents died, *mis ab*—grandparents raised us in Cozumel, and then Timo and Isabella here. My classes. I can't pay for my classes." Marco bent over the sink, looking like he was going to puke.

Silver put a hand on Marco's shoulder and made a tentative pat on his back. "Want to shower?"

Marco looked up at him with a lopsided smile. "But you're not washing it for me? No." He tossed the washcloth in the sink. "I can't—I can't think about anything, it all goes…." He raised a finger and spun it around like an out-of-control carousel.

"So don't."

They went into Silver's room. Marco perched on the edge of the bed like he didn't know what to do with himself. Silver didn't give the cue, but his mind called up his first night, trying not to sneeze, hidden with the dust bunnies under Marissa's bed until her parents left for work and she could drive him into Shrewsbury to the bus stop. He still owed her for the ticket.

Silver gave Marco a gentle shove, and he sprawled back. "Does this mean a pity fuck?"

Silver choked. The first thing that came to his mind—*Where did you hear that?*—made him feel a hundred years old.

"No."

"Pity blow job?"

"Not happening." Silver stretched out on his back next to Marco.

"Is that your boyfriend? The one with the long hair?" Marco rolled on his side, supporting his head with a cocked elbow.

The boyfriend part of it was debatable but not worth getting into with Marco. "Yeah."

"He's cute, but not what I thought you would like. He's… quiet. I thought someone strong with nice muscles." Marco made a biceps flex.

Silver pictured the cuts over Zeb's hips, how he should have licked them yesterday when he had the chance, remembered the power in his thighs, the unfamiliar damage to his hands. "He's strong enough."

"Thank him. And thank you. For saving me. Again."

"Thank Quinn. I didn't do anything."

"But they helped me because of you. Because it's your family."

It's only because of the judge. The protest came immediately to mind, but Silver didn't say it. Because they kind of were. A family.

Marco rolled onto his other side, facing away. Silver figured Marco was crying again, but he obviously didn't want Silver to see.

Silver stroked a hand through Marco's curls. "Is it always this bad?" Marco asked.

"At first. It gets better." Maybe Silver should lie. But Marco deserved to know. "But it always hurts." He put an arm around Marco and held him until he fell asleep.

Chapter Twenty

SILVER JERKED awake. He'd never intended to fall asleep. Marco was breathing deeply, curled in a tight ball like a kitten. Checking his phone, Silver found out he'd only been out for about twenty minutes, and Eli had sent a text every two minutes.

I didn't mean for you to fuck him. What are you doing up there?

OMG cops R here!!!

It's OK. Quinn does responsible suburban home-owner well. Jamie showing up helped.

Brother didn't call cops. Nosy neighbor.

Mrs. Murdoch. Sounds like a character on a sit-com. We're getting pizza.

Silver slipped downstairs. Voices in the dining room had him headed there in time to hear Jamie complain, "Christ, why the hell can't these damn kids wait till they leave home before they announce they like dick? Like we did."

"That's your solution?" Quinn's growl was so different than his usual calm voice.

Silver saw a little of what got Eli so hot and bothered.

"How much of a choice do you think I had?" Eli said. "I didn't announce it. I couldn't fucking hide it." He glanced up as Silver came in. "How is he?"

Silver shrugged. "Asleep." He clamped down on a sigh of relief when Zeb came in from the kitchen. Silver had expected him to have taken off after the showdown was over.

Zeb met Silver's eyes and gave him a smile that made him feel like the only person in the room.

Jamie slammed back against his chair. "And in the meantime you're going to run a home for wayward youth? I think the cops thought you were running a stable of boys out of here."

"The problem is that there isn't anyplace in the city for them to go." Zeb leaned against the archway to the kitchen. "Like a safe house."

"Well, Quinn can't take 'em all in. Do you even have a bed for this one?" Jamie jerked a thumb toward the ceiling.

The doorbell rang, and Quinn pushed to his feet. "We can handle it." He paused to rest his hands on Eli's shoulders for a moment, then went into the hall.

"I'll get napkins." Eli shoved back from the table, glaring at Jamie.

Silver followed Eli into the kitchen, pausing to whisper, "Don't take off, okay?" to Zeb. As Silver opened the fridge, he asked Eli, "Beer or soda?"

"His Royal Asshattedness can deal with iced tea."
Eli got down some glasses.

"Um. Thanks. For bailing out Marco like that."

"Quinn did it. I had no idea what the fuck we were
going to do." Eli leaned his back against the counter
and shoved his bangs out of his face. "He gets kind
of—I think he's trying to help me, back then? Not that
it makes any sense."

Since Silver wondered if Zeb had been doing the
same thing when he got in Timo's face, it did. But
explaining that to Eli was too complicated, so Silver
nodded.

Eli sighed. "Man, can you imagine if we'd had a
place like that to go to instead?"

"A place like what?" Silver stepped around him.
"Plates?"

"Yeah. A place like Zeb said. For queer kids with
no place else to go."

Was that what Zeb was talking about? Silver must
have missed that part of the conversation.

"Sounds like more social workers. And what if
the kids' parents try to get them back?"

"Zeb says they have them in other cities. There
must be a way. That would be tons better than the
shithole where we met."

"I guess." Silver thought it sounded epically
delusional.

"I take it I missed some excitement," Gavin said
from the doorway.

"Gavin." Eli bounced over and kissed him. "We
thought you were the pizza guy."

"Sorry to disappoint."

"You? Never."

Gavin picked up a couple of the glasses from the counter but didn't take them anywhere. "Where did you two meet?"

Eli shuddered. "Homeless shelter. It was January, cold as fuck, and the place was packed. Everyone screaming, babies, winos, crazy people."

"Trading a blow job to fat and bald for a sweaty twenty and a hotel room looked pretty damned good after that," Silver said.

"A Scylla or Charybdis decision." Gavin nodded. Then saved Silver from asking if those were STDs by explaining, "Mythological monsters. There should be some other option."

"Tell me about it." Silver carried the plates and napkins out to the big table.

"I got an old air mattress. I'll bring it over for you," Jamie was saying to Quinn as they came in.

Zeb still hadn't claimed a seat, so Silver joined him in leaning near the kitchen door. "Great. Drive safe." Eli thunked the pitcher of iced tea on the table. "We'll save you some pizza."

"I meant—" Jamie slung an arm around the back of his chair and looked up. Whatever he saw on Eli's face had him sputtering. "C'mon, kid—Eli. Are you serious?" Jamie glanced around like someone was going to bail him out. "All the way to Dundalk and back?"

"Use your lights," Eli suggested.

Jamie stood and kicked his chair back, scrubbing a hand across his face. "Look, what I said about staying closeted—"

"It's fine." Eli smiled, but it was mostly teeth. "Or it will be when you get back here with that air mattress."

Jamie growled deep in his chest but started for the door.

Gavin raised a hand in goodbye.

Jamie turned back, grabbed Gavin, and kissed him hard and long. "Wish you'd been here earlier."

"I doubt my influence extends to keeping your foot out of your mouth." Gavin put a hand on Jamie's face.

"Maybe not, but you give me something else to do with my mouth." Jamie winked, and they were kissing again.

Zeb's hand landed on the small of Silver's back, fingers wide, palm a warm, solid weight. He wondered if Zeb had spent time around other couples. It had been something Silver had seen in the bars, but it had taken some getting used to around Eli and Quinn, the way they kissed and touched, not just before fucking but all the time, in front of other people, comfort and connection in every brush of fingers or lips.

"Maybe there won't be any pizza left," Eli said loudly.

"I'm going, princess." Jamie saluted and left, the door closing with a muted *thud*, then popping back open.

"Pizza guy's here," Jamie called, then shut the door again.

"You guys gonna sit or stand around all night?" Eli said as Quinn went to the door. Silver thought about stealing Jamie's chair but shifted down so he and Zeb faced Gavin.

Eli plunked himself at the opposite end from Quinn, who came back and slid the pizza to the middle, like it was some kind of choreographed dance.

Silver didn't know why that irritated him tonight. "For someone as heterophobic as you, you do a great imitation of Mr. and Mrs. Suburbia."

"Which might bother me except for where I have a dick and Quinn likes to suck it while also having a dick of his own." Eli flipped open the lid and scooped out a piece from the sixteen-cut. "And it feels pretty damned queer with his dick up my ass."

Quinn shook his head and then gave Eli a crooked smile. Eli toasted him with his pizza.

"What is the stick up yours?" Eli said to Silver. "Or is it that there isn't anything up yours with your date being screwed up?"

"Shit, Eli." Silver couldn't believe how hot his cheeks got. He dropped the slice he'd just grabbed. Talking about it with Zeb sitting right there was a whole lot more personal than anything he'd done on camera for who knows how many guys to jerk off to.

"What?" Eli licked cheese and sauce off his chin. "Since when do you get embarrassed about sex?" He glanced over at Zeb. "Oops. Is it a religious thing? No offense."

"None taken." Zeb pulled a piece of pizza from the box.

Without giving Zeb a chance to answer, Eli said, "Or... oh. You're not doing it. Sorry." He looked like he meant it. Then he said, "Well, when Jamie gets back with the air mattress—"

"For fuck's sake, Eli." Silver was so very sorry he'd brought it up.

Eli grinned. "I thought you were feeling stifled by the imitation heterosexuality. I mean, I wouldn't want Marco to have bad role models."

"I doubt he could have better," Zeb said.

Surprised in the act of stuffing his face, Eli had to swallow before he answered. "Are you blowing smoke up my ass?"

Zeb seemed to consider it. "I wouldn't dream of it."

Eli laughed. "Well, I wouldn't go that far. It'd still be better if there was a place like you said they have in other cities."

"What's that?" Gavin leaned forward.

Eli had taken a break to eat again, so Silver got a chance to answer. "Zeb was talking about how there's no place in Baltimore for gay kids who get tossed out. But other places have them."

"I looked up New York and Los Angeles," Zeb explained. "They offer meals, emergency beds, and other kinds of housing along with medical care and case management."

Social workers. Always a catch. But Silver thought of that kid, Eddie, ready to knife someone over the possibility of a trick. After swallowing a mouthful of pizza, he asked, "How old?"

Zeb pulled out his little notebook. "Ages twelve to twenty-four in LA, sixteen to twenty-four in New York."

"Probably has to do with state agencies like Child Protective Services, what they're willing to sign off on. They'd want to keep their piece of the pie." For a guy who never had to worry about a meal or a bed, Gavin seemed to know a lot about it. "But there are always workarounds in Baltimore. Once the immediate need and solution is identified, there are ways to get things done."

Eli reached for another slice. "Immediate need is sleeping upstairs. I'm open to solutions."

"What would have been the most immediate need to you back then?"

"Shower and a bed," Silver said right as Eli said, "A bed and clean clothes."

"Meals?" Gavin asked.

"Yeah, but those were a lot easier to come by than a bed."

Silver thought of the clinic. He'd gotten his test because a guy he'd seen a bunch of times out in front of it offered him ten bucks if he took it and came back for the results and one counseling session.

"Still might not get people to come in, though. I left the one shelter because I figured they'd track down my parents."

"So an element of trust is required. Spreading the word that it's a safe haven." Gavin nodded.

"And medical care. I'm not saying give the kids an HIV test when they come in, because they won't stay, but yeah. Eventually you'd need that." Silver thought of Eddie again, the scar on Tanner's face. "Some might come in fucked-up, beaten, or cut."

Eli was leaning forward in excitement, as if someone had really put him in charge of this made-up shelter. "Fed, healthy, and off the streets. Then what?"

"If they're as young as twelve, there's still a lot of school left," Zeb pointed out.

"And if not, a GED," Quinn added.

Silver managed to keep from rolling his eyes as he gnawed on his crust.

Zeb must have seen the aborted frustration because he put a hand on Silver's thigh. "Job or higher education, with transitional housing."

"What the fuck is transitional housing?" Eli said.

"It's partially supervised and subsidized, where someone comes to check to see if you need help," Zeb said. The guy had really done his research.

"And makes sure you're following all their rules," Silver added.

It had started off interesting, but now the whole thing was making him a little crazy. It might be fun for the rest of them to get riled up about some wild idea, but not Silver. It cut far too close to where Silver kept his wishes and what-ifs. Life was a lot easier when he didn't get his hopes up.

"Couple blocks from the bars? What do you think, Silver?" Eli's question dragged Silver back to their fantasyland.

"Huh?"

Zeb rubbed Silver's thigh. Not in a wish-we-were-alone way. More like he was trying to calm Silver.

"Where would be a good place for the shelter? Where would it get more drop-ins?" Eli said.

"Between the bars and the Greyhound bus stop. Or near a metro line." Silver squeezed Zeb's hand, then got up, grabbing the pizza box. "You guys done? I'll wrap the rest of this up for Marco and Jamie."

After a round of nods, Silver carried it into the kitchen, hearing Zeb say, "A wardrobe or something where kids could get fresh clothes or find stuff to wear on job interviews would be good too."

Maybe Zeb hadn't picked up on Silver's mood after all. Wishful thinking. It was fucked.

"I'd be great at that," Eli said.

"They might not all have your flair." Quinn's voice was amused.

Silver went back and forth clearing the table while the rest of them made lists of what the shelter should have first. Good thing Marco was upstairs sleeping instead of sitting around the table getting his head gassed up on dreams.

The counters were wiped, the dishwasher loaded, and still they yammered on. Silver banged out through the back door.

It smelled like thunder outside, but there wasn't much of a breeze. The clouds made it look closer to dark than it was. Silver swatted a mosquito as he sat in one of Eli's swivel chairs and twisted back and forth.

The anger burning Silver's throat was familiar, but the target wasn't. Not his useless parents, not Zeb for turning away. More at himself. He'd had more choices than he knew, but he hadn't wanted to look. Maybe not something as perfect as the dream house they were busy building on Eli's phone and in Zeb's tiny notebook. But he'd been so angry, he hadn't wanted any help. Maybe those assholes at Path to Glory had brainwashed him into believing he deserved to suffer. Or maybe he'd just been pathetic enough to punish himself for them.

He heard the kitchen door but kept swiveling back and forth, staring at the tops of his Chucks. It didn't matter who he hoped it would be. It would be whoever it was.

"We're missing your valuable input." Gavin settled himself in another chair.

Silver only heard the action, engrossed in observing the marks on the rubber-covered toes. How had they lasted this long? He'd whined about the right brand back when his mom had bought them almost four years ago. He'd had no idea what they'd see him through. Guess they were pretty good kicks. They were fraying here and there, and his toes left bumps in the rubber, but they still worked.

"I'm doing this, Silver. I can make it happen."

Silver snapped his head up to look at Gavin. There could only be one thing he was talking about.

Gavin nodded. "I've worked enough charity boards for museums and nature conservancies." His tight-lipped smile offered an apology. "I know how to get funding, what arms to twist, and who to flatter for permits." He stopped and looked directly into Silver's eyes. "This is something I believe in. I'm good at what I do. But you know what the needs really are. I hope I can rely on you for that input."

Silver managed to swallow the confusing mess of shame and pride and nod back.

"I regret it won't be fast enough to help Marco, and I'm sorry it wasn't in place to help you."

Silver finally had enough control of his voice. "Why?"

"Not only do I think you'd be of incalculable value to the project, but if you'll forgive me being mawkish, you are its inspiration."

Silver shook his head. He was very definitely not an inspiration.

"I recognized something of myself in you when I met you. With a less fortunate birth, I might have found myself in similar circumstance."

"I doubt it," Silver said.

"A good thing too. As I've come to know you better, I realize you have an inner strength I could only hope to emulate in your situation."

Silver remembered Zeb saying *I've always seen something amazing in you, Silver, like a light to draw me in*.

"Can I count on you to make sure this is done right?" Gavin lowered his gaze.

"Yeah." Silver snorted a laugh. "I can see why you're good at the arm-twisting and flattery. How much of that was bullshit?"

Gavin's eyes held an answering laugh. "Less than ten percent, I assure you."

"Isn't your boyfriend going to have something to say about it?"

"I'm sure he'll have a lot to say on the subject. But I think he will find himself backing the plan with his usual intensity."

Silver recognized Zeb's silhouette the instant it appeared in the kitchen door. He came down the steps. "I thought you had gone up to check on Marco until he came down."

"How is he?" Gavin asked.

"Hungry enough to finish off the pizza." Zeb stood behind Silver's chair.

Silver had no trouble recognizing the next silhouette either. Jamie banged through the door and out into the twilight.

He folded his arms on the back of Gavin's chair. "So. I hear you've found a new cause."

Gavin tipped his head back. "I have."

"Won't the dwarf wedge mussel people miss you?" Jamie stared down. The two of them might as well have been alone for all the attention Jamie spared for anyone not named Gavin.

"I spare no appreciation for such a noble crustacean, but I'd like to do something with personal meaning."

"Thought you were."

Gavin frowned.

"The hospice," Jamie explained.

"I'll still be doing that."

"Not surprised." Jamie leaned down to kiss him, Spider-Man style. "Come on. That kid ate all the rest of the pizza. You fill me in while I fill up at a drive-thru." He pulled Gavin up out of the chair and started for the driveway before turning back with a typical Jamie exit line. "Enjoy the air mattress. It's a single."

Zeb wasn't touching Silver, but he felt Zeb everywhere. The grip of his fingers over the back of the chair, the sound of his breath over the cricket chirps, and most of all the solid warmth of him, welcome even in the sticky air. A blend of steady reassurance and tingling awareness. It was something he'd like the chance to get used to.

"Sorry we didn't make the movie." Zeb's words felt weighted like the air.

Silver was too. And then he was surprised at how sharp the regret was. A longing that hollowed his gut and was about so much more than a lame movie. Straight people could take dating for granted. No wonder queers either fucked and moved on or moved in. When were they supposed to learn how to date when being out together in the wrong place at the wrong time could get them beaten up? Eli's heterophobia made a lot of sense.

"Yeah. Maybe I'm not cut out for dating." Or moving in, according to Quinn. Not that Zeb had asked.

Was sneaking around—more than only the lie about his age—what had made it so easy for it to fall apart? Even Marco now had a chance to fall in love the first time in the open, with people who would understand.

Silver stretched his legs out. "Thanks for helping out with Marco. Getting in his brother's face like that." He paused, staring at a spider scuttling along the table edge. "I know you did it for me." What the hell. Might as well put the whole thing out there. It didn't look like they were going to be having sex anytime soon. "And I know it's because you're still riding the guilt train." It was the truth. He wanted to know if Zeb knew it too.

Zeb stepped around the chair and stood between Silver's legs before leaning back against the table. The spider made it by an inch.

A boat-shoe-covered toe nudged at Silver's ankle until he looked up to Zeb's face. "I did do it for you. For a second I was ready to throw a punch at him for shoving you. And yes, I'm always going to wish I could go back and fix that night, but that isn't why I wanted to protect Marco. I wanted to show you that I've changed."

"How do you mean?"

"I had a lot of shame back then. About being gay."

"And that wasn't shame when you let my parents call you a pedophile?" The first rumble of thunder was only a vibration down in the bones of Silver's ears, a low, deep warning. He expected Zeb to look away, but he didn't.

"Even then. I thought letting them confront me was something I owed them. It was a mistake. But I'm changing. I'm learning from men like Eli and Jamie and Quinn and Gavin. And you."

Silver slumped back in his chair. The sky had gone deep twilight with clouds. "Yeah, well, stick to Gavin as a role model."

"He seems to think just as highly of you."

"Jealous again?"

"No. It would be impossible not to like him."

If Silver didn't know how dark and deep Gavin's cynicism ran, the guy would be perfect for Zeb. Polished. Smart. Undamaged.

"You should be with someone like him. A nice guy."

"I want to be."

Zeb's easy agreement slammed into Silver's chest, knocking the wind out of him.

Good thing he was already sitting down.

Zeb leaned forward, his hands bracketing Silver's neck where it rested against the chair. "You *are* a nice guy."

Silver wanted to brush the praise away, force the reality that nice guys in Zeb's world didn't do bareback porn just to stay off the street.

Zeb loomed closer, hands on Silver's shoulders. "No, screw that. I've had nice guys. I've dated and taken my time before ending up in bed with them." Silver's skin prickled with gooseflesh.

Zeb's hands moved onto Silver's shoulders, intensifying the charge racing through his body. "None of them made me crazy. None of them made me feel like I couldn't breathe right until we kissed. None of them made my whole body hum with the need to touch. You do." Zeb's grip shifted to Silver's forearms and pulled him to his feet. "You turned my life upside down, and I couldn't put it back together in any way that made sense without you."

Silver wanted to believe him, believe in what kept driving them together, that this halo of electricity around them could somehow make everything all right again. But in the meantime…. He swallowed back the spark of tears in his throat. In the meantime, they were kissing.

He tangled his fingers in Zeb's hair, keeping him leashed to an exchange of breath and taste. Zeb parted his lips, drew Silver's tongue inside. The groan that met him, the hands that dragged his hips forward, whether their connection was special or not, Silver knew what Zeb was asking, even before he tore his mouth free to whisper, "I want you inside me."

Chapter Twenty-One

SILVER KNEW he should say something back. Something real about his feelings, about having missed this for too long. But with his cock draining the blood from his brain, he could only grab Zeb's ass through his khakis and mumble, "Okay."

The sky opened with a solid crack that stunned Silver's senses like a shot to the back of the head. The instant his heart started again, rain drowned them in an inverted ocean.

Inside the lighted house were towels and safety—and questions and decisions and delays.

Silver grabbed Zeb's hand and ran for the garage, kicked open the side door, and then sealed them inside. He didn't want time to think, for uncertainty to seep in and wash away how right everything had felt a minute ago. He stripped off his shirt and tossed it. Zeb did the same before they slammed together, mouths and fingers frantic, like they had to find a way into each other.

Silver couldn't get enough of the rain taste and ozone smell on Zeb's skin. Sweeter than fresh laundry and shower water, carrying a rush and threat of energy from the storm, it drowned out the moldy-leaf-and-oil odor hanging in the close air. Everything was sharper, burned hotter under clammy skin. Silver raked his teeth across Zeb's nipple, squeezed his ass through the soggy cotton.

"Yes." Zeb groaned it into Silver's ear, hot breath on hair standing on end. "Now, now, now, now." Zeb tore at the front of Silver's shorts, impatient fingers yanking the rivet out of the button.

Zeb went to his knees to deal with the rest of the barriers, not even bothering with the boxer briefs as he pulled Silver's dick through the slit and into scalding-wet heat.

The contrast of mouth with dank, clinging clothes made Silver jump, hips flexing back and forth. Zeb gasped and sputtered, and it took every bit of control Silver had left not to force his way in, make that muscle convulse around the head of his cock as Zeb fought for breath. After a moment Silver eased back, rubbing the head across Zeb's lips, while Zeb's tongue tried to recapture him.

With a floundering hand, Silver found the light switch. One glance at the floor made Silver haul Zeb up and steer him toward the workbench. It was only few steps, but in the space of those seconds Silver's chest got tight, an anxious wave threatening to flood his brain with a million doubts and questions.

Zeb spun back and kissed him, and there was some proof to Zeb's earlier words. The kiss fed Silver fresh oxygen, sharp as a winter rush of it when you

surrender to need over warmth and peel the scarf from
your face. He clung to Zeb's shoulders, their hair dripping rain into the kiss.

Zeb wriggled a little, and then his slacks brushed
damp and heavy over Silver's legs on the way to the
floor. Grabbing Silver's hand, Zeb shoved a condom
and a small lube packet into his palm.

"What kind of movie were you planning on?" Silver asked against the prickle of Zeb's jaw.

Zeb's breath came out in a huff, and he lifted his
head to give Silver better access. "Anything that got
us here."

As Silver reached forward to put the condom and
lube on the bench, Zeb turned away, hands braced
wide on the plywood, lean back and muscular ass on
display. Silver ran a hand down Zeb's spine. Drops of
water from his hair sparkled as they found paths along
that length. Silver lapped one with his tongue, and
then followed another all the way down, until his lips
rested in a silky patch of hair at the top of Zeb's ass.
They'd tried a lot of new things together in those six
months. But not this. A teasing flick of Silver's tongue
made Zeb groan and arch his back.

A flash lit up everything like one of Eli's polar-
ized images, and then a shock wave of thunder shook
the building, the echoes and rumbles lasting another
minute. After another blast that shook the windows,
the bare light bulb popped and went out.

When Silver's hearing came back, the rain was a
solid wall of sound until Zeb's harsh plea came out of
the dark. "Don't stop."

Silver licked the little indentation. "I think I can
find my way by feel."

Spreading Zeb's cheeks, Silver swiped the crease with his tongue. The muscles under his hands quivered. Another lap, wetter, a long, flat press against the hole. It was hard to tell if Zeb's shocked gasp being audible over the rain meant that he'd never been rimmed or that he really liked it.

Pushing down on Zeb's back got his ass up higher. Silver stopped teasing and focused his licks on the tight space he wanted into, breathing in Zeb's sweat, his ass, all of it flavored by the cool rain. The taste was almost like his cock and balls, but darker, more intense. Zeb's legs shook, and Silver wrapped one arm around Zeb's hips to keep him steady. Silver moved his mouth like in a kiss, darting just the tip of his tongue inside, the muscle shifting and twitching in response.

Zeb's ragged breathing reached Silver over the rain, changes in length and pitch helping guide him on how much, how far to push. Zeb's ass was soft and open, breaths deep when Silver kissed and sucked. The stab of his tongue made Zeb shake, his breath almost a whine.

Wetting a finger, Silver used it next to his tongue, humming and licking until the pressure eased enough to slide it in. He dropped to his knees so his mouth could reach the smooth skin right behind Zeb's balls, then ran his tongue over the sac, drawing one and then the other in his mouth while fucking with his finger.

"God, Silver, please." The drawn-out last syllable disappeared in another blast of thunder.

Zeb's pleading and the burst of electricity drenched Silver in power, confidence. Blood rushed everywhere, hot and full and loose like he'd had a hit of amyl. Silver flowed up Zeb's back, lips below his ear. He pressed a second finger to Zeb's hole, rubbed, then pushed the tip in.

"Please."

"Please what?"

He didn't know which of them liked it more. Zeb being forced to say it, or Silver hearing the filthy words from Zeb's mouth.

"Fuck me. Please fuck me."

Silver did his own groaning when he had to tuck his cock back in to get those too-fucking-tight boxer briefs down his legs. Slapping his hand around on the plywood, he picked up a sliver and finally the lube and condom.

Another moan from Zeb distracted Silver enough that he forgot to worry about how his cock would react to the latex sheath until it was already rolled down to the base. It felt a little weird coating it with lube, the slick glide on his hand but not feeling it on the skin, like trying to jack a mirror image of his cock.

He used every last bit of the lube on his fingers and around Zeb's hole, working it inside him as his back bowed and he pushed up.

"Fuck. Now."

Silver grabbed Zeb's circling hips and held him steady, using the other hand to line them up.

He'd thought the condom would make things harder. But in the pitch-black with nothing but the feel of their bodies and the sound of Zeb's breath to guide him, Silver was even more aware of the pulse and twitch of muscle that told him how fast to go and when to back off.

He sank in, only the head, and then the clamp of muscles telling him too much, too soon. He eased out and smoothed a hand down Zeb's back and over his hip. Rubbing the tip over Zeb's hole, Silver felt Zeb relax again, ass softening enough to let Silver in. Another breath as he waited for the pulse and softening that would let him slide home.

Then he was in deep. Everything hot and tight and pulsing around him. Zeb so perfect around Silver's cock. Clenching on him, shaking under him. Sucking air in such quick breaths that Silver found himself echoing the rhythm.

In the back of Silver's mind, a tiny alarm shrilled. There was something he was supposed to be worried about, something he had to be careful with, but with his belly pressed against Zeb's back, balls brushing Zeb's, it was all Silver could do to hang on against the need to fuck. To drive in hard and deep until his balls emptied.

The pressure eased, and Silver shifted his hips, making more room inside Zeb's body.

Zeb's breathing slowed. "So good. You feel so good in me."

Silver started a slow rolling motion, but Zeb's hand came down on Silver's where it rested on Zeb's hip.

"Just fuck me."

Silver nodded against Zeb's back, snaking an arm under his chest, wrapping his hand around the opposite shoulder for leverage. He pulled almost all the way out and slammed back in. Zeb's hand tightened on Silver's.

They blew out a simultaneous breath. "Yes."

It didn't matter how long it had been. This was as easy and as impossibly good as the first time. So good Silver was afraid he was going to come almost as fast as he had then. Pressure, exquisite rippling friction, gripped his cock along every inch, clinging, milking him with every thrust. The heat inside him ramped up a thousand degrees. He needed Zeb just as out of his mind.

Using the grip on Zeb's shoulder, Silver shifted them, rocking a little side to side, until he heard the gasp that told him he had the angle he needed. He lowered his head to Zeb's shoulder and pumped his hips.

A final squeeze and Zeb's hand was gone. Silver's ears strained to hear the slap and slide of Zeb's hand on his cock. It was Silver's turn to beg. He fucked as hard and fast as he could, but the more he tried to drive Zeb over, the closer Silver got to the edge. He held it back, internal muscles almost cramping with the effort.

"Come for me." Silver turned his head, lips brushing Zeb's hair. "Want to feel you come around my dick."

Zeb bucked forward, body jerking like he was pile-driving an ass under him. Silver put his mouth on Zeb's collarbone, sucking a small bite into it.

He gasped and shuddered, ass suddenly soft before it locked down hard, pulses constricting around Silver's cock, pumping him up and over the edge. He let himself go over. A few hard pumps of his hips and then he slammed deep, filling Zeb's ass with come.

A wave of panic brought him back to earth. No. The condom. It was still there. He flooded the condom. His infected spunk was safely contained. Gripping the base to keep it on, he pulled out of Zeb's ass.

Zeb tensed, grunted, then looked over his shoulder, eyes glittering in the dark. "What—oh."

Silver pinched the tip and stripped the latex off his dick. Since his brain was no longer hijacked by his dick, he was starting to think dragging Zeb in here probably hadn't been the best plan.

"Silver?"

He stepped back toward Zeb, dropping the condom on the workbench and putting his other hand on Zeb's shoulder. The wood chip in his middle finger slid in deeper. "Hope you didn't get slivers. Guess this wasn't—maybe we should have—"

"I came so hard I thought the top of my head would blow off." Zeb turned and wrapped his arms around Silver's waist. "Nothing could get through the skin on these hands." With a squeeze, Zeb added, "And we had the bed and the candles last time."

Silver's laugh was barely more than a hard breath. "Yeah, we did."

Zeb put his hand on Silver's cheek. "And I've never felt closer to anyone than I do right now."

"But it's always going to be complicated." Silver gestured in the direction of the condom. "Even if you fuck me, you'd have to wear one."

"Maybe we could just focus on what we do have. What we've found again." Zeb's hand fell away. "Unless I'm the only one feeling like that."

"No." Silver rested his forehead on Zeb's shoulder. "You're not the only one."

Pulling wet pants back up over recently swollen body parts made for a really uncomfortable trip back into the house. Silver tried switching on the kitchen light, forgetting the power was out. He patted his way through the kitchen to the bathroom to flush the condom. He'd half expected Eli to pounce as soon as they hit the kitchen door, but he and Quinn and Marco were lying in wait, Marco on the air mattress, in the living room.

"Thought maybe you got washed away." Eli glanced up from the tablet, face reflecting in blue and white.

"We were in the garage." Silver shivered. The AC wasn't running, but the house was still cool enough to chill his wet skin.

"I know. I saw the light when I went to check."

"Was your *date* good?" Marco tipped his flashlight in their direction. "Eli told me you'd had plans tonight."

"Seriously?" Silver didn't know who he was more exasperated with, Eli or Marco or himself for giving them so much ammunition. His boxer briefs were tucked in the front pocket of his cargo shorts, and he hadn't bothered with a shirt. Zeb looked even more... fucked. Untucked, stained shirt and wrinkled slacks.

"Let me have that for a minute." Silver yanked the flashlight away from Marco. To Zeb, Silver said, "C'mon," and started for the stairs. Dealing with the Inquisition would be easier after they cleaned up.

Zeb pulled Silver back. "Uh."

"What?"

"I can't stay."

They had to do this with a fucking audience? Silver backed Zeb toward the dining room.

"I don't have another change of clothes. And these are—"

"Trashed," Silver finished for him.

"I'd invite you home with me, but...."

Silver nodded. He didn't want to hassle with Quinn and his overdeveloped sense of responsibility. Plus there was Marco. He was only there because of Silver. It wasn't exactly fair to stick Eli and Quinn with babysitting duties.

"When's your next night off?" Zeb asked.

"The day after forever? I don't know. I'll see the new schedule tomorrow. And text you."

Silver wasn't sure who moved first, but the space between them disappeared, foreheads pressed together, arms around each other's waist. Not kissing, but sharing breath.

"Name the time and I'll be there." Zeb's hands rested on the base of Silver's spine, one stacked over the other, hot on his cold skin.

He wanted to believe in that touch, like he wanted to believe in the promise. "I go in front of the judge a week from today. The sixteenth. I'd like you to be there."

"What time?"

"One o'clock."

"I'll be there." Zeb's prompt answer didn't seem possible. Silver knew the last day of school was June 18. Quinn had been counting it down on the kitchen calendar.

Silver didn't know he'd leaned back until he realized he was searching Zeb's eyes for the truth.

"It's another assessment day. The kids are gone by eleven forty-five. I'm supposed to be there, but as long as my paperwork is done, I can get it off."

Silver nodded, and Zeb kissed him. "You're not going to jail."

Silver didn't trust his voice, so he nodded again.

Zeb tipped up Silver's chin. Like in the garage, the kiss gave him the air his tight lungs wouldn't let him have.

Silver stepped back sooner than he wanted to. "I'll go get your stuff from upstairs."

"It's right here." Zeb pointed the flashlight at the laptop bag in the corner of the dining room.

"Right."

Nothing felt right. Zeb might feel like finding each other again put his life back together, but as far as Silver was concerned, all the pieces were still up in the air.

Quinn met them in the hall and took the flashlight from Silver. "I'll walk you out."

None of it was Quinn's fault, but with potentially a week left of freedom, this whole setup felt like a leash around Silver's neck. Was he really going to spend it going to work and studying for some stupid test?

He stood at the open door as Quinn and Zeb went down the steps through the steady rain. "Don't take the Daddy role so seriously, Quinn. It's not like I was a virgin."

Eli came up behind Silver. "I think he's kind of worried Marco's brother might show up again. Told me to not go anywhere alone for a while. Like I can't take care of myself."

Silver heard the eye roll in Eli's voice. Zeb turned back for a second, shaking his head and smiling.

As the possibility Silver was just starting to put some hope in got in the car, his brand-new responsibility came up and bit him in the ass.

"How old were you when you weren't a virgin?" Marco asked, holding another flashlight.

Silver knew how Marco would react to the answer but admitted the truth anyway. "Seventeen. But not for lack of trying a lot sooner."

Marco sighed then turned the light on Eli's face. "Fifteen, but we're not talking about it."

Marco frowned.

Silver put a hand on Marco's shoulder. "I guess we need to get you a phone. And some clothes. How long are your classes paid for?"

"I don't know."

Silver hoped it was the way the flashlight made shadows that put the haunted look in Marco's eyes.

"We'll go to the college and talk to them."

"We'd better start early, then," Eli said. When Silver looked at him, Eli added, "You said clothes. And this will make Quinn happy while I be your bodyguard. Nine o'clock?" At least it would keep him from obsessing over how many days of freedom he might have left. And it would be nice making sure Marco had things a little easier than Eli or Silver had.

"Yeah. That's fine."

Chapter Twenty-Two

OUTFITTING MARCO with a few basics was more fun than Silver had expected. Free to be himself, Marco felt less like a responsibility and more like a friend again. Silver and Eli split the costs of a couple changes of clothes and a prepaid phone with one hundred minutes on it. When Eli found a pair of alarmingly tight and tiny shorts for Marco and announced they'd be perfect for Pride, Marco's delight at realizing he'd be able to go made Silver sorry he'd miss seeing it. Being in Mount Vernon meant the restaurant was packed all day during Pride.

Marco went from bouncy to pinging off the walls when the trip to the Bursar's Office let him know his fall classes had already been paid for. Silver tucked the big packet of financial-aid information into his backpack.

"I don't need to pay again until November," Marco pointed out, as if the money would magically appear by then.

Of course, despite Marco's obliviousness, Silver didn't have grounds for criticism. Marco had been homeless for less than a day, and he still knew more about his future than Silver. Until less than a month ago, Silver hadn't really believed he had one.

"After your friend's shelter opens, I can move in there."

Eli's eyes met Silver's. "That might not be for a while. But we'll manage something."

Marco nodded, smile still bright. He had complete trust in Eli. And why not? If it weren't for Eli—

"C'mon." Silver steered them east. "I owe you another freaky ice cream."

"You owe me a hell of a lot more than that. But we can start with some ice cream." Eli winked.

SILVER'S WORK schedule was perfect. That is, for someone trying to save up enough money to cover the first, last, and security on an apartment. For someone who wanted to spend maximum time with his sort-of boyfriend before he left for six weeks or indefinitely, the schedule sucked. He had the Monday of Doom—otherwise known as his court date—off, having made it clear he had an appointment he couldn't miss. But that was it—until after Zeb was gone. He had a call out to the other waiters and had offered to take any weekend shift Kaivon didn't want for the entire summer to be able to leave by four on the day before Zeb left.

Figuring Marco's endless questions were probably making it hard for Eli to get anything done, on

Thursday Silver brought Marco down with him to work. Marco had two summer school classes starting at three twenty. Quinn and Eli were going to drive down to pick him up to make sure Timo didn't cause any problems. They all must have reminded Marco three times each to call campus security if Timo showed up.

Seeing Marco peering at his laptop at a back corner table, Silver realized how much he'd been asking of Zeb when showing up that night on the run from Path to Glory. Full responsibility of someone not even legally able to vote. Food, clothes, school. If Zeb had taken him in, it wouldn't have been much of a relationship. Being dependent on Prince Charming for everything might have worked for Cinderella and Eli, but for Silver and Zeb, it would have been a disaster. Right now there was a chance to salvage things, assuming everything worked out on Monday.

His phone buzzed in his pocket, and he ducked into the toilet to answer it.

The *yeah* rising to his lips got substituted for a nervous *hello* when he saw the number. Did lawyers ever call with good news?

"Don't panic."

The lawyer's first words had the exact opposite effect. Obviously there was something to panic about.

"The court date has been rescheduled," the lawyer said.

"Why?" Because if everything was going to work out like people told him, no one would need more time.

"The Branson trial is taking longer than anticipated, so Judge Rosen's cases have been adjourned to

July. I'd rather wait and have her hear us than take our chances with a different judge."

"Okay." Not like it was up to Silver. That's what Gavin was paying this guy for, to make sure Silver had the best chance of not going to jail.

"You'll receive a criminal summons at the address you left with the court." The address he left with the court. As if Quinn would let that be a front.

"What's the new date?"

There was a crisp sound of pages turning. "July 14."

Another month of not knowing? Of waiting to so much as start to figure out if whatever he and Zeb had found again could turn into something like what Eli and Quinn had? Or Jamie and Gavin?

He'd been counting on having a decision before Zeb left. So they knew where they stood. Now he couldn't ask for anything. Had nothing to offer, not even the freedom to make his own decisions.

"I'm confident Judge Rosen will approve the plea bargain," the lawyer said into the long pause.

"Thanks for letting me know."

The lawyer clicked off.

In that moment, it felt like it was already over. He was standing up there, and they were going to take him away. Everyone saw through him. Saw how little it mattered what happened to him. A space between his shoulders burned as if all those eyes were peering into him. Seeing nothing.

He turned around. Marco was behind him. "Is—are you okay?"

"Yeah. I'm fine. But you should head back up so you aren't late for your class. You need anything?"

Marco held up his bus fare card.

"Right." Silver peeled off a bunch of ones from his tips. "Load it up."

"Thanks, *cuate*." Marco stood on his tiptoes and kissed Silver's cheek.

Silver started to issue another warning, but Marco rattled off, "Be careful, pay attention to everyone around me, and call security if Timo shows up to make trouble."

Silver nodded. Marco scooped his backpack off the table and waved as he slipped out the door.

There weren't many early diners. Kaivon came on at four, but they only had one table each at four thirty. Silver nodded at Kaivon to let him know he was taking a break as he went out through the kitchen to the alley.

He leaned against the wall and closed his eyes for a second while he thought about starting smoking. He probably would have to if he went to jail, to keep from going crazy. But he hated the taste.

Everything about it reminded him of the blow job he'd traded to get out of Path to Glory. And for the truck ride home. The clinging stench had lasted longer than the bitter taste in his mouth.

A familiar red Pontiac came down the alley. Silver met it as it stopped. "I was just going to text." Zeb leaned out his window.

Despite the smile on Zeb's face, Silver asked, "What's wrong?"

"Nothing. I know you don't get out until ten, but I wanted to see you."

Silver leaned in and kissed him. He hadn't meant for it to turn into anything, but before he knew it, the kiss was wet and hot and making it hard in more ways than one to think about going back in to hand out burgers.

Zeb's hands bracketed Silver's face as he pulled back. "What if I asked you to fuck me up against that wall?" His chin pointed toward the wall separating the restaurant's alley access from the pawn shop next door.

Silver crooked a half smile. "I'd ask if you were friends with Benjamin." Zeb's brow went bumpy in confusion.

Silver smoothed it with a thumb. "Got a hundred on you?"

"Oh. A hundred?"

"Well, in the daytime, I'd make you spring for a hotel. Too risky. Be lucky if we don't get arrested again just doing this." Though his black clothes and white apron identified him as a waiter, with the privilege of leaning in a car window to have a conversation. "You're off the hook on showing up for my court appearance, though."

Zeb had been stroking Silver's cheeks. Letting go, Zeb sat back, eyes wary. "For what?"

"My court date got moved to July. So you don't have to be there, since you won't be around, right?"

"Silver, I'm sorry. I made the commitment before I saw you again."

"I know." Silver looked down at his forearms folded on top of the door. The hairs stood up as the AC rushed out, summer sun turning them white.

"Do you want me to do something about it?"

Only the most selfish prick in the world would say *Please turn your back on a bunch of kids with cancer for me.* But was it awful to wish Zeb wanted to? That he'd at least say he'd rather stay?

Silver shook his head. "I've got to get back to work." He pushed himself away and tapped on the doorframe. "Thanks for coming down."

MONDAY, WHICH was supposed to hold all the answers, came and went. Silver didn't have to work that day, but Zeb did. He came to dinner, though, along with everyone else, since Eli had already purchased supplies in preparation for a Celebrating Silver's Freedom cookout.

Eli also handed off the tablet loaded with pictures he'd taken at Pride. Damn, he was good. Somehow Eli had managed to take shots capturing more than the way it looked, but the way it felt. Being queer and open and proud of it. Marco stood next to Quinn in those microscopic shorts, not facing into the camera, but with his eyes on something beyond it. The joy on his face was so apparent Silver felt an answering warmth in his own chest.

Zeb was in the next shot. Hair pulled back and a little off his neck, in a green T-shirt and black shorts. Relaxed, happy, wearing his real smile. Zeb at a Pride parade. Things did change. Silver doubted Zeb would have gone to the parade if it weren't for knowing Eli and Quinn—and not only because they gave him a ride.

Silver lowered the tablet to get a real-time look. Like a typical teacher, Zeb was talking with Marco about his classes. Silver tuned in to the neighboring conversation, where Nate grilled Gavin about his plans for the shelter. Kellan's exclamations of *awesome, man* made his opinions clear, but despite his casual tone, Nate was excited too. He didn't even have a fit when Kellan ate a real meat burger.

"It'll be better when it's the party for the right reason," Eli said as Silver handed over the tablet.

"Yeah. Thanks for…." He gave up and gestured. He wasn't exactly sure having committed a crime and not going to jail was something they should make a big deal of, but Eli loved making one anytime he could. Silver tapped the back of the tablet. "You're pretty fucking awesome at that."

"I am." Eli nodded. "Zeb staying tonight?"

"It's your house."

"It's your bed." Eli winked. "I was going to say it's your ass, but I realize that's not the case."

Party-cookout-whatever, Silver felt more comfortable acting like he was at work. He got the orders for cheese or no cheese, carried stuff in and out of the house, and made more sweet tea when they ran out. When the burgers hit the table, he slipped into the house, figuring he could get started on the dishes.

Detouring for a piss stop, he washed his hands and shook them dry. The heat and humidity always made the hair over his forehead do its very own Elvis impersonation. Pausing in the mirror, he smooshed it down with a wet hand, but it sprang back up.

"Fuck it," he muttered and yanked open the door.

Like they were back on the yacht, Zeb stood in front of the door.

Silver got caught up in staring at how green and gold Zeb's eyes looked right then and almost missed what he was waving between two fingers.

A hundred dollar bill.

Silver locked a hand around Zeb's wrist and pulled him inside.

Zeb laughed. "Not much more room than on the boat."

"Not much. Potentially a bigger audience, though."

"You raising the price?" Zeb's voice was still full of humor. "I'll expect a really good time."

Silver hadn't given much thought to a future boyfriend's opinions of his porn and hustling career. Neither Jason nor Austin had cared, and though Silver had been modeling by then, they knew about the other work. But anytime he'd thought about Zeb back then, Silver had pictured the disappointment and a little righteous disgust.

Not Zeb laughing while waving a Benjamin.

"You're getting a good time." Silver plucked the hundred out of Zeb's fingers, then stuffed it back in his front pocket, digging around his keys before claiming a quarter in exchange. "But I'm afraid it'll cost you this."

Zeb leaned in, hands sliding up under Silver's shirt. "A whole quarter, huh? You better be worth it."

"Oh, I am." Silver had Zeb's fly undone, shorts and boxers off and his cock in hand in less than a breath.

"Prove it."

Zeb was already half-hard, and Silver took him the rest of the way there. Thumbing the slit and smearing precome, he worked the spot right under the head until Zeb put a hand on the mirror to steady himself. His head dropped back, sharp pants coming from his throat. Silver licked along the bony line, feeling the vibrations under his skin. Scraping his teeth over Zeb's jaw, Silver made his way to an ear to murmur, "Up against the wall, wasn't it?"

His answer was mostly a moan, but there was an *uh-huh* in it somewhere.

"Kick your shorts off." Silver opened the cabinet, silently thanking his horny friends for keeping lube in multiple places. He'd made his own condom purchases earlier in the week.

Zeb leaned ass-out against the wall opposite the toilet. Silver took advantage of the position to tease and stretch Zeb's hole with a well-lubed thumb.

The muscle gave and then tightened closed around the base. Soft and hot and slick. Silver groaned.

Zeb let out a shaky breath.

Silver pumped his thumb in and out, watching the quiver in Zeb's back muscles, the way he dipped then arched his head in time to the movement of Silver's hand. Everything he'd missed in the dark garage.

It was going to be even better when he got to watch Zeb's face. Silver grabbed his hips and turned him around. Zeb's eyes widened. "Oh yeah, like this." Silver answer the unasked question.

Zeb bit his lip, and Silver leaned in to kiss it. "Don't worry. I'm a professional."

"How?" Zeb rested his hands on Silver's shoulders.

"Get one leg around my waist and I'll lift you."

Zeb nodded. He got one leg pretty high, making it easy to grab his ass and slide him farther up. Zeb wrapped his other leg around Silver's waist, fingers digging into his shoulders for balance.

"Now sink down onto my dick." Arching his back, Silver pressed up against Zeb's hole.

"You... didn't... say... I'd... uh... have... to... work." Zeb's words were sandwiched between gasps as he worked the head inside.

Silver adjusted his grip on Zeb's ass, holding him open. "Oh, sh-it." Zeb sank deeper.

Silver clenched his teeth and waited.

"Just do it. Fuck me," Zeb urged, ass squeezing Silver's cock and hands almost as tight on his shoulders. "Fuck me right through the wall."

Silver's brain shorted out for a second. The fist-like grip on his dick and Zeb groaning something so dirty sent Silver's hips slamming up and in. Zeb's moan was closer to a shout, his eyes popping open.

Silver froze.

Zeb's fingers dug in deeper. "Don't stop. It's just...." Now his voice went too soft to hear.

Silver leaned closer. "Tell me."

"Different like this. God."

"Yeah." Silver smiled. "Hang on." He drove his hips up harder, faster. Watching the shift of sensation in Zeb's face, hearing it in his moans, feeling it in the pressure from his fingers, his legs, and oh fuck, his ass, Silver was drowning in it. In him. Sweat on his lip, on Zeb's to lick off, the change in the angle making Zeb drop his head back into the wall with a solid thud.

His eyes blinked open, then closed, like he barely noticed. "It's so. God."

Silver knew. Suspended on a dick like that, your weight forcing it deeper, the angle making everything tight, endless pressure on the gland.

He watched it build in Zeb. The sharpness in his jaw, the painful squeeze of his shaking fingers.

Silver rolled his hips, the change in friction making them both groan.

Zeb's eyes opened wide again. Like he couldn't believe what was happening. Silver kept up the motion, and that sound was definitely a shout.

Zeb dropped a hand to his dick, but he was already shooting and sending thick, creamy ropes onto Silver's shirt, one glob landing up near his shoulder. Zeb kept shuddering and bucking after he was empty, knuckles grazing Silver's belly as Zeb stroked and soothed his dick.

Silver started to disentangle them, but Zeb tightened his legs. "No. Finish in me."

Silver wasn't going to argue it. Not when Zeb's ass was still pulsing tight and quick on Silver's cock.

He meant to go easy, didn't want to hurt him, but the twitch on Silver's cock was so damned sweet. The way the outer muscle fought against him on the way in made him lose his mind. He pistoned up, every flex of his ass as he drove in taking him higher, until another ragged groan from Zeb sent Silver over the top, pounding his last few strokes in as the orgasm pumped out of his dick, so hot and sugary good.

After they cleaned up and went back outside, Silver kept his arm around Zeb's waist, daring any of their friends to make a smart remark. Jamie's arched brows retreated when Silver gave him smug right back.

Eli laughed and shook his head. "I'll get the ice cream."

Marco put his head down on the table, covering it with his arms. "I really need a fuck."

Chapter Twenty-Three

SINCE QUINN didn't have to be at work at the ass crack of dawn, he was still hanging around a cup of coffee in the kitchen when Silver made it downstairs on Thursday morning.

Silver sat down across from him. "Zeb's driving out to the camp tomorrow."

Quinn closed the laptop he'd been using and regarded Silver over a mug. "He is."

"Does he have a job here next year?"

"Shouldn't you ask him that?"

"I did." Silver cooled his palms against the tabletop. "He said he did. As far as he knew."

"It's the only answer he can have until he gets tenured. They can cut him any time."

"That sucks."

Quinn nodded. "It does. But I think they like him. The kids did well on the assessments. No serious screaming from parents over grades. If he doesn't make a habit of getting arrested, he should be fine."

Silver rolled his eyes. "Right. 'Cause that's Zeb's style."

"He continually surprises me." Quinn knocked back a slug of coffee.

Silver took a deep breath. "So he's leaving. I'm getting out at four thirty today, and he's picking me up. And I'm going to spend the night there."

Quinn put his mug down but didn't say anything. He didn't have to. He had the whole teacher look going for him.

"I'm not going to take off. I know you take this court thing seriously. I won't fuck anything up."

Quinn leaned back. Silver waited him out. "Guess we'll see you tomorrow, then."

THE RIDE back up to Zeb's apartment was so quiet Silver started fiddling with the radio, alternating between any station not on commercial and the Christian rock CD Zeb had in the player. At the end of every song, Zeb made a sound like he was about to say something, but nothing ever came out. When he wasn't punching the buttons on the dash, Silver had to wipe his hands on his work slacks. The nervous flutter in his stomach that had started when he talked to Quinn over coffee had become a clanging alarm bell, the clapper swinging in time with the cross hanging from the rearview mirror.

There was a bunch of stuff to be said, worked out. But Silver wanted to skip all of it. Skip ahead to the part that didn't need any fixing. Where their bodies talked. Bodies, and at least on Silver's end of things, his heart too.

If Zeb thought Silver was going to start the conversation, the guy was out of his mind. No way was Silver risking ever feeling the way he'd felt that night again. No way was he going to ask—beg—for something and give Zeb the chance to tell him no. And working with kids with cancer was important. Silver got it, yeah, but Zeb should at least want *them* enough to say he didn't want to leave.

Instead, when the door of Zeb's little apartment closed, all he did was go to the kitchen and stare into the fridge. "Grilled cheese sound good?"

Silver took in the big duffel and professional-looking tall backpack lined up against the wall near the door. "Yeah. It's fine."

They had grilled cheese and canned tomato soup. But Silver left most of it uneaten. Living with Eli and Quinn had gotten Silver over the urge to stuff himself until he almost puked, a habit born out of not knowing when the next chance he'd have to fill up would be. Silver wasn't full now. But every minute that passed in silence felt like he was swallowing back volcanic rock to burn his throat and smolder in his stomach. He wiped greasy fingers off on his work slacks and pushed the food away.

"I'm sorry. I don't think I could ever measure up to Eli's cooking," Zeb said.

"It's okay. I should have said I had something at the restaurant after the lunch rush." *Should have said* made it not be a lie, right? Silver had been trying like hell not to give Zeb a reason to ever throw lying back

at him. Glancing over at the gear near the door, Silver
added, "So you do a lot of hiking at the camp?"

"They have a bunch of different programs for the
kids. Hiking, horseback riding, swimming, boating. I
like taking them out backpacking. They're surprised
at how much they can do."

"So you'll be coming back with supersexy muscled legs?" *You'll be coming back* being the part Silver
most wanted the answer to.

"I hope you'll think so."

Okay, so there was that. Zeb planning on coming
back and wanted Silver to still be interested.

Zeb put his hand over Silver's on the table. "It's
only six weeks. Quinn said he'd help if you had any
questions about the GED test."

Right. Because the GED was what was keeping
Silver up nights.

He'd had enough. Leaning forward, he grabbed
Zeb's shirt. "Let's go to bed." Zeb nodded.

But it wasn't anything like the first time Silver
had been here, when they'd been so hot for each other
they'd barely made it to the bed. For fuck's sake, they
stopped to brush their teeth, though it was only six
o'clock.

Silver watched Zeb tuck a few more things in a
toiletry bag.

"I'll have my phone." Zeb met Silver's eyes in the
mirror. "I don't know how much cell coverage there
is—not much if I remember correctly."

Since Silver wasn't going to hear the right answer
to the question he was too scared to ask, he decided he
didn't want to hear anything else but moans.

He pulled Zeb into the bedroom, pushed him onto the bed, and landed on top. Their kiss was full of fake mint at first. Then the toothpaste mask slipped away, and it was just them. The way Zeb kissed. The way he tasted. The way it was old and new at the same time.

Too much.

It wasn't fair, having this back only to lose it again so fast. Silver knew better than most people that life wasn't fair. That same knowing told him six weeks could change a hell of a lot.

He lifted his head, wanting to find the camera-lens distance that would insulate him from the cracks forming in his insides.

Rearing up, Silver focused on getting them out of their clothes efficiently and methodically, like the best of any Todd Pike Production. Zeb moaned and squirmed on cue. A tease of nipples and a light stroke on his cock had it throbbing in Silver's hand. Everything was going along, until a glimpse at that familiar face, the darkening of Zeb's eyes, dragged Silver back to where everything was raw, scraped feelings.

He barely stopped himself from shaking his head. Instead he braced himself on his hands to slide down Zeb's body. A blow job would keep them both distracted.

But Zeb captured Silver's face, freezing his movement. "What's wrong?"

"Nothing." Silver forced up a smile and tried to turn to kiss Zeb's fingers, but the grip was too strong to move without a struggle.

"It feels like you're not here."

"I'm about to suck your cock, Zebadiah. How much more here can I get?"

Instead of shoving Silver's head down with a *Don't let me stop you* like any guy not Zeb would, he pulled Silver close and kissed him.

All right. His mouth wasn't the only way to drive Zeb crazy. He shifted his hips, lining up their dicks and sliding them together. Zeb met his thrusts, groaning into Silver's mouth.

Zeb's hands gripped Silver's ass, urging him closer. Silver rocked them together, mouth sweeping along Zeb's jaw and up to his ear. "Can I suck your dick now?"

Zeb rolled them onto their sides, bringing a thumb up to rub across Silver's lips.

Silver added a little persuasion, tongue flicking out and then swirling over, finishing with a noisy suck down to the bottom knuckle.

Zeb threaded his free hand through Silver's hair, the soothing tingle of it making everything so much worse. "Is that all you want to ask me?" Zeb whispered.

"What the—Christ. Can't we just fuck?"

"Fine." Zeb's voice was flat. He pulled away and then settled himself belly-down on the mattress.

Silver reached out, but his hand froze in the air over Zeb's shoulder. Silver's fingers craved Zeb's warmth, the brush of skin that had somehow managed to make him feel safe for the first time since—

But his feet ached to hit the ground running. Take off. Safety was in getting as far away as fast as possible.

"Silver?" Zeb's voice was gentle.

Silver was afraid too much would spill out in answer, but his voice was deep and low, and thank God, steady. "I just—I want as much of you as I can get before you're gone."

Zeb rolled onto his side. "Okay." He ran his hand through Silver's hair. "Okay. You know, if I hadn't already signed on—"

"I know." Silver let out a sigh. It wasn't the I'll-stay-if-you-want-me-to he'd wanted to hear, but he'd take it. "I want you to fuck me."

Zeb's mouth twisted in a smile that did just as much twisting of Silver's insides. "Okay. I think I can handle it."

Silver had been fucked a lot. Like a thing bought and paid for. Like a pretty object arranged to the best angle. And back when he and Zeb had first done it, like Silver was a prize to be handled carefully.

Now, Zeb fucked him like a man.

Two fingers slicking and stretching, mouth making Silver twist and shift, chasing one sensation and then the other. Ripples of pleasure from his ass, tingling in his dick, a shivery echo of both when Zeb licked and sucked a bite into Silver's belly.

A bristly jaw brushed Silver's dick. "I'll come."

"That's the plan." Zeb's breath, hot and sticky on the head of Silver's cock, made him buck closer to Zeb's mouth.

Zeb gave him the torture of one long lick, mouth clamping over the head for a perfect shuddery moment that was over too soon, leaving Silver gasping.

Waiting for Zeb to roll the condom down seemed to take forever. When he knee-walked up, Silver hiked his legs into his chest. Zeb snugged his dick up close, but he didn't push in.

Silver looked at him, and Zeb gave him that crooked smile again. The one that meant he was laughing at himself. "Want to be kissing you when I go in."

Silver lifted his head off the mattress to meet Zeb's kiss. He didn't need the distraction, but Zeb did. He groaned the instant the tip pressed into Silver's ass. Curling up farther, he tried to capture Zeb's tongue and his dick.

"Fuck," Zeb whispered. His muscles trembled under Silver's palms. "Feel good on me."

Silver smiled into the kiss, earning a quick bite of his lower lip.

"Behave." Zeb's words were breathy. "I'm concentrating."

"It's not calculus." The in-between was a little uncomfortable, the way Zeb's dick got wider halfway down.

"You're not the only one who's trying to save up some memories," Zeb answered through gritted teeth.

Save them for what?

Silver might have asked it out loud, but then Zeb drove all the way in, a solid, warm shock against Silver's gland, a burn and ache from the stretch. Zeb stayed deep for a breath, kissing Silver with a firm, possessive mouth that made him want to ask for so much more than Zeb's cock to fill his body.

Silver moved first, and Zeb matched him, working them together. The friction turned from pain to the perfect stretch, nerves pulsing in an endless loop of pleasure.

Zeb gasped in his ear, and it felt like it could have come from Silver's throat, their bodies in complete sync.

Zeb clutched Silver's thighs, lifting his ass, then lowered his calves so they rested on Zeb's shoulders. It forced Silver tighter, pushed Zeb deeper, his constant stroke making Silver's dick pulse.

Zeb leaned down, eyes so intense it added to the shiver in Silver's belly. He reached for his dick. Zeb grabbed the headboard and nailed Silver to the mattress. There wasn't any other way to say it. And everything he'd promised himself about knowing it could be the last time and trying to last vanished in his need to come right the fuck now.

"Yeah, Jordie. Come for me."

Like he could stop. One more thrust, the right stroke on his dick, and it burst loose, hot and sharp, ripped from where their cocks seemed to connect on the downstroke. Then a bolt of it through his dick, pulsing from base to tip, jizz scalding where it landed on his skin.

"God, yes." Zeb's eyes fluttered closed, hips slamming forward over and over. "Love you, Jordan. God, I love you."

The satisfaction drifting on the chemicals in Silver's blood turned from sweet to bitter. It wasn't the first time a guy had had said *I love you* when he came. And as usual, the guy wasn't really talking to him.

Zeb had collapsed with his forehead on Silver's shoulder. Silver pushed at him. "*Mmph.*"

God, had Zeb fallen asleep? Silver cranked his neck and squinted, glimpsing an eye through a mess of tangled hair.

Zeb made another noise, a happy sigh. "Hey."

"Hey," Silver said back.

"Give me a second while I remember how to move." Zeb's lips brushed Silver's chest.

"Nah." Separating didn't seem so important anymore. After all, wasn't that the whole point of being here, to spend this last night with Zeb?

His body on Silver's was warm and solid, matching the pulse of Zeb's cock still in Silver's ass. Instead of a weight pinning him down, Zeb anchored him. Anchored them both right here. Even if it was only for a night.

SILVER WOKE up cursing his bladder. He tried to drift back into sleep, but the insistent fullness dragged him awake. Easing out from under Zeb, Silver staggered into the bathroom.

The annoying toiletry bag on the sink forced him to be more awake than his need to piss had.

He could look in it. See if Zeb had packed condoms. But that wasn't the kind of boyfriend he wanted to be. And he really did want to be a boyfriend. Wanted it even knowing how much risk, how much pain it could bring. He wanted it with the same intensity of the clueless teenager he'd been the first time.

It was dark now, but the hall light shined into the bedroom, a wide parallelogram of it on Zeb, like a spotlight. He was about to join him in it, when he saw the condom on Zeb's thigh. On his way back from flushing it, he noticed the sliding doors of the open closet. Looking to see what was still here wasn't like checking for condoms in a zippered bag. He stared in.

A few pairs of dress pants, shirts and ties, and a lot of empty space. Like the one in his gut when he thought about Zeb being gone. He'd been on his own for years. Why the hell should it matter so much now?

"Silver?"

He'd wondered if Zeb was going to go back to calling him Jordan. "What are you doing?" Zeb asked.

"Nothing." Silver climbed back into the bed.

Zeb pulled Silver into warm skin. The contrast made him shiver. "I'm coming back."

Silver nodded against Zeb's chest. "It's only six weeks."

WITH A ten-hour drive ahead of him, Zeb wanted to be on the road by seven. At six forty-five, they sat in front of Quinn's house.

"I'll text you when I hear what the judge says. Or I guess if I'm in jail, Eli will." Silver unlatched his door.

"Silver."

He turned back.

"I feel like—" Zeb scraped a hand over his jaw. "Is there something else I'm supposed to say?"

"No."

And it wasn't a lie. Zeb had to go. Silver had a test to study for. A judge to please.

And Marco to worry about. It was just the way things were.

Silver leaned over and gave Zeb a quick kiss. "See you in six weeks."

Chapter Twenty-Four

"YOU GET a week to go all emo," Eli announced when he came downstairs.

"Fuck you." Silver had baked some french toast. Mostly because he was bored standing in the kitchen at quarter of seven with nothing to do.

"I take it back. If you're going to make breakfast, you can mope all you want. I hate cooking breakfast."

"Fuck you sideways."

"Mmm. Sounds good to me." Eli grabbed a cup of coffee. "By the way, we had a little excitement last night."

Marco slid into the kitchen in his bare feet. "Timo showed up outside my class yesterday."

"Shit. What did he do?"

"Made an ass of himself," Eli said.

"He asked if I was tired of having to get fucked to have a place to sleep."

"Did you call security?"

"No."

"Marco, you don't know what Timo might—oh fuck."

Quinn came into the kitchen with a purple circle under his eye.

"Quinn was with me," Marco said, grinning, like Eli's boyfriend didn't have an ugly black eye.

Eli started, but the three of them talked at once. "I was meeting Nate to do a shoot on some program the college was doing and—"

"He got way worse than this." Quinn pointed to his eye.

"Quinn walked me to class, and Timo was there."

Silver sank into a chair. "Please tell me no one got arrested."

Quinn shook his head. "No one saw."

Marco chirped, "Quinn took him aside. The bathroom. Then he fucked him up."

Quinn winced. "The important thing is he won't be back."

Eli was practically vibrating as he tried to pretend he was okay with what had happened.

Silver glanced at Quinn's scraped and swollen knuckles. "I'm sorry."

"Why are you sorry? My brother is a—a—asshole." Marco landed on the right insult. He smiled. "Now he's a bloody asshole." His brows drew together. "I mean bruised." His cheeks got pink. "I mean—" He shook his head. "Oh, but Timo swung first," he added like he'd been prepped for the witness stand.

"What if he decides to press charges?" Silver looked at Quinn, who shrugged.

"He won't." Marco sounded positive. "He has a record."

Silver's appetite for french toast shriveled like a ninety-year-old's balls. He couldn't stay there anymore, looking at Quinn's bruises. Quinn, who was the calmest person Silver knew, involved in a fist fight in a bathroom. A fist fight he wouldn't have been in if Silver hadn't dragged him into this. "I need to head downtown for something."

Eli gave him a narrow-eyed stare through bangs.

"I'll take my pill and grab something to eat on the way."

"One week."

"Yeah. I got it."

Silver started in the direction of the bus stop, but he was only walking to burn off the urge to scream. He was a magnet for shit. And now it was splattering on his friends.

How the hell could families act like this? Turn their backs on their own kids, get violent with their own kids because of who they fucked? It was such shit. Silver was tired of it.

He wasn't the only one. Quinn didn't know Marco, but he was willing to stand up for him. Gavin too, in his way.

Maybe things wouldn't have gone down like they did if Gavin's shelter had been there for Silver. Or Marco. Silver stopped walking. If he was so sick of this shit happening, maybe Silver owed it not just to whoever came next but to himself to make sure Gavin's idea happened.

If the shelter did it right, kids would have a place to go. A place to feel safe. But it could just as easily go wrong. Kids like the ones he'd hung out with off Eutaw Street would never trust it. Eddie and his butterfly knife wouldn't trust some social worker with a bunch of forms.

He stopped and hauled out his phone.

When Gavin picked up, Silver had a hope that what he was interrupting would piss Jamie off.

"It's Silver. Are you still thinking about the shelter for homeless gay kids?"

"I'm up to my… eyeballs in paperwork for it right now. I have a board in mind, but there are fifteen forms to fill out for every step."

"I want to run it."

"I'm sorry?"

Okay. Maybe that was a little much. Silver hadn't really known it was what he was planning to say until it came out. "I mean, I want to be a part of it. I'll volunteer or whatever. But if you just put social workers or whatever in charge, kids'll be afraid to come in."

"Thank you. That's exactly the kind of thing I hoped you'd help with. I have one more question for you."

"Yeah?"

"Why couldn't you run it?"

Silver thought about it for a second. He didn't have a GED yet. And he'd probably have to take some college courses. He could handle some school. But then what, he'd be in an office? "Me do the paperwork?"

"Paperwork is the tedious but easy part. After all, I can do that. But someone making the decisions who has had the actual experience would be invaluable. I'll send over some information, like a job description. See if it's something you want to think about."

"I do. Want to think about it, I mean."

"Does this mean you found your passion?"

Silver didn't know if he would call it a passion. Not like the way Eli felt about his pictures or the way Zeb talked about teaching. But if it meant Silver was tired of seeing crap go down and pissed enough to do something about it, yeah. And maybe that's how a passion got started. By wanting.

"I think I did."

Chapter Twenty-Five

SUITS WERE a lame clothing choice for Baltimore in July. How was everyone in the courtroom not dripping with sweat? Gavin had vetoed Eli volunteering to take Silver shopping, but since Silver had decided to pay for this particular wardrobe upgrade himself, they went to a discount store. It wasn't like he could compete with what was on his lawyer anyway.

Sweat trickled between Silver's shoulder blades and pooled under the new tie, worn a lot tighter than the token knot he threw on for work. Despite the sweat, going in front of the judge was easier this time. There were no guarantees, but having friends—family—on his side helped him face what might happen.

He grabbed a deep breath now as he and the lawyer went through the little gate Silver might not get to go back through. Here at this table, the lawyer would tell the judge why Silver shouldn't have to go to jail.

After putting a deposit on an apartment, the fine they were expecting would clear out the new savings account Silver had opened, but he'd be free. And when Zeb came back, Silver would be ready to see where things could take them.

The judge peered over her glasses and lowered the folder in her hand. "Jordan Barnett, the charge is Violation of Maryland Code 8-303, possession of a fraudulently altered government identification document with intent. This misdemeanor charge carries a fine of five hundred dollars or six months in jail. Do you understand that, Mr. Barnett?"

Silver had used lip balm and drunk plenty of water, but his lips still felt stuck together, and he stuttered a little. "Y-yes, Your Honor."

"How do you plea to this charge?"

The first words were out, but the second ones weren't any easier. "Guilty, Your Honor."

"Do the people have a recommendation?" The judge looked over at the assistant district attorney.

The opposing lawyer had a sneer that reminded Silver of a high school bully. "Three months in jail and three years' probation, Your Honor."

Even though the lawyer had warned Silver, the words still felt like a punch to the gut.

Now it was their turn. "Your Honor, I would like to share with the court some circumstances regarding Mr. Barnett's situation."

The judge nodded sharply, pulling off her glasses.

"Mr. Barnett has no prior criminal record, not even a traffic violation. Mr. Barnett did not obtain a fraudulent identification with the intent to violate legal restrictions on purchasing alcohol. He was estranged from his family before the age of eighteen and was unable to access his own identification. Since his last appearance, Mr. Barnett has maintained a fixed address and has achieved employment. He is registered to take the GED exam next month and intends to pursue further education. He has signed a lease for an apartment in the city. We ask for dismissal."

"What will you be studying, Mr. Barnett?" the judge asked.

Gavin had emailed a job description, complete with the qualifications. Counseling was just talking. But the other part, that would be a lot of use, knowing what the laws were and how to get around them.

"Criminal justice, Your Honor," Silver said.

"Are you planning on becoming an attorney?" The judge slid her glasses back on her nose.

"No, Your Honor. I hope to keep people from needing one."

"A noble sentiment." The judge examined her papers. "Jordan Samuel Barnett, you have entered a plea of guilty to the charge of possessing fraudulent government identification. You are hereby sentenced to six months…."

Silver's hearing faded out in a rush of blood, a waterfall of sound. Jail. The whole sentence. Six months of jail.

"…remain within this jurisdiction for the full six months. And, Mr. Millhouse, I expect to be apprised of the results of each step."

Silver was still having trouble hearing. It made him feel off balance. He flinched when the lawyer shook his hand. Kind of a ballsy gesture when the guy hadn't helped much.

"Do you understand all that, Mr. Barnett?" The judge was looking over her glasses at him again. "Stay in the area, keep your job and your apartment. And I'll be looking to see the results of your GED. Any missteps and you'll serve the full sentence."

"I'll brief my client, Your Honor," his lawyer said.

But the judge was looking at Silver. He wasn't going to jail. All he had to do was what he was going to do anyway.

"Yes, Your Honor."

As the lawyer led Silver back through the gate, he said, "It's probation before judgment. You comply with the court's expectation, the main one being not getting arrested again, and at the end of the term, you're free. Going forward, you won't have to say you were ever convicted of a crime." The lawyer shook Silver's hand.

This time he returned the motion and pressure. He wasn't going to jail.

He hadn't been able to really let himself believe it until this second. Still wasn't sure he wasn't going to wake up under the blue-striped cover at Quinn's house, or worse, wake to find himself in an orange jumpsuit.

He turned to look for Gavin, to thank him, and stubbed a toe on the bench. First his hearing went. Now his eyes. Standing next to Gavin was Zeb. This was definitely a dream, because Zeb was way the hell out in the Allegheny Mountains of Pennsylvania.

Eli grabbed Silver's arm and tugged him down the aisle. "Better get while the gettin's good."

"Who are you, my grandfather?" Silver muttered as they left the courtroom.

No one was out in the hall, but when Silver hit the marble stairs and saw Zeb standing down in the lobby with Quinn, with their friends, he felt like he really was in a movie. The kind with a happy ending. And for once Silver didn't want to be watching it from a distance. He wanted to be in it. Feel everything up close. Even 3-D wasn't going to cut it. He had to have the real thing.

Silver looked down at his suit. Yeah, he supposed if he ever did it for real, Eli would be the one to give Silver away, the one he would want at his side.

Quinn put a hand on Silver's back, Marco clung with a quick hug, even Jamie threw a friendly punch at Silver's shoulder. He needed to thank Gavin, needed to thank them all. Without his found family, Silver would already have been dressed in orange. But knowing that didn't slow Silver down as he walked through his friends to stand in front of Zeb.

If Zeb's hands weren't in his pockets, Silver might have flung himself on him.

Instead he just stared. Zeb's hair was in a ponytail, but he was clean-shaven. "You're here."

"Seemed like a pretty important day in my boyfriend's life. I thought I should be here."

"Boyfriend?" Silver asked. He was two-for-two in the stupid department.

Zeb grabbed Silver's hand. Warm. Solid. Real. "Pretty amazing guy too. Have to say the prick of an ADA took a few years off my life, but you should have heard what the lawyer said about my man. All that he's managed in two months. Impressed the judge too."

"He had some help," Silver said.

Zeb shook his head. "I am so incredibly proud of you." He pulled Silver into a hug. "I love you."

Silver took a deep breath. Sandalwood. Whoever said you couldn't go home again was a moron. It was right here. He swallowed. "Love you too." Like Zeb could have missed noticing that.

Zeb squeezed harder.

Silver pulled back enough to say, "Are you coming to the party, or do you have to start back to camp?"

Zeb released him. "I think I have to go to the party. At least to give you a ride." Silver glanced around. Everyone else was gone. They headed for the door. "What's with that tone?" Zeb sounded hurt. "Didn't you hear me say I love you?"

"And I love you, but I know how important being at the camp is to you. Like teaching."

Zeb stopped him before the metal detectors. "You're important to me, Silver."

So after kicking Silver in the nuts for four years, the universe decided to hand out all the goodies on the same day. He supposed maybe he could not be completely selfish and make sure Zeb knew what he was getting into.

He tugged Zeb outside and took a deep breath. The oppressive city heat had never felt better. Because he was free to be out in it—and to bitch about it.

"Have you thought about what having a boyfriend means?" Silver asked.

"I'm hoping it means you in my life as much as possible. Plus, really awesome sex." Zeb grinned.

"I mean for teaching."

Zeb's brow rippled. "Quinn has a boyfriend."

"But Quinn has been there long enough that they can't just fire him. Zeb, stuff gets out. You know it does. And if the parents find out your boyfriend has HIV—"

Zeb stopped walking. "If I lose my job, I'll get another one."

"You heard the judge. I can't leave Baltimore."

"So I won't either." Zeb started down the pavement again.

What had happened to the guy who had been afraid to bump arms in public?

They reached the parking garage and started up the stairs. They'd get in the car and go to the party and sneak off and fuck. Why couldn't Silver just let it go at that? He was like a kid whining about having to go to the toy store. But if he got to have what he wanted and it got taken away again....

"If you're with me, everyone's going to think you're positive too."

Zeb froze. "Is that what you think? Silver, I don't care what anyone thinks. I don't care how people see me. Unless the problem is how you see me."

"I just want you to be sure." At Zeb's narrow-eyed look, Silver blurted, "You can think about it and tell me when you come back in August."

Silver thought he knew every expression on Zeb's face, but he couldn't read this one. Zeb didn't give him much time, striding toward his car on level three. "About that. I'm back."

Silver jogged after him. "What?"

"I mean, when I told them I had to leave today, I also told them I wasn't going to be able to come back." His voice echoed among the cars.

"But—"

"I don't need three weeks to think about it. I love you. I never stopped loving you."

Silver stopped. "If it was so easy to get out of, why did you leave?"

Zeb turned and leaned on his car. "You didn't ask me to stay. And after—I didn't think it should be up to me. Well, screw that. I'm not waiting. I'm asking now. I want you. I want us. I want it all. Are you in?"

Silver's head floated loose on his shoulders at the same time that his feet stuck frozen to the ground. But it wasn't a bad feeling. Sometimes standing still was good. He'd been running away from so much crap, it never occurred to him he had something to run toward. He could hang on to what hurt, or grab a chance to have what he'd wanted from the minute Zeb had made the first *Star Wars* reference. But a chance to have it without the lie that had cost them so much time. Without the need to lie because they already knew the worst and loved each other anyway.

Silver's feet found the answer first. He jogged up to Zeb and grabbed his face, startling a huge smile. "I think you'd better get this car rolling before they have a real reason to arrest us."

Zeb popped the locks, and Silver ran around to the passenger side. Across the roof, Zeb gave Silver that special, just-for-him twisted grin. "You know, since we've waited all this time, you think the party could wait a little longer?"

"Sure." Silver slid in, grabbed the GPS and threw it in the back seat. "We'll just tell 'em you got lost."

Author's Note

To OUR great misfortune, there is no real Gavin Montgomery available to create a safe space for homeless GLBT youth in Baltimore, but there is YES, a drop-in center for youth, which welcomes GLBT teens: www.yesdropincenter.org. Like most social programs, they always need help. If you're in good shape and want to share something with them, they have an Amazon wishlist and other ways to help on their page: www.yesdropincenter.org

Let's hope someday no one has to face the choices that Silver did.

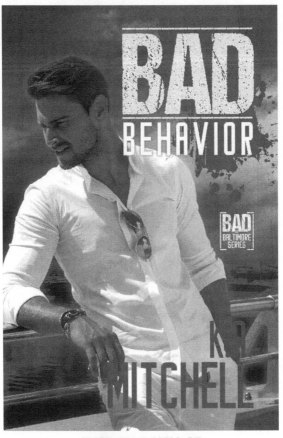

Bad in Baltimore: Book Five

In a lifetime of yes, no is the sexiest word he's ever heard.

After one too many misunderstandings with the law, wealthy and spoiled David Beauchamp finds himself chained to the city by the GPS and alcohol sensor strapped to his ankle. Awaiting trial, cut off from usual forms of entertainment, he goes looking for a good time—and winds up with his hands full, in more ways than one. The situation only gets more complicated when he's summoned for a random drug test and comes face-to-face with the dominant man who took him for one hell of a ride the night before.

Probation Officer Tai Fonoti is used to handling other people's problems, but he's horrified when one of the extra clients his boss dumps on him is the sweet piece of ass he screwed the night before. It makes getting a urine sample a pretty loaded situation. Tai's unique brand of discipline has Beach craving more. But while Tai relishes laying down the law in the bed-room, the letter of the law stands between them and kinkily ever after....

Available now at
www.dreamspinnerpress.com

Chapter One

THE PREMATURE ejaculation of a Second of July firecracker exploded out of the night. Without a backward glance, Beach stepped from the steam of a Baltimore summer into Grand Central and took a deep breath of sweat, spilled booze, and sweet, sweet testosterone. The opportunity for a nameless fuck on the nearest convenient surface was one of the reasons Beach loved having sex with men. Women were not without their charms, though the *maybe, maybe not* dance could get tiresome. But men, especially the men who came to Grand Central, weren't there for that kind of dance.

After waving over the bartender, Beach paid for a local bottled beer he would be scrupulously obedient about not drinking and scanned the sparse weeknight offerings. He knew exactly what he wanted—or at least, he would when he saw it. He could never say for sure what would catch his eye. All he knew was he had to find it.

Tonight more than usual.

His gran always said Beach had ants in his pants when he fidgeted, unable to keep still or hide his boredom at being stuck anywhere for any length of time.

And stuck he was. In Baltimore. Until his lawyer managed to work a deal with the DA over something that had created far more inconvenience for Beach than it had for any of the birds on the sanctuary he'd allegedly trespassed on.

But the trapped feeling wasn't all that had pushed him out the door tonight. He was looking to forget the voicemail he'd gotten while in the shower.

Hope you'll take some time during celebrating the Fourth to think about your old man spending his twenty-fifth year in exile from his country.

As if Beach could avoid thinking about his father, when an effort to bring him home had taken him to the bird sanctuary and was the whole reason why Beach now possessed a cane and custom-fitted ankle jewelry courtesy of the Maryland Department of Corrections.

And this jittery sensation that he had to do something right now or come out of his skin.

The itch burned like an infection in his blood, a desperate fever heat. Without any chemicals to take the edge off, not even a sip of beer, it was impossible to ignore.

But there was always something better than beer or chemicals if you knew where to look. Something exactly like… that. A crinkle at the corner of an eye. Warm tan skin over broad cheeks.

Beach shifted off the barstool to make a better appraisal. The object of his fascination leaned over a pool table. Jeans showcased a firm ass, and a tank top showed off intricately patterned black ink from shoulder to elbow. Though it also served to draw attention to the massive muscles on the arms and the breadth of chest that turned the hot ache under Beach's skin to fire. Whether a guy was a top or bottom, Beach had never had any trouble getting exactly what he wanted. And he wanted that.

The man became aware of Beach's greedy stare and glanced over. If Beach hadn't already been determined, the smirk would have done it. The eyes, the not-quite-smiling lips, the black slash of his brows. All of it together promised he could bend Beach in half, make him beg the Lord for mercy, and smile all the way through it.

Beach tipped the bottle toward the man, then brought it to his lips, suggestion in the way his mouth covered the rim. Without losing any of his smirk, the man turned back to his pool game, lining up his shot. Beach didn't know much about pool, but he had a fair understanding of physics, and the shot was at a difficult angle.

When the man spread his arched fingers on the felt to make a bridge for his cue, the strength on display from fingertips to shoulder made Beach's mouth water. He barely refrained from fanning himself in an imitated swoon. A dip in the music let him hear the sharp click of the colliding resins, the softer thud of ball on bumper. The resurging volume of music couldn't drown out the groan from the man's opponent. Beach's target lined up another shot, and with a shake of hands, the game was over.

As the man rounded the table, Beach transferred his weight to his good leg and contemplated leaving the blasted cane against the bar. He already felt hard muscles under his palms, heard the slap of their flesh as their bodies pounded together. The itch that had driven him here rushed to his cock, pulsing hungry and insistent. Catching the man's eye, Beach tipped his head in the direction of the bathrooms.

The smirk grew more promising, more pronounced on the man's handsome face, leaving Beach more determined to see the man follow through on it.

Then the man plucked the plastic triangle off the wall and began racking the balls for another game. He might as well have racked the ones hanging heavy under Beach's dick. The bastard had turned him down in favor of another game of pool. It was a damned sorry state of affairs when men came to Grand Central to fondle billiard balls instead of each other's.

Beach dragged his bad leg back up onto the barstool and had almost opened his mouth to order several double Maker's Marks when the ankle shackle on his other leg caught the footrest. Right. Even that consolation was denied him. And nothing but the threat of the absolute loss of freedom was enough of a deterrent to keep him sober.

With a disgusted sigh, he slammed down the bottle he'd been using as a prop and placed a different order. "Bourbon and soda. Hold the bourbon. And keep 'em coming."

Beach grew aware of a few other approaches as he drank his utterly impotent soda. But he wasn't interested. All he could see was that damned smirk. The mesh-and-block-patterned tattoo on the solid shoulder. He had developed a craving, and nothing else would satisfy, though his wounded pride kept him from glancing back toward the pool table.

When three glasses of soda made another need equally insistent, he clamped a straw between his teeth and slid off the stool, propping his cane under the bar. Affecting the rolling stride he'd developed to mask his limp, he headed for the men's room. He should probably get it checked out again, but a few weeks in a coma and then surgery to put a rod on his snapped tibia had exhausted his tolerance for doctors for the foreseeable future.

The day he needed support to stand long enough to drain the snake was the day he went off a bridge headfirst on purpose. He was shaking himself dry when he heard the door open, but before he could tuck and zip, a hard body clamped around him, and a hand covered Beach's on his cock.

There couldn't be two men in the bar with a chest like the one Beach felt against his back. But he snuck a glance at the arm around him to be sure. There was the same intricate tattoo, ending at the elbow.

He felt the voice before he heard it, gravel-rough and smoky-smooth like the best bourbon. The voice alone could harden a man's cock at ten paces.

"Give you a hand?"

Beach's dick had never had much pride. It was all ready to forgive the earlier insult, jolting forward at the offer. "Near missed your chance. Thought you weren't interested."

"Like hell." Sweet Lord, the voice was sin. "But *I* make the first move."

"You can move it anyway you like if your cock can cash the check your mouth is writing." Beach pulled his own hand away.

The hot grip was all his cock needed to shift from leaping to lunging for attention, dragging his hips forward in search of friction.

An arm wrapped around Beach's hips and pinned him back, denial and promise in the press of a cock against his ass.

Beach's friend Gavin would probably be able to predict the exact inches and circumference from that brief grind. All Beach knew was it was solid, hot and thick, and felt damned good. He pushed back to indicate he was on board with the plan. All he got for an answer was a grunt as he was dragged backward into the end stall. The wider one with the rails. The man wasn't rough—not by Beach's standards—simply forceful as he shoved Beach face-first against the tiled sidewall. There was a stone window ledge to lean on, or to grip if things got as wild and fast as he hoped they would. That the other man wanted to take charge was no hardship. The more responsibility someone else took, the more Beach was free to focus on how good everything felt.

Except there wasn't any feeling good at first. Beach had been ready to go since he set his eyes on his prize, but a hard dick didn't automatically make his ass soft. He hadn't been fucked since before his coma. This was where chemicals were so damned useful, right here when he was trying to trade the discomfort of a thick callused finger jamming lube into him for the tingle he knew would happen if that finger curled the right way.

It didn't.

His jeans were snug enough to stay bunched under his ass after the man had shoved them out of the way, and they made it tough to spread his legs to accommodate the added stretch of another finger. Beach wiped his forehead on his forearms where they rested on the window ledge and tipped his ass up, looking for that good pressure, the way the muscles would give and the nerves would start singing praises louder than the sanctuary choir on a Sunday morning.

He didn't get it.

He shifted more of his weight onto his whole leg, wondering if he wanted to turn around and see the size of what the man behind him was sheathing in latex before it went up his ass. Then the man grabbed one of Beach's hands and put it on the smooth, covered flesh. Maybe the guy meant to prove to Beach the condom was on, maybe it was to give Beach some lube on his hand to help him work his own cock, but as Beach's hand closed around the dick a few inches from his hole, all he could think of was the heft and the width spearing into him. The strain that had been balanced between a throbbing hunger and a gut-churning tension snapped. Beach spiraled into a hot, dizzy space where pain and pleasure were all part of the same beautiful sensation to send him out of his head, better than any drug ever could.

He released the man's cock and held himself open, rocking back onto the blunt head, wanting to push them faster into the rhythm of the fuck, those few moments of perfection where nothing existed but pleasure.

Beach wanted to rush them, rush himself past the first moment of I-can't-take-this, but a bruising pinch on the swell of his ass made him lurch forward. Before he could spin around with an affronted remark about not being a cocktail waitress, the man wrapped an iron-muscled forearm around Beach's waist.

"I make the first move, remember."

It was a statement, not a question, but Beach nodded. Beach didn't know how he could forget anything said in that voice. He should have had it available to read him his textbooks in school. Should hire the man to record the latest board of directors' update.

He wished there'd been a need for more negotiation, the kind of dance he'd come here to avoid. Because then the voice would roll over them, fill the air like fog, the kind thick enough to grab on to. He waited, hoping he'd get rewarded with more of it.

When it came, it curled inside him, an added sensation to build the agony of waiting. "Good." The voice trailed over him, a hand stroking down his back, rubbing the pinched spot for a soothing instant.

Then the arm around Beach's waist pulled him back, forcing his hips out so torso and legs made a comfortable angle. Beach smiled, imagining the man lining himself up with the same care he used on his pool shot, and hoped his skill translated.

It did.

It really did.

The first push had the head in, smooth and easy at first, until the man held them there. Beach's nerve endings, his pulse, his muscles all screamed the reminder that they were doing this without any of the usual enhancements, that this was the only part about getting fucked he wished he could skip, the sting of too tight focused right there in too small a spot, straining tolerance to the limit. This was the part so easy to forget once everything was friction and heat and pressure.

A harsh breath stuttered, echoed into the tiled space, and the rasp in Beach's throat let him know it came from him. He'd half a mind to tell this smirking prick what he could do with his first moves and weird pauses. But they were almost there now, and hell if Beach would back down from a challenge.

The man moved, finally, but it seemed to take forever for him to work it in. The scrape and burn had faded, leaving an even emptier craving. The damned bastard better have stamina to make up for the torturously slow entry.

Beach gripped that window ledge with all the strength in his fingers as his ass swallowed up the thick length. By the time the man's balls swung into Beach's, his manicure was shredded.

Beach shifted a bit under the grip keeping him tight against the other man's hips, wanting more, more room in his ass, more movement between them, every bit of sensation. One of the man's hands was flat on Beach's chest, the other pinning them together at the hips. Beach was sure the man felt the leap of his heart as someone came into the bathroom, letting in a blast of music before the door swung shut, muffling it again. A scrape of shoes, the sound of a zipper.

No patron of Grand Central would be shocked to stumble over men fucking in the bathroom, so Beach couldn't explain why tension had his muscles locked, his teeth clenched to hold back any sound. After all, fucking had been about the only item not on the list of things forbidden until his trial.

As the stream splashed into the urinal, the man behind Beach used his mouth to shift aside the hair from Beach's neck, kiss away the sweat, then draw the already tight skin into teeth, sucking a burning mark to make Beach's ass throb harder around the rigid heat inside it.

The chuckle the man outside the door gave as he washed and shook dry his hands made Beach's cheeks flush, as if this was the most outrageous thing he'd ever done—instead of something mildly impulsive.

His exhale as the door closed behind the other man was full of relief.

"What's the matter? Didn't want to share?" The voice purred against Beach's back, across the bite on his neck and into his ear.

Something insaner than usual had gotten into Beach since he'd glimpsed the crinkle of eye above tanned cheek, leaving him damned near broken to saddle, but he found his footing.

"Starting to think there's nothing here to share. You all talk? Have to go that slow to keep from shooting soon as you get it in?"

Beach expected a rough, if not violent reaction, a quick withdraw and a slam forward, finally getting the pounding he'd been looking for, what he'd known he needed when he parked his car down here on Eager Street.

But despite an even tighter clamp from the man's arms, it was only a long, smooth, and—damn him—perfect stroke. He shifted Beach, lifting him up and back a bit more. No wonder the guy was so good at pool. He knew his angles, that was for hell sure. And Beach didn't care if the guy was playing Beach's body like he owned it; that was what Beach had wanted. This, all of this, was the answer to the itch that had been driving him out of his skin. Steady, deep pressure, exquisite burn on the back stroke. The hand on his chest found a nipple under Beach's shirt and pinched until Beach gasped, hand dropping to work his cock. He could manage to whisper all kinds of sweet things to a partner when he was the one driving his dick into them, but right then all he could handle was an endless repetition of harsh breaths and moans.

The build inside made his lips and tongue start to shape the word *please*, as if he couldn't manage his own climb. It was like he'd forgotten his dick was in his hand. He shivered and started working it, hand and fingers providing all the friction he needed to turn the pressure inside into one hell of an explosion.

The grip of fingers around his wrist was as tight as a handcuff but warm and alive. It didn't bruise as it tugged, dragging his hand back up to the ledge to join the other, leaving his cock bobbing and pushing on nothing but air.

"No."

Beach considered himself a pretty open-minded individual, but if there was one word he was downright prejudiced against, it was that one. The barest hint of it had him either openly defiant or looking for a way to dance, charm, or twist his way around it.

He chalked up his reaction to the voice. Had to be the purr of it that made him suck in a gasp as his balls grew tighter, instead of the word creating the urge to tell the guy to fuck himself from now on in.

He didn't even yank his hand free, although the pressure of the other man's hand atop it wasn't enough to keep it resting on the ledge. Since he hadn't been disappointed this far, he'd see what the guy had in mind.

"Better be worth it."

The answer was a faster thrust, a renewed sting of skin against teeth on his neck, and a drag of nails against his nipple as a hand found its way under Beach's shirt. All of it drove electric jolts to spike into his cock, without the answering friction of his hand to ease him through it, to give it a place to build to.

Too much and not enough. But damn, it felt good. He rocked back to meet the thrusts, not caring anymore if the angle was perfect. He needed. Needed rougher and harder to hold back the hunger to come, spilling from his cock and balls, shaking into his hips and belly and arms and chest until he trembled with that much want. The sensations kept building without a crest to ride them out.

What was the plan here? Because Beach was pretty sure orgasms were the endgame, and he was more than ready to collect his and say thanks and good night.

He started to tug his hand free, and the man's fingers interlaced with his, cock still slamming into his ass deep and hard. It wasn't that Beach couldn't get himself off with his left hand; it just wouldn't be as much fun. And as much as he wanted to defy the bossy son of a bitch, his curiosity won out. Maybe the guy would come and then suck Beach off, which was an appealing scenario.

Beach tightened his ass against the thick pressure, earning himself a gasp that heated his ear.

"Yeah."

Okay. Beach worked his muscles and drove back harder, increasing the burn of friction for himself and earning the pleasure of constant strokes over his gland. So hot, melting with it, drowning in it. He gave up trying to free his hand, breath whistling out of him.

"Come." That voice.

He wanted to. Fuck, how he wanted to. But he couldn't. Not without—"Now." There was a threat curling under there.

It sparked something inside him, cranked the urgency way past the red line, and still Beach couldn't. He'd fucked guys who could. He didn't happen to be one of them.

"I can't." The admission dragged at him, sinking him into a chill of disappointment and shame. His body remembered there was a big fat cock in his ass, that both his nipples hurt, that his balls were aching and full.

"Don't have a choice." Despite the harsh command, the man's hand soothed and petted across Beach's chest, soft lips and soft beard teasing at his neck under his ear.

The man released Beach's hand and laid a hot palm low on his belly, so damned close to where it would be of some help, and kept fucking him.

Beach looked at his freed hand with fascination, wondering why he didn't simply grab his dick and finish, then shut his eyes as the man's rhythm shifted, short quick hard.

"Now." The man growled it.

Tension and yielding in a giant tangle. Straining for it, knowing one thing would be enough to free him, but he didn't know what it was until the solid punch of it shocked him. It was everywhere. In his ass. His balls. His dick. Oh God, so sweet and hot and electric in his dick. A powerful jerk wrung the first shot out of him in a burst of light behind his eyelids, and then all the aftershocks, each one its own slice of heaven as he came back down. Beach found himself wishing their audience had stuck around, because that certainly deserved a round of applause. He'd clap himself as soon as he got his coordination back and got what now felt like a cannon out of his ass.

His bad leg was shaking with exhaustion. Hell, everything felt shaky. Still, he could manage a hand job, though, or even a suck if he sat on the toilet to do it.

The pleasure faded away. There was no high on earth like an orgasm, but the price was that you didn't get to stay there long, and there was no way to up the dose right away. That was the only downside to sex. The sorry, sagging aftermath. He leaned forward in an effort to get the man's dick out of his ass and found himself wrapped up in something between a hug and a restraint.

"No."

There was that word again. "I could—"

"No." He stretched Beach's hands back out to the ledge and fucked him.

It hurt. Not in a God-I'm-dying-get-it-out way, but it definitely wasn't comfortable. And there was no reason Beach couldn't stop it. The man obviously could have won in a battle of strength, but Beach knew the man would let him go if Beach made it an issue.

No. It had never been a sexy-sounding word before. And even if there was no way Beach was going to be getting off from it, something about this felt good, despite the scrape of the cock in his ass. The man's hands trailed down his arms, his shoulders, the sides of his chest to land on his hips.

"Good," he murmured in Beach's ear, following the comment with a choked groan. "So good."

Beach's dick ached as it tried to get back in the game, but he had to content himself with the tingle from the man's pattern of caresses, the way his breath and beard tickled Beach's neck. The surprising warmth from listening to the man's control began to shatter. Beach put a hand back, urging the man closer. Faster.

"Yeah."

The raw feeling in the smoky voice made Beach tighten his muscles around the cock fucking into him, dragging out another stuttered "Good" before he felt the man come, the lock and snap of muscles, the convulsive jerk of hips. Beach rode it out with him, and when the man finally pulled out, Beach swallowed back the burn of disappointment. He wiped his forehead on his forearm, still holding on to the ledge to relieve the pressure on his leg.

The condom hit the water in the bowl, and the roar of the flush echoed around the stall, but Beach thought he heard "That was sweet" before the man brushed a kiss against his cheek and left.

It took a few minutes before Beach was ready for the world. His leg throbbed, a spiking pain underneath like a fresh break. His next round of sex would be horizontal, definitely.

By the time Beach decided he didn't look or walk quite so rode-hard-and-put-up-wet, the man with the tattoos, goatee, and velvet-sin voice wasn't lingering around the pool table or anywhere in the barroom. Which may have saved Beach the humiliation of forcing his number on the man and begging him to schedule a repeat.

After retrieving his cane, Beach made his way out to his Spider, dropping the top as the engine purred and rumbled. He'd always imagined the sound like a tiger getting a belly scratch. Now it reminded him of the gravelly notes in the voice that had whispered in his ear in the bathroom. The one that had told him no and made Beach listen. He was shaking off his stupidity and putting the car in gear when his phone went off.

He let himself enjoy a few more moments of a fantasy where the man had recognized Beach somehow, found his number, and was calling to set up something blissfully horizontal and twice as hot. But it was only a computer-generated voice. Female, impersonal. But to Beach it always held a bit of a derisive sneer as it told him to report to the probation office for testing tomorrow. Thank God sex was the drug that didn't leave any traces.

TAI'S COMPUTER had barely finished moaning and grinding to life that morning when Sutton dumped a bunch of files on his desk.

"Here's your latest share from the Bob fallout."

Tai scanned the pile. "Eight?" And two of them were thicker than average. "Overtime authorization come with them?"

His boss shook his head. "Sometimes you gotta take one for the team."

"Or eight." Tai hauled the files closer. Everybody had more shit now while Bob was suspended and Leslie was out on medical leave. His mom was fond of saying the only reward for a job well done was another job, but Tai hadn't ever noticed her slacking off, house or hospital.

Top file was some sixteen-year-old busted for shoplifting. When Tai flipped through and got a look at the parents' occupations, he was surprised they hadn't been able to make it all go away. Then he got a look at the priors. Some people loved wasting second chances, and third, and fourth. But that wasn't something he had to get to right away.

The next one was a mess. Bob must have been shoving it to the back while he spent his time drinking and driving around underage girls. Tai was still sorting through the file when switchboard called to tell him David Beauchamp was reporting in. The name meant nothing, which meant he was one of Bob's. Tai yanked out the file and ran through it.

David Beauchamp at thirty-four was where that sixteen-year-old was headed. Charges dismissed, violations and misdemeanors all reduced by the intervention of more money than everyone in this office would make in a lifetime. Beauchamp's sole occupation was to keep the family lawyer in business. Tai moved through to the present. Christ, Beauchamp had been the one to take the header off the bridge back in March, then get busted in May for criminal trespass out on Fort Carroll. The office got one or two of those cases every damned year. Most of them urban adventurers looking for online fame with videos of the dangerously crumbling fort. Tai wished the island would sink the fuck back into the bay. Failing that, become Anne Arundel county's problem. They had enough shit to deal with here.

Beauchamp had been seen as a flight risk and had substance-abuse issues, so they'd slapped a monitor on him to track his whereabouts and to read alcohol intake. Tai checked the monitoring system on the computer. No ethanol alarm, but Beauchamp had been flagged for location last night.

All the chances in the world, and all the advantages, and Beauchamp still had to act like an asshole. Maybe Tai would just throw him back at the judge for violating probation terms. Except given the way things worked for a guy like Beauchamp, he'd be back in Tai's office the next day with a shit-eating grin on his face.

As the man made his way in front of Tai's desk, Tai glanced around the computer screen enough to catch a glimpse of a cane. The grip on it, the light drag in his step, said it wasn't only decoration, but it could be a sympathy game.

A vocal gasp made Tai think the limp and cane were part of the same pity ploy.

"Sit down." Tai spat out before he flipped through the file again, looking for the medical reports. Coma, fracture of the tibia—the jump off the bridge? No, the trespass on Fort Carroll. So Beauchamp wasn't just a party boy, he was a klutzy one. Tai went back to the monitor.

"Want to tell me your whereabouts last night?"

"I would think you already know the answer to that, Officer Fonoti." Beauchamp's voice was amused. These cases made Tai sick. Give him a street punk any day over someone who'd had everything handed to him and threw it away. "Since our whereabouts happened to coincide so forcefully."

Tai snapped a look at the man in the chair. No. No fucking way. Admittedly he hadn't been paying much attention to the guy's looks after ascertaining the basics—fuckable and asking for it. It had been a good time, the guy playing along like he knew the ropes. He'd bet it wouldn't have taken much to get the guy to drop to his knees and kiss Tai's boots. But last night there hadn't been a cane. Tai hadn't been interested in a lot of details beyond getting his dick up a nice— God, he'd been tight—ass. Tai tugged on his pant leg to free up space. He couldn't get his brain to connect the smug bastard in front of him with the eager, obedient screw he'd had last night. The way he'd groaned and shook and how hard he clenched down. Tai had to tug on his pant leg again.

Despite all the evidence, Tai took another look at the program on the monitor. Beauchamp, David A. had been at 130 West Eager Street from 8:52 until 10:38. Tai had gotten there at seven thirty.

"I was informed my probation officer would be closely monitoring my activities, but I didn't realize how closely," Beauchamp said with a slow blink, a smile curving over an unshaved chin.

Tai had been threatened by gang leaders, self-labeled drug lords, and your basic foaming-at-the-mouth douchebags with anger issues. He'd listened to sob stories about hungry children, cheating girlfriends,

and backstabbing friends. If any of that could screw
with his judgment, he wouldn't have been able to do
his job. And he was good at his job. He knew the rules,
knew about the boundaries with clients. Hell, it didn't
take the Corrections and Probations Officer's Manu-
al to figure out the rule on fucking probies. Just one
word. Don't.

"Mr. Beauchamp—"

"Call me Beach. Everyone does."

Tai looked away from where white teeth bit
down on a pink tongue in a cheeky smile. "Mr.
Beauchamp—"

"Beechem. That's how you say it. Beech. Em."

The heat in his gut drove Tai to his feet. He
glanced down at his hands on the desk, knowing he
had slapped them there, but only from the sting in his
palms, the echo of the sound. He stared a little longer,
taking a deep breath for control, battling the instinc-
tive desire to put his hand on Beauchamp's neck and
remind him where the power really rested and do it in
a way that had nothing to do with supervising a client.
Of course, if Tai allowed himself such an extreme reaction over the slightest challenge, Beauchamp was the
one in charge. He peered down. The amiable expression on Beach's—Beauchamp's—face didn't change
at all. But his gaze made a leisurely journey from Tai's
thighs to his face before he raised his brows.

"According to the conditions of your pretrial probation, you are to remain out of bars."

"But I didn't have a drink of anything…fun."
Beauchamp's eyes focused on Tai's crotch. "Didn't
my lovely ankle jewelry tell you that?"

Tai glanced over at the monitor, though he already knew the answer.

"Where's Bob? Not that it isn't charming to run into you again, albeit under these circumstances, but I thought I was working with Bob."

Bob? "Officer Meade is not working with this department right now."

"Now that is a shame. We were getting along so well."

Tai had been about to resume his seat, but the phrasing made him wonder if Beauchamp hadn't been getting more from Bob than supervision.

"Drug test. Let's go." Tai grabbed a sample kit from the cabinet and started for the door. Having to piss under supervision like a toddler was humiliating enough to take the starch out of most of the assholes Tai dealt with. But as Beauchamp pushed open the men's room door, Tai realized how epically this was going to backfire. He busied himself in tugging on his gloves, avoiding the memory of his last trip to the men's room with Beauchamp.

Beauchamp stepped up to a urinal and grinned at Tai. "Hold it for me?"

"Excuse me?" Tai stepped away from where he was blocking the door.

"My cane." Beauchamp held it out. His tongue caught in his teeth for an instant before he added, "Well, it's either my cane, the cup, or my cock, but I was trying to keep things professional."

Tai snatched the cane and handed over the sample cup. Beauchamp faced him as he unzipped. Tai tried to glance away, but the action made him appear more pathetic.

Beach shrugged. "Not like you haven't seen it."

"Get on with it."

It was only a small hitch in Beauchamp's breath, but in the tiled room it echoed. And the echo reverberated right to Tai's balls. Tucking the cane under an arm, he kept an eye on the mirror set up to make sure the probie couldn't sub out from a tube secreted somewhere and waited.

When a minute passed, Tai leaned back against the doorframe. "Shy bladder?"

"Not as a rule." The response was sharp. "Uh." There were a few variations on that sound before Beauchamp said, "Tell me what happened to Bob."

"It's none of your business." Tai pushed away from the wall and turned on one of the faucets. "Some inspiration."

"Yeah, thanks." Beauchamp's voice was polished, smooth as silk, with a hint of the Carolinas in it and an ever-stronger promise of a laugh waiting to happen.

"Relax and concentrate."

"Not helping."

Tai made a living reading truth, fear, or desperation in people's voices, their faces, their body language. Right now Beauchamp was projecting all three. And that came overlaid with the awareness Tai should never have of a client. To know he liked it hard and dirty with a commanding voice in his ear.

The sooner this was over with, the sooner Tai could be in Sutton's office, passing Beauchamp on to another PO. That was what he told himself, but it was only half the truth as he took a step to put himself close enough to growl into Beauchamp's ear, "Do it. Now."

There was the sexy hitch in his breath again, and then Beauchamp obediently filled the cup, lifting it away as he splashed the rest into the urinal. He held up the cup, cheeks pink, looking at Tai's shoes. "Uh."

With a heavy sigh, Tai handed him the cap and a paper towel. "Wipe it off."

"Right. Sorry."

When the cap was twisted on and the outside was as clean as it was going to get, Tai took it, slapped on a label, and they both signed the seal on it before he passed back the cane. "Your curfew is eleven, and you're due for a home visit. Better be there. And stay out of bars."

"That's it?" Beauchamp sounded disappointed.

"That's it."

With a raised-brow leer, Beauchamp used the cane to swagger out as Tai held the door. "I can't tell you how much I'm looking forward to that home visit, Officer."

K.A. MITCHELL discovered the magic of writing at an early age when she learned that a carefully crayoned note of apology sent to the kitchen in a toy truck would earn her a reprieve from banishment to her room. Her career as a spin-control artist was cut short when her family moved to a two-story house and her trucks would not roll safely down the stairs. Around the same time, she decided that Ken and G.I. Joe made a much cuter couple than Ken and Barbie and was perplexed when invitations to play Barbie dropped off. She never stopped making stuff up, though, and was thrilled to find out that people would pay her to do it. Although the men in her stories usually carry more emotional baggage than even LAX can lose in a year, she guarantees they always find their sexy way to a happy ending.

K.A. loves to hear from her readers. You can email her at ka@kamitchell.com. She is often found talking about her imaginary friends on Twitter @ka_mitchell.

Email: ka@kamitchell.com
Twitter: @ka_mitchell
Website: www.kamitchell.com
Blog: authorkamitchell.wordpress.com
Tumblr: kamitchellplotbunnyfarm.tumblr.com

BAD
COMPANY

BAD
BALTIMORE
SERIES

K.A.
MITCHELL

Bad in Baltimore: Book One

Some things are sweeter than revenge.

"I need a boyfriend."

Hearing those words from his very straight, very ex-best friend doesn't put Nate in a helpful mood. Not only did Kellan Brooks's father destroy Nate's family in his quest for power, but Kellan broke Nate's heart back in high school. Nate thought he could trust his best friend with the revelation that he might be gay, only to find out he was horribly wrong and become the laughingstock of the whole school. Kellan must be truly desperate if he's turning to Nate now.

Kellan's through letting his father run his life, and he wants to make the man pay for cutting him off. What better way to stick it to the bigot than to come out as gay himself—especially with the son of the very man his father crushed on his quest for money and power. Kellan can't blame Nate for wanting nothing to do with him, though. Kellan will have to convince him to play along, but it's even harder to convince himself that the heat between them is only an act....

www.dreamspinnerpress.com

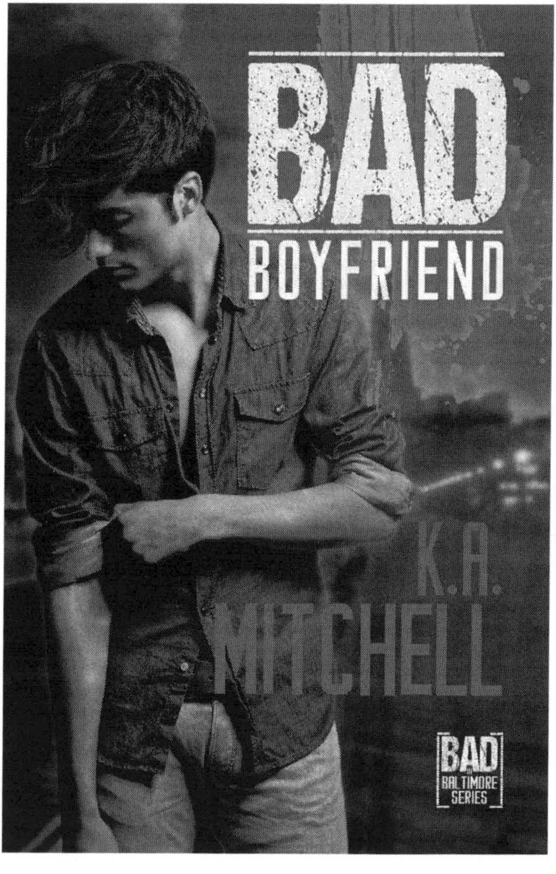
BAD
BOYFRIEND
K.A.
MITCHELL
BAD
IN
BALTIMORE
SERIES

Bad in Baltimore: Book Two

Causing trouble has never been more fun.

Eli Wright doesn't follow anyone's rules. When he was seventeen, his parents threw him out of the house for being gay. He's been making his own way for the past five years and he's not about to change himself for anyone's expectations. For now, romance can wait. There are plenty of hot guys to keep him entertained until he finds someone special.

Quinn Maloney kept the peace and his closeted boyfriend's secrets for ten years. One morning he got a hell of a wake-up along with his coffee. Not only did the boyfriend cheat on him, but he's marrying the girl he knocked up. Inviting Quinn to the baby's baptism is the last straw. Quinn's had enough of gritting his teeth to play nice. His former boyfriend is in for a rude awakening, because Quinn's not going to sit quietly on the sidelines. In fact, he has the perfect scheme, and he just needs to convince the much younger, eye-liner-wearing guy who winks at him in a bar to help him out.

Eli's deception is a little too good, and soon he has everyone believing they're madly in love. In fact, he's almost got Quinn believing it himself....

www.dreamspinnerpress.com

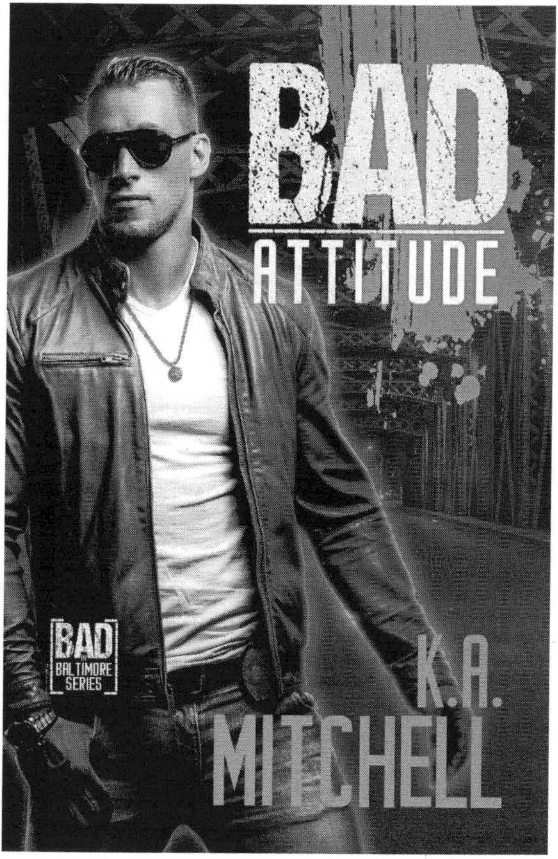
BAD
ATTITUDE
BAD IN BALTIMORE SERIES
K.A.
MITCHELL

Bad in Baltimore: Book Three

Saving lives never used to be this complicated.

Gavin Montgomery does what's expected of him by his wealthy and powerful family—look good in a tuxedo and don't make waves. When a friend takes a leap off a bridge, Gavin tries to save him, only to fall in with him. At least at the bottom of the river he won't feel like such a disappointment to his family. But he's pulled from the water by a man with an iron grip, a sexy mouth, and a chip on his shoulder the size of the national deficit.

Jamie Donnigan likes his life the way it is—though he could have done without losing his father and giving up smoking. But at least he's managed to avoid his own ball and chain as he's watched all his friends pair off. When Montgomery fame turns a simple rescue into a media circus, Jamie decides if he's being punished for his good deed, he might as well treat himself to a hot and sweaty good time. It's not like the elegant and charming Gavin is going to lure Jamie away from his bachelor lifestyle. Nobody's that charming. Not even a Montgomery....

www.dreamspinnerpress.com

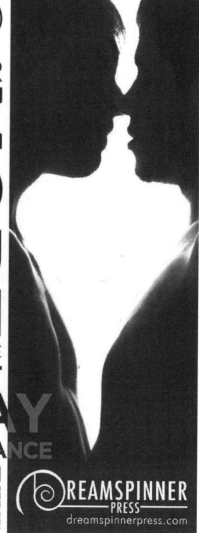